BLOOD HUNT

By Christopher Buecheler

Part 2 of the II AM Trilogy

Blood Hunt

http://www.iiamtrilogy.com/
http://writing.cwbuecheler.com/

ISBN-13: 978-1463774042
ISBN-10: 1463774044

Blood Hunt is a work of fiction. Names, places, and incidents either are a product of the author's imagination or are used fictitiously.

First Edition: September 1, 2011

Cover Art by Karla Ortiz
Cover Design by Christopher Buecheler
MasterPlan font by Billy Argel

HAVE YOU READ THE FIRST BOOK?

Blood Hunt is the sequel to **The Blood That Bonds**. If you have not read the first book, there's good news: it's free! Head to **http://www.thebloodthatbonds.com** to download it – it is available for every major eReader, including Kindle, Nook, iBooks, Sony Reader, Kobo, and more. You can also purchase the print edition.

DEDICATION

For my parents, Bill and Leslie.

ACKNOWLEDGEMENTS

As is the case with most books, this one would never have reached its present form without the efforts, enthusiasm and encouragement of many people. It's a privilege to list them here, and I can't thank them enough for all that they've done.

- My wife Charlotte. She is my best friend, my toughest critic, and my muse. Her love and faith in me keep me going on these projects.

- My editor Lauren, who did double-duty in a very short time-span, hunting down copy errors and suggesting ways to make the book better. If there are any flaws left in the text, be sure that they are my fault and not hers.

- My cover artist, Karla, who really saved my life on this one, working with a completely unreasonable deadline. I love her vision of Two, and I hope you do too!

- My trusted readers: Charlotte, Nora, Joost, Trevor, Caryn, Charles, Diana, and Kim (to whom I also owe thanks for some copy-editing of her own). Their feedback helped greatly in identifying what needed to change between drafts.

- My fans, who've provided constant feedback and support on social networking sites, reviewed my books on the web, and sent me their thoughts via email. It is amazing to me that there are so many of you out there. It's incredibly motivating, and I've worked hard to make sure this book was worth your patience. I sincerely hope you enjoy it!

PART I

CHAPTER I

Voices in the Dark

Tori Perrault shifted position, arched her back, thrust her hips. Breathing hard, she glanced down. Tangles of dirty-blonde hair, dark and damp with sweat, framed the edges of her vision, swayed with the motion of her body. A droplet caught briefly on her lower lip and trembled there, reflecting what dim light there was in the room, then fell to burst on the chest of the man below her. Occupied as he was, he didn't notice.

Tori felt him gripping her buttocks, pulling her against him, straining. Her lip curled in an unconscious snarl as she tilted her head back, eyes closed, trying to focus. Trying to *feel*. The sweat, more a response to the room's heat than to either exertion or stimulation, rolled down her body.

"Oh, Christ, baby ..." he moaned, his voice high and weak and strained, and Tori knew he would finish soon. She tried to tamp down her annoyance; he was almost done, almost *there*, and she was still *here*. She was just starting to get into it.

She tried to tell herself that it wasn't his fault. She required so much effort, so much time. Her body had spent twelve years in a heightened state of sensory awareness beyond human conception; was it any wonder that this return to something resembling "normal" felt empty and dull? It would take time for her to adjust to her current state – perhaps even years. Surely, though, her ability to feel would return eventually.

The lump of muscle below her had short brown hair and dark eyes, and if she'd known his name at the beginning of the evening, she had forgotten it since. Burned away by alcohol, perhaps, or apathy. Maybe he'd never told her. She didn't care now, knowing that he was nearly *there* – she just wanted it to be over.

Here it was. His hands clenched tight with a pressure that might have been painful to someone else, and he thrust deep within her and held there. His breath caught and he leaned his head back, baring his throat, groaning. Tori could see his veins throbbing. *This is the part where I tear your throat out,* she thought, a bright flash of adrenaline streaking through her, there and then gone. *No, not that. Not anymore.*

He let out a long, groaning exhalation, and Tori felt liquid warmth flood her. A moment more and the hard thing inside her began to go limp. She leaned down, kissed him once, and rolled off without ceremony. She sat staring out at nothing as he groped for tissues, heard the scrape of a lighter as she reached for the bottle of cheap tequila on the nightstand. She drank from it directly, coughing a little.

He tapped her shoulder. "Smoke?"

Tori accepted one of the two lit cigarettes he held, put it to her lips, dragged, still staring at the far side of the room. The sheets pooled in her lap, leaving her breasts exposed; she could feel the man glancing at them from time to time as he sat beside her, saying nothing. Tori sat. Smoked. Stared.

"Good?" she asked after a while.

"God damn, baby."

"Good. Stop calling me baby."

"Uh ... 'kay."

"What's your name again?"

"Tom."

"You gonna be here when I wake up, Tom?"

Tom was silent. The right side of Tori's mouth, the side he couldn't see, lifted up in a brief smirk.

"That's what I thought," she told him. "You left your ring on the sink. Don't forget it."

"Oh. Didn't think you saw that."

"I see everything." Tori flicked ash into an empty glass on the nightstand.

"You pissed?"

Not about that, thought Tori. She told him no.

"Cool." Tom yawned, stubbed out his cigarette, and rolled over on his side, facing away from Tori. Within minutes he was asleep. Tori sat. Smoked. Stared.

I see everything, she had told him, and it was true. There was little that escaped Tori's notice. When your eyes could read newsprint from across the room and your mind could recall events as a series of detailed snapshots, it was hard *not* to notice everything. The trick for Tori wasn't paying attention, but making herself stop.

She closed her eyes to focus on her body, still stuck in a state of arousal she no longer wanted. Rapid heartbeat, hard nipples, warm and wet between her legs. She supposed she could try to finish the job herself, but the prospect seemed unappealing. She instead went to the bathroom, cleaned off the mess that Tom had left, and returned to the bed without waking him.

Across the room was a window, facing out into an alley. Across the alley was the blank face of a brick wall, illuminated only by the dim glow from a streetlight somewhere near the front of the building. Sitting in the dark, staring out the window, Tori could make out each individual crack in the masonry. She passed the time by counting them.

The warmth between her legs began to fade, finally, and Tori took another swig from the bottle, willing sleep to come. Three quarters of the alcohol was gone, and Tom had barely touched it. A woman her size should have been hanging over the toilet right now, or heading for the emergency room. Tori's head swam a bit, but she was far from drunk. She smirked again. Drank again. Sat. Smoked. Stared.

She was glad Tom would be gone when she woke up. It was better when it went this way. Tom had what he wanted from her, and Tori had escaped from her parents for an evening without needing to play the awkward morning-after game. She had no more desire to feign any sort of connection with Tom than he did with her.

Somewhere his wife was lying cold in her bed, waiting for him, and he was here, asleep in a motel next to a strange girl he'd just fucked. Tori supposed this should bother her, but it didn't. She found it difficult to care about the wife, or about Tom, or about anyone else for that matter. She cared for her parents, annoying though they could be. Then there was Two, more of a sister than any biological relation could ever have been. After that, who? Rhes and Sarah? Molly? Surely they were wonderful people, but Tori had known them so briefly that she sometimes had a hard time picturing their faces.

The friends she had once known in Ohio were all new people. Gone or grown. Married. Raising families. Tori had existed in a kind of suspended animation for the past twelve years, and they had passed her by. Her body was still twenty-one. They were all in their mid-thirties. The girl who had once promised to someday stand as Tori's maid of honor was dead, killed in a car accident. She had left behind a husband, two daughters, and a house.

Tori glanced at Tom and felt guilt, though not about his wife. No, it was for her parents; they would be wondering where she was. Her mother especially. At times like this Tori felt remorse, but it would be a different story when she was home. She was fighting with them more and more often, frustrated by their concern, smothered by their love. It had only been six months since her return after more than a decade of darkness and madness and death. Was it right for her to feel so constrained, so pressed upon, or was it simply a selfish reaction to good intentions?

Tori sat. Smoked. Stared. Eventually her body cooled. Eventually she slept.

* * *

She woke gasping, sweating, shaking from a dream that she couldn't remember. It was still dark, still night, and she grappled with panic, disoriented by her unfamiliar surroundings. After a moment, memory filled the darkness: Tom and the motel. Right.

He was gone. She could see that the other side of the bed was empty, but even without the light leaking in from the street, she would have known. There was no warmth there, no sound of breathing other than her own, which was slowly returning to normal.

Tori ran a hand through her long, golden semi-curls, tousled and damp with sweat. A glance at the digital clock on the nightstand told her that dawn was still more than an hour away. Plenty of time to get home, sneak quietly in, and catch a few more hours of sleep before work. This was not an uncommon occurrence; Tori needed very little rest, perhaps four hours of sleep each night. Her body seemed to want no more.

She slid out of the bed and moved to the bathroom, sat on the toilet, relieved herself of the night's alcohol intake. When she was done she stood for a moment, naked, posing for the mirror. She had the sort of waist and hips that mannequins and magazines made every young woman pine for, though few could ever hope achieve. Bright blue eyes, full breasts, her only visible blemish a strawberry-colored birthmark on the inside of her left thigh. The blood had erased everything else. *Baby,* she thought, *you oughtta be in pictures.*

Tori knew she was attractive, and knew she was lucky to be so. She understood this in a way that was detached, not arrogant. It was useful to be attractive, but beyond that it was not of great importance to her. Tori had seen too much, known too much, lived too much to hold such concerns. Far more interesting, in her opinion, were the secrets hidden behind her form. She flexed, looking herself over, searching for any sign of what she was. There was no outward evidence of her interior strength. No bulging muscles stretched her skin, no veins stood out like roadmaps.

There was no indication that the naked woman in the mirror before her, long-legged and shapely, could bench-press nearly four hundred pounds. No sign that she could run a six-minute mile without becoming winded. There was no sign at all of what she had been for twelve years, no exterior hint of the changes that more than a decade of vampirism had made to her physiology. Abraham's blood had worked within her, changing her, and those changes had not entirely reversed after her return to humanity. It had been too long, the blood too strong, for its marks to be completely wiped out.

The cigarettes, the booze, the sex ... nothing fazed her, hurt her, made her sick. Tori had not so much as come down with a cold since her return to Ohio. She had slept unprotected with more than three dozen men without becoming pregnant or catching any sort of disease. Sometimes she felt like a superhero. Other times she wondered what the point was. She could not be too overt with her abilities; to do so invited all sorts of unwanted questions. She could drink and smoke and fuck without repercussion, yes, but she spent most of her time trying to hide the gifts that the blood had given her.

This is how Clark Kent feels, she thought as she made her way back to the bedroom. *All that time spent pretending* not *to be Superman. Fantastic.*

She was pulling on clothing, nearly ready to leave, when the voice came without warning into her head, overwhelming her thoughts in a rush like a tsunami, the words strung together and incomprehensible, ranting in a nonsense language.

SasemapestrovahPestrovahNankefalsonsaNanaguivesonsa.

Tori stumbled, put one hand against the wall and the other against her forehead to steady herself. When the voice came to her, it was usually as a whisper at the back of her mind. This was direct, loud, and for a moment Tori felt sure her knees would buckle under the onslaught. She made a small cry, closed her eyes, and tried to fight against it.

And then it was gone.

She was sitting on the bed, though she couldn't remember moving there. Sitting and shaking, the prickly feeling of cold sweat on her spine exacerbated by the rough cotton t-shirt she was wearing. Her heart was pounding, her breath coming in ragged gasps.The superhero feeling was gone. Left in its place was nothing more than a scared little girl, nervous and shaking, wondering what was wrong with herself. Tori dressed quickly, glanced one last time around the room, and left.

* * *

Her room was dark and bare and cold, not much more inviting than the motel she had left. There was a double bed on a steel frame at one end, a cheap desk at the other, adorned only with a laptop and a set of speakers. Tori's mother often pressed her to decorate, but to Tori that seemed as though it would bring an unwelcome sense of permanence. This was not her home.

Tori loved her parents, was glad to be back with them, but could not see living here in their little ranch house, in this forgotten part of Ohio, as anything more than the most temporary of situations. After a dozen years of living in the woods surrounding Abraham's palatial estate, Tori had come to value both freedom and solitude. The two-bedroom, single-bath house offered little respite from the presence of her parents. She shuddered to think what it would be like when her father retired.

She was pulling her clothes off when the knock came. *Great*, she thought, rolling her eyes. It would be Mona, of course – her mother. Tori was convinced that her father Jim would someday sleep through the apocalypse. She debated pretending to be asleep, decided against it, and opened the door.

"Hi, Mom."

Mona was a short woman, plump from years of hearty, home-cooked meals and no lack of desserts. She had been beautiful once, like Tori, though not nearly so tall, and unlike many beautiful girls she had also been kind and friendly. She still retained a sort of glow about her that made most people feel comfortable. She was the type of woman, Tori reflected, that one thought of when somebody mentioned their grandmother. Kindly and concerned, Mona looked at Tori, and the worry in her eyes was touching.

"It's very late, Tori."

"I know. I'm sorry if I woke you ... was I making too much noise?" Tori knew she wasn't, knew that Mona didn't sleep well even under the best of circumstances. Her mother confirmed this.

"No, no … I heard the car pull in. I just wanted to make sure that everything was all right."

"Everything's fine, Mom."

Mona's eyes searched Tori's face for some hidden truth. "Your eyes are all puffy and … and you smell like cigarettes."

Good, Tori thought. *Better than smelling like Tom.* Out loud she said, "I was at a bar."

"Until five in the morning?"

What could Tori say? *I was trying to drink myself blind when I met this guy, and I was horny and bored, and he was cute, so I took him to a motel and fucked his brains out. You know how it is, Mom.*

Instead she shrugged, said, "We went to the diner for a snack and coffee. Got to talking."

"We?" Mona raised an eyebrow.

"Mother …"

"I'm sorry, you're right. You're an adult and it's none of my business. I just worry, angel."

The guilt flared back up and Tori sighed. "I don't want to hurt you or Dad. You know that. I don't want you to be scared. What happened before, when I disappeared, I … trust me, it can never happen again."

"I wish you'd tell us more about it. Your friend's story, it … it doesn't explain much."

At first her parents had eaten up the explanations that Two and Tori had proffered. It was not until later, after much consideration and, Tori suspected, many sleepless nights on Mona's part that they had begun to question. Tori felt anger warring with her guilt.

"No. There's nothing more to tell, and you need to forget it, Mom. You can't let it eat at you. Why won't you trust me?"

"I do trust you, dear. I just—"

"You just worry. Right. Stop worrying."

"I can't."

Tori sighed. "I have to work at ten."

Mona frowned. "You don't get enough sleep."

"I'll get what I need, if you'll let me."

Mona looked at her for a long time, and Tori wondered what it was her mother was seeing. Surely not the daughter she had sent off to college twelve years before, a bubbly, vivacious girl who had been quick to smile and friendly to everyone she met. What must Mona think about this new version of her daughter, the one who was brooding, angry all the time, harsh and judgmental?

Tori looked back, unflinching, saddened by the knowledge that the changes within her must be hurting and confusing her mother, but unwilling to divulge what had happened, how she had become what she now was. At last, Mona dropped her gaze and nodded.

"Good night, dear," she said to the girl who had once been her daughter. "I love you."

"I love you, too, Mom," Tori said. She moved backward, and let the door close with a small thump. She turned the lock mechanism, moved to her window, opened it and lit a cigarette. From the hallway she heard her mother sigh and shuffle off, making her way back to bed.

* * *

Tori worked in a nondescript industrial park in Lima, Ohio as an administrative assistant for a dentist, and her job seemed to her the epitome of everything that was wrong with her life in this place. It was boring, slow-paced, unchallenging, and meaningless in the grand scheme of things. Patients came in. Tori retrieved their files. The doctor checked their teeth. Tori marked down their next appointment date, filed the papers, moved on to the next patient. This kept her busy for perhaps twenty minutes out of every hour.

Most of her time was spent sitting at her desk, answering phone calls and playing solitaire on the single computer in the office, waiting for her next cigarette break. The doctor frowned on the smoking, of course. Tori supposed this was hardly surprising, coming from someone who cleaned teeth for a living, but she also knew that she was better at the job than any of the previous girls he had employed, and probably nicer to look at. She felt safe for the time being, if not content. The job paid her few expenses, bought her booze and cigarettes, and provided a reason to get out of the house and away from her parents. What else was there?

Her father had asked her, once, when Mona was out of earshot, if Tori had ever thought about returning to college. She had been a student in good standing at Syracuse University before her disappearance. They would likely take her back. Did that still interest her?

Tori had sighed, frowned, shrugged. Did it interest her? No. She had spent her two years there cheerleading, taking liberal arts courses, and dating a nice young finance major. She had no further interest in cheerleading, could not think of a single course of study that would hold her attention, and the finance major was now thirty-five years old, divorced, and living with a mistress just over half his age in Manhattan. Besides, Mona would have a heart attack if Tori announced any intention to return to the school from which she had been abducted. Why spend the money? Why deal with the stress? Why bother? There was no point.

Tori wished sometimes that she could explain her ennui. She wished she could articulate the feeling of desperate, hopeless, helpless apathy that seemed to have consumed her since Two's return to New York. She was here, going through her days mostly by rote, her only real escape the assortment of bars downtown, located not far from I-75 and a reliable source of new, anonymous partners with whom to spend the night.

She didn't know how to put it into words, this feeling, heavy like a weight around her neck. Nor could she think of any means of escape. She suspected that moving to New York, though the most obvious course of action, would only leave her equally empty and many times as broke. Two was there, and perhaps that was something, but when Tori thought of seeing her friend again some indescribable feeling, half-hidden, impossible to identify or understand, welled up inside her in protest. At these times, faced with this sudden pain that she wished neither to contemplate nor comprehend, Tori would simply turn her thoughts to other matters.

She was on break now, sitting outside in the early September warmth, smoking a cigarette and purposefully not-thinking about these things. Sometimes there were other people out there, in the space between her building and the one next door, smoking and chatting. Sometimes Tori would have to make small talk, a process that did little more than frustrate her. Today there was no one, and that was good. She sat on a stone bench, staring up at the sky, smoking and trying not to think at all.

Nan pareson sa, the voice said at the back of her mind, and Tori barely noticed it. This was more common than the blast that had knocked away her senses at the motel earlier that morning, and Tori had become used to it. She supposed she should be more concerned about hearing phantom voices, even when they were quiet. Tori supposed she should be more concerned about a lot of things.

Nan Kefaleson sa. Nan effriteson sa. Nan afalmeson sa iae vilestro cheo tuvi kashituvre ma vishtati a nav.

Nonsense words in her head, and that crawling feeling of being watched. She had investigated this sensation in the past. It was this, more than the voices, that made her uncomfortable ... this feeling of eyes crawling over her, appraising her. It was not like being at the bar. Tori was used to having her breasts stared at, or her legs, or her rear. This feeling was similar but not the same. Greedy and covetous, but not sexual. Whoever was coveting her wanted her for some other purpose.

She had spent time searching, but if someone was out there watching her she had been unable to find them, and eventually Tori had given up looking. If schizophrenia was a side effect of all the changes vampirism had wrought on her body, there was little to be done about it.

She smoked the cigarette down to the filter in just a few short minutes, wanting to be away from the sensation. The voices were usually weaker indoors, and the feeling of being watched usually left her entirely. She felt a wave of relief and grim humor as she escaped back into the confines of the office building that she had so recently been desperate to leave. Upstairs, a half-finished game of solitaire was waiting for her.

* * *

Her father was out in their back yard grilling steaks when Tori arrived home. She could smell potatoes baking in the oven, and a large pot of corn ears was steaming on the stovetop. Tori glanced out through the screen door, watching her father tend the grill for a moment, then grabbed two bottles of beer from the fridge. She opened both and brought them with her out to the yard. The mid-September air was warm, but there was a scent of autumn on the breeze.

"Hi, Daddy," she said, holding a beer out for him. He turned and smiled. Tori took her height from Jim, and her blue eyes. His hair, once brown, was now mostly grey. Two years away from sixty, her father was still in reasonable shape, with a broad chest and only the slightest hint of a belly. He was wearing a battered pair of jeans and a grey mechanic's shirt.

"Thanks, sweetheart. How was work?"

Tori shrugged. "Same old, same old. You?"

He smiled. "Still got a job. Can't complain."

The economy in Lima and the surrounding area had been on a downward slide for several months. Many people had been fired, laid off, or transferred. Still more had simply moved on, looking for other opportunities. Tori's father worked for a plant on the outskirts of the city that manufactured tanks for the military. He spent most of his time maintaining Cold War–era electronics that there was no money to upgrade. It was a relatively safe, stable job, and Tori hoped it would last until he could retire.

"I suppose that's the truth," she said, and she sipped at her beer. It still felt strange drinking around her father, like she was getting away with something she wasn't supposed to do.

"Your mother said you came in late last night."

Jim's back was to her, so Tori couldn't read his expression. She grimaced, then took another drink, opting not to respond to the statement.

"Don't want to talk about it?" Jim asked, after her silence made it obvious that no reply was forthcoming.

"Not really."

"We worry about you, hon."

Tori sighed. Why did people always ask if you wanted to talk about something, when they were going to push on regardless of your answer?

"There's nothing to worry about," she told him. "I'm a big girl. Believe me, I can take care of myself."

"That may be true, but you're still young—"

"I'm thirty-three."

"No, you are not." Jim's voice betrayed unexpected tension. There was silence again for a moment, and then her father continued.

"You're not thirty-three. You're twenty-one, the same as you were when ... when you disappeared. I don't know why, and I don't know how, but don't stand here and deny what I can see perfectly well. I know what thirty-three looks like, what it sounds like, what it acts like. You're the same girl who went away to her junior year at SU and disappeared."

"Not the same girl ..." Tori managed to keep her voice subdued.

Jim sighed, the sound curiously broken. Defeated. "No, I suppose not."

"Do you believe I'm your daughter?"

"Yes. I ... yes."

Tori shrugged. "I don't know what else I can do for you, Daddy. I *am* your daughter ... but not the same one that I was. You say I'm the same girl, that I haven't changed or grown, but that's not really true. Just because I look the same doesn't mean I'm the same inside."

Jim sighed again, drank his beer, refused to meet her eyes.

"Did you like the other girl better? Is that what this is about?"

She wouldn't have been shocked if the answer was yes. Sad, perhaps, but not shocked. She *knew* that Mona liked the other girl, the Tori who had earned a letter on the cheerleading team in high school, much more than this one that had returned to her.

Jim shook his head. "No, Tori, that's not what this is about. I loved you then, and I love you now, different or not. It's just ... we're so confused, Tori. We're worried about you, about how you're living,

13

about what could've changed you like this and still somehow kept you the same."

"I told you, I don't know. Two found me wandering around in New York. I don't remember anything."

Jim looked up now, meeting her gaze. "If you could say that to me without looking away, I might have an easier time believing it, but you never have."

Tori considered trying, right there, but knew she would fail. She was not the same girl she had once been, but some things hadn't changed. She had never been able to look her father in the eyes and lie to him.

"Daddy ..."

"Why can't you tell us the truth, Tori? That's all we want. I don't care what it is – I'll support you through anything, and I hope you know that."

"I know."

"Then why lie? Or if you're not lying, why hide so much? Why avoid so many questions?"

Tori looked away. "You would never in a million years believe the truth."

"Try me."

"No."

Jim put his beer down and sat on the edge of the picnic table, pressing his palms against his head in frustration. His breathing was haggard; dry and weary. Tori felt like crying. She turned her back to him.

"I think maybe I should move out," she said, hating the shakiness in her voice. She hoped that Jim couldn't hear it, that he wouldn't try to use it against her to get the truth. It would only hurt them both. She would never tell him about Abraham, about Theroen and Melissa. She would never tell him about the things she had done, the things that she still sometimes did in dreams and memories and fantasies she refused to even acknowledge.

"Tori ... "

"No, listen. I think it's too much stress, having me right here on top of you like this after so many years away. Too much stress for you, too much stress for me. *I can't tell you!* I can't. If you won't accept that, and won't believe what Two and I told you from the start, then maybe it would be better not to have me here reminding you every day."

"I already lost my daughter once ... you're going to go away again so soon? Where will you go?"

"I don't know. Columbus, maybe. Or Chicago. Or ... or New York."

"What is there for you in New York?"

"Two is in New York. She has a life there. She'd help me get started. Your steaks are burning."

Jim stood up, flipped them over, drank again from his bottle of beer. "Two. So she's stealing you away from us again?"

The feeling of tears was gone in an instant. Tori turned on her father, furious. "Don't you *ever* accuse her of that. She had nothing to do with that."

"How would I know? All I've heard from either of you, about who she is or where she came from, is lies."

"She saved my life. She believed in me when anyone else would've given up; when everyone else *had* given up. Do you think I'm different now? You have no *idea* who I was, what I did, how I lived. You have no idea. Don't you dare blame that on Two."

"I don't know who else to blame."

"Why do you *need* someone to blame?"

Jim raised his voice for the first time in the conversation, shouting in frustration. "Someone took my daughter away from me!"

They stood in silence for a moment, and then Jim shook his head. When he spoke, he was under control again.

"Twelve years, Tori. It may not matter to you ... those years seem to have passed you by, but that's almost twenty percent of my life. I'm going to die sooner or later, and I'll have missed *twelve years* of watching my daughter grow, and change, and live. I can't ever have those back. They're gone. *That's* why I need someone to blame. I can't blame you, and you won't let me blame Two. You won't tell me anything else. All I have left is blaming myself for letting you go away in the first place."

Tori felt her emotions turn again, this time as a physical force, something that pulled and tore at her. She shuddered, sat down next to her father, took his hand. "Daddy, no. It's not your fault. What happened to me ... it's like getting hit by lightning."

Jim looked at her again. Tori could read concern, and care, and anger, naked there on his face. "At least with the lightning, I'd know what happened."

"And I'd be dead. Which is better? Me alive and you not knowing what happened ... or the alternative?"

"You know the answer," Jim said.

"Yes. But my staying here is driving you and mom crazy. It's ... not doing great things for me either. It's probably best that I go."

"Have you talked to your mother about this?"

Tori laughed, though the sound carried little real humor. "You think *our* discussions are tense? She and I don't know how to talk to each other anymore. Not like we used to."

Jim nodded, standing in silence, considering.

"Take some time to think it over," he said at last.

"I will. I only really started considering it a day or two ago. I might call Two, ask her what she thinks."

She saw her father stiffen a bit at this, but he said nothing. Tori stood up.

"It's really not her fault. I don't know if you'll ever believe that, but it's the truth. The only thing Two's ever done that's hurt me was when she left me here, and I know why she did that."

"She knew you belonged here."

Tori grimaced, resisting the urge to roll her eyes. "Temporarily, yes. Not forever. Whether I'm thirty-three or twenty-one, I can't live here forever."

Jim pulled the steaks off the grill and put them on a plate. "Let's eat," he said, without much enthusiasm.

"Will you tell Mom? About me maybe moving out? I don't think I can ... not without fighting with her anyway."

"If you want me to, I will."

"OK. Daddy?"

"Yes, sweetheart?"

Tori gave him the best smile she could muster, but she knew it had come out sad and weak. She could see in her father's eyes that it hurt him to look at it, and thought she knew why; it was exactly the sort of expression that the old Tori could never have made.

"I'm sorry," she said.

Jim returned her sad smile, shook his head, and glanced toward the screen door that led into the house. "There's nothing to apologize for, baby. Let's eat."

* * *

Dinner had been a silent affair for the most part, and Tori was glad to be done with it. Mona had returned from a trip to the grocery store, and had busied herself preparing vegetables. As Tori and Jim entered, she had looked at her husband, and Tori had read the glance like a highway road sign. The talk had been expected, and Mona had left them alone for that reason.

Tori had braced herself for a flood of questions, but none came. Instead, there had been a few attempts at light conversation, but nothing sustained. Tori had excused herself after a helping of steak and a small potato. As she walked up the hall, she could hear the soft clink of silverware as her parents resumed eating, still not saying anything. She assumed they were waiting until she was out of earshot, or out of the house entirely.

Chalk one up for Mona, she thought now, changing out of her work clothes and into a comfortable pair of jeans. Her mother was a sweet woman, but rarely knew when to keep her mouth shut.

She could hear her parents murmuring and might have been able to piece together individual words if she tried. It didn't matter. In the long run, she knew she was right, and her father knew it, too. Mona might never understand it, but there was little that could be done to prevent it.

Tori sat at her computer, idly browsing websites, trying to ignore the noises of her parents' conversation. She had, for a time, looked carefully for websites relating to vampires, but it had rapidly become apparent that if there were any to be found, they were careful not to reveal it. Most of the people she found claiming to be creatures of the night were little more than angst-riddled teenagers. Of the very few who had sounded halfway serious, all had proven ignorant of a simple test, a single sentence, sent by email.

"I know the *Eresh-Chen*," she had told them, and not one of them had responded with anything other than puzzled curiosity. Tori knew little of vampire society, but even in her previous, animalistic state, she had picked up enough to know that this was important. Theroen's blood, passed on to Two, had meant something. A real vampire would have known that the term existed, if nothing else. A real vampire would have responded with more than confusion.

Eventually Tori gave up on the computer, stood in front of her mirror, put on eyeliner. She knew she shouldn't be going out, not with her parents already concerned, not on a Thursday, not when only two days had passed since the last time. It didn't matter. She needed to be away from here, needed to go somewhere with music and smoke and alcohol. The conversation with her father had left a tense knot inside of her that demanded the touch of skin against skin. Maybe tonight she would find someone who would be able to satisfy her.

She looked herself over in the mirror, half listening to the murmurs in the background. Mona and Jim discussing the fate of their daughter, no doubt. She wondered how much Jim would divulge of what she'd said, and how much he would keep to himself. In the end, she decided it didn't matter. Satisfied with her appearance, Tori left the room.

The voices stopped immediately, and she walked through the living room in silence. As she neared the door, Mona asked, "Are you going out, Tori?"

Tori rolled her eyes, turning to face her parents. "Yes, Mom."

"We had hoped you would stay to talk."

"Not sure that's a great idea tonight."

Mona looked to Jim for support, but he shrugged. "Maybe she's right, hon. Let it sit a while."

Her mother looked pained, but after a moment her shoulders slumped a bit. "All right. Well, be careful, dear."

"I will."

Tori could feel both pairs of eyes burning into her as she turned, opened the door, and stepped through it. The cool night air was a relief. Inside, the murmuring voices started up again.

* * *

The week bled into the weekend. Tori spent most of her time outside of work at bars and motels. There was little pleasure to be had, but she seemed unable to stop, propelled into these activities by a need within her that she couldn't identify. Was this life? Was this the way she would spend the rest of her days? Trying to get drunk? Trying to get off?

On the following Monday night her parents held what felt to Tori afterwards like an intervention, and she supposed that feeling wasn't too terribly inaccurate. They *had* to have guessed what she was doing with her nights; if not the boys, then at least the booze. What else was there to do in the evenings but drink? Tori had no friends to speak of, and she wasn't the type for bowling leagues.

It began as Tori was leaving for the bars. The atmosphere at home had grown decidedly worse over the course of the past week, due not to the conversation but to the lack thereof. The house seemed draped in silence since her talk with her father the week before, as if both sides were waiting for the other shoe to drop, but neither wanted to be the one to drop it. Her mother must finally have become tired of waiting. Tori didn't think Jim would ever have gotten around to it without his wife's prompting.

"Tori, we'd like to talk to you," Mona said as Tori left the bathroom, wrapped in a towel. "Do you have some time?"

Tori knew in an instant what was coming, thought about arguing, decided against it. This had to happen sooner or later.

"OK, give me a minute to pull on some clothes," she said, and headed for her bedroom. She could feel Mona watching her go, and Tori allowed herself a moment of annoyance. It wasn't as if she was going to bolt directly for the front door should her mother's eyes stray.

19

Jim and Mona were waiting for her in the living room, sitting together on the couch. Tori looked at them for a moment, apprehensive, before sitting down in a recliner that faced them.

"All right. Bring it on," she said. Jim looked away, as if uncomfortable with what was about to happen, but Mona seemed undeterred.

"Your father and I think we've waited too long to talk to you about your behavior, Tori," Mona said. She was pitching her voice carefully, trying to sound stern without being too judgmental. Tori, who could pick up vocal nuances unnoticeable to most people, could hear that her mother was nervous, but determined to go on. She kept her own voice neutral in her response.

"OK."

Mona pressed on. "You go out drinking a lot, even for someone as young as you are."

Jim stirred for a moment at this, then settled. Tori nodded, shrugged, said nothing.

Mona continued. "It's not that we want to run your life. You're not a child ... you can do what you want. But we're very worried about you, Tori. You drink, you don't sleep, you come home at all sorts of hours and refuse to tell us anything about where you've been or what you've been doing."

Mona was gaining steam as she spoke, getting on a roll.

"You're smoking all the time now, there's no sense in hiding that. You're never in a good mood. When you're home, you're either asleep or brooding. You hold down a job, but you clearly don't like it."

"Clerical work isn't exactly a stimulating career," Tori interjected.

"It's not a career at all, and you know it," Mona replied. "It's just something you're doing because you feel like you're supposed to. Tori, that's our point ... this life you're living, it can't be healthy for you."

Something about this struck Tori. It was the truth, of course; her day to day actions couldn't possibly be good for her, and yet ...

"It hasn't hurt me yet," she said.

"We don't want it to get to that point."

"And what exactly would you suggest I do?"

Mona paused, looked at Jim for support. He took her hand, squeezed it, nodded. Mona continued.

"We'd like you to see a therapist."

Tori rolled her eyes. "Oh, Christ ..."

"It could help," Mona said.

"No, Mom. Not happening."

"Hear her out," Jim said.

"Why? I don't want to waste your time, or mine, or a doctor's."

"This is hardly a waste of time," Mona said.

"There is absolutely nothing a therapist could do for me," Tori said. She could hear anger creeping into her voice, and some small part of her cried out against it, but she seemed powerless to keep it out.

"Please, Tori." Jim looked tired and old, a man of fifty-eight having a talk he had hoped never to have with his daughter. Tori tried to force herself to relax.

"OK, fine. You want me to see a therapist, and you want me to hear you out. Got it. Go ahead, make the pitch."

"The 'pitch' is that you're not healthy," Mona said. She saw Tori take in a breath to respond, and cut her daughter off. "Oh, physically you're fine. You seem to be in great shape, though Lord knows how long that's going to continue if you keep smoking and drinking the way you do. It's your emotional state we're concerned about, Tori. You won't *talk* to us."

"I *can't* talk to you," Tori said.

"That's not true," Mona replied.

Tori made a sound of frustration, shook her head, looked to her father for help. "Yes it is. Jesus Christ, mom ... this isn't the same thing as when I was eleven and needed a training bra, but I was too embarrassed to ask."

"We understand that, Tori."

"No, you don't. If you did, you'd let it go. I'm fine."

"You're not fine, and you need to stop pretending you are. Whatever it is that happened to you, Tori, it changed you. It made you ..." Mona paused, at a loss for words.

"That's what this is about, really, isn't it? It's because I'm different, and because you miss the bubble-headed idiot you sent off to school."

Mona looked as if she'd been slapped. "Tori, your father and I love you."

"Then stop trying to change me."

"We're not trying to change you. We're trying to help you."

"This isn't helping."

"We couldn't think of anything else. We're scared! We're scared that you're going to run off to New York. Behaving like this, in that city, can get you *killed*. Who will look after you?"

"I'm an adult. I don't need looking after. We've been through this ... repeatedly. I guess it's not sinking in. Are we almost done?"

Mona was slow to anger, but Tori's attitude had finally taken her there. "Why?" she snapped. "Are we cutting into your drinking time?"

"Mona—" Jim began, but Tori was already talking over him.

"Yes, Mom, that is *exactly* it. I'm so very desperate for a beer and a smoke that I simply must abandon this otherwise *scintillating* conversation. I apologize, do go on! I believe you were accusing me of being crazy?"

"I never *said* that!" Mona cried. "I never said you were crazy. Don't you go twisting my words, assuming things I never said!"

"That'd be crazy," Tori muttered. Mona shot her an angry look, but opted to otherwise ignore the comment.

"This is not going well," Jim said. "Perhaps we should save it for another night."

Tori sighed. "Daddy, it's not going to be any better some other time. If Mom has things to say, then she should say them. It doesn't matter. I'll be out of your hair in a week and this won't be a problem anymore. I can make it faster than that if you want."

"We don't want you to go anywhere, Tori," Mona said.

"You may be disappointed," Tori replied.

"This sarcasm isn't helping anything!" her mother snapped, and Tori felt anger boiling over, taking control. She let it happen, almost thankful for it.

"Fine. I think we're done here, then," she said, standing up and walking toward the door. She wasn't ready to go out, hadn't put on any makeup or even brushed her hair, but this needed to stop before she said something stupid.

"You're leaving?" Mona asked.

"What else is there to do?"

"You could sit and talk instead of fighting with us."

Tori paused at the door, her back to them, and sighed. "Talk about what, Mom? My job? My friends? My life? It's ... empty. My life is empty, and this place is empty. There's nothing here for me."

"We're here!"

Tori turned to face them. "You're not enough. I'm sorry. I'm so sorry, but it's the truth. I love you both, but you're not enough, and you have to let me go. If you don't, I'm going to go insane."

It was Mona's turn to roll her eyes. "There's no need to be melodramatic," she said.

"Melodramatic?"

Tori felt her eyes narrow, felt her fists clench. She took a step back into the room, grappling with her emotions. "Is ... is that what you think this is?"

"What is it about your life that would drive you insane?" Mona asked. She was still angry, Tori could hear it in her voice, but there was something else there, too. A sliver of doubt, as if her mother knew she had overstepped her bounds.

"You know nothing about my life. Nothing." Tori was trying not to yell, only barely succeeding.

"You won't *tell* us anything!" Mona cried. Jim put a hand on her arm, but she shoved it away, glaring at her daughter.

Tori closed her eyes, looked at the floor, tried to get herself under control. When she thought she could speak without shouting, she looked back at her parents.

"I can't."

"Tori, please—" her mother began.

"I *can't!* God, please listen to me! I can't tell you. Not what I was, not what I did. You don't want to know, and I don't want you to know. Don't make me *hurt* you like that."

"Better you hurt us than hurt yourself," her father said, his voice.

Tori smiled, but she had started to cry.

"Hurt myself ..." she murmured, and laughed. "No, you don't need to worry about that. I can't hurt myself. I've tried and tried. I've been trying ever since Two left."

Neither Mona nor Jim seemed able to find a response to that, and after a moment Tori laughed again, still weeping.

"I'm indestructible. Do you understand? I smoke two packs a day. I drink *bottles* of alcohol every night. God ... I fuck like a *rabbit!* No protection. With men who might be bringing me to the motel to cut my throat."

Jim and Mona were still silent, staring, unable to respond. Tori grinned at them through her tears, savage, hating herself for what she was saying but unable to stop.

"Is that what you wanted to hear? Nothing can kill me. Nothing can help me. Nothing can change me. I'm already dead."

She drew a hand across her eyes, stared at her parents, unable to change the painful expression her face had contorted itself into. More a grimace than a grin now, really, but was there even any difference? It didn't matter. She could see fear in their eyes now, their expressions those of people who have been thrown with sudden force badly out of their element.

"Now you *really* think I'm crazy," she said, "but I don't care because there's the truth. You asked for it. Tori died on a winter night, in a mansion in Binghamton, at the hands of a monster. All that was left was another monster just like him. I did horrible things and I *loved* doing them, until Two showed up. She saved me, and she brought me here to you, and then she left me here, empty, and I hate her. I fucking *hate* her for saving me and then leaving me all alone."

"Tori, I don't understand ..." Mona was at a loss, shocked and scared, pale and shaken.

"Of course you don't understand!" Tori roared at her. "That's what I've been telling you all along. You'll never understand. No one understands, except Two, and she left me. She *left* me!"

Tori looked around the room, jaw clenched. It seemed as if at any moment the walls would cave in on her, collapsing and burying her, trapping her here forever. She put her hands over her eyes.

"I have to go," she said, and turned to make her way toward the door. Stumbling, barely able to see through her tears, needing only to get out. She heard her mother call her name.

"I have to go!" she cried, and then she was out into the night air, racing across her yard, pulling herself into her car. Roaring engine, screeching tires, rushing wind. Tori left her parents still sitting bewildered, trying to understand this last outburst, and drove out into the night.

* * *

The miles rolled by underneath the wheels of her car, but where was she going? To New York? No. She was not yet ready to say to Two the things she had said to her parents. It was hard enough to admit to herself this hatred she felt for Two, who had left her here in this grey world with no pleasure, no pain, no hope. She would not be able to say the things she needed to say. Not yet. She wondered if she ever would.

Tori drove, cried, tried to sort out what to do. It seemed a thousand voices clamored at her at once, each demanding her attention. One voice wished only to rend and tear, to hurt things, to take satisfaction in strength and savagery. Another whispered promises of salvation at the bottom of a bottle or, failing that, at least escape for a time. Another murmured incessantly, unyielding, desiring nothing more than the smell of sweat and the feel of a man's skin. There were other voices; some advocated that she keep driving, others that she turn back. Whispers and shouts and screams offered everything from solace to suicide, and Tori listened to them all, unable to choose from the options offered up by her own traitorous mind.

Old habits finally won out over indecision, and Tori found herself in a city parking lot, across the street from a row of bars, looking herself over in the car's rearview mirror. She could barely remember the drive, wasn't sure she wanted to be here, but could think of nowhere better to go. With a feeling that was very much like relief, Tori surrendered to habit, let the training of so many previous nights take over. Inside there would be a bottle. Inside there would be smoke. Inside there would be men, some of them too drunk and busy staring at her breasts to notice her blotchy cheeks and bloodshot eyes.

When he was asleep next to her and she sat in bed, still hot and awake and unfulfilled, Tori smoked and sat, staring out the window with her preternatural eyes. She tried not to think about who she had been. She tried not to think about who she was now. She thought instead about Two, the only person left that she loved and the only person left that she despised. When the voices began in their nonsense language at the back of her mind, she paid them no attention. When sleep finally took her, she did not dream.

Tori lived in motels for four days before returning home.

* * *

"Dad? Daddy?"

Tori leaned in through the front door, her voice tentative. She had hoped to catch her father before he went to work, while somehow avoiding Mona. Over the past few months, Jim had been better equipped to talk to her than her mother. He would probably not understand her leaving, would not agree with her that it was what she had to do, but in the end he would accept it. He would let her go to whatever destination she had chosen, though what that destination was Tori could not say.

There was no response to her call, and this seemed odd. Her mother didn't sleep well, but it was possible that she was still angry and purposely not answering. Her father, though, was nearly always up at this time. It was almost dawn, but all of the lights were off, the house silent. She flicked the switch to her left, more out of habit than out of any need for light, but nothing happened.

Tori felt a shudder run up her spine as she stepped through the door and into the silent house. *Relax*, she told herself. *Bulb's burned out, and they're asleep. That's all.*

26

Something made a crackling noise under her feet. Tori looked down, then up above her head. The front hall lamp, a glass dome containing two light bulbs, had been shattered, the broken stumps of the bulbs still jutting from their sockets. The tiny things crunching and snapping below her feet were pieces of the broken glass.

"Mom?" Tori tried again, registering vague and distant surprise at the amount of tension in her voice.

There was a noise from the bathroom, just a single sound, small and lonely, but to Tori's ears it was like a gunshot. She jerked, gasped, whirling in that direction before she fully realized what she had heard. The faucet had been leaking all summer; her father hadn't gotten around to fixing it yet.

Tori was struck by a sudden urge, so strong it was nearly impossible to resist, to simply turn around and run. She didn't understand it, but the sound of the dripping faucet had filled her with a slow and crawling dread. Mealworms inching up her back, snakes churning in her stomach, a cold and mold-coated floor against her skin. Abraham had made her feel like this, when she first met him, before he bit her and stole her life away.

She fought down the urge to flee, turned instead and glanced toward the kitchen. When she saw the hand, she felt no rush of surprise, but the crawling feeling intensified. It was just a hand resting on its side, the arm attached to it blocked from view by the lip of the kitchen door. Just a hand, but it told her everything in an instant. The fingertips were dark, even for this low light, and curled slightly. Beneath them the floor was black and slick. Tori let out a low moan and, taking steps on legs that seemed unwilling to obey, walked to the kitchen door.

Mona Perrault – *Mom* – lay on her side, eyes wide and staring, in a pool of semi-congealed liquid that looked like ink in the dim confines of the kitchen. Mona's throat was not so much cut as torn out, a ruined mess of flesh and cartilage. Her wrists were crisscrossed with a pattern of slashes, and her other hand, the one that had not been visible from the living room, clutched still at the edge of a cupboard door, reaching toward the telephone.

Tori stared, feeling stupid and slow, not yet ready or willing to comprehend the sight before her. She looked away from the body, toward the counter, and reeled backward as if dealt a physical blow. Her feet slipped out from under her on the slick floor and she fell, cracking her head against the oak cabinetry, barely noticing the pain.

Sprawled across the counter was a thing that had once been her father. This thing, like Mona, was missing its throat, covered in blood, eyes staring blankly out at nothing. Where Mona's wrists had merely been slashed, Jim's had been reduced to tattered strips of skin and muscle, his palms and fingers also lacerated. His arms were stretched out before him, bound at the wrists, his face frozen in an expression not of fear or hate or horror but of desperation. He seemed to be looking at her for help, for salvation, and Tori was consumed with the desire to get away from those staring eyes and whatever accusation she might find there if she looked too long.

She scrabbled backward on her hands, moving like a crab, making nonsense sounds of negation and slipping on the wet floor. She reached the living room and would have kept going if not for the pain that lanced up from her left palm, too strong to be ignored. More glass from the broken lights, this time embedded deep into her flesh. Tori held her hands up before her and saw in the first light of day, shining in from the bay window, that they were streaked with crimson. These bright, new streaks mixed with Mona's older, darker blood. Between her fingers, Tori could see both faces, both pairs of eyes. They stared out at her from the kitchen, from the place where both of her parents had been butchered and now lay dead.

Looking at those eyes, Tori began to scream.

CHAPTER II

A Walk in the Rain

The borough of Brooklyn sat brooding under a wet blanket of stratus clouds, muttering and grumbling, longing for sun. Summer was turning slowly to fall, and New York was preparing now for the wet, and the cold, and the long nights of winter. Not even October yet, and still there was a bite to the wind that snagged in the corners of jackets, a heaviness to the rain better suited to the short, grey days ahead.

Rhes Thompson, out walking because the atmosphere at home was more dismal even than this rain, could've done without it.

"Figures. First the phone call, then the fight, and now I get God pissing down the back of my neck. Some fucking day."

Rhes looked mainly at the wet concrete in front of him, letting his feet carry him where they would. He was not out on any errand, had no real destination, was simply walking without a plan.

The day had started out well enough, waking under heavy covers to the pleasant sound of light rain against the windows. His girlfriend Sarah next to him, warm and naked, her chest rising and falling against his arm. Down the hall their ward, Molly, slept peacefully, the demons of her past held at bay for the time being. Outside was grey and miserable, no doubt, but inside they had comfort and warmth.

And breakfast, which he had been in the process of cooking when both girls had come wandering down the stairs. Molly had announced that she would be leaving at noon to spend the day, and night, at a friend's house. Sarah had said she wanted to visit a new exhibit – tactile art for the blind – being featured at MoMA. This had sounded fine to Rhes, and so the plan had seemed complete. Then Sarah had suggested the phone call, and everything had gone to hell.

A honk, the sound of wet skidding, a muffled curse. Rhes looked up to realize that he had wandered into an intersection without really checking for traffic first, and had nearly been run over. He waved, ducked his head, put on an apologetic face. *Sorry, my bad.* The driver rolled his eyes, shrugged, motioned him along. *Eh, whaddaya gonna do about it?*

His mind was not on the roads, and Rhes resolved to walk more avenue blocks, crossing fewer streets. He found himself wishing for his old neighborhood, Bedford Stuyvesant, and the thought amused him. Fewer cars during the day, certainly, but even he hadn't been comfortable going far from the apartment at night. Their new place, a two-bedroom duplex in Park Slope, was beautiful and safe, but his feet had not yet learned the roads.

Rhes liked to walk, even in the rain. He was not a quick thinker like Sarah, but he often had success working out problems when given the time. Walking served this need, though in this instance he was not sure the problem could be solved, no matter how long he worked at it. It was not the fight that worried him, not really; the occasional argument was inevitable. It was the girl who had caused the argument, who was at its core, that he was pondering now.

When he had first met her, Two had been a pretty, perky young woman who had adapted quite well to the life she had chosen for herself. He hadn't always approved of the ways in which she earned her living, but overall he had thought her smart and well-equipped to survive life on the city streets. Then had come the heroin, the pimp, the prostitution. She had fought through all that, amazingly, with the help of a lover, and come through to the other side scarred but alive. For a short time, the Two he had known seemed to have emerged. She had stormed off to Ohio with Tori, determined to return the girl to a normal life.

When she had come back to New York, though, Two had been different. Pensive, preoccupied, and obviously unhappy. Her lover was dead, and with each passing week it seemed that Two slipped further into despair. There was no cure for her ailment that Rhes could provide, no gift he could give that would lift her spirits. Two pined for the life she had been shown, that which had been given to her for the briefest of moments by this man, Theroen. He had opened a vein in her throat, drank her blood, and replaced it with his own. He had made her like him, and then he had died, and now she was alone.

* * *

"Why don't you call Two and ask her if she wants to go?" Sarah had asked him, and Rhes remembered the immediate sinking feeling in his stomach. There had been a time when her suggestion wouldn't have been needed. As soon as the decision to go had been made, Rhes would have been on the phone to invite Two. That time was long gone. They barely saw Two these days.

"Yeah," he said. "OK."

"You don't want to?"

"Can't say I'm looking forward to it, no."

"She might want to come, Rhes." Sarah's voice was soft, and she shrugged. "You never know ..."

"No, you never do. I'll call, Sarah."

So he called, and let the phone ring. He was expecting to get her voicemail, leave a message, never get a call back; this had become standard procedure. Two never wanted to do anything at all, these days, and answering the phone seemed to rank particularly low on her list. He was surprised by the click that said someone had picked up.

"Yeah?" her voice was fuzzy.

"Two? It's Rhes. Sorry ... did I wake you up?"

Rhes glanced at the clock above the stove. Almost one.

"Yeah. S'OK, don't worry about it. What's up?"

"Sarah and I are headed out to MoMA to check out the new exhibit. Figured we'd call ..."

31

Rhes let the words hang, the invitation implicit.

"Thanks, Rhes. I'm going to skip this one, though."

Two's voice was dead and distant, on auto-pilot, as if she was reading the words from a cue card. It reminded him very much of speaking with her during her addiction. Against his better judgment, Rhes spoke again.

"Look, Two … are you OK? We haven't seen much of you lately."

There was a moment of silence. When Two's voice came across the line again there was a slight chill in it. Rhes wondered whether this was an improvement over the apathy.

"I'm fine, Rhes. Rain's got me down, is all. I'm not ready for summer to end."

Me neither, Rhes thought. Out loud he asked, "You're still sober, right?"

Silence again, and then, "Yes, Rhes."

"Two …"

"You want to come over and check for needle marks? I'll let you." Two's voice was dead again.

"No. I believe you. I just … Two, if there's anything we can do …"

"There's not."

It was Rhes's turn for silence. He couldn't think of a response to this, which pretty much confirmed its truth. After a moment, without thinking, he said, "Molly misses you."

Two made a sound that was less a sigh than a noise dead leaves might make rattling across pavement.

"I miss her, too," she said, and hung up.

Rhes looked at the phone for a moment, felt anger welling up inside of him, fought against it and lost. He slammed the phone down hard, smashing his fingers in the process, which did little to improve his mood.

"I'm guessing that didn't go well," Sarah said from the living room.

"No. No, I don't think that 'well' is the word I'd use," Rhes said. He wandered over to the fridge, got himself a beer, and sat down at the kitchen table.

"Is she OK?"

"I don't know."

"Are *you* OK? It's ... kind of early for beer." Sarah was blind, but had heard the sound of the bottle opening.

"I don't know," Rhes repeated.

"Hon ..."

"Just give me a minute, Sarah! Christ."

Sarah gave him about ten seconds. "What did she say?"

"Nothing. I mean, she said that she didn't want to go, and then I asked her if she was OK, and that pissed her off, or made her sad, or whatever it is she feels these days. So then I got *really* stupid and asked if she was still sober."

"Is she?"

"Of course she is; that's not what she wants. Anyway, she's not going to the stupid museum. This whole call was a waste of time."

Sarah had gotten up and was standing in the doorway. She frowned. "Well, Jesus, Rhes, you could've handled it better."

"Really? Wow, I thought I was doing great, but God knows the expertise you've demonstrated lately has been amazing. In fact, wasn't this phone call your idea in the first place?"

"Yes, it was my idea," Sarah replied, her voice icy, "and no, maybe I haven't been handling her well lately ... but at least I'm trying."

"Your trying is driving her further away."

"And your sitting around on your ass isn't helping bring her back!"

Rhes could feel the beginnings of a headache behind his temples. He didn't want to be doing this.

"She's my friend," he said, trying to keep his voice level. "I don't want to hurt her. I hate hurting her."

"But you can't help her if you won't even talk to her. If you won't do anything ... where are you going?"

Rhes had gotten up and was crossing the kitchen. He dropped his beer bottle into the sink and headed toward their front hallway. Sarah's head turned as she followed the sound of his movements.

"I'm taking a walk."

"What about the museum?"

"Not in the mood, Sarah," Rhes said, pulling on his jacket. "Maybe next weekend."

"Great. That's fucking great." Sarah tossed the book she had been holding into the living room and stormed off up the stairs, still talking as she went. "Go walk and be pissed off, then. I'll just blow my weekend sitting around doing nothing."

My heart bleeds, Rhes thought, but he bit his lip and stayed silent, slamming the door behind him as he left. Outside the weather was miserable but, at the moment, it seemed more appealing than staying in.

* * *

"You feeling any better?"

Rhes searched the tone of Sarah's voice for any malice, found none, and shrugged. The apartment was cool and dim; Sarah didn't require any lights and hadn't noticed the setting sun. Rhes pulled his shoes off in the front hallway, turned on the living room light as he entered, and flopped down on the couch.

"Yeah, a little. I'm sorry for yelling."

Sarah was sitting across from him in an easy-chair. "S'OK," she said. "I was being … a little unreasonable myself."

Sarah's voice was nonchalant, but Rhes smiled to himself. It was a rare occasion when she would cede anything of the sort in their arguments, and Rhes considered it a small victory whenever it happened. He didn't respond immediately, and the two sat in quiet for a time before Sarah sighed and spoke again.

"What're we going to do about her, Rhes?"

Rhes shook his head. "I don't know. I hate saying that, but I've got nothing else. I went out, I walked, and I thought about it … and I just don't know. I don't think there's anything we can do for her."

"She's shut us out completely … it's even worse than before! Why won't she let us help?"

"How would we help? What can you do for her? What can I do for her? We don't know anything about this."

Rhes closed his eyes and leaned his head back, resting it on the top edge of the couch. Finally he said, "We can't make her into a vampire."

Silence fell between them, the absurdity of his final statement hanging over the room. Of course they couldn't make her into a vampire; there were no such *things* as vampires, or so they had believed until Two had presented them with enough evidence to change their minds.

There were the objects from the mansion, countless items that Two had sold in order to fund her new life. There were the records – hard to locate and to trace, but available for the right price – of Abraham and his children's existence. There was the fact that Two had shrugged a serious heroin addiction off in a matter of weeks and seemed to have not the slightest interest in ever returning to the drug, something that Molly still struggled with on a constant basis.

And of course there was Tori, the girl whose mind had been cracked by vampirism and who Rhes himself had watched return more and more to humanity with each passing day. Her tales of the mansion, of the things she had seen and done there, had been simultaneously fascinating and repugnant, and they had hammered home the point to Rhes and Sarah over and over again. Yes, there were vampires. Yes, Two had been among them.

No, that didn't make it any easier to talk about.

Sarah finally broke the silence. "I don't suppose we can do that for her, no."

"I don't know what's left except to let her go, but I just can't do it. It hurts."

"I know, baby. I don't want to let her go either."

"Maybe Tori could help her?"

Sarah shrugged. "Who knows? Tori spent most of her time running around naked in the forest, doing things she's pretty ashamed of. I don't think she has quite the same impression of it all that Two has."

"Probably not," Rhes said. He stood up and headed toward the kitchen. After a moment, Sarah followed him.

"You want me to make dinner?" she asked.

"I'll do it. What do you want?"

"First? A hug. After that, maybe spaghetti."

Rhes gave a small laugh, crossed the kitchen, and put his arms around Sarah. She held him tightly in her own, resting her head against his chest.

"This sucks," she said.

"You're the one who asked for it."

She laughed a little. "Not that. I mean this whole thing with Two. Why should we even care, Rhes? It's not like she wants us to. She'd be happier if we didn't."

"Yeah. But we care because she's our friend, and we can't make ourselves stop. We know who Two is when she's healthy and ... and right. We like that person a lot, and what we're seeing now is someone else."

Sarah nodded, let him go, moved to the cupboard and pulled a pot from it. She walked over to the sink, filled the pot with water, set it to boil on the stove. Her spatial awareness never ceased to amaze Rhes, who had trouble crossing an open room in the dark without finding a way to hurt himself. He took a package of spaghetti from the pantry closet and laid it on the counter.

"The person we're seeing now is creepy," Sarah said. "There's some open sauce in the fridge."

"Thanks. Yes, it's creepy. It's wrong and sad and frustrating, which is why I sometimes have to bang shit around and take walks in the rain."

Sarah turned her head as if looking at him, an action still ingrained from her childhood, when she'd been able to see.

"That was my fault," she said. "I'm sorry."

"No, it was both of our faults. And Two's fault. And probably if I wanted to get real worked up about it, I could find a way to blame Jesus, too. But it doesn't really matter ... it's just a touchy subject because we don't have any answers."

"Maybe we should stop letting her close us out. I dunno ... maybe go talk to her in person, grab her by the shoulders, slap her around. Make her realize there's still a whole world out here and that she should stop living with the dead."

"Works in movies," Rhes said, shrugging. "Don't know about real life. I think she's likely to just give you that laugh of hers, the one that's all sarcastic and pissed off, like you should quit wasting her time."

"Yeah, well, so I get the laugh. Big deal. I've gotten it over the phone a ton of times since she came back that last time, when she said the place had burned down. I could deal with the laugh if I thought what I had to say was going to have any effect on her."

"Think it will?"

Sarah paused for a minute and leaned backward against the counter, arching her back and stretching, which caused her sweater to press tight against her breasts. Rhes paused with his hand outstretched over the pot of water, ready to drop a handful of spaghetti in, taking an opportunity to admire the view she was unintentionally providing. There was a lot to admire; Sarah was five-eight, in good shape, with straight red hair that she was currently keeping at shoulder length and a cute spread of freckles across the bridge of her nose. Rhes had met her when he had stopped to ask if he could pet her guide dog, Jake, during jazz night at a local coffee shop. By the end of the evening, he had thought he might be falling in love.

"Quit staring at me like that," Sarah said with a laugh. Rhes rolled his eyes and dropped the pasta in to the water, stirring a few times.

"Quit *standing* like that, then. Anyway, you're not supposed to know I'm looking!"

"Right, right ... one of the perks of dating a blind chick. We've got crazy hoodoo, though. We know what you're doing."

"At the moment, what I'm doing is waiting for an answer to my question."

Sarah smiled at him as he poured tomato sauce into a pan and set it on the stove.

"I'm getting to it. Add some oregano and salt and stuff to that. It's not so great right out of the jar."

"Yes ma'am."

"To answer your question, no ... I don't think confronting her will accomplish anything, but I'm not averse to trying it."

"Mmm. I'm not sure I can handle seeing her again in person. The last time was brutal, and that was, like, two months ago."

"Yeah," Sarah said. "But on the plus side, she's probably even more detached than she was, so at least she might not start crying again."

"You noticed that, too?"

"Pretty sure the only person who didn't notice was Two. She just kept right on talking in that dead voice."

"So how'd you know?"

"She started sniffling."

Rhes shook his head, amazed. "I would never have noticed that."

"You don't need to. You've got all five senses available to you."

"Yeah, but I—"

The phone rang, cutting Rhes off. He reached over and picked it up, stirring sauce with his free hand. On the other end of the line he could hear someone gasping for breath, and realized after a moment that he whoever he was listening to was weeping.

"Hello?" he asked. Sarah looked up, immediately aware of the change in his tone.

On the phone, the person seemed to be struggling to gain control of their tears. Finally Rhes heard, "Z'iss Rhes?"

"Yes, this is Rhes? Who's this?"

"S'Tori."

"Oh, hey! Tori, are you OK?"

There was a pause and some snuffling. Rhes thought he heard tissues being pulled from a box, rapid-fire, one after another.

"No, 'spose not," said Tori.

"What's wrong?"

"D'you know where ... where Two is?" Tori's words were slurred, and not just from crying. Rhes thought she might be drunk.

"No, sorry. I called her this afternoon and she was home."

"Not now," Tori replied.

"Did you try her cell?"

"Juss rings an' rings. Stupid. I need to t-talk to her *now*."

"Well, if I hear anything from her I'll tell her to call you. Is there anything I can do to help you?"

"Too late ... Rhes, 'sallover now. They're gone. Oh, no. No."

Tori began to sob again. Rhes listened, feeling bewildered.

"Who's gone? Tori? Who are you talking about?"

"She left me!" Tori shouted. "Left me here, and now they're gone and she's not there. You tell her, Rhes. You tell her it's all her fault."

"Tori, what happened?"

"Gotta go."

Tori hung up on him. After a moment, Rhes set the phone down in its cradle and returned to stirring the tomato sauce.

"... the *hell* was that about?" Sarah asked him.

"Not sure. She was super drunk, and crying so hard I could barely get what she was saying. Except when she started shouting about how Two left her there and that it's all her fault."

"I heard that part all the way over here," Sarah said. "What's all Two's fault though? Should we call her back?"

"Probably."

Sarah waited a moment. "You uh ... gonna?"

"You know those scenes in movies where someone goes 'I've got a bad feeling about this,' and they're always right?"

Sarah nodded.

Rhes frowned. "That's how I feel right now."

* * *

Sarah made the call, but Tori wasn't answering her phone, nor was there any kind of voicemail or answering machine. After letting it ring for nearly five minutes, Sarah gave up, returned the handset to its cradle, and helped Rhes bring dinner to the table. They ate without saying much, contemplating the day's troubling calls, wondering what was happening to their friends.

"I guess we should check the news," Rhes said when they were done. "You get the TV, I'll get the 'net."

It hadn't made the New York news channels, but it didn't take Rhes long to hunt down what had happened on the Internet. He found the story on a local news site and read it to Sarah, feeling her hand gripping ever tighter on his shoulder as the article explained that, though the police would not reveal the exact nature of the crimes, Tori's parents had most certainly been tortured before their eventual murder.

When the article reached Tori's alibi, Sarah's hand relaxed. "Oh, thank Christ," she said weakly.

"Did you think she did it?" Rhes asked. He wasn't trying to accuse her, and thought he had managed to keep any suggestion otherwise out of his voice. Sarah didn't seem offended.

"Yes. Well, no, I mean ... I didn't think she'd do something like that, but you have to consider the possibility. You know what she was. It's not that hard to make the leap."

"No, it's not, you're right. My brain just hadn't made it yet. She's safe, though. Coroner says they were hours old when Tori found them. She was at that bar during most of it ... eight witnesses there, and then the other guy."

"The motel attendant, after, right. I'm sure she was thrilled to have *that* written in all the papers. But yeah, I know she didn't do it. I was just scared that she might have, for a minute."

"I know. God ... what do we do now?"

Sarah looked bewildered. "I have no idea. I don't think we can just pack up and go to Ohio, at least not for a couple of days. We've got work, and Molly's got school ... but Tori's going to need all kinds of help, and I don't know if she's got anyone out there or not. We have to find Two first."

"Why didn't Tori call us before? Christ, it's been more than a day already."

"Don't know. She's probably not thinking very clearly, and really, she didn't even want to call us. She wanted to call Two. We were the backup plan."

"Ok, so what now?"

"We find Two." Sarah looked very concerned.

"Tori said she's not home."

"Tori said she's not *answering*. That doesn't mean she's not home ... not at all. She may not be *able* to answer. Hon, we have to find her. This is really bad. I don't think it's random coincidence that something like this is happening to Tori. If someone's targeting her, don't you think that Two's in danger?"

"Oh. Shit, Sarah ..."

"Right. Let's go."

Rhes and Sarah left their dishes on the table and headed for Manhattan.

CHAPTER III

Manhattan by Moonlight

Two was drowning in blood.

The liquid ran down her forehead in rivers, pooled in the corners of her eyes, dripped past her lips and swirled hot on her tongue. Eyes shut, she opened her mouth wide and drank, drank, searching for the source, bathing in blood, immersing herself completely. Yet even in this bliss, this joy, this beauty, there was still that cold ball in her stomach. There was still the dull grey veil that sucked the life from her vision, even with her eyes shut. It covered her dreams, destroyed her fantasies, brought her always back to harsh reality.

This isn't real.

Yes it is.

No.

Two turned off the shower and rested her head against the slate tiles that lined the wall. The liquid running from her hair, dripping on the floor, steaming on her pink skin was water, not blood. There was no blood for her, or at least none that mattered. There was only her own, being pushed through her veins by a heart not yet slowed to stillness by sickness or accident, age or apathy.

The blood was gone, buried and probably burned to ashes below the bones of what had once been a lavish mansion situated in the forests of southern New York state, near the Pennsylvania border. The blood was buried there with the man she loved, the vampire Theroen. She had not had the courage to explore the charred remains of the mansion to find out whether his body had survived the blaze.

It didn't matter anyway. Ashes to ashes, dust to dust; Theroen was dead.

When she had arrived at the mansion and found it burnt to the ground, she had sat there for a time on the hood of her car, smoking cigarettes and looking at the pile of charcoal and ash that had, for a few short months, been her home. It was during this time of reflection, as she replayed over and over in her mind the events that had lifted her up from the streets and brought her salvation only to leave her alone again, that it seemed the grey veil had descended to cover her sight. The cold feeling had begun to gnaw at her stomach, the first stirrings of despair. The house was gone. Theroen was gone.

That part of her life was over, and now all that remained was the time ahead, time that seemed to stretch like a vast sea, calm and still and empty. She could not forget the warmth of the blood, could not take that taste from her lips. Life under the sun offered no comfort, but she knew that the task before her was daunting. Finding another vampire would be difficult. Convincing that vampire, or any other, to bring her back into the world that she longed to inhabit might well prove impossible.

When she returned from Ohio she began her search in earnest, and in the following weeks, as the last vestiges of hope faded and the icy despair within her grew, Two began to withdraw. She did it intentionally, to protect her friends and herself. She could see that she was hurting them, and this saddened her, but she couldn't lift the grey veil, couldn't shake the grief or erase the pain. She couldn't bring back what she had lost, and her friends' attempts at consolation seemed only to drive this home all the more clearly. So she had established distance, losing herself in the cold and the grey, giving in to the apathy that her brain had begun to produce in a last attempt to counteract the sadness and hopelessness that threatened to overtake her completely.

The tile was growing cool against her skin as the warmth from the shower dispersed, and goosebumps were prickling up on her arms. Two sighed, opened her eyes, and began to dry herself off.

* * *

The light on her phone was blinking. Voicemail, probably Rhes again. Two ignored it, not wanting to deal with him. Rhes had managed to hurt her, a little, the first real emotion she'd felt in some time. She had thought she'd inured herself to everything at this point, but when he brought up Molly there had been a few seconds where the pain had resurfaced, bright and clear, like sunlight shining through good crystal.

Two had sighed and forced herself to shut it out, and shortly thereafter the conversation had ended. She had sat for a time on her balcony, as she often did during the afternoons, smoking cigarettes and sipping on a glass of bourbon, and then had taken her shower. Tonight she would walk, as she did every night, with no real hope of finding the thing she was looking for, but with nothing else to do, and no real reason to do anything else even if there had been.

At last the sun was setting, and she could begin. Two had to wait for it before starting her search because of the nature of what she was hunting. Theroen had told her that only some vampires could abide the sun, and that of those, few preferred to spend any significant time underneath it. When the last sliver of red had dipped below the horizon and dusk covered Manhattan, Two would begin her walk. She never planned, never mapped out a route or decided on a path. She let her feet move her according to random whim, the timing of the street lights, the movement of the crowds.

Two leaned back and glanced at the clock sitting by her phone, noting that the sun should fully set in another thirty minutes. The light on her phone blinked and blinked, as if chiding her for not checking her messages. She thought about listening to Rhes apologizing for upsetting her and grimaced, then got up, crossed the room, picked up the phone and hit the button. The moment the automated voice broke into its scripted greeting, Two quickly pressed the series of keys that would clear the mailbox, waited for confirmation that this was done, and slammed the phone back into its cradle. She walked out onto her balcony again, lit a cigarette, and stood watching the traffic down below turn fuzzy and indistinct in the dimming light. Time crawled. Two smoked.

"I hate you," she said to the crowds of people on the sidewalk below, to the cars and trucks and limousines that crawled along Sixth Avenue towards the theatres to the north. It wasn't true, of course; there was nothing left anymore but the ghost of this feeling, and of countless others. She didn't hate these people, nor envy them, because she didn't care. Her body survived, even as she drove it into the ground, subsisting for the most part on cigarettes, bourbon, and water. She waited for the sun to set, thinking of Theroen.

"There are vampires in Manhattan," he had told her once. "I know few of them, unfortunately. Abraham keeps me from interacting with them any more than is absolutely necessary, but I have met three or four of them. There is a council that he sits on ... lords over, I imagine. He's the oldest vampire in this country by hundreds of years."

"What does the council do?" Two had asked.

"According to Abraham, most of what they do is pointless deliberation and setting meaningless laws. It does seem a bit absurd. Abraham is their chief, yet he follows no law but his own, and never has. Of course, it's to his advantage to be the head of the council. If nothing else, it allows him insight into any plotting that might be done against him."

"Are most of the vampires like you, or like him?"

"Neither, really. They are individuals, people like you and I, though shaped somewhat by their bloodlines. There are four types of vampires: Eresh, Ashayt, Ay'Araf, and Burilgi. The basic mechanics are the same ... we drink blood to survive and use blood to reproduce, but there are substantial differences in physiology and psychological makeup."

"You and Abraham are both Eresh, right?"

"We are. He is, so I am, so shall you be. Obviously, given the differences between Abraham and I, it would be a mistake to say that the blood within a given vampire determines who that person is. Still, it has some effect. Ashayt vampires are often spiritual or creative, and can be prone to depression. The Ay'Araf are warriors, for the most part, people who not only excel at conflict but actively seek it out. They value strength and speed, mastery of fighting skills, and are often callous or abrupt, uninterested in politics or self-expression. Amusing, really ... Ay'Araf himself was a priest and a poet."

"There's so much to learn," Two had told him, and she remembered his smile; that maddening, subtle grin that made her want to grab him, hold him tight, kiss him until her lips were raw.

"There is all the time in the world," Theroen had replied. The words had sounded so sweet, then, coming as they did from his mistaken belief that he had started Two down the path to immortality. Now they seemed to her only deeply ironic. "All the time in the world" had turned out to be little more than a handful of weeks.

Two watched the last hint of sunlight fade from the sky, watched the streetlights flicker on, watched as her own reflection grew ghostly, pink and blue and purple in the afterglow of the sunset. Her one-bedroom condo in SoHo, modest by New York standards, lent her views of Sixth Avenue and Prince Street. The evening crowds were thick, a sea of people seeking dinner or entertainment or both. Perhaps her vampire was out there, somewhere.

Maybe tonight, she thought, and then laughed. It was a harsh, angry little sound. Yes, maybe tonight she would find what she was looking for, and if not, then maybe the next night. It didn't matter. She would search until she fell dead on her feet, even though she no longer believed that she would ever meet another vampire. There was nothing else to do and, as Theroen had once told her, she had all the time in the world.

* * *

The rain had stopped and now the city was cool and damp. The sound of water rushed from the sewers below her, trickled from the walls to her left, echoed from little streams of the sidewalk. New York steamed and smoldered and stank, and Two paid it no attention. She had lived her entire life in this place, and it seemed to her there was no more natural a setting in the world.

It wouldn't have changed anything, the rain; she would have gone on her walk even in the midst of a tempest, but at least now there were people on the streets to survey. She would not have to spend the entire night ducking into bars and clubs to catalog the people within. Two zipped her leather jacket against the wind, thinking of a time when she would not have even perceived the chill. With a bitter grin, she lit a cigarette and began to walk.

The evening passed. Two's steady but aimless path took her through SoHo and Little Italy, moving in a general eastward direction until she reached Second Avenue, where she turned north, heading up into the East Village, past Union Square, and into the Flatiron district. Finding this area nearly deserted by Manhattan standards, she made her way west along 18th Street. She scanned each passerby as she went, looking for the right combination: pale face, oddly luminescent eyes, an ethereal sense of balance. Everywhere she walked, Two looked for vampires and found none.

This did not surprise her anymore, though it still pained her. She had spent more than enough time doing the math, figuring out the odds, coming to the understanding that in a city of twenty million, the relative handful of vampire inhabitants would be almost impossible to locate. There might even be several hundred – she had no way of knowing for sure – but Two saw more people than that in a given hour of walking. The probability was akin to the needle-in-a-haystack conundrum, except the needle and each individual piece of hay were in constant motion.

When she reached Ninth Avenue she turned north again, moving along the border between the Garment District and the neighborhood the city government was trying to rebrand as "Clinton," but which would, she knew, always remain Hell's Kitchen. The fabric shops gave way to theatres, the streets overloaded with garish neon signs and old-style marquees. Two found it possible, even likely, that the type of vampire she was looking for might frequent the New York theatre scene, but she found herself unable to face the crowds of tourists and so turned left instead, making her way to Tenth Avenue via 48th Street before turning south.

Near midnight she stopped for a slice of pizza, more out of the need to fuel the rest of her walk than out of any desire to eat. She sat on a stool at a counter, looking through the plate-glass window in front of her, watching the people walking by. It was a Saturday night, and the New York nightlife was in full swing. Two knew that there were still four good hours of searching left to her.

She continued her walk south, listening to the sounds of cars passing, people talking, music blaring from the open doors of various restaurants and bars. She was headed toward the entrance to the Lincoln tunnel, an area not well-regarded, but was not afraid. She had not been afraid of New York in a long time, not since the days before the needle had gotten hold of her. The city's dangers paled in comparison to those she had faced on the grounds of the mansion. There was nothing in New York more dangerous than Abraham.

She passed this relative dead zone without incident, still checking everyone she passed for the telltale signs of vampirism. Even the drunk and quite possibly homeless man urinating on the side of a building, near 36th street, did not go without scrutiny. He responded to her stare with a leering grin and a beckoning wave of his hand. Two wordlessly declined the implied invitation, continuing her walk.

The neighborhood slowly grew upscale as she made her way south, skirting the edge of the Meatpacking District and moving down into the West Village. The wind freshened and Two shivered, but not from the cold. She was feeling a curious doubling sensation, something like *déjà vu* but not as strong, nor so disorienting. She had not been here before, had not lived this moment already in some past life, but she knew this feeling just the same. She was shaky, tense, excited; she hadn't felt these emotions in what seemed like years.

Two thought back to an evening last October, when a hand had fallen suddenly on her shoulder and a voice had whispered her name. She thought of waiting on the curb outside of Darren's building – waiting for her destiny, as it turned out – and she wondered if she was remembering correctly how it had felt then. She thought it had felt like this.

* * *

The club on Hudson Street made its presence known two blocks away; the blue glare from its myriad neon lights bathed the street, the buildings, and the nearby trees in icy hues. The ground floor on both sides of the street was occupied by commercial space, but above the shops and restaurants were numerous apartments. Two wondered briefly how anyone in these buildings could sleep with the light from the club shining so brightly, and thought of the heavy blackout curtains that had lined all of the windows in Abraham's mansion.

The face of the club was nothing but glass, and all of this had been painted jet black. The neon blue lights converged above the entrance to form words: *L'Obscurité*. Two wondered if it was a Goth club. She'd been to many, in the early days of her search, before considering the fact that only one of the vampires she'd known, Missy, had seemed a fan of that particular subculture. Theroen had been a fan of black clothes and heavy eyeliner, but that was the extent of his interest.

Two hadn't been able to understand the young men and women she'd met, obsessed with death, morose and often disturbed. While it was true that the vampires she had known were trapped in darkness, the world that Theroen had shown her was not a place of grim and Gothic depression. Vampires were not cold, dead things; they breathed. Their hearts beat. Their lives could mean warmth, love, and immortality; there was little, if anything at all, to do with death.

I'm going in, she thought to herself, though she couldn't say why this particular place had brought about that strange, familiar feeling within her. The club's entrance seemed to call to her, drawing her near, as if pulling with a magnetic force. Two had relied on her instincts for so many years that she no longer questioned them. When they told her to go inside, she listened.

49

L'Obscurité was not a Goth club, much to Two's relief. The clientele was upscale and Two, in a pair of jeans and her leather jacket, felt underdressed. She moved through the crowds on the dance floor, inspecting faces, avoiding eye contact. She had to pass through two rooms to reach the bar, but it was quieter back there. The music had become a part of the overall background noise, no longer assaulting her ears or shaking her entire body with pulsing thuds.

"Girl, you do not have a drink. It is my pleasure and my *duty* to put one in front of you."

The bartender was young and black and beautiful, his muscles filling out a leather t-shirt and matching pants. Two thought he was wasting his time tending bar when he could've been modeling. His head was bald, and when he smiled at her his white teeth cut through the haze of neon and black light that colored the mist from the fog machines by the stage. They were dazzling and Two smiled back, almost despite herself.

"OK. What's good?" she asked.

"It's all good, honey, but the specialty of the house is the Cup of Blood."

Two shuddered. She tried to stop herself, but couldn't. It seemed she had lost all control of her body for that brief moment as the spasm passed through her.

The bartender raised an eyebrow. "Hey now, did I scare you? It's not *real* blood. You OK?"

Two took a breath, squeezed the back of her neck once to relieve the tension, and got a grip on herself.

"Yeah. Yes, I'm fine. Sorry ... what's the Cup of Blood have in it?"

"Whiskey, cherry liqueur, little sour raspberry syrup, bitters. It's dark red. Good stuff."

"That's fine. One of those, then."

The bartender nodded and moved away to make her drink. Two turned her back to the bar, leaned against it, looked at her hands. They were shaking, and she took a few deep breaths. *What the fuck is wrong with me?*

The other customers seemed relatively normal. There was a lot of money on display in the form of clothing, jewelry, and expensive haircuts, but the bar's DJ had attracted a share of younger, less well-dressed customers as well. One of these, a young man with short hair dyed blue, seemed to notice her. He stood up from his table of friends and wandered over, trying to look casual and doing a terrible job of it.

"Haven't seen you around before," he said, leaning against the bar next to her. "I like your jacket."

"Never been here before, and thanks. I like your hair," Two said, smiling. She felt alive tonight, able to connect with these people in a way that she hadn't in ages. This young man held no interest for her in the way he was hoping, but she wasn't offended by his presence as she might normally have been.

"My name's Jeremy. So uh ... can I buy you a drink?"

"You can buy the one I already ordered, if you want. Here it comes now."

Jeremy nodded, motioned to the bartender that he was covering Two's drink, and then to his own glass. "Jack and Coke, please."

The bartender smiled, took the glass, moved away again. Two sipped at her drink. It wasn't bad; a bit sweet after weeks of nothing but straight bourbon.

"Thank you, Jeremy."

"No problem."

There was a pause. Two sipped at her Cup of Blood, watching the people in the other room writhe in time with the music. The bartender returned with Jeremy's drink, took two twenties in return, made change and moved on. Jeremy leaned with her against the wood of the bar.

"Can I ask your name?" he asked at last.

"Sure. It's Two, like the number."

"That's cool."

"Thanks."

There was another silence, slightly awkward. Two was having a hard time not laughing.

"Can I ask you something, Jeremy?"

"Shoot."

"You the type who's easily offended?"

"Mmm ... don't think so."

"OK, then I'll be honest. You're cute, you seem sweet enough, and the hair's a nice touch ... but I'm not looking to get lucky tonight. If that's what you're after, you should pick another girl."

Jeremy looked at her for a moment, eyebrows raised. Two couldn't tell if he was shocked, angry, or amused.

"Sorry," she said, shrugging.

Her hopeful paramour smiled a little, then broke out into a full-fledged grin. He glanced over at the table full of his friends, all of whom were pretending not to watch in a way so obvious it bordered on ridiculous. Jeremy laughed to himself.

"What's funny?" Two asked.

"I'm gonna get a lot of shit when I go back over there."

"Why's that?"

"We're visiting from upstate. Never been to the city before ... none of them think we have a shot at meeting any women. They think New York girls don't give a shit unless you drive a Jag and shower them with diamonds."

Two smiled. "Come here ..."

She stood up on tip-toe, wrapped her arms around his neck, and kissed him, long and slow and in full view of his buddies, who began whooping. Laughing, Two let him go. Jeremy looked at her, happily surprised but unsure how to proceed. Two waved at the table full of guys, then turned back to the young man in front of her, still grinning.

"It was nice meeting you, Jeremy. Thanks for the drink. Go sit down, and tell your friends I said that they're a bunch of pussies who don't know anything about New York girls."

"I ... yeah, OK. It was nice meeting you, too! I'll tell them."

Two watched him go, gave one last wave, and turned away from the group, surveying the rest of the room. She sipped at her drink, laughing to herself. It took a moment to feel the eyes on her, not from Jeremy's side of the room, but from the other, in one of the darker corners.

Two looked up, meeting the eyes of a young woman sitting by herself at a table, and understood the girl's amused expression immediately: this person had witnessed the incident with Jeremy, had understood it, and had found humor there. Two read this in the eyes, the grin, the entire set of the woman's body.

Her second realization took a moment longer, but when it happened Two felt her entire frame go rigid. The woman regarding her with that amused, detached expression was young – so young that Two wondered if she was even old enough to legally drink. She was also beautiful, with hair that was either dark blond or light brown, pale skin, and large eyes that seemed to catch all of the light in the room and absorb it, collecting it in a soft glow. They were ageless, these eyes, and Two recognized in them something she had not seen since Abraham's death.

She was looking into the eyes of a vampire.

Two's heart seemed to halt in her chest before giving a single, excruciating throb. She wondered, in some small corner of her mind, if she was going to die. She tried to force her heart to keep beating, tried to make herself breathe, tried to do anything other than stare. Her right hand was clutching her cocktail glass with such force that she feared the stem would snap in half. Her left hand hung limply at her side.

No, she thought. *It's impossible.*

She had to know, had to be sure, had to confirm what she wanted so badly to believe. Two felt like shrieking, throwing her glass in the air, and bolting across the room to fall at the feet of this woman, begging for the gift, pleading for the blood. She couldn't do that, of course, and so she simply stood and stared.

Eventually the girl across the room glanced at her again, and Two had all the confirmation she needed. It was those eyes that gave it away. No one else was likely to notice; the difference was too subtle, otherwise this woman would not be out in the middle of a crowded club. Two had seen vampire eyes before, however. She had possessed them for a time. She knew exactly what they looked like.

The vampire woman focused on Two, cocking her head to one side and narrowing those eyes. She had clearly not been expecting this continued scrutiny, and her smile faded from her lips, becoming a frown. She looked at Two in wary suspicion, then stood without warning and moved toward the door.

"No!" Two cried. She left her drink on the bar, forgotten, and began to push her way through the mass of people between herself and the vampire. She tried to keep the other woman in her sights, but it was a losing battle. The girl moved with an ethereal grace that Two couldn't hope to match even in the best of circumstances. To make things worse, it seemed that tonight she had lost any of the natural finesse she might once have possessed.

Before she had even reached the dance floor, Two had lost track of the woman. She felt frustration rising, despair on its heels, and tried to shove these things to the back of her mind. She made her way to the door and finally burst out into the cool night. There were tendrils of mist rising up off the wet pavement, and Two turned right and left, looking down the street as far as she could. There was nothing but the traffic and a tight cluster of people smoking near the front of the club. The vampire was gone.

Two stood there on the sidewalk, hands clenching and unclenching, panting, listening to the throb of music from the club behind her. She closed her eyes, trying to retain control, not wanting to cry in front of strangers. She tried to remind herself of what Theroen had told her: vampires were just extraordinary people. They became attached to certain places, certain areas, just like normal human beings. They had favorite spots and didn't often range far from home.

Two forced herself to relax. She opened her hands, unmindful of the burning crescent marks her nails had dug into her palms. Shaking, she reached into her jacket, brought out a cigarette, and lit it. She dragged, breathed, stared out into the fog, feeling suddenly exhausted. She wanted to go home, to sleep and dream of Theroen and of the blood.

"See you tomorrow," she said to the empty street, and she began the walk home.

CHAPTER IV

The Children of the Sun

Tori put her parents into the ground on a Wednesday afternoon, five days after she discovered their bodies. She supposed that for some people the time after such an event might have seemed an eternity, but to Tori it was little more than a blur. She remembered being interrogated by the police and finally being released in the early evening, to drive first to a liquor store and then to a motel. Tequila had burned away most of the following days, leaving huge gaps in her memory. She thought she might have called her friends, before deciding that doing so might put them in danger. She had also managed, somehow, to plan the funeral.

She knew she had gone back to the house at some point after it had been cleaned up. She knew she had tried to sleep there. She remembered spending the night curled up on the couch, every light in the house burning bright, drinking and weeping as she leafed through old photo albums. Her father and mother stared out at her from these pictures, happy and healthy and alive. Here, too, was the old Tori, the girl she once had been, the girl that Mona and Jim had loved so much.

The love was there, stamped on their faces in every picture, so clear and obvious that Tori wondered how she had never noticed it. She would become lost in the pictures for a time, and then would stumble across something that reminded her of the sad, confused love she had returned home to. This, in turn, would cause that painful wrenching sensation within her as she realized again that

55

even this love was now gone, taken from her by someone or something. She had finally left the house at sunrise, taking a suitcase and moving back to a motel.

The police were hunting for clues but finding little. Tori's alibis were strong and she had established them immediately. No, she couldn't possibly have been murdering her parents sometime during the night in question, because she had been busy drinking herself blind and having sex with a random stranger. Admitting this to a group of police officers had been unpleasant, but it was better than being considered a suspect in her own parents' deaths.

Her story had checked out, of course. Tori was not a murderer, not in this life. She did not hate her parents and had never wished them dead. If anything, she had loved them too much to share her past with them. She had tried to shield them from it, and she wondered now if this heartache was some kind of penance she must pay for the things she had done, for the people she had killed.

The priest droned on about God. Tori was not crying; she felt as though she had emptied herself of tears completely in the past week. There was only a deep, hollow ache within her as she looked over the twin caskets being lowered into the ground. It was warm out, pleasant, and that made things somehow worse. Funerals were supposed to take place in the rain and the cold. The earth had no right to be celebrating now.

There were few people at the wake, fewer still at the burial. Jim and Mona had been well-liked by those who knew them, but neither had been particularly social. Jim had made a few close friends at work and Mona played bridge with a small group of women whose sons and daughters had gone to school with Tori once upon a time. Jim's only brother, Frank, was unable to attend the funeral. He was an Army Captain, called into active duty in Iraq, and couldn't secure leave. Mona's two siblings, a brother and sister, had both passed away at some point during Tori's absence.

Those friends and well-wishers that could attend did, and Tori had welcomed them as best she could. A few remembered her from her childhood, but they had all seemed perplexed. Tori looked too young to be Jim and Mona's child, and she seemed different somehow from the girl they had known. She had handled this, and everything else, to the best of her abilities, and now it was almost done. Soon there would be nothing left to do but get on with her life.

Tonight, though, Tori had no interest in doing anything of the sort. She wanted the funeral to be over, the crowds dispersed, so that she could drive across town to the house in which she had grown up, take one last look around, and then close the doors until the estate sale. There was a big bottle of tequila sitting on the nightstand in her hotel, and Tori had been thinking about it since the moment her alarm had roused her from sleep.

* * *

The man waiting by her car was tall and thin, grey at the temples, perhaps in his mid-forties. He was wearing a dark suit, expensive and well-cut. His high cheek bones, hooked nose, and intent eyes gave him a sharp, predatory look that reminded her of a hawk. Tori did not recognize him.

"Miss Perrault?" he asked, and Tori heard a ghost of a British accent in his voice.

"Yes ... I'm sorry, have we met?"

"We have not. My name is Charles Porter. I was sorry to hear about your parents."

"Did you know them?"

"No, young lady. I read about them in the newspaper."

Then why are you here? Tori thought, and frowned at her own hostility. Charles mistook her expression.

"I'm sorry, have I upset you? I understand that this may not be the best of times."

Tori shook her head. "No ... no, sorry. It's been a difficult couple of days."

"I can only imagine."

"Can I help you with something, Mr. Porter?"

"Please, call me Charles."

"Right. Charles, then, and you can call me Tori. Now that we're good friends, what do you want?"

Charles smiled at her, but his eyes remained intent. "Very direct. Good. I represent a small group that takes special interest in cases like yours."

"So, what ... like a lawyer?"

"No, we're not lawyers. We're a private company that does not frequently contact people who are not already aware of us. In this instance, we deemed it both necessary and prudent."

"What type of company, exactly?"

"My employers value my discretion. I think you will come to value it as well."

"I'm not interested in discretion. What I'm interested in is leaving. Since you're the one who stopped me, and not the other way around, why don't you cut to the chase and just tell me what you want?"

"We believe we can help you with the problems you are most certainly going to run into while you investigate this tragedy."

"I see. So you're a private detective, or a vigilante, or just some nutbag who thinks it's a good idea to sell me his services on the day of my parents' funeral. Thanks, Charles, that's great. Not interested."

"I am none of those things," Charles said. His expression was amused, not at all perturbed by Tori's anger or lack of tact.

Tori considered this for a moment, then shrugged, opening her car door. "Fine, you're not. This is the part where I drive away. It was *lovely* meeting you. Don't call us, we'll call you."

"Stop, Tori."

"No thanks."

Charles put a hand on her door and held it open, looking down at her.

"If I tell you who we are, will you stop behaving like this and listen to what I have to say?"

"I don't care who you are," Tori said. She wondered if she were to use her strength to jerk the door shut, whether this man would let go or have his fingers crushed. She was about to try it, and he seemed to sense this. Charles took his hand from the door, smiled, and spoke in a low voice.

"I represent the Children of the Sun, Tori," he said. "We kill vampires. Vampires like the ones that murdered your parents."

He's trying to get a reaction out of me, Tori thought and then, on the heels of that: *Well, it worked.*

She could feel her pulse racing. Her entire body seemed charged with electricity, rigid, unable to move. Tori sat in her car, hands welded to the steering wheel, trying to gain control of herself. Charles let her take her time.

Finally, when she was able to breathe again, she croaked out a few words.

"What did you say?"

"By your reaction, I'd say you heard me clearly, and understand very well that I speak in the utmost seriousness. I'll not repeat myself, not out here in public, not even in the light of day."

Tori was silent, trying to digest this piece of news which seemed to confirm the things that she had only begun to guess at. *Vampires like the ones that murdered your parents*, Charles had said. Yes, that seemed to be the case, and Tori had a good idea why. In December of the previous year, a vampire god had been killed, and Tori had played an active role in that murder. She had always feared retribution, but had never thought that her parents might be targets.

"How do you know?" she asked after a time.

"We know many things, Tori. We know about Abraham, for example. We know how he lived, and how he died. We know that at least one of his children remains unaccounted for."

Tori felt a chill run through her. "If you know anything about me, you can guess that I'm not exactly a fan of people who kill vam— people in your profession."

"If you knew more about yourself, and about what has happened to you, you might be fonder of us."

"I didn't have much opportunity to learn."

"We may be able to fix that."

"So you're not here to kill me?" Tori asked.

Charles gave a small chuckle. "Good Lord, no. We don't kill humans."

"I'm not like other humans."

"No? Perhaps not, but you are one of us nonetheless, and none of my people would raise a finger against you. We're quite interested, however, in learning your story. Perhaps one day you will tell it to me."

"Maybe."

Charles smiled at her, but now his hawkish eyes glittered. "This is neither the time nor the place to enter into that particular discussion. I am only here as an emissary, Tori. The Children would like to help you, if you'll let us."

"So what's next, then?"

"We should meet somewhere less public than this parking lot. Perhaps your parents' former house, if it's not too painful for you?"

"It's possible. I need to think about this."

"Take your time, but I must warn you that you are in danger."

"I can take care of myself."

"Of that I have no doubt, Tori, but you've seen the brutality that these things are capable of. If they come at you in numbers, you may find them a match even for your talents."

Tori considered this. "OK. Fine. How do I contact you?"

Charles handed her a card, and for one absurd moment Tori wondered if it actually read "Vampire Hunter." She glanced down at it, then back up at Charles, whose amused expression told her he'd understood what she was thinking. The card contained nothing more than a phone number.

"Call that," he said. "Whenever you are ready to talk, someone will be there to answer."

Tori looked at him for a moment, frowning. "How much danger am I in?"

"I cannot say for sure. The things that did this are not stupid; I do not think the stupid ones would care about your transgressions. It is likely that they will wait for a time before carrying out any further action against you. How long that will be is anyone's guess."

"I'll risk it."

Tori could feel something building inside of her, a storm of such intensity that it frightened her, made her wonder what she might do if it was let loose. She needed to be *away*. Away from Charles, away from other people, away from the world. She would go back to her motel, lock herself in, and crawl into the bottle.

"I look forward to hearing from you, then," Charles told her. "It was a pleasure meeting you, and I'm sorry it had to happen under such grievous circumstances."

"You and me both. Goodbye, Charles."

"Take care."

In her rearview mirror, Tori could see Charles watching her go. He held his hand up once, just before she turned, and then he was lost from view. Tori drove on in silence, going over what he had said again and again in her mind, picturing how it must have happened, the way the vampires must have treated her parents. Inside her, the dark storm grew.

* * *

Angry. Violent. Drunk. Tori lay in the corner, naked except for a pair of panties, where she had fallen when she had lost her balance while tearing around the motel room. She had thrown a lamp into this corner earlier, and her landing had shattered the porcelain base. Picking the tiny shards from her skin, struggling to make her fingers obey her brain through the alcohol haze, had done little to improve her mood. Her arms and legs and body were now dotted with small drops of blood.

Her hands were soaked slick with the substance, making it hard to hold on to the heavy bottle as she raised it to her lips and drank. The liquid inside was select silver tequila, 100 proof, and the bottle held a liter and a half of it. Tori had made it about two thirds of the way through.

She swallowed, rubbed her mouth on her arm, lay back against the wall, staring up at the ceiling. Her eyes were far away, her mind trapped back in the home she had shared with her parents, imagining their last moments, events she had not been able to prevent.

Vampires had butchered them like cattle, for crimes they had not even known about, much less committed. Vampires had murdered her parents and left Tori alive to bear witness to the atrocity. Soon, she thought, they would come for her, but not until she had been made to bear all of the pain and loss they had caused her.

Tori wanted to mutilate, desecrate, destroy. She wanted to find the creatures responsible for her parents' deaths and pull their eyes from their sockets, tear their limbs off, gnaw the skin from their bodies. She wanted to bathe in their blood and listen to their screams of mercy before casting them, still writhing and very much alive, upon their pyre. Tori swigged from the bottle again. The world spun.

Anger whipsawed to grief as she thought of her parents again, recalling the expression of desperation on her father's face. Tori let out a sound somewhere between a scream and a sob, felt hot tears stinging at her eyes, and drove her left hand hard into the mound of porcelain shards lying on the carpet. Tiny daggers drove into her flesh, piercing and slashing, and Tori barely felt them. She swigged from the bottle again.

Her hand was bleeding anew, pieces of the lamp sticking helter-skelter out from it in all directions. The blood pooled in the cracks between her fingers and dripped to the floor, staining the carpet. Tori upended the bottle over her hand, liquor cascaded down to hit her flesh, and her hand became a white-hot ball of fire. Here, *at last*, was something she could feel. Tori hissed through her teeth, grimacing, holding her hand out in front of her, willing herself to contemplate the pain.

She was going to find the things that had killed her parents and subject them to pain like this, only on so much larger a scale. The pain in her hand was only the smallest taste of the agony she was planning for them.

Tori continued to use the bottle, alternating between hand and mouth, and after a time the pain began to drift away. With it went Tori's vision; she was blacking out, and was happy for it. She had consumed enough alcohol to kill a normal human being, all in the hope that she might be given this chance to sleep, this chance to forget – if only for a small while – that look in her father's eyes. At last her wish was being granted.

The bottle fell from the numb fingers of her right hand, hit her leg and flopped to the carpet, the remainder of its contents sloshing out onto the floor. Tori's head lolled back. She slumped against the wall and slept.

* * *

In the morning, things had improved. The storm of the night before had passed, though a cloud of rage and hatred still loomed over her. Physically, it was as if the previous night had never happened. This was the first time Tori had done major damage to any part of her body since Two had saved her. She was startled by how quickly the lacerations on her hand had healed.

I'm still mostly vampire, she thought, looking at herself in the mirror. Her arms, face, breasts, and belly were smeared with tequila and blood, but even the deepest gashes on her hand had faded completely. The alcohol itself had left only a very minor headache, which Tori knew would fade after a glass of water and a shower. She was fine.

The motel, on the other hand, was a mess. Shards of porcelain littered the carpet, accompanied by tacky spots of dried blood. There was a hole in the wall that she couldn't remember making but knew hadn't been there when she had arrived. Tori didn't care. She would deal with the bill when it came.

She showered, rinsing away the evidence of the previous night's masochism, thinking about the pain she had felt in her hand and the pain she would bring to her enemies.

"How can you trust him?" she asked the empty bathroom, filled with swirling steam and the sound of rushing water.

"You can't, but it's not like what he's saying is really surprising," her own voice answered back.

This was true. She could not trust this random stranger claiming to represent a group of vampire hunters, at least not without learning more about him and his organization, but she didn't need trust to see that he was telling the truth. Throats torn out, wrists slashed; the murders had been about *blood*.

Some small part of Tori's mind, perhaps the part not yet fully dominated by anger, thought that she should call Two again. There was no one else on earth who could understand Tori's situation, no one who would be able to give better advice, and Tori allowed herself to consider the option for a few brief moments before shutting it out. No, Two was safe in New York. Better to not involve her. Impetuous, instinct-driven – Two would come flying out to Ohio within hours, no matter what Tori asked her to do.

I can handle this on my own, Tori thought with a touch of bitterness. Two had left her here in Ohio and, for better or worse, gone back to New York. There was no sense in involving her now.

Tori stepped out of the shower and dried herself off, brushed her teeth, performed the other tasks that went with her morning shower. She left the bathroom naked and dressed quickly. She fished the card Charles had given her from the pocket of her jeans, picked up the phone, dialed the numbers.

The first ring had barely begun when her call was answered. The voice at the other end of the line was not Charles, and the words were not a typical greeting.

"Please speak only to answer my questions. Our representative mentioned a potential meeting place to you yesterday. Do you remember it?"

"Yes, I ... yes," Tori said.

"Do you find it acceptable?"

"Yes."

"Be there at noon today."

"I will."

"We look forward to working with you."

There was a click, and the line went dead. Tori looked at the phone, shrugged, and hung up. *Yeah, sure ... I look forward to working with you, too.*

Of course, she hadn't made that decision yet. She would meet with Charles, yes, but that was no guarantee that she would accept his offer for help. She wanted more time and a lot more information before making any kind of decision.

It was already eleven thirty, and her parents' house was miles away. Tori took her purse, shut off the light, and walked out the door. She left her belongings behind, expecting to return that evening. She would never see any of them again.

* * *

Charles was waiting in the driveway when Tori arrived, standing beside a muted grey Mercedes. Getting out, Tori glanced at her own car, a used economy import, and raised an eyebrow.

"Guess your business is pretty profitable?"

"It has its perks. Hello, Tori."

"Hello, Charles."

"I trust you're feeling better than you were yesterday?"

"Maybe. Still far from good. I have a lot of questions."

Tori unlocked the front door and held it open, but Charles gestured, indicating she should go first. Tori shrugged and went ahead.

"I will do my best to answer them," Charles said, following her into the house.

"Good. Question one: now that you have me somewhere private, is this the part where you try to club me over the head or something?"

"Heavens, no."

"OK." Tori made her way to the kitchen with some trepidation, but found herself feeling strangely detached. The house had been cleaned once the police investigation was through, and it now seemed more like a place she had seen in a movie, or visited in a previous life.

"Can I get you something to drink?" she called, filling the coffee pot with water and watching her guest through the doorway that separated the living room from the kitchen.

Charles was looking at the pictures hung on the wall. "What are you having?"

"I'm making coffee. I think we'll be here a while, don't you?"

"I do indeed. Coffee would be very nice."

"Fine," Tori said. "Who killed my parents, Charles?"

Charles settled down on the living room couch and looked at her through the doorway, a small smile on his face.

"Still direct, I see. Very well. If I knew the exact names of the vampires in question, I would be happy to give them to you. I do not. To the best of my knowledge, there are none living in the vicinity of Lima. The ones that did this must have come from somewhere else. New York, most likely. That is where their council is located."

"There's a vampire council?"

"I'm surprised you're not aware of it, actually. Abraham sat at its head until his death."

The electric coffee-maker began to bubble and hiss. Tori stepped back into the living room and sat down in a recliner. "How much do you know about my time with Abraham?"

"The only thing we know for sure is that you spent more than a decade at his mansion. Our sources have told us that you were a vampire, once, but I can see with my own eyes that you are not anymore. We were hoping you might be able to shed further light on what exactly happened to Abraham and to his children."

Tori pursed her lips, considering this. Charles sat on the couch, legs crossed, hands folded neatly in his lap. He let her take her time, not anxious. His calm demeanor reminded her of Theroen.

"Not just now, Charles. I'm going to hold off on telling any stories for a bit."

"That is fine."

"Are you sure it's a *group* of vampires that killed my parents, and not just one?"

"The forensics work that the police have done indicates that ... forgive me, Tori, but this is somewhat graphic. Can I speak plainly?"

Tori made a motion with her hand. *Go ahead.*

"The work shows that your father was held by his shoulders for a substantial period of time, and that he experienced heavy bruising in that area. The police believe he was struggling so much because he was forced to watch the murder of your mother. This would indicate at least two assailants, likely more."

Tori grimaced, her mouth suddenly bitter. She swallowed once, took a deep breath, and nodded. "OK."

"I am sorry for you pain. The Children share my sympathy."

"Thank you. Tell me about the Children of the Sun."

"We are an order that dates back nearly six hundred years. Our origins are Incan, though obviously we've expanded our ranks."

"Obviously, since you're white-bread British."

The corner of Charles's lip raised momentarily in a slight smirk. He continued.

"We were initially an order of Incan warrior-priests, formed and trained to deal with the Ngembe plague."

"What's ... how did you say it?"

"En-gem-bay," Charles annunciated. "They were a race of vampires that, as far as we know, originated independently of the Eurasian strain that you are familiar with. The Ngembe acted like a virus. They would infest a civilization and grow rapidly to epic proportions, reaching saturation in only a few decades. This would lead to their near extinction as entire communities full of vampires starved to death, or murdered each other for blood. A few would manage to move on to a new civilization, carrying this blood-plague with them, and the cycle would begin again."

"How long did this go on for?" Tori asked.

"Centuries. Look at a timeline of South American culture, and you will find that it is full of civilization fragments. They build their way up to dominance and then ... simply disappear. The disappearance of the Olmec and the emptying of the city of Teotihuacán are two famous examples, but there are several others, and we believe the common element in their sudden disappearance from the timeline is an infestation by Ngembe vampires. We have dated them at least as far back as eleven hundred BC, but there may yet be earlier examples."

"Are there any Ngembe left?"

"No. The Children wiped them from the earth in the fifteenth and sixteenth centuries."

"How can you be sure?"

Charles spread his hands. "How many vampire cities have you seen lately?"

Tori rolled her eyes, stood, and headed for the kitchen again. "What do you take in your coffee?"

"Black is fine, thank you."

Tori returned with two mugs and handed one to Charles. She positioned herself again in her chair, sitting cross-legged, sipping at her coffee.

"So the Ngembe vampires come into existence at some point and start wiping out entire cultures ..."

Charles nodded. "Yes."

"And then the Incans figure out what's going on and form a group to stop it."

"Yes. There was a city discovered in the Andes Mountains in Peru just last year, a sister city to Machu Picchu, that we believe was a training ground for the original Children."

"So they destroy the Ngembe and then what happens?"

"Cortez arrives in the new world, and his coming eventually decimates the native civilizations. We have reason to believe that both an Eresh and an Ay'Araf vampire were among the Spanish forces under Pizarro who conquered Peru. They would perhaps have been inclined to assist in wiping out a group specifically formed to kill vampires."

"I don't know what those words mean. 'Eresh?'"

"Did Abraham teach you nothing at all of vampire history?"

"No, and I wouldn't have had the capacity to understand it anyway. Let's just ... we're not at my part of the story yet, Charles. Your people were right: I was a vampire once, but for now you should assume I'm just a normal human who has no idea what you're talking about."

"Very well. Abraham is, or was, an Eresh vampire, as is everyone descended from him. It is one of the four dominant strains of Eurasian vampire. Ay'Araf is another strain."

"And they came to South America? I mean ... isn't that a long trip?"

"Quite, but if they managed it carefully, a pair of them could easily survive on a ship's crew, along with its supply of rats. At any rate, they were alive when they reached the new world. They discovered the Children and, fearing what we might do to them, essentially instigated the destruction of Incan society. Most of the Children were murdered or imprisoned. The rest fled north, eventually making their way into what is now the United States of America around the time of the Revolutionary war."

"And they're still around today."

"They have been based in the US for more than two centuries, and operate branches in many areas of the world."

"And in all this time, no one's ever heard of you. No one from the Children has ever thought 'hey, I could totally sell this' and brought the information to the History Channel or something?"

"If someone had told you, Tori, before Abraham abducted you, that they were a member of an order of vampire hunters that had existed for almost six hundred years, how would you have reacted?"

Tori considered this and nodded, laughing a little. "OK, valid point. I'd have thought they were nuts. But I know you're for real. So tell me, what have they been up to, Charles? Six centuries of killing vampires?"

"More or less. Unfortunately, we have been forced to operate in secrecy and from a position of limited strength. We've not been able to stem the tide as much as we would prefer. Powerful vampires like Abraham arrived from Europe, where we had no presence, and the Children were simply unable to combat them as they had the Ngembe, or the early Burilgi immigrants. We have spent much of the past two centuries waiting for a weapon to wield against them. Now, at long last, they have drawn us right to one."

"Really? What is it?"

Charles tilted his head and looked at her, eyebrows raised.

"Why, surely you've guessed, Tori," he said. "It's *you*."

CHAPTER V

Blood of Eresh

The phone was ringing again. Two didn't want to answer it.

She had slept for nearly six hours since returning to her apartment, but she felt as though she had only just closed her eyes. The events of the previous night seemed to have given her temporary respite from the cold, dead feeling that had been her constant companion for so many months. Last night she had felt humor, contentment, and the incredible thrill of spotting the vampire. Now she was exhausted, but filled with a strange sense of hope.

In the other room, the ringing stopped, her voice mail greeting no doubt playing to whoever was on the other end of the line. *This is Two. I'm not answering right now. Leave me a message.* A few moments later the phone beeped, and the message light began flashing. The phone immediately began to ring again. Two considered answering it, but in the end the call went to voicemail again, and this time the caller gave up.

"Life's a bitch," Two muttered into her pillow, and rolled over on her stomach, falling almost immediately back into sleep.

A sense of nervous anticipation pulled her back awake a few hours later, in the early afternoon. It lay like a tight, hot ball in her belly, and after a few minutes of tossing and turning, Two gave up and rolled out of bed.

Breakfast – actually something of a late lunch – consisted of a glass of water and a couple pieces of toast. Two ate little on a normal day and the current state of her nerves had done nothing to improve her appetite. She wandered around her apartment in an oversized t-shirt, taking breaks to stand on the balcony and smoke, thinking about vampires and waiting for dusk.

She wondered if the vampire would return to the club. Two worried that she had squandered what might have been her only chance, losing sight of the woman in the crowd. She tried not to dwell too much on this possibility, but her nerves were eating away at her. There were so many questions. Even if she found this vampire again, would the woman talk to her? Would she grant Two's wishes? Would she simply kill Two and be done with it?

There was a time when this latter option might not have bothered Two, might even have appealed to her. There had certainly been moments in the past few months where she would have welcomed the chance to escape into oblivion, but she felt alive again for the first time in so long, and with that feeling came the desire to extend that life, to make it last as long as it could. Forever, if possible.

At seven, Two took a shower. She dressed in a pair of black slacks and a cream-colored blouse, trying to look a little classier in case that would help her cause. She wrapped herself as always in the leather jacket Theroen had given her, made sure she had her keys and cigarettes, and left her apartment as the sun began to slip below the Manhattan skyline. She would walk for a time, as she always did, and when night had fully fallen and the time seemed right, she would make her way to the bar.

* * *

L'Obscurité throbbed like a young heart in the center of Manhattan. Two stood before it, finishing a cigarette and looking up at the neon sign. It was warmer this evening, with no rain, and there were small groups of smokers scattered around the sidewalk in front of the club. Two scanned them for the girl with luminescent eyes, but didn't see her. This wasn't particularly surprising; the vampire had probably not even left her home yet.

The same bartender was working, and he smiled as she moved toward him through the thin, early-evening crowd.

"I guess we made a new fan. Welcome back. Nice shirt."

Two flashed him a grin. "Thanks! You remember me?"

"I remember everyone. It's why they pay me the big bucks. I'm Thomas."

He reached his hand out over the bar, and Two shook it.

"Hi, Thomas. I'm Two."

"Name like that, now I'll never forget. You busted up outta here pretty quickly last night. Trying to catch up with someone?"

Two decided that honesty was the best policy, at least to a degree. "Yes, actually. A girl I saw last night looked familiar, but she left before I could see if we'd met. She was sitting over there, real pale ... I think her hair was light brown. Darker than mine, anyway."

"Lotta girls come in here every night. You didn't see her outside?"

"By the time I got out the front door, she was gone."

"Maybe she went out the side exit."

"There's a side exit? Where does it go?"

Thomas paused, eyebrows raised. "Out the side?"

Two rolled her eyes, laughing. "Well, yes Thomas, thank you ... but wouldn't I have still seen her on the street?"

"Maybe not. That alley connects both sides of the block. She could've gone the other way."

"Oh, shit. OK, if I see her again and can't get to her in time, I'll check the alley."

"Sounds good. So what's your poison?"

"Woodford Reserve, one ice cube, and a glass of water."

"Not a fan of the Cup of Blood?"

"Too much sugar." Two gave him a dazzling smile. "I'm sweet enough already."

Laughing, Thomas went to make her drink. Two surveyed the bar. It was quieter than it had been the night before, and the clientele had thinned considerably; the next day was a work day for most of the world. There was no sign of Jeremy, the boy she had kissed, and Two was glad. He probably would have felt obliged to make awkward conversation, and she wasn't interested in that tonight.

Her bourbon arrived, and Two leaned against the bar, tapping her foot to the music and watching the people. Thomas kept himself busy cleaning dishes and organizing the bar, but Two felt him glance at her from time to time, checking the status of her drink. *Big tip for Tommy,* she thought.

One drink became two, and two became three as Two waited. She was pacing herself, not drunk, passing the time by watching the bar's one television, which was muted but had the closed-captioning turned on. No one was hitting on her, even though she was obviously alone, and the alcohol had helped to unwind the knot in her stomach. She felt warm and comfortable. Perhaps the vampire would show, perhaps not. There were worse ways to spend an evening.

Thomas touched her shoulder, and Two glanced over at him.

"I think I'm good, thanks," she said, glancing at her drink, which was still half-full.

"Just wanted to let you know that I think your friend might be coming soon. If it's who I think it is, she usually shows up around now. Her usual routine is to order a glass of wine and sit by herself, people watching. Seems a lot like you, actually; doesn't really talk to anyone. She just watches."

"She is a lot like me, I think. Or at least, like I used to be. Thanks, I'll keep an eye out for her."

It didn't take long. Little more than ten minutes after Thomas had spoken to Two, the girl walked through the front door of the bar. Two's heart seemed to do a crazy summersault in her chest before settling into a steady, rapid pulse. She tried not to stare, but couldn't help herself. The vampire looked directly back and, far from being startled by Two's attention this time, she only raised one eyebrow and smirked.

Two tried to match her gaze but, after a time, felt awkward and looked away. She saw that Thomas was already pouring a glass of red liquid – too thin to be blood – and he set it down in front of the vampire woman as she reached the bar.

"*Merci*, Thomas."

"*Pas de problème. Comment ça va?*" Thomas answered back. His pronunciation and accent were smooth.

"I am well, thank you."

The woman leaned against the bar and glanced around, sipping her wine. None of the three spoke for a time. Thomas cleaned. The vampire seemed caught up in her own thoughts. Two watched the crowd and stole looks at the woman at the other end of the bar. Finally, the vampire spoke.

"The wine is good, Thomas. I have things to do this evening and can't stay long. I will see you again soon."

"Come back anytime, snowflake. You're always welcome here."

The vampire smiled at him, and looked directly at Two for the first time since entering the bar. After a moment she turned and made her way toward a hallway near the back of the bar's middle room.

"I'd say that was an invitation," Thomas commented, polishing a glass.

"Doesn't matter, I'm going anyway," Two said, pulling on her jacket.

"Best move quick. That girl disappears in a heartbeat."

Two left cash on the bar. "Keep the change, Thomas. Thanks."

"Pleasure's mine."

Two moved through the crowd, into the hallway, and toward the door at its end. Somewhere outside, the vampire was waiting for her.

* * *

The alley was dark, and damp, and smelled like mold. It stretched for perhaps twenty meters in either direction, opening up to streets on either side. There were other doors that opened out into it, but all seemed locked tight. The vampire was nowhere to be seen.

"You're kidding me," Two said, running a hand through her hair. "You have *got* to be fucking kidding me! Where did you go?"

She moved down the alley toward the rear of the building, kicking boxes and old newspapers out of her way. There was no sound but the noise of her progress and the bass thuds coming from the club. Two reached the end of the alley and peered down the street. Nothing.

"God damn it, don't *leave* me here!" she shouted back at the darkness, but there was no response.

Two began walking back up the alley, muttering to herself.

"Fine. Fuck you and fuck your stupid vampire bullshit. Fuck your stupid games. I'll come back tomorrow, and the next day, and the next day after that. I'll keep coming back until you talk to me."

There was a sound like rushing wind, something heavy hit Two's shoulders, dragging her toward the ground. The motion was fast, disorienting, and Two was sure that she would hit the hard cobblestones of the alley floor. Instead, she found herself cradled in the arms of the woman from the club.

"I'll speak with you now, since you request it," the vampire said, her voice icy and detached. "You know what I am, and we can't have that. I'm sorry ..."

"Wait!" Two shouted, and took in air to speak more, but it was too late. With one swift motion the vampire grabbed Two's chin, forcing her head back and exposing the veins of her neck. The vampire lunged forward and Two felt a brief spike of pain, like fire lancing out from where the vampire had bitten her to touch every nerve ending. After a moment, the pain was replaced with warm, pulsating waves of pleasure that coincided with her heartbeat.

Two felt herself being drained, felt her life being stolen away from her, felt blackness overtaking her. It didn't seem to matter, anymore, caught in this comfortable embrace. She thought to herself, *At least it's over. At least it's finally done.*

She did not expect the abrupt end to the sensation, nor the sudden plummet to the unforgiving stones below. She was dimly aware that she must still be alive, because hitting the cobblestones hurt. Two looked up, groggy, and tried to clear her vision. The vampire was backing away from her, eyes wide with confusion and surprise.

"*Tah ama vamper. Sa pare tah ama vamper. Ashi?*"

The words meant nothing to Two, but she forced herself to respond anyway. Her mouth grudgingly formed the words.

"Told ... toldjoo to ... wait."

"*Ashika moritas*?!" the vampire cried.

Two was fading rapidly, but she forced herself to a sitting position. Her head spun, and she leaned against the side of the building for support. The walls of *L'Obscurité* throbbed and hummed against her back.

"I don't speak ... whatever language that is, sorry," Two said.

The woman seemed to have regained some of her composure. She was regarding Two with curiosity.

"You have vampire blood," she said.

Two's vision was fading now, the world going first grey and then dark. She laughed. The sound was more like a sob, and with it went the last of her strength. Two slumped to the ground, and her last words were a whisper.

"Not anymore."

* * *

Her body twitched, twisted, shifted to a different part of the bed. The sudden cool of the sheets brought Two up from the depths of sleep, and her first thought was: *I don't remember buying silk ...*

This wasn't her apartment. The events of the previous evening began to play like a film against her eyelids, flickering at first, growing stronger as she left sleep behind. Memory drove Two's eyes open and she sat bolt upright in bed, eyes wide and panicked. The vampire had attacked her, but must have stopped in the nick of time. Two knew she had been on the edge of death the previous night, but now she was alive and resting in a bed.

Was this, then, the vampire's home?

Two swung her legs over the side of the bed, surveying her surroundings. She was in what looked like a modest spare bedroom in a high-rise condominium, well-furnished but not lavish. The dresser on which her clothes were piled was oak, and there was a pretty standing mirror in one corner. She recognized a painting on the wall as a Monet print, but a very good one, chosen to match the rest of the room's decor. The clock on the nightstand stood at eighteen past ten, the darkness of the room confirming that it was night.

Two was wearing a sea-foam green nightgown that had bunched itself up around her hips while she slept. She stood, smoothing the gown out, and rolled her eyes as folds of extra fabric pooled at her feet. Whoever the gown belonged to, she was significantly taller. Two took a step and nearly fell to the floor. Her legs were shaky, weak, not willing to hold her. She steadied herself with a hand on the foot of the bed and took another step toward her clothes.

"Lost a lot of blood, I guess," she muttered, taking small, slow steps across the room.

Standing by the chair, Two pulled the nightgown off and replaced it with her blouse and slacks. Everything was still in its place: wallet, keys, cigarettes. Two wanted one of the latter but decided against it. Her life had been spared; she could at least do her host the courtesy of not lighting up in the house.

There was noise coming from out beyond the door, and Two stood in front of it for a moment, listening. Her legs were feeling better, and Two thought that getting some food into her system might help even more. She wondered if vampires kept anything edible in their kitchens. The noise from behind the door sounded like a televised sporting event, nothing that should have given her pause. Two turned the knob and opened the door.

The apartment was larger than she had expected based on the size of the bedroom in which she'd awoken. The hall contained entries to two more bedrooms and a bathroom. At its end, Two could see what looked like a substantial kitchen and dining area. The living area was adjacent to this, out of view, but light from the television flickered, reflecting on the stainless steel appliances.

"Come on, come on," a man's voice said, and then, "yes!"

Two walked down the hall and turned the corner. The living area of the apartment was better furnished than the guest bedroom. Before her were two overstuffed couches and a recliner set in front of a gigantic flat-screen television with a complete surround-sound stereo system. One wall was dominated by a massive aquarium filled with corals and tropical fish. Against the other wall were three large, oak bookcases, filled almost to bursting with hard-bound books. Some of them looked ancient.

On the couch, watching the television with his back to her, was a young man of perhaps twenty-five. He had long hair, somewhere between brown and red, that was pulled back into a ponytail. Two could not see his face. On the television, a team in black uniforms was moving around on a basketball court.

"Quit wasting time," the man said to the television, his accent Irish. "Sure, it's the pre-season, but a game's a game. Stop pussying around."

"Excuse me—" Two began, her voice tentative, and the man interrupted her without looking.

"I'm trying to watch the fucking game, Na—"

He paused in mid-sentence and looked suddenly over his shoulder at her. This man was another vampire, there could be no doubt. If the speed of his movement hadn't told her, his eyes would have. They were bright green like Two's, but ageless, reflective. Vampire eyes.

"You're not Naomi," the man told her. "She isn't home."

"No, I'm not Naomi," Two replied.

"What the fuck is this? You're not even a vampire!"

"No, sorry."

The man stood up, frowning. Two took a step backward, not enthusiastic about the look she saw on his face.

"What are you doing here?"

"I don't know. I mean … I just woke up. In the guest room."

"Well isn't that fucking brilliant. She goes out an' doesn't even bother to tell me that she's left dinner in the other room."

Two shook her head. "I'm not dinner. That's … not why I'm here."

The vampire smiled at her and actually licked his lips.

"You're human, and you're here with me alone. If you weren't dinner before, girl, you are now."

"Wait!" Two took another step back, and bumped against the countertop that divided the kitchen from the living area.

"No," the vampire said, still smiling, and leapt at her.

78

For the better part of her life, Two had been forced to let instinct dictate her actions. She had long ago learned to trust her impulses, and they had thus far saved her from death on several occasions. Had she taken the time to think, it would likely have brought only her murder at the hands of the vampire sailing through the air toward her. Instead, Two let instinct and adrenaline think for her, pushing up with her arms and falling backward over the counter behind her into the kitchen.

She hit her head hard on the tile floor and saw stars dancing in her vision as the vampire flew over her and landed on the stove with a crash. Still acting on instinct, Two was up and moving in an instant, away from the vampire and toward the front door of the apartment. She heard him shouting profanities behind her.

Two would have died anyway, no matter how good her instincts, if luck hadn't been on her side. The vampire was simply too fast, was in fact already up from his landing and reaching out with his long arms. He caught her hair in his hand, and Two gave a yelping shriek of pain and fear as he pulled her backward off her feet.

He caught her before she could fall, spun her, and pushed her chin back with his powerful hands, exposing the same vein that the vampire woman had latched onto. Two knew she could not survive another feeding, and she beat her fists against his chest, terrified and furious, but it did no good. She was helpless.

It was a voice that saved her, an angry shout that stopped her attacker in mid-bite, teeth only inches from Two's skin.

"Stop! *Farake,* Stephen! *Mishke kel, vi ma kovre sa tarseson munta teo maje.*"

The vampire, Stephen, looked up and smiled.

"Oh, it's not as bad as all that, surely," he said.

"I am serious, Stephen," the voice, a woman's, snarled. "Release her. Right now!"

Stephen seemed to consider this for a moment, and then did what he was told. He let go of Two without warning, and she plummeted to the floor with a squawk of surprise. She pulled herself slowly to a sitting position and looked to see who had saved her. The vampire woman from the bar was looking down at her. She spoke, her voice now restrained.

"Hello, child of Eresh. I am Naomi, and I apologize for last night – and for my idiot friend who does not know how to mind his manners."

Stephen was now propped against the counter, looking amused, not at all perturbed at having lost his opportunity to feed. He laughed. "Your idiot friend isn't the one who left a human in the guest room without bothering to tell anyone, Naomi."

"I made the assumption that you know me well enough to realize that if I'd wanted her dead, she would be dead."

Stephen shrugged. "She's food."

"She is not."

"She's not a vampire. Look at her."

Two, who had been trying to regain control of her heartbeat, grabbed the counter and hauled herself to a standing position. She scowled at the two vampires and said, "She's getting tired of listening to you talk about her as if she's not standing right fucking here."

Stephen's grin broadened. Even Naomi smiled a bit.

"Again, my apologies," she said. "May I ask your name?"

"My name is Two. Like the number. How do you know I'm an Eresh?"

"I could taste it."

Stephen laughed again. "Oh, the great Naomi attacked an *Eresh?* That's genius. Brilliant! Senior Councilor Naomi Ames, unable even to tell a vampire lord from a common human."

Naomi gave him a cool, disapproving look. "As you said yourself, she is not a vampire. Nevertheless, there is trace enough of it still in her veins that I was able to discern it. I wonder, Stephen, would *you* have been able to do so?"

"Don't know. Don't care. She's got Eresh blood in her? Very well then – she's safe. No hard feelings, human?"

"I said my name is Two."

"Yes. Two, like the number. You may call me Stephen. Or at least, you could if we were to continue this conversation. I am bored to tears, Two-like-the-number, and am going back to my basketball game."

Stephen stood, waved once, and moved back to the couch.

Naomi shook her head, sighed, and said, "Again, I must apologize for my companion."

Two shrugged. "Whatever."

"You were someone's fledgling once, yes? But your sire has abandoned you, or died, and you have become human again."

Two nodded. "Yes, that's what happened."

"May I ask who your master was?"

"He wasn't my master at all. He was my ... my lover, I guess. His name was Theroen Anders."

Naomi took an involuntary step back, an expression of shock flashing across her face as if Two had slapped her. Two looked at the vampire woman for a moment, confused, and then felt understanding flood her mind. Of course this woman would know that name. Grey eyes, amber hair ... Two's legs felt shaky again. She leaned against the counter for support.

"Oh," she said, her voice weak. "I get it. You're *that* Naomi. Theroen thought you were dead."

Naomi shook her head. "No, not dead. I would have contacted him, but Abraham forbade it and I was ... disinclined to go against his wishes. It was *you,* then ... the one who destroyed Abraham."

Two looked away, afraid of the judgment she might see in Naomi's eyes. She nodded. "That's right. I killed him. I'm sorry."

Naomi took a step forward and Two looked quickly back at her, trying not to flinch. To her surprise, the vampire was smiling.

"Sorry? I doubt that. I doubt that very much. Learning of that bastard's death was the best news I've had in decades. I can only imagine how enjoyable performing the actual deed must have been. I ... Two, are you all right?"

Two had gone pale and was visibly shaking. She held on to the counter like a sailor trying to weather a particularly violent storm.

"I think I'm going to throw up," she said, her voice miserable. "Or pass out. Maybe both."

"Sit down. No, on the floor, just sit down. Breathe deeply."

Two did as she was told, sitting down, head bent, staring at the floor. Finally, she was able to gain some measure of control.

"I'm starving," she said after a time.

"Yes, and bruised, and far too low on blood. You shouldn't be moving about, and I should know better than to be bringing up traumatic moments from your recent past. I'm sorry, Two, there are just so many questions. We have so very much to discuss."

Two laughed. It was a tired, grey sound, but there was some humor there, where none had been for many months.

"Yeah," she said. "No kidding."

Naomi helped Two to the unoccupied couch and instructed her to lie down.

"Thanks," Two said, following the orders. "Do you have anything to eat? I guess probably not."

"We have human guests occasionally. There might be something. I will check."

Naomi moved into the kitchen. Two could hear her opening cupboard doors.

"Who's playing?" Two asked Stephen.

Stephen glanced over at her, one eyebrow raised. "Do you actually care?"

"No. Sorry for interrupting your game before."

"Quite all right."

There was a moment of quiet. Naomi's voice called out from the kitchen, "She's expecting you to apologize for trying to kill her, now, Stephen."

"It may be a long wait. Tell me, Two, do you apologize to your turkey sandwich before you eat it?"

Two smiled. "No, and I'm not expecting an apology. I've been on your side of the fence. I know what it's like."

"You were an Eresh, not an Ay'Araf. You do not 'know what it's like' for us."

"Oh, yes," Naomi said, returning to the living room. "The unending hardships thrust upon the warrior caste. What they always forget to mention is that they're the ones making things difficult.

Two, I have a bag of cheese-flavored popcorn and a frozen chicken patty. Do either of those appeal to you?"

Two was ravenous. "Yes, either. Both. Right now, I think I'd eat cardboard soaked in water. I'll pay you back."

"Lord forbid we give up our chicken patty without compensation," Stephen muttered.

"Enough," Naomi told him, and returned to the kitchen.

"She's always so serious. You'd think after four hundred years she'd ... make it! Yes!" Stephen's interest had once again been drawn to the basketball game.

Two lay on the couch, feeling weak and shaky. Her head spun with questions, so many that she was not sure where to start. At last, she began with something pedestrian.

"How old are you, Stephen?"

"Three hundred and twenty-seven years."

"How long have you been in this country?"

"God, are we to make small talk now? I'm trying to watch this game."

Two rolled her eyes. "Do you work at being a prick?"

"No," Stephen said. "It comes naturally."

Naomi returned to the room with a plate and a can of soda.

"It was 7-Up or a three hundred-dollar bottle of wine. I figured the former would go better with the popcorn," she said, setting the food down on the coffee table.

"That's fine. Thanks." Two sat up, fought off a wave of dizziness, and picked up the food. She tried not to wolf it down but had little success. Naomi watched her, amused, waiting.

When Two was done, the vampire woman asked, "Better?"

"Much. Thank you. Best chicken patty I've ever had."

Stephen did not look away from the screen but laughed.

"He's pretending not to be interested," Naomi said, "but he's not doing a very good job."

"The two of you aren't making it easy to ignore you," Stephen replied without looking away from the screen.

"It's a summer game, Stephen. It doesn't even count. The woman who killed Abraham is lying next to you on the couch, and you're worried about summer basketball?"

"It's pre-season, not summer league. This is the one who killed Abraham?"

"Yes. Weren't you listening earlier?"

"To you? Lord, no."

Naomi made a sound of frustration. "Two was Theroen's fledgling. She's the one who freed us from Abraham."

"Freed you?" Two asked.

"In the metaphorical sense," Stephen said. He was looking at Two with new interest. "Abraham did not own us, but he sat at the head of the vampire council. As such, he held all *civilized* vampires in this country in some level of control."

"God, there's so much I don't know," said Two. She ran a hand through her hair and glanced around. She felt dazed from the loss of blood, the hit on her head when she had fallen on the floor, the adrenaline, and the sudden return of emotion to a life that had seemed so empty. Two covered her face with her hands, fighting tears.

"Are you all right?" Naomi asked gently, as if she already knew the answer.

Two shook her head, keeping her hands where they were.

"He's dead," she said at last. "He's dead and I couldn't stop it."

"Abraham?" Stephen asked.

Two sobbed once, unable to answer, fighting to retain control.

Naomi answered for her. "No, Theroen."

"Ah. So it was like that, then."

Two took in a deep, shuddering breath and looked up at them with eyes that were hard and glassy, filled with anger and sadness and hate.

"It was like that," she said. "I loved him, and Abraham took him from me. Now he's gone, and you're my only hope."

"Never been someone's only hope before," Stephen muttered. Naomi glared at him.

"This isn't funny, Stephen. I'll not tolerate your attitude, even if Two is willing to put up with it."

Two shrugged. "I don't really give a shit. As long as one of you can fix me, you can say whatever you want."

"Fix you?" Naomi looked perplexed.

"Bite me. Drain me. Give me blood. Make me what I was. Can either of you do that?"

Naomi and Stephen looked at each other, considering this request. When Stephen spoke, his voice was slow and cautious.

"We are ... both at an age where we can produce fledglings, yes. We are neither of us Eresh, so we could not make you what you were, even if we could do what you ask, which we can't."

Two looked up at him, not understanding. "Why not?"

Naomi spoke up. "It's ... I'm sorry, but it's forbidden."

"What do you mean 'forbidden?' Vampires make fledglings all the time, don't they?"

"Yes. Well, not all the time, but they do make fledglings. You're right. That's not the issue, Two."

"Then tell me what the problem is so we can figure out a solution."

Naomi and Stephen exchanged another glance, and when Stephen smiled at Two, she could read the apology in his eyes.

"You've been marked by a vampire. Any vampire would be problematic, but your original sire was the heir apparent to the Eresh dynasty. A lord among lords. Theroen may not have known what he was, but everyone else does. We are not permitted to touch you."

Two was too stunned to feel anger, or sorrow, or much of anything. She felt the empty, dead feeling creeping back over her. "But ... why?"

"It's against our laws," Naomi said. "The Code of Eresh-Kigal states it very clearly. *A vampire's claim to his or her fledgling is absolute, and no other vampire shall interfere.*"

"No other vampire ..." Two murmured, considering this.

Stephen frowned. "None who follow the laws of the council, anyway, which effectively rules out all but the Burilgi. Believe me, Two, what you know of vampire life holds little similarity to what the Burilgi are. You do not want that."

Two stared at the floor a moment. When she looked back up at them, her eyes were burning with rage.

"He's fucking *dead!*" she shouted. "He's not coming back. He's not going to come climbing up out of the fucking ashes to make me whole again. How can it matter?"

Naomi sighed. "I know what it is like to lose a sire, and a lover, and a friend. You know who I am, so Theroen must have told you of his time with Lisette."

"Yes," Two said. She was shaking again, this time from anger at these two vampires and their idiotic laws. "I know about Lisette. I know *all* about Lisette."

"Isaac stole her from us, from Theroen and me, when we were still young, because of the very same law that prevents us from touching you."

Two shook her head. "It was Abraham who burned her, and he didn't do it because of some stupid law. He did it because she took something that belonged to him and it pissed him off. The law was just an excuse to get Isaac to do the dirty work for him so he could trick Theroen into coming back. He told us that, before the end. I heard it from his own mouth."

Naomi stiffened, her considerable pallor whitening even further. After a time she spoke, in a voice that was distant and strained.

"It is ... good that he is dead."

Two rested her palms against her forehead. "He was an evil, horrible monster. He took everything I had, and now you're sitting here telling me I can't get it back. What do I do?"

"I'm sorry. We're sorry. It's ... Two, if I could bring him back for you, I would."

Two looked down again, and to the two vampires it seemed then that a change came over her. Though she barely moved, it was as if all the life had fled from her body.

"Sorry doesn't help me," she said. "Nothing can help me anymore. I can't have Theroen back, and no one else can help me. So what's left? Nothing."

"We will do what we can to help," Naomi told her.

Two looked back up at them, sighed, shrugged.

Blood Hunt

"The only thing left you can do for me is kill me."

CHAPTER VI

Tori's Choice

"You want me to kill vampires for you?"

Tori stared at Charles, unable to believe what he had just said. He looked back, head still tilted, watching her with a slight smile on his face. When Tori realized no explanation was coming, she forced herself to speak again.

"I can't ... I mean, why would I do that? They're not all like Abraham. They're not all like these things that murdered my parents. I'm here to take care of my personal business, not to become some sort of vampire assassin."

Charles looked her in the eye. "What if I told you that you're wrong? That most of them *are* like Abraham? What if I told you, Tori Perrault, that there is a council of vampires – the *Kharas Mach* – that rules over nearly all of the vampires in this country? What if I told you that they ordered your parents' murder to punish you for your crimes against Abraham?"

Tori opened her mouth to respond to this but found herself at a loss for words. After a moment she closed it again, clenching her teeth. It couldn't be ... and yet, didn't it make sense?

"They are a blight," Charles continued. "A plague. A threat against humanity. They will eventually destroy us, if we don't destroy them first. You are a human again, Tori. Will you sit here and allow that? Will you tell me 'no' and go on your way and wake to find them there one night, ready to bind you with chains and drag you to your death?"

"No, I—"

"Will you do nothing as other young women are torn from their lives and their families, to be thrust into misery and despair? Or perhaps you would have them return, as you have, to a bleak world where there is nothing left for them but the pursuit of raw, empty pleasure?"

Tori started at this, and Charles continued, "Yes, we know all about that. We know about the drinking, the smoking, the men. We thought at first that it would pass. We believed that you were merely readjusting to human life, but it's only getting worse for you, isn't it, Tori? You lust for the thrill you once had: the pleasure of the kill, the taste of blood."

"It's … not like that," Tori said. She closed her eyes and put a hand against her forehead, trying to get her bearings. Was what Charles had said true? Had some council of vampires ordered the murder of her parents? Her innocent, harmless parents?

"It *is* like that, I think. You don't want to admit to such bestial thoughts and desires, but they are within you. That was vampirism's gift to you, the gift given by the creatures who made you, the same creatures who held your father down and *tore his throat* from his body!"

"Stop it!" Tori shouted. "I'm not like that! Not anymore!"

"You are repulsed by your own desires, I understand, but do not deny their existence. Do not lie to me. You will not escape this nightmare without our help."

"I don't need any help," Tori said, knowing it was a lie, her voice low and broken. What was there for her now? What was there but an unending procession of empty, hopeless days?

As quickly as his mood had changed, Charles now snapped back into his calm, smooth, polite tone.

"Of course you need help. Tori, it begins now, with this simple choice. You are beset upon by evil, and as strong as you may be, you are not strong enough to face it alone. Our enemies have, through their reprehensible actions, delivered you to us and given you this choice.

"You can choose to send me away now, send me from your home and wait huddled in the dark for the inevitable end. They *will* catch you. They *will* kill you, and before they do, they will hurt you. They will make you give up the names of those you care about. When death has come to look like bliss compared to the pain they will put you through, you'll tell them anything they want to know, and they'll use that knowledge to go and hurt others. This is what they do."

Tori stared at him. Charles contemplated his manicured fingernails for a moment, looked up, met her gaze.

"You can make that choice, and I won't stop you. Under ordinary circumstances, I might even admire your bravery, but these circumstances are nothing of the sort. These things are not a shadow in a child's closet, or the imagined monster under the bed. They are very real, and they will come for you. Is this what you want, to stay here alone until they come for you?"

Tori shook her head.

"Then come with me. Let us together bring a scourge down upon these creatures, these terrible things so willing to destroy lives and shatter families. Come with me to meet the other Children – come and learn, if nothing else. You have been travelling this path alone. I cannot offer some other, easier journey, but I can promise that with the Children, there will always be a hand there when you need it."

Tori closed her eyes and thought of Two. What would Two choose, if given this chance? What would she do?

A cold voice, this one belonging to no one but herself, spoke up in her mind. *Two would leave you here. She would go back to New York and leave you here to go insane, leave you to watch your parents die and your life crumble. Isn't that the choice she already made? Isn't that what Two would do?*

"It is time, Tori," Charles said. "I must depart, with you at my side or not. There will be no second offer. Will you come now, and meet with the Children, or will you stay here and meet your death?"

Tori took a deep breath, wiped her arm across her eyes, opened them and looked at Charles.

"I'll go with you," she said. "I'll go and meet the Children."

Charles breathed in a deep breath, smiled, nodded as if the conclusion had been forgone. He set his cup of coffee down and stood. Tori stood with him. Together, they left her parents' house behind.

Christopher Buecheler

PART II

CHAPTER VII

Broken Door, Broken Window

Rhes Thompson couldn't feel his legs. It wasn't that they weren't there; he could see them, crossed beneath him on the plush carpet lining the hallway outside of Two's apartment. Any feeling they'd once had was now long gone, and it was this sensation that had pulled him up out of sleep.

"Sarah," he said. "Baby, you gotta get up. I can't feel my legs."

"Whuzzah?" Sarah mumbled, stirring. She took her head from his shoulder and yawned. "Where are we? Rhes, this isn't our room ..."

"No. We're in Two's hall, remember? We're waiting for her to come home."

It had been six hours since they had read the news report on Tori's parents and five hours since they had reached Two's condo in SoHo, followed another resident inside, and set up camp in the hallway. In that time, they'd seen no sign of their friend, and had eventually fallen asleep leaning against the wall.

"Oh, yeah, that's right. Sorry."

"S'OK. Do you think you could move for a sec? I fell asleep and lost all the feeling in my legs. I like them too much to let them get gangrene."

Sarah laughed and shifted, taking her weight off of Rhes. She drew her knees up to her chest and wrapped her arms around them. Rhes had to use his hands to uncross his legs.

"Gonna suck when they wake up," Sarah commented.

"I'm trying not to think about it."

"Did Two ever come back?"

"I don't think so. At this point, I think we have to give up for the night. We called, we came over here, we sat in front of her front door … I don't know what else to do. It's almost three in the morning."

"It's OK, Rhes. I'm sure she's fine. We'll get in touch with her eventually."

"How do we know she's not lying in there right now, hurt or dead?"

Sarah shrugged. "We don't. But we just talked to her this afternoon … police won't do anything about it yet. You going to break down the door?"

Rhes considered the possibility for a moment before answering. "No, I guess not. If we don't hear from her for another few days, though …"

"If that's the case, we'll come back and try to get in. I'm with you. Can you walk yet?"

"No way. They're just waking up. You've got at least ten minutes of listening to me … agh … bitch and moan."

Sarah grinned, slid up next to him, and kissed him on the cheek. "Poor baby. You *were* the one who said he'd stay awake, though."

"Yeah, I know. Ow! Why does the human body … ow, ow, ow … do this?"

"Think vampire legs fall asleep?"

"I can't even keep track of it all. Half the things Two told us about Theroen don't jive with the Dracula creature-features I used to watch as a kid."

"More than half," Sarah agreed. "But she did also say that there was more than one type of vampire, and that Theroen was unusual."

Rhes massaged his legs, biting his tongue and making faces. "Right, Theroen. It's hard to think of him as a person and not some creepy monster, no matter what Two says about him, you know?"

"I know. He seems to have been good, though. Better than good, really. I'm angry about what's happening to Two now, but it's not his fault. If he hadn't saved her, she'd have probably OD'd by now or something."

"Probably true."

Rhes grimaced and pulled himself to his feet. The prickling feeling in his legs was finally beginning to recede.

"You ready to go?" Sarah asked, standing as well.

"Almost. I'll call Two tomorrow before I go to work, I guess. Worst case, I just get the stupid voicemail again and leave another message."

Sarah nodded, then arched an eyebrow. "Can you walk yet? I need to work out some of this frustration, and Molly's away for the night. Maybe we can ... make some noise."

"Walk? Put it like that, and I think I can run."

Sarah grinned, turned, and started toward the elevator, tracing her fingers along the wall to keep her bearings. Rhes took a moment to admire the view and then, still wincing at the prickles in his legs, followed behind her.

* * *

Had Rhes and Sarah stayed for another forty minutes, they would have encountered their friend, still alive and healthy, excited for the first time in months after her first brief encounter with a vampire. They had no way of knowing this, of course, and so returned by cab to their home in Brooklyn. After the sex, which had been as loud as Sarah could make it and very good, Rhes lay awake, thinking about his life and his friend. Was she simply gone without a trace, like it had been when Theroen had first taken her? Even if they eventually found Two, was there really anything he could do for her?

It didn't matter. He had to try, if not for Two's sake then for Tori's. Somewhere, Tori was dealing with her own hardships, and

Rhes knew that she had been through things that he simply couldn't comprehend. He and Sarah wouldn't be able to help her the way Two would.

Now what? Rhes's brain asked him, over and over again, as he lay in bed staring up at the ceiling. *Now what?*

He didn't know, and that was the primary source of his frustration. He could have handled an undesirable answer, if such an answer had been obvious. It wasn't. Should he forget her? Some days he wanted to, thought it would be for the best. She would not have been the first friend to fade from his life. He didn't want to forget her, however. He wanted to save her.

Rhes loved Two – not in the way he loved Sarah, but in the fierce and protective way that he would have loved a younger sister. The idea that she was suffering some sort of hurt he couldn't help her with bothered him a great deal. That she might be in danger, real physical danger, was ever on his mind. Sarah understood this and shared most of his concerns, and Rhes was thankful for that. It would have been easy for her to let Rhes's relationship with Two drive a wedge between them.

He glanced over at his sleeping girlfriend, tousled and sweaty and beautiful, her arms wrapped around one of his. She always fell asleep like that, gripping his arm, holding him to her. The feeling was so comfortable now that Rhes had difficulty sleeping without it.

Two was not driving them apart as he had once feared she might. Rhes and Sarah had been together for three years, and he loved her more now than he ever had. He tried not to think about losing her because it made him feel confused and frightened, emotions with which he was not generally familiar. Sarah, for her part, found ways to make him understand that she felt the same. Sometimes it was words, but more often it was gestures, like wrapping his arm up in hers before falling asleep. *You're mine*, this told him, *and you're not going anywhere.*

It was when he thought about losing these things that he believed he could understand some of what Two must be going through. Her relationship with Theroen had been short, but they had bonded at a mental level unavailable to normal human beings, and his death had clearly scarred her deeply. Rhes supposed a psychiatrist might be able to lend some insight into how she could heal, but he believed that dragging Two in that direction would make irrevocable cuts to the ties of their friendship. At the same time, she was shoving them away anyway, so maybe ...

Rhes sighed, stared, thought.

"Gonna go nuts, if you don't stop," Sarah murmured, her voice fuzzy from sleep, hoarse from her earlier cries. There was concern there, and a kind of loving exasperation, but also understanding. She pressed up against him, still holding his arm, and kissed his neck.

"I know," he said. "You're right."

"Love you, Rhes. Worried." Sarah was still as much asleep as awake. She was mumbling into his neck, muffling her words.

"I know. Don't."

"Can't help it."

"I know. I love you, too, Sarah." Rhes knew he didn't say this often enough, and hoped he made it clear in other ways. He felt Sarah's smile against his skin.

"I know."

* * *

The next night took him to Manhattan. Several blocks north and west of where Rhes now stood, Two was lingering outside of *L'Obscurité* for the second time in as many days, nervous anticipation tightening her guts, making her heart race. Just a few dozen feet above her, from an apartment window, the vampire Naomi watched her with curiosity. Six hundred miles away, Tori Perrault sat drinking and weeping, leafing through old photographs in the living room of the house she had shared with her parents, who had now been deceased for nearly sixty hours.

Rhes, aware of none of this, knew only that it had come down to what now seemed inevitable. He was concerned enough about his friend's well-being that he was preparing to kick in the door to her apartment.

"Do you know what you're doing?" Sarah asked, sounding nervous.

"Sure. Well, no ... but I've seen it on TV a couple times."

"Oh. Fantastic, Rhes."

"Look out. I'm going to get a running start."

Sarah took a few steps backward. She opened her mouth and Rhes knew she was going to ask him to reconsider. He didn't want to do that; he knew that if he did, the fear of what might be waiting for him inside the apartment would never let him go through with it.

"I'm going," he said, and charged forward, leading with his right shoulder and aiming low so that the maximum impact would happen near the door-knob. The wooden door gave way with a splintering crack and Rhes, off-balance, fell forward into the condo's dark entranceway with a thud and a grunt. He lay there on the floor for a moment, breathing.

"Should I laugh or call an ambulance?" Sarah asked. She knelt down beside him and put her hand on his back.

Rhes rolled his eyes and pushed himself up off the floor. "Let's hold the laughter until we're sure Two's not here."

"OK."

Rhes glanced at the alarm system. If it had been activated by his entrance, there was no outward sign of it, and he guessed that Two had never turned it on in the first place. He glanced around the hallway, trying to see.

"Where are the fucking lights? I can't see anything."

"Welcome to my world," Sarah muttered.

Rhes paused, glancing over at Sarah. The regularity with which her blindness came up in casual conversation seemed to have increased lately. Where the simple act of flipping a switch would make things much easier for Rhes, it would change nothing for Sarah, and it seemed that this sort of thing was bothering her more than it used to.

Sarah, aware that Rhes had paused, shook her head. "Not looking for pity, hon. Just musing. The light switch is behind you, near the kitchen door. I heard Two use it the last time we came over."

Rhes looked where she had told him to, found the switch, and turned on the lights.

"Does it bother you when I say stuff like that? I'm not trying to be insensitive or hurtful, I just don't think about it most of the time."

"You were just looking for a light switch. It's not like you shouted out 'Jesus Christ, I feel like my cripple girlfriend!' or something."

"Sarah ..."

She sighed. "Look, we can talk about the many cons of blindness later if you want. For right now, it's really OK, I promise. Let's focus on what we came here for, all right?"

"Yeah, you're right. I need to search this place."

"Yes, you do, and we both know you can do it quicker if I stay out of the way. That's fine. Get me to the couch and I'll hang out there."

Rhes led her forward, glancing into the kitchen as they passed it. It was empty, the only sign of human use a half-empty bottle of bourbon and an empty bottle of water. The hallway opened out into a small living room, sparsely furnished. Two hadn't been much for decoration even before any of this had begun, when she had been a vibrant, mischievous kid of seventeen living with Rhes in Brooklyn. Much had changed about her since then, but not that.

"See anything suspicious?" Sarah asked, sitting down on the couch, her back to the large picture window where, only a few hours before, Two had stood waiting for the sun to go down.

"Nope."

Rhes moved quickly around the living room, looking behind the couch. There was no indication of any struggle and no sign of Two, other than another bottle of bourbon, this one unopened, sitting on the small table she had stuck in what architects and realtors liked to call the 'breakfast nook.'

"I'm going to check the bedroom," he said.

"Knock yourself out."

The search ended quickly and without result. Rhes checked Two's bedroom, her bathroom, her closets. He looked into the bathroom and found nothing out of the ordinary. Two was not here in any capacity, and certainly not lying dead in a corner somewhere.

Rhes returned to the living room, trying to be happy that he had not found any sign that his friend was in trouble. Instead, he was mostly frustrated.

Sarah had been reclining on the couch. She sat up straight as Rhes returned.

"Not here, huh?"

Rhes leaned against the door-frame between the hallway and the living room, blowing air through his pursed lips in aggravation.

"No, she's not here. I have no idea where she is, but she's not here. Her voicemail light is blinking … probably from me filling it up."

"You want to listen and be sure?"

Rhes shrugged. "No. Don't know her password anyway, and who cares? Two obviously doesn't give a fuck about anything anymore. It's probably time to stop worrying about her and just let it go."

Sarah considered this for a moment before asking, "You mean that?"

Rhes raised his head. He was going to tell her no, of course not, he didn't mean it at all. He was, in fact, already considering where else he might search for his friend. He was going to explain this to Sarah, but instead he found his glance shifting from his girlfriend to the window behind her. There was something not right happening, though for a moment the sight was so absurd that his mind seemed unable to process it.

A pair of eyes, burning bright with malice, were staring at him from behind the pane of glass, eighty feet up the side of a building where no human being could possibly be.

"Jesus Christ, Sarah, get down!" Rhes roared. He took what he knew would be a futile step toward his girlfriend. Behind her, the thing at the window reared back, maintaining some impossible grip with its feet, and brought both hands forward, palms out, crashing into the glass.

Rhes heard each noise as if it had been plucked out individually, separated from the general cacophony and accentuated. First, the splintering as fissures opened, then the crash as the window burst inward, and finally the pitter-patter noises of individual squares of safety glass hitting the carpet. Rhes took another long, impossibly slow step, still shouting, still watching as the thing at the window now reached out to grasp at Sarah with the elongated talons of its fingers.

Time seemed to snap back into place at that moment, and Rhes heard the sounds of the attack receding as his pulse began to thud in his ears. He could still hear the wind outside, rushing in through the now-shattered window. Sarah had begun to scream. The thing, whatever it was, gurgled out laughter that sounded like sewage passing over river stones. Rhes took another step, found that this one seemed fast enough for him, and shifted his weight, springing forward. He shouted something incoherent, but it was enough.

The creature that had been headed for Sarah now turned to look at him instead. Rhes, unafraid and well beyond the point of no return, flung himself into the air. He had time to contemplate the possibility that he might send both himself and this monstrosity soaring out through the broken window in a suicidal dive to the pavement below. Instead, acting on instinct, the thing grabbed him out of mid-air, falling backward and to the side. They landed on the carpet, grappling with each other.

Rhes wanted to shout for Sarah to run, but there were long fingers wrapped around his throat, throttling him. He jerked his head back and then slammed it forward, connecting with the creature's skull. Stars shot through his vision, but Rhes forced himself to shove forward with his hands. The grip on his neck was broken, and Rhes rolled away from the thing.

There were two more crashes, from other windows in the room. The lights went out. Sarah was sobbing, somewhere.

"*Sa liraset karecomar zhi nav,* Jason," a voice said. The words echoed out from the dark, rotting and guttural. Rhes scuttled on hands and knees toward the sound of Sarah's sobs. When she felt him take her hand she jerked and then, realizing who it was, wrapped her arms around him.

There was a cough from near the couch and a shuffling noise. Silhouetted against the light from outside, Rhes saw the thing he had wrestled with getting to its feet. It gestured over at him, looking at its companion.

"*Karecomar pare culdad chesas vi nenka korare. Epilate.*"

"*Vame toh ker pove eso filan,*" the first speaker answered back. "*Sa pirnate echi bombar estibe sa?*"

"*Na se nen estibas,* Saul.*"

"*Listro baje gaso.*"

A third voice, thick with glee and malice, spoke from the shadows near Two's bedroom. "*Tao lirasemo ma emoar* Saul. *Teas hagimen ukia eso pikoti taravas.*"

The first voice spoke now in English. "Good. Take her. I will deal with the other."

"The fuck you will!" Rhes shouted.

"Big words from someone kneeling on the ground and staring out into the dark," said the first voice, but the figure it belonged to made no immediate move forward.

Sarah was breathing hard, gripping his arm tightly but otherwise in control. Rhes kissed her forehead. "Pretty sure there's going to be a fight, hon."

"I figured that one out. Are you going to win?"

"Doubt it. Two's vampires were stronger than God, remember?"

"These aren't Two's vampires."

"Guess we'll see, then."

"Will someone call the cops?"

"Doubt it. This is New York, city of brotherly indifference."

"I love you, Rhes."

"I love you too," he replied, glad to have had the chance to say it, knowing they were probably both going to die in this room.

"That's very sweet," said one of the vampires. In his mind's eye, Rhes could see the mocking smile on its face.

"Push yourself into the corner," Rhes told Sarah. He stood up, in front of her, watching as the black shapes began to advance.

"We can make this quick," the one he had fought with said.

"Don't do me any favors."

He saw the figure shrug. "Have it your way."

* * *

Rhes felt like he was being beaten with aluminum baseball bats. He was hurt, but not yet badly, and managed to stumble away from his attackers, bouncing off the couch and catching himself against the wall. Breathing sent a sharp pain stabbing up through his side, and he wondered if his ribs were broken.

He hadn't given them the chance to get close to Sarah, had instead charged the entire group without warning, tackling the figure in the center. When they had landed, Rhes was on top, and he had pounded his fist into the side of his opponent's head once, twice, a third time. Something had grabbed his arm and hauled him backward, and Rhes had found himself taking some comfort in the recognition that these creatures were not nearly as strong as the ones Two had described.

Rhes was a bouncer by profession, but he was not a fighter by nature. Now, though, energized by fear and a sort of instinctive hatred for the things that were attacking him, he was prepared to do whatever was necessary to stay alive. He pushed himself off of the wall, advancing again. The shadows closed the distance – they were very fast – and began to pummel him again. It hurt, a lot, but he tried to ignore it, swinging with his own fists and hoping to connect. Though it seemed much longer to Rhes, the fight lasted only a few seconds before he was thrown clear again, bruised and bleeding.

"Get the girl," the one that seemed to be in charge said, and one of the shadows broke off from the pack and moved toward the corner where Sarah sat huddled. She cried out Rhes's name.

Shouting, he charged in that direction, but the other two vampires intercepted him and began to pummel him again. Rhes couldn't feel the blows now, wasn't even paying attention to them. All he seemed able to focus on was Sarah's screaming. Was she hurt or just afraid? He felt his body weakening, but it seemed distant, unimportant.

Sarah's screams were cut off, but not by any action of the three vampires. The one vampire had only just grabbed her by the shoulders and yanked her to her feet when a shout came that overrode all of the other noises in the room, cutting them off and giving pause to all of the apartments' occupants. The words were in a language that Rhes and Sarah could not understand, but they took the meaning just the same. Someone had arrived, and he was not happy.

"San mortemon nanta hortati. Ayme chemtapon!"

Rhes was aware of movement, faster by far than these things that had assaulted him seemed capable of. He was suddenly freed from his attackers' grip, and it was only then that he realized his legs would no longer support him. Rhes toppled to the floor, landing on his back on the plush carpet. The world seemed to be spinning even though it was too dark to see it. He heard confused shouting in a mix of English and the vampire language. Then the screams began, hideous and agonized, but Sarah's voice was not among them. The sounds were interspersed with thick, wet thudding noises that Rhes associated with the butcher shop down the street from his apartment.

And then, as quickly as it had begun, it was over. There was only breathing and blackness.

CHAPTER VIII

Set in Motion

"Let me be sure I have this right. You claim to be the girl that Theroen chose to make his bride?"

Stephen's voice was tinged with incredulity and something that bordered on disgust. The tone of his words cut through her despair, and Two looked up at him, eyes narrowing.

"That's right. Why?"

"I'd not expect such poor taste from an *Eresh-Chen*."

"Stephen Connelly!" Naomi hissed. She couldn't seem to find the words to begin chastising him. Two only tilted her head, looked at Stephen, waited for his explanation.

"For Christ's *sake,* Naomi, listen to her. 'Kill me,' she says. What a great load of weak, pathetic bullshit."

"You will not speak like this to the one who killed Abraham!"

Naomi was on her feet now, blocking most of Two's view of Stephen with her rump. Two supposed that many a man and likely no small number of women had admired this view over the centuries. Currently, Two was more interested in what Stephen had to say than whatever Naomi had to flaunt. She leaned to one side and watched.

Stephen was looking up at Naomi, his expression skeptical. "Aye, she says she killed him. I cannot believe that anyone capable of such an act would then simply roll over and give up at the first sign that things might not go the way she wants them to."

"You have no idea what she's been through."

"I don't *care* what she's been through!"

"Stephen, I—" Naomi began, and Two interrupted.

"What are my options?"

Stephen looked over at her and said, "I haven't finished thinking of them all, I'm sure, but I'll give you what I've got off the top of my head. Let me assure you that none of the ones coming to mind include lying down and dying."

Two motioned for Naomi to sit down and looked again at Stephen.

"Good," she said. "So tell me."

Stephen shrugged. "You are *Eresh-Chen*. That means 'child of Eresh' in our language, but that's not all it means. That title is reserved only for a select few. You are part of an unbroken line that has been traced for almost five thousand years."

"What does that mean?"

"It means many things. First, it means that every point in that line, from Eresh through Abraham to Theroen and yourself, are first-children. As far as we know, Eresh was the first *vampire*. By blood, you are her direct heir, and blood – 'tah' in our language – is the only thing that has ever mattered to us.

"If you die, the line dies. There are some – and at times I've been among them – who would dearly like to see it happen. Abraham was an oppressor, a thing of pure evil, and we had only Naomi's word that his son was anything else."

"That should be enough," Naomi muttered.

"And for me, it is. That and your *lovely* personality," Stephen said, flashing her a brilliant grin.

Naomi rolled her eyes. "You'd think the word of a member of *Kharas* would carry a bit more weight."

"I don't understand why any of this matters," Two said. "I'm a human. Whatever blood was in me is gone, at least mostly ... Maybe there's enough so that Naomi could tell I'd been a vampire once, but that's about it."

"That doesn't matter, or at least it shouldn't. Two, you're *Eresh-Chen*. Not only that, but you managed to kill one of the oldest vampires left on the planet, a being who had kept the entire American council under his boot for centuries. You have more of a right to the blood than anyone else in the world. You're going to let them deny you that because of some foolish law from five thousand years ago?"

Two leaned forward, met Stephen's gaze, did not look away.

"I'll ask again: what are my options?"

Stephen nodded. He sat back on the couch and began to tick the items off on his fingers. "First, I'd try appealing to the council. If that fails, then second, I would try to find a vampire who doesn't obey council laws. If that didn't work, then the third thing I'd try would be to take the blood by force. And fourth, if pressed, I would start killing vampires until the council relented."

"Stephen ..." Naomi was looking at the floor, shaking her head.

"I'm not advocating those last few, Naomi. She asked me what I would do, other than give up and die. Those are my answers."

He returned his attention to Two, He began to speak but stopped, his hands first opening and then folding. He reconsidered and started again.

"I don't know how to put this, Two. There has never been a case like yours that I know of. Only Eresh vampires revert to humanity, and Eresh vampires are rare. Those few in history who might have been in a similar situation were usually killed at the same time as their masters. There has certainly never been another *Eresh-Chen* in this position.

"If the council says 'no,' there are other options. Most of them will be dangerous, since you'll be breaking our laws, but you've already broken several of those and seem to have come through all right."

"What laws did I break?" Two asked.

Stephen glanced at Naomi, who took a breath and spoke up.

"The person who killed Abraham is technically wanted for questioning. You've broken statutes thirteen and fifteen of the scrolls, and triggered statute twenty-seven."

"Oh, go ahead an' recite them, Naomi. You know you want to," Stephen said, amused.

"They're wordy. In a nutshell, thirteen says you can't kill an elder of your line. Fifteen says you can't kidnap a fledgling. Twenty-seven says that any human who becomes aware of us should be brought before the council to explain themselves, particularly if they're actively seeking us. That was a later addition, after the council was formed, when we had some trouble in the eighteenth century."

"I didn't kidnap a fledgling," Two said. "She came with me willingly."

Naomi shrugged. "That is one of many reasons why we want to question you, not kill you."

Two rolled her eyes. "This all sounds like I'm going to need to meet with your council, sooner or later."

"You're already meeting with one of them," Stephen said. "Luckily, I suspect you'll find she's one of the most sympathetic to your case."

Two turned to Naomi. "You're on the council?"

Naomi nodded. "My predecessor, William, stepped down earlier this year, after the death of Abraham. As one of the eldest and strongest vampires in America, he would have assumed leadership of the council, but he did not want it. He said that he was worn down from so many years of dealing with that monster, and I don't blame him. As his apprentice, I was next in line for a council position. I do not possess the political clout that William did, Two, but I will help you argue your case if you wish."

"Good," Two said. "OK, Stephen, you're right. Giving up and dying isn't an option. But this had better work. I want back in. This humanity shit just isn't doing it for me at all."

* * *

"You're sure you can do this?" Naomi asked, concern in her voice. Two found her worry amusing; only the night before, this same woman had intentionally attacked Two and nearly killed her.

Two lit a cigarette. She could hear *L'Obscurité* throbbing just across the street. Naomi's apartment looked directly down upon the entrance.

"Yeah, I'm OK. Little shaky, is all. I appreciate the chicken, but I need more food. I could just go home if you don't want me coming back to your place."

"I do not think it is safe for you at home. I have my doubts that I'm the first vampire to notice you and your search. There are many Burilgi in this city. Hundreds, maybe, but you would not have identified them like you did me. Many look like normal humans. The others are so disfigured that they try to stay out of sight."

"Well, then this is the other option. We hit the *bodega*, and I grab some burritos, a pack of smokes, and a six-pack of beer."

"Perhaps you could round out your vices with a box of condoms and a copy of *Hustler*," Naomi said. Her voice was dry, but when Two glanced at her, there was a ghost of a smile on the vampire's lips. Two laughed.

"I'm not the most perfect person in the world," she admitted. "Theroen saved me from a bad place."

"Nobody's perfect," Naomi replied. "We all have our demons."

"Yeah, I guess. You seem to have done pretty well for yourself since what happened with Lisette."

Naomi glanced down at her, raised an eyebrow.

"Did he tell you much about those days? About ... us?"

"You and Lisette?"

"Lisette and me. Theroen and me. Lisette and Theroen."

"Yes and no. He told me the important stuff, I think. I didn't get a day-by-day account of your adventures, but I know how he met Lisette, and how he met you."

A faint blush rose in Naomi's cheeks. Her eyes were far away. "I never loved him like Lisette did, but Theroen and I had our moments."

Two sighed. "I loved him like Lisette did."

"I believe that," Naomi replied. "One does not attack an elder like Abraham without good reason."

Two shook her head. "No, definitely not. I killed him for what he did to Theroen. Not just at the end, but all the way through ... he murdered Lisette. He kept Theroen locked away from the vampire world. He created these deranged sisters and forced

Theroen to take care of them. He tried to kill me just as a parting gift to his son. He was evil. He was purposely, consciously evil, and he enjoyed every minute of it."

Naomi nodded. "I know. I have spent more time in Abraham's presence than I would wish on anyone. It *galls* me that I never guessed at his involvement in Lisette's death."

"Not much you could've done anyway," Two said. She could see their destination, a small grocery and convenience shop of the type that could be found all over the city, at the end of the block.

"No? You were able to do something."

"I didn't know anything about your laws, and I had a *ton* of luck on my side. Luck and heroin."

"What?"

"That's how I did it. I had heroin available to me, strong stuff, uncut. I managed to throw some of it at his face and he breathed a lot of it in. It uh ... fucked him up pretty good."

Understanding dawned on Naomi's face. "Of course! Eresh vampires don't handle opiates well at all. Something in the chemical composition causes a lot of structural damage."

"Yeah. Enough damage that when the time came, I managed to cut his head off."

"Two, that's fantastic."

Two shook her head. "No, it was horrible. Theroen was dead. Melissa was dead. Tori was nuts. Even after Tori got better, she went home to her parents. I had no one left."

"Surely you have other friends?"

"A few, yeah. None who could understand."

Naomi considered this. "So you withdrew from them and went hunting for someone like me."

They had reached the *bodega*. Two pitched her cigarette butt into the gutter and nodded.

"Yeah," she said. "Hunting. Exactly."

* * *

The plastic bags crackled at Two's side as they walked. One contained a six-pack of beer, the other a bag of chips, three huge beef burritos from a brand called Captain Chorizo, and a carton of Camel lights.

"What's happened to Tori?" Naomi asked.

Two shrugged. "She's in Ohio, living a normal life with her parents. Took her a while to turn human again. Actually, I guess it never fully happened. She got her brain back and she doesn't need blood anymore, but she's crazy strong and fast. Theroen said she was really physically advanced for a vampire her age to begin with, and I don't think she lost much of it in the conversion back. I get letters sometimes. Emails."

"Does she miss being a vampire?"

Two hesitated. "I don't think so? She's never said so, anyway, but she has started talking about how restless she is. Could just be Ohio doing that to her, though. Lima's ... not New York."

"Was she with you when you disposed of Abraham?"

"Yeah. I think she saved my life, actually. She bought me a couple more minutes, and I think if he'd gotten to me before that, the heroin wouldn't have done enough yet. I chopped his head off, but it was like hitting stone, even after the drugs were in him. Hurt my arm really bad."

"I imagine so. An *Eresh-Chen* more than two thousand years old? It's a miracle that you weren't killed."

Two shrugged. Miracle it might have been, but at the time she had simply been acting on instinct, as was so often the case.

"Do you know about the vampire races?"

"Theroen told me some of it. I know there are four of them, and that you're the second type ... starts with 'A' I think."

"Ashayt, yes. Lisette was an Ashayt vampire, and so am I. We are the poet caste, not as strong as the Eresh or Ay'Araf, but skilled in other areas. Our senses, particularly our sight and hearing, are very good indeed."

"Poet caste?"

"Oh, that's just from the scrolls. There are certain proclivities that run in the bloodlines. The Eresh are usually very strong, mentally and physically, and the majority of them are very wise and balanced people, though I'm sure you can think of one glaring exception. Ashayt vampires are often writers, poets, painters ...

people who love the arts. Stephen is an Ay'Araf, the warrior caste. They love physical competition of all sorts."

"That explains the basketball," muttered Two.

Naomi nodded. "Yes, and the soccer. And the football. And the rugby ... and even baseball, though he says it's not a true sport since there's so little physical contact. I don't know if I've ever seen Stephen watch any television outside of the sport networks."

"Doesn't that get old? How long have you been living together?"

Naomi shook her head. "We do not 'live together.' Stephen is a guest in my apartment for the time being. The council has him here in New York because somehow, despite his personality, he holds a great deal of sway with American Ay'Araf. There are some minor internal struggles happening right now, and a friend and fellow council member requested that he come to America for a few years."

"He sounds Irish. I guess he hasn't been here very long?"

"He moves back and forth. He'll spend a decade in Ireland, then a few years here, then a year back in Ireland, then another five years here ... it gets quite maddening, actually, trying to keep track of where he is."

"The council is making him stay with you?"

"No. I ... Stephen and I have been friends for a long time and I don't mind the company from time to time. I've not really lived with anyone, in the sense you mean, since Lisette died and Theroen returned to Abraham. But I enjoy his visits. On the surface, he can be aggravating, but there's a good man down below."

"Ah. So are you two, you know ... together?"

Naomi smiled. "No. Even if we were romantic, there is no 'together' for Stephen. I'm lucky to still be able to make love, Two. Most Ashayt and even a good deal of Eresh vampires can't. I don't believe I've ever encountered an Ay'Araf who is capable in that department."

"Oh, right. Theroen mentioned that it was uncommon. I guess my idea of what being a vampire is like is sort of different."

"Quite. You are the first *Eresh-Chen* in almost five hundred years. There will not be another until such time as you make a fledgling."

"Which will be kind of difficult if we can't convince your council to bend the rules."

They had reached Naomi's building. She held the door open for Two, smiling confidently. "We shall convince them."

* * *

The rest of the evening moved by with startling speed. Naomi excused herself to go feed, and Stephen said he'd already done so but should she want to bring anything home that *wasn't* a child of Eresh, he wouldn't complain. Naomi told him she would do no such thing.

Two ate her second meal, went outside for another cigarette, and returned to lie down on the couch and watch basketball with Stephen. She didn't ask him questions, and he didn't offer any commentary of his own, other than to occasionally yell at the television. Two could sense, though, that he was impressed with her unexpected silence.

Her time working with Darren had taught Two a lot about reading people's personalities. She thought that she understood Stephen, and wanted to use this understanding to stay in his good graces. If he had the ear of the council, she wanted him to say positive things about her should they ask him about this human girl who wanted to be a vampire. So she stayed quiet, and after a time Stephen made conversation on his own, as Two had thought he might.

She had been half-asleep on the couch – a plush, luxurious, overstuffed piece of furniture upholstered in something that felt like a cross between flannel and corduroy – daydreaming about how it would be when she was a vampire again. She would be strong, confident, unafraid. Two was certain of this. She wondered how Tori would react, and was drifting off to sleep pondering this when Stephen's shout woke her up.

"Pass the Christ-forsaken ball, ye great drooling *retard!*"

Two noted in an absent way, as the adrenaline rush that had caused her to jump nearly out of her skin was fading, that Stephen's accent thickened when he was excited. She let out a shaky breath, laughing a bit and saying, "Jesus ..."

"Oh, sorry. Scared you, did I? It's this game ... they have the best jump-shooter on the very planet, wide open, and their idiot center never finds him when the double comes."

"That's a bitch," Two said, her voice dry. She rolled over on her side and looked first at the television, then at Stephen.

If the vampire had realized that Two had no idea what he was talking about, he didn't seem to care. "Aye, it is indeed, but what ... shoot! *Shoot!* Good."

"Uh, wasn't that the other team?"

"Yes. It's the accomplishment I care about, especially during the preseason. I want a game that's decided by one basket, and I want them to fight for every point in between. Who wins matters little, though I'll admit to developing some rooting interests as the season goes on."

"Ah." Two kept her voice noncommittal. In truth, she'd never paid attention to any organized sport and didn't particularly care. If asked, she would have said she wasn't *against* them, but rather had never taken the time to become interested. No one had ever asked.

Stephen was explaining his opinions further. "It's the battle. The test of wills. Which warrior will prevail? Not as good as a real fight, of course, but better than the make-believe in movies or television shows."

"I bet if there were gladiatorial games, you'd watch," Two said.

"Watch. Attend. Compete if I could."

Two smiled. "Not surprised."

Stephen glanced over at her, saw her grin, and returned it.

"I'm not the hard one to understand," he said. "That's Naomi's department."

"She doesn't seem that tough to figure out."

"No? Maybe not, but you've only just met her. There's a lot to her beyond the politician, if you go digging. That's why I like her.

She's better than most on the council by a fair amount, certainly better than the coward she replaced."

"Not a fan of William?"

"No, I ... hold on. Pass! Look at this lummox – he's not hit a shot all night. *Pass the ball!*"

On the screen, a pale-skinned giant took what looked even to Two's unpracticed eye like a very ugly shot. The ball clanged off the front of the rim and Stephen swore in disgust, pitching a throw pillow at the television.

Two felt her smile widening. Stephen looked at her and shrugged. "Three hundred and twenty eight years, and I still haven't grown out of throwing things around."

"So that's what ... sixteen-hundreds?"

"Tha's right. I was born in 1676, on the western coast of Ireland. My parents met there after Cromwell – may his rotten soul burn in the deepest pit of Hell for all eternity – sent all the true Irishmen to Connacht. I met my patron twenty years later, and the next year he made me into what I am."

"Did you want it? Or was it forced on you?"

"I wanted strength and power. I didn't fully understand the type of power that was being offered, and when first I woke to find what I had become, I will admit I was somewhat ... concerned."

"Only concerned?"

Stephen laughed. "Terrified, actually, but not for long. I grew to love what I had become. My patron was a good warrior and a good mentor. He spent many years teaching me the skills I would need to survive and thrive amongst the Ay'Araf, and we parted ways amicably enough after about eighty years or so. I see him from time to time when I'm in Europe, though last I heard he was on an extended trip to Asia, attempting to establish another council in China or Japan. I doubt he's succeeded – the warring factions there are even less fond of outsiders than they are of each other."

"The council ... right. Do you know when I'll be able to meet them?"

Stephen shrugged. "I believe they meet once a month. I tend to lose track of the days, but it feels like about two weeks since the last meeting happened. Naomi will be able to tell you exactly."

"OK." Two lapsed back into silence, letting Stephen watch his basketball game and trying her best to follow the action on the screen.

"Who's the best?" she asked after a few minutes had gone by.

"Depends. Best at what?"

Two looked at him and spread her hands wide. *I'm trying here ... help me out.*

Stephen grinned. "The tall one, there. Not exciting, but he's the best."

"Skill is better than flair?"

"Skill is all that matters to me. He knows how to win. If they need rebounds, he gets rebounds. If they need points, he gets points. If his guards are hot, he gets them the ball. The best of warriors do whatever is necessary."

"What are *your* skills? Do you play basketball?"

"Against mortals? Rarely. I'm too fast and strong. Against other vampires ... it's not my game. I'm not a tall man, Two."

Two laughed. "Fair enough."

"Mainly I fight, as most Ay'Araf do. I was trained first as a swordsman, then later I traveled to Asia for a time to learn martial arts. This century I've focused primarily on boxing and firearms, though I keep my other abilities honed."

"Who do you fight?"

"Anyone who's interested. Mostly sparring and shooting competitions with other Ay'Araf warriors. Occasionally an Ashayt or Eresh will come in for some training, but there are few of them. Sometimes when one of the Burilgi groups goes berserk, we're permitted to hunt them."

"Hunt? Like animals?"

"The Burilgi *are* animals, and barely that. They're leeches. Our race would be better off if we exterminated them all. I ... shoot, *shoot!*"

Two was desperate for information, but she was still weak, tired from the blood loss and the events of the evening. Her head was spinning from all of the new knowledge. She let Stephen watch his game in silence and, when it ended, went out for another cigarette.

"Game's over. I'm done shouting for the evening," Stephen said as Two lay back down on the couch. He was flipping through a magazine.

"So what now?"

"Now I go and meet some friends at one of our clubs. Then perhaps fighting."

Two sat up, eyes wide. "Take me!"

Stephen shook his head. "Not until you've seen the *Kharas*. The council."

"Please!"

"Two, there's nothing there for you. They would consider you food, as I did. This is not your world, not yet. Naomi will help you get it back, and when she does I will be happy to take you wherever it is that you would like to go."

Two considered this, asked, "Is that a promise?"

"Aye. Now go to sleep. You look like the walking dead and, trust me, I'm intimately familiar with what that looks like."

"I'll wait for Naomi," Two told him, lying back on the couch. When Stephen glanced over at her five minutes later, she was asleep.

CHAPTER IX

Sixteen Stitches

In the dark there was breathing, and the sound of cloth on metal, and footsteps.

"Who's there?" Sarah asked. "Who are you? Please ... who's there?"

"You are no longer in danger." The voice, male, was young but ancient. Sarah couldn't explain it, but Two would've recognized the quality immediately. She would have thought of Theroen.

"Please, I ... is Rhes OK? I'm scared." Sarah hated this, feeling like a rabbit caught in a snare, blind and trapped and so afraid. Not for the first time in her life, she cursed her lack of sight, convinced that things would be better if only she could see.

"He is breathing. Beyond that, I don't know."

"Who are you?"

"My name is Jakob." He pronounced the first syllable with a *zha* sound.

"Did you ... kill those other people?"

"It's best that you not think of them as people. *Burilgi povromos chappati.*"

"But did you kill them?"

"I did."

Sarah considered this. She knew that it was no less than they had planned for her, but it was hard to find pleasure in their death nonetheless. What she mostly felt, in addition to the fear of this unknown man, was an overwhelming sense of relief.

"Are you hurt?" Jakob asked her.

"No, but I need help. I've lost track of where I am in the room. I'm ... I'm blind."

"I know."

"You do?"

"I suppose it could be a fashion statement, but you're wearing a pair of sunglasses in a darkened room."

"Oh. Right. What happens now?"

Jakob's hand grasped hers, and he helped her to her feet. "You could start by telling me your name."

"Sorry. I'm Sarah. Thank you for saving us."

"Think nothing of it. The things that attacked you are garbage, and I'm glad they gave me an excuse to put them out of their misery. The one on the floor – you said his name is Rhes? – he fought well, all things considered."

"Yes, Rhes. Is he hurt? Will he be OK? Rhes, can you hear me?"

She heard coughing from a spot perhaps fifteen feet to her left, and realized after a minute that Rhes was laughing.

"No Sarah, I'm not OK. I feel like I just got worked over by Lennox Lewis."

Sarah let go of Jakob's hand and made her way slowly over to Rhes, stopping when she felt him reach out and touch one of her feet. She knelt down and touched his face. Rhes hissed, took her hand, and moved it away from his split lips.

"Oh, baby," Sarah said, and began to cry. She ran the tips of her fingers over the puffy flesh around his eyes. His left eyebrow was tacky with drying blood.

"That cut is bad," Jakob said from behind her. "It will require stitches."

"Yep. I think the one on my leg is worse. Something sharp got me there. Fingernails, maybe ... or teeth. They were vampires, right?"

Sarah nodded. Jakob said, "Yes."

Rhes looked up at him. "You too?"

"Yes."

"But not the same."

"No."

"OK. Sarah, honey, it's OK. I'm not dying. I'm just banged up. Here, help me sit up."

"You're too heavy for me to lift and you're *way* more than 'just banged up' and I can't even see you and I *hate* this!" Sarah's voice was miserable. She yanked her glasses off and rubbed furiously at her eyes with the back of her sleeve, as if the tears were something filthy that needed to be scoured away.

Rhes glanced up at Jakob, little more than a shadow in the dim light. The vampire extended his hand. Rhes took it and struggled to a sitting position.

"Can we have, like ... two minutes alone?" Rhes asked him. "I appreciate your help. Seriously. I am scared to death of you, but I'm pretty sure you saved our lives. I just need to talk to my girlfriend for a minute. Believe me, we're not running anywhere. I don't know if I can even walk."

"Take your two minutes, but then we must go," Jakob said, and wandered over by the broken windows, looking out at the city.

Rhes turned to Sarah. She was still crying, staring down at her lap with her blind eyes. He touched her cheek.

"I thought they killed you," Sarah said.

"They didn't."

"No, they just ... just *broke* you. I want to hold you and kiss you, but I'm afraid I'll hurt you."

"You probably will. I don't care. I don't ever want to hear you screaming like that again. I thought I was listening to them murdering you. I thought ..."

At a loss for words, Rhes took her face in his hands and, very gently, kissed her. She wrapped her arms around him, and Rhes tried not to flinch back at the sudden pain that lanced through his body from what seemed a hundred different sources. Eventually, Sarah took her lips away from his and pressed them into the space between his neck and shoulder.

"I'm worthless," she said. "All I could do was lie there and scream."

"All I could do was get the shit kicked out of me."

"If I could see, we could've run."

"No. Jakob saved us, period. It wouldn't have been any different."

Sarah sighed and let go of him. She rubbed her eyes again and put her glasses back on.

"I want to go home," she said. "I don't know where Two is. I don't care. We're not going to find her."

"Whoever Two is, if she's the one the Burilgi were here for, there is a good chance that she is already dead," Jakob said, walking back to where they sat.

Rhes looked up at him. "You might be surprised, but we'll worry about that later. I need to go to a hospital and get some stitches. And some painkillers. Then I'm going to go home and sleep for three days. Can you help me to my feet?"

Jakob nodded. "If need be, I will carry you. Let's go."

* * *

There were sirens in the distance, but the trio encountered no one in their flight from Two's building. Leaning against Jakob, Rhes was able to limp along. Sarah followed, slightly behind, holding Rhes's hand and trusting him to lead her. Jakob took them down the stairs and out the rear exit of Two's apartment building. From here they cut through an alley and out onto Sixth Avenue.

"Do you have a car?" Rhes asked.

"Not here. I can make arrangements for transportation as soon as we are far enough away from the building to not risk an encounter with the police."

"OK."

"Rhes, what's wrong?" Sarah asked, her voice strained with concern and frustration. "Why are you breathing like that?"

"Don't know. Everything hurts."

"His ribs are broken," Jakob told them.

"Those fucking ... stupid ... I wish I ... if they ..." Sarah was incoherent, unable to form a sentence in her anger. Rhes found himself laughing at her.

"They're dead, baby. Think they got what was coming to 'em. Please don't make me laugh."

"How can you *laugh* at this?" Sarah exclaimed.

"I am so fucking happy that we're both alive right now, you have no idea. I'd dance if I could."

"Rhes, they broke your ribs! They bashed in your face. Who knows what else they did to you?"

"Yeah, I can feel the ribs. And the face. And the leg, both arms, something in my back ... even the place where Two's friggin' coffee table got me in the back of the knee. My body is a symphony of pain!"

Rhes began to laugh again, the noise sounding more and more like a disturbed giggle than real humor.

"He's in shock," Jakob said. They were well away from Two's building now.

"Can't people die from shock?" Sarah asked.

"People can die from a lot of things."

"I don't want him to die."

Sarah could hear the smile in Jakob's voice as he said, "If he seems headed in that direction, there are things I can do to help."

"Don't you even fucking think about biting him!"

Rhes had stopped giggling. "I bow to her authority on that one," he said. "Part of the whole 'soul mates' deal."

Jakob laughed. "I won't do anything without consulting both of you first."

"Good," Rhes said. "Ouch. Jesus Christ, this hurts so bad! Can we stop walking yet?"

"Yes," Jakob said. They stopped by a news stand, and he helped Rhes shift his weight to the wooden wall.

"Never a cab when you want one," Rhes muttered. He touched his eyebrow and winced.

"Stay here. I'm going to make a call." Jakob pulled a cell phone from his jacket pocket, dialed, and wandered away as he began to speak. Rhes got his first decent look at the vampire who had saved them. Jakob was perhaps five-eight with dark brown hair cut to shoulder length. He had heavy brows, dark eyes, and olive skin that made Rhes think of the Mediterranean. He was powerfully built, and wore a long, dark trench coat. Rhes assumed that whatever blade the vampire had used was housed underneath to avoid arousing suspicion.

Sarah brought Rhes's hand to her lips and kissed the back of it. "How you doing, soul mate?"

Rhes smiled. "I'm all right, soul mate. A little loopy. He's probably right about the shock ... I feel like I did the one time I dropped acid in college, right before it really kicked in and I spent the next five hours staring at the wallpaper. You OK?"

"No, not really. I'll survive."

"You don't have to beat yourself up over this, hon."

"We've still got a date to talk about how much I hate, hate, *fucking hate* being blind. For right now, let's worry about you."

"You sure?"

"Positive. I've been dealing with this for almost twenty years. One shitty night isn't going to change anything. It's just a shitty night."

"OK. You want to change the subject?"

"Yes."

"You suppose Molly's OK?"

"I told her we'd be out late, and not to worry unless we weren't back in the morning and hadn't called. She asked if we were helping Two, and I figured the truth wouldn't hurt, so I told her that we were trying."

"Good. She'll be fine."

"Yeah."

They were quiet for a moment, resting against the news stand.

"Sarah, will you marry me?" Rhes asked.

He couldn't look at her, was afraid of the expression he might see on her face, but he heard her pull in a sharp breath of air that wasn't quite a gasp. Her grip on his hand tightened.

"Yes. Yes, I will."

"I'm sorry to ask you here, like this. I have a ring at home and I wanted it to be special, but I ... I needed to know the answer now, in case anything else happens. I don't trust our friend on the phone."

"I understand. It's not *exactly* how I imagined it either, but I'll take it."

"I don't care if the rest of my life lasts five minutes or fifty years, I want to spend it with you."

Sarah was crying again. "Let's shoot for fifty years, OK? Or maybe eighty."

"OK. Sarah, I'm so sorry."

"For what?"

"Everything. All this bullshit that you got stuck with when you decided to get involved with me. Prostitutes and heroin addicts and vampires. Jesus, I thought you were going to say 'no.' I really did. I feel like all I've done is fuck up your entire life. I've been scared to ask you."

Sarah laughed through her tears. "Dummy. You could've asked any time in the last two years and I'd have said yes. I knew from the third month in. I was just waiting for you to figure it out. I don't blame you for this, not for any of it."

"Then why are you crying?"

"The last person I saw in the mirror was this ugly little redhead eight-year-old with a bowl haircut and fucked up teeth. That's who I still see when I think about myself. Just an ugly blind girl who never even had a date until she met her current boyfriend."

"You are the polar opposite of ugly."

"That's not the point. The point is that now here you are, beaten to shit by fucking *vampires,* and you're more worried about proposing to me than you are about internal bleeding. That makes me so happy, even though it also makes me want to punch you. I've been waiting for this practically since I met you, Rhes, because I *love* you!"

"Do me a favor then?"

"Anything."

"Put your arms around me and kiss me and say 'Yes, I will' again?"

"Won't that hurt you?"

"Probably. I really don't give a shit. Will you marry me, Sarah Taylor?"

Sarah grinned and gently embraced him. Trying her best not to hurt him, she kissed him, and said, "Yes, I will."

* * *

"I hate to break up whatever is happening here, but I must," Jakob said as he returned. "I've called a friend who lives not far from here. She will take us to the hospital."

"Why are you helping us, Jakob?" Rhes asked. He was pale and shaky, but the strange, drug-like confusion seemed to be receding.

"You needed help."

"That doesn't really answer the question. Why were you there? How did you even know we would be there to help?"

"I didn't. I was not there to help you – I was there to find this friend of yours. I'd heard that the Burilgi were looking for her, because she has been poking her nose into places where she does not belong."

"Were you there to hurt her?" Sarah asked.

"You might say that I was there to determine whether she needed to be hurt or not."

Sarah frowned, not happy with this answer. She said, "Two was one of you, once. Do you know that?"

Jakob raised his eyebrows in what Rhes thought was honest surprise. "What do you mean, 'was'? There is no 'was' for us."

"Doesn't that depend on the vampire?" Rhes asked.

"Oh, I thought you meant one of my people specifically. Well, I suppose it might be possible for an Eresh, but I don't—" Jakob's eyes kindled suddenly, and he leaned forward. He seemed about to grab Rhes by the shoulders and then stopped himself, aware of Rhes's injuries.

"This girl ... do you know what happened to her? Do you know her story?"

"We know a lot of it," Rhes replied.

"Her sire, the man who made her a vampire ... what was his name?"

"Theroen Anders," Sarah said.

"God. Dear God ..." Jakob's voice trailed off as he searched for a lie in each of their eyes. When Jakob was satisfied, he said, "This is not good."

"Great. Does that mean it's necessary to hurt *us* now?" Sarah asked. She didn't sound afraid, but rather disgusted, tired with the entire affair.

Jakob drew back, ran a hand through his hair, looked around as if trying to get his bearings. It was the first gesture Rhes had seen him make that looked fully human.

"If the Burilgi catch her and find out what she is, it could be very dangerous for her, and for everyone she has told. You are in tremendous danger."

"You didn't answer my question, Jakob. Are you going to hurt us?"

"I don't believe so. In fact, if she has been caught already, I may be your best hope of living through the week."

"That's comforting," Rhes muttered. "How do we even know we can trust you?"

"If I wanted you dead, could I not simply kill you?" Jakob asked. "That course of action holds no interest for me. What is important now is determining whether your friend is still alive."

"That's what we were trying to do. She's not home," Sarah said.

"Did you see any evidence of a previous attack?"

"No," said Rhes. "The place was pretty much spotless. The windows were all still fine when we got there. I think the people ... the things that you killed were the first ones there."

"Speaking of which," Sarah said, "are we fugitives now? There are three dead people in the apartment, and our fingerprints are all over the place."

"It will be taken care of," said Jakob.

"You can just 'take care of' the NYPD?" Rhes asked.

Jakob grinned. "People who live for hundreds of years make lots of friends."

Rhes shut his eyes, shook his head, and said, "Jesus, Sarah, wake me up, would you? This is just too fucking bizarre to be real."

"I was about to ask you to do the same thing," Sarah replied. "To be honest, part of me is dead-convinced that this is all some sort of massive, elaborate joke on the blind lady."

Rhes made a noise of discomfort. "Where's your friend, Jakob? I don't think I can actually stand up for much longer, wall or no wall."

Jakob glanced up the street. "I believe the Cadillac sedan three lights up is hers."

"Good."

They were quiet for a moment, and then Jakob said, "So. Your friend is not home. She has not yet been abducted by the Burilgi, unless they were uncharacteristically subtle about it. That begs the question: where is she?"

"Out walking. It's what she does," Sarah said.

"Do you know where she walks?"

"I think it's different every night. Random. She's looking for people like you."

Jakob rolled his eyes. "Fantastic. So we've only a few million people to comb through."

"She always comes home," Rhes said. "Can you post someone to look out for her?"

"I can and will."

"Why do you care if one human gets killed by these Burilgi things, anyway?"

Jakob glanced over at Rhes. "She killed a ... a demigod that had been ruling our council for several hundred years. Whether that deserves prosecution or some sort of reward is a matter of some debate. In either case, I know many people who would like the opportunity to talk with her."

"Judging from what she told us of Abraham, go with reward," Sarah said.

Jakob shrugged. "It's not my decision to make, at least not alone. Come, my friend is here."

Struggling against the pain, Rhes shifted his weight back to Jakob's shoulder and let the vampire help him toward the car.

* * *

Jakob was sitting in the front passenger seat of the car, speaking to someone on his cell phone. He had not introduced the car's owner to Rhes and Sarah, nor had she made any greeting of her own. Rhes was stretched out across the back seat, his head in Sarah's lap, only half conscious.

"I don't care if she left orders not to be disturbed, Karl," Jakob was saying. "I need the number to Naomi's private cell, and I need it now. Something has happened that will be of great interest to the council."

"You suppose that's Theroen's Naomi?" Sarah asked Rhes.

"Whuh?" Rhes looked up for a minute, then put his head back in her lap. Sarah stroked his hair.

"Never mind, baby. Just relax."

"I asked you to marry me, right?" Rhes asked, his voice fuzzy.

"You did, Rhes."

"You said 'yes,' right?"

"Sure did."

"Good deal." Rhes seemed to settle into sleep.

Sarah laughed to herself. *Yes, good deal,* she thought. *Good deal if we ever get out of this bullshit and back to anything resembling a normal life. Me and Rhes and Molly, and maybe a little brother or sister for Molly to—*

"Oh, shit!" she said out loud.

"One second," Jakob said into the phone. "What is it, Sarah?"

"Our ... we have a girl who lives with us. She's still at home. Is she safe?"

Jakob looked concerned. "Probably, yes, but I'd rather not take any chances. I won't have anyone wake her up, but I will put her under guard. Karl, are you listening? Yes, two of them. Ay'Araf. Where do you live, Sarah?"

Sarah hesitated for a moment, and then gave him not only their address, but the safety word that she and Rhes had worked out with Molly for emergencies. Jakob gave this information to Karl, and said, "If you can't get me Naomi's number, at least tell her to call me if she checks in."

He hung up the phone and glanced at his friend, who kept her eyes on the road but slowly shook her head.

"We're nearly there," said Jakob. "How is he?"

"Asleep. Still breathing. Thanks for the help, Jakob. Does your friend have a name?"

"She is not comfortable with humans. I'm sorry ... bad experience about sixty years ago with an overzealous priest. She'd prefer to remain anonymous. It's best if you think of her as a taxi driver on this occasion."

Sarah raised her eyebrows. "OK, then ... well, thanks, ma'am. For what it's worth, not all of us are going to start digging out the garlic and crosses the minute we come in contact with a vampire."

"She knows. Please do not take offense, Sarah."

Sarah shrugged. "You're helping Rhes ... far as I'm concerned, you could have Hitler driving the car."

Jakob smiled, nodded, said something to his driver in their vampire language. The woman laughed. Sarah considered asking about the joke and decided against it. What did she care? These people were not like her, and it really didn't matter if one of them didn't care to make friends.

She felt the car slowing and guessed that they had reached their destination. Jakob confirmed this, saying, "We're here. Is he all right?"

"Beats me. He's still alive. What's the story? What am I telling them?"

"Take the cash out of his wallet. We were at a bar, he was meeting us there. When he didn't show up, we went outside to see where he might be. We found him in the alley, beaten up and robbed."

"Works for me. Think they'll buy it?"

"Depends on how well you sell it," Jakob said. He got out of the car and opened the right-side passenger door, near Rhes's feet.

"Rise and shine, sweetheart," said Sarah, tapping Rhes on the shoulder. Rhes groaned.

"I'm going to let these people decide how to get him out of the car without causing him undue pain," Jakob said. He went inside.

"My whole ... fucking ... body hurts," Rhes said from her lap. He sounded groggy, but better than he had since they'd left Two's apartment. "I'm not kidding. I mean every last thing. Pick a thing. It hurts. Guarantee it."

"Toes?" Sarah asked.

"Yep. Those hurt."

"Small of the back?"

"That too."

"Roof of your mouth?"

"Burned the *shit* out of it this morning with a cup of coffee."

Sarah laughed. "Poor Rhes. They'll have something good for you inside, hon. Darvocet or Vicodin or something."

"Mmm ..." Rhes murmured.

Sarah could hear clattering outside. Jakob's voice said, "They're bringing a stretcher."

She felt Rhes's head leave her lap and heard people speaking to him as they transferred him to the stretcher. A man's voice near her said, "Ma'am, your friend says you can't see. Can I help you out of the car?"

Sarah shrugged and held out her hand. "Hey, sure, why not. Be careful with my boyfriend, please. I'd like to keep him."

The man laughed. "We'll do our best."

* * *

"Eleven stitches in the leg, five in the eyebrow. Two broken ribs. Broken finger. Two black eyes. Abrasions all over the place. Light concussion ... and enough bruises that he looks like a patchwork quilt. Forgive me, Ms. Taylor, but the term we normally use for this is 'had the crap beat out of him.'"

The doctor was young. Sarah could tell by his voice and manner of speaking that he wasn't much older than she or Rhes. He seemed to be in a decent mood, which helped Sarah relax. She leaned back in her chair, took a deep breath, let relief wash over her.

"So there's nothing terrible?" she asked. "He's not bleeding internally or about to barf up his own spleen or anything?"

The doctor, Jamison was his name, laughed. "No, nothing like that. He needs two weeks of rest – no hitting the gym or even lifting anything heavy at home – and another couple weeks of light effort so those ribs can finish healing. That's about it. They really stomped him. Did he see anything?"

Sarah didn't like lying for Rhes, but he was out cold in the hospital bed to her left, exhausted from the beating and the painkillers. "He said they jumped him from behind, and he never got a good look after that. It was dark out there."

"Unfortunate. I'm sure you'd like to press charges."

"I'm just glad Rhes is safe. People like that usually get what's coming to them eventually."

Jakob was standing behind her, in the corner at the far side of the room, looking out the window at the city below. He made a coughing noise that Sarah thought was a laugh.

"You didn't see anything, did you, sir?" Jamison asked.

"I'm afraid they were gone by the time we got there. They were probably gone before we even went out to look for him. The gentleman at the door said no one had come running by, so they must have gone the other way."

The ease with which Jakob's lies rolled off his lips amazed Sarah. He sounded so convinced of what he was saying that she found it difficult not to believe his sincerity despite knowing the truth.

"All right," Jamison said. "Well, I'm afraid visiting hours are over and I'm going to have to ask you to leave, Mr. Kasavan. Sarah is his fiancée, but you're not."

"No, I'm not. That's not a problem, doctor."

Sarah heard Jakob start across the room. He brushed against her coat on his way, slung over the foot of the bed, and Sarah's hearing, honed to pay attention to things that sighted humans might not bother with, heard something drop into the folds of fabric. Jakob continued moving, stopping next to her.

"He'll be fine. I will call you later, Sarah."

Sarah nodded. "OK, Jakob. Thanks for your help."

"It was nothing." Jakob left the room.

Dr. Jamison spoke up. "I've got to move on, but I'll be back to check in later this evening. I'd like to keep Rhes here overnight, just to monitor him. He can go in the morning. Just keep him out from behind the wheel of a car while he's on painkillers."

"That's easy – we don't own one," Sarah said.

Jamison laughed again. "We're at low capacity at the moment, so Rhes gets his own room. You're welcome to the second bed, if you want it. But my guess is—"

"I'm not leaving this chair," Sarah said.

"And there we go. I'll talk to you later, then." She could hear the smile in his voice.

"Thank you," she said as he left.

It was less than ten minutes later when the cell phone that Jakob had dropped into her coat began ringing. Sarah reached over, picked it up, and flipped it open, hoping that would answer the call.

"Yeah, it's Sarah."

"I didn't have time to get your own number, so I gave you my phone," Jakob said. "I've had some updates. Molly is asleep, safe and under guard. We don't know where your friend is, but nothing we've heard suggests that the Burilgi have taken any special prisoners this evening. We will watch her apartment and wait for her return."

"Good."

"When you and Rhes are discharged, what are your plans?"

"I hadn't really thought about it. We're going to go home, he's going to call in to work and go back to sleep. I'm going to figure out what to tell Molly. Are we in danger?"

"Not during the day. Sarah, I know you don't trust me and I take no offense, but I will make you an offer: we can guard you at night, at least until we find out what has happened to your friend and know whether you are in any further danger. You will not see us unless you are attacked, but you will be kept safe."

"You know where we live now, Jakob. I already trusted you with that."

"Yes."

"Then why don't you come by tomorrow night and we can talk things over. You can also pick up your phone."

"That would work. Is eleven too late for you?"

"Eleven is fine. We'll expect you then. Thank you again for saving us. We may not trust you completely yet, but we know we owe you our lives."

"I'm glad I was there to help. Try to get some sleep, and I will see you tomorrow. Goodbye."

"I will. Goodbye, Jakob."

Sarah hung up the phone and blew air through her pursed lips. Vampires, beatings ... this might be old hat for Two, might even be what the crazy girl was out looking for right this second, but Sarah wanted nothing more to do with it. She had a life in which she was largely happy. She had a fiancé with whom to share that life. What did she need from vampires?

Protection, it seemed. Sarah wondered if Jakob was really any safer than the creatures that had attacked them earlier, and she decided it didn't matter. Fate had delivered them here, into the hands of a vampire who at least seemed intent on keeping them alive. There was little she could do about it.

The night wore on. Sarah called the nurse's station and asked if some food could be brought up from the cafeteria. Twenty minutes later she received a surprisingly good cheeseburger and some french fries. Dr. Jamison checked in and said that Rhes seemed fine, and that they should be dismissed whenever he was ready in the morning. Sarah thanked him again.

Some time in the night she took his arm in hers and wrapped it up. She drew her knees under her, rested her body against the side of the chair she was sitting in, leaned her head against his shoulder, and slept.

CHAPTER X

Expensive Tastes

"What in the fuck happened here?!"

Two stared in awe and dismay at what had once been her living room. Where before there had been giant glass windows looking down on the streets of SoHo, there were now only heavy plastic tarps duct taped to the window frames. Scattered below these on the carpet were thousands of shards of safety glass. Her furniture was overturned, and there were huge maroon splotches on the carpet and walls.

Stephen was squatting by the stains, inspecting them. "Don't touch anything. It looks like there was a fight, and someone got hurt … probably killed. This is blood, and a lot of it."

"Who the hell was in my apartment getting killed?"

"Hopefully, no one you knew," Naomi said. She was standing near the door, by the police tape, making sure that no one was coming.

"Well, no shit," Two replied. She peered around the room, still too shocked to do much else. Stephen had moved on to inspecting the windows.

"Do you see the way this glass is spread out? Someone knocked this window in from outside."

"What could do that?"

Stephen glanced over his shoulder at her. "I could, if I had the right equipment, but my bet is a Burilgi … a lot of them have nasty fingernails. Good for climbing."

"So you're saying vampires broke into my apartment."

"That's what I'm guessing, at any rate."

Two laughed. "That's great. I spend five fucking months searching, and get nothing. I finally find two of you, and a bunch more come looking for me in the same damn week."

"I told you that you might have encountered Burilgi and not known it," Naomi said. "It is very possible that they knew you were searching for them, saw it as a threat, and came here to stop you."

"Well, that would explain the break-in at least. What about the blood?"

"Someone else was here," Stephen said. "Someone with a knife of some sort. See the blood sprays on the walls? They're too thick to be claws or teeth; sheets like that would have to come off a good-sized blade."

"You train as a cop or something?" Two asked.

"I'm a warrior, as I've mentioned. I know about fighting, and the results thereof. I've seen men hacked to pieces with machetes in Zaire and claymores in Scotland. It looks like this."

"So someone wasn't just killed but was *chopped up* in here?"

"Multiple someones, I think. My guess is two or three."

"Well, what the hell does *that* mean?" Two was peeking her head into the other rooms of the apartment. They were dark and empty.

"It means we need to get in touch with the council, right now," said Naomi.

"Why?"

"Should be obvious," Stephen told her.

"Pretend like I'm stupid."

"Pretend?"

Two extended her middle finger. Stephen grinned at her.

"What can kill two or three Burilgi vampires, Two? There's not much. Another group of Burilgi vampires? Possible, but though they often fight amongst themselves, it's unlikely that they broke in here to do it. A skilled Ay'Araf could handle three Burilgi with ease. So could an Ashayt or an Eresh, but the former aren't much for fighting and there's presently only two of the latter in the entire city, so it probably wasn't them."

"That," said Naomi from the hall, "is precisely why we need to contact the council."

"Wouldn't they call you?" Two asked.

"Only two or three people know my private number, and I asked not to be disturbed. To be honest, Two, before you dropped in on us, I'd been planning on taking a vacation. It's been a while since I saw France."

"France. That's right ... Theroen said you and Lisette were both French."

"Yes."

"I'd like to go someday."

"Perhaps we can do so together."

Stephen moved past Two, touching her on her shoulder as he went, signaling for her to move toward the door.

"That's all well and lovely, but it can wait," he said. "Right now, let's be gone, before someone calls the police back. Did you need anything from here, Two?"

"Well, I was *gonna* grab some clothes, but ... no, I'll buy new stuff. Better not to take anything, right? I'm probably a missing person and I think I'd like to keep it that way for now."

Naomi nodded. "A wise policy. If our guesses as to what transpired here are correct, then the council can help you straighten out this issue. They will give you an alibi and ensure that no legal action will be taken against you. I do not detest the Burilgi the way that Stephen does, but you'll find few members of the council that are particularly sympathetic to them, especially if they're threatening you."

"All right," Two said. "I'll go buy some stuff to wear, and while I'm doing that, you can make some phone calls and find out what the hell is going on."

"Very well," said Naomi, already reaching for her phone. "Let's go."

* * *

The vampires had suggested this trip to her apartment on the third night that Two had spent with them. After she had fallen asleep on Naomi's couch, Two had spent the rest of the night and most of the following day there. She had awoken during the following afternoon, ravenous, and treated herself to a burrito and a beer. Naomi had woken shortly thereafter, as had Stephen. Two had spent most of the second evening in deep conversation with Naomi, as Stephen had almost immediately excused himself to attend a football game.

Two enjoyed talking with Naomi. Their experiences with Theroen gave them common ground, and from there the conversation had flowed naturally. Naomi seemed to enjoy Two's sarcasm and outspoken nature. Two found Naomi's more reserved approach calming and pleasant, similar to how Theroen's demeanor had made her feel.

Eventually both women had gone to their beds, happy to know each other and content to spend the time between then and the next council meeting as friends. For Two, it was a welcome change after months of self-imposed solitude.

Now they were standing in a pricey SoHo boutique. The store had closed an hour ago, but Naomi knew the proprietor. The woman, dark haired and stunning even in middle-age, seemed to understand that they would make it well worth her while to allow them in to shop. She was leaving them alone, sitting at the counter with a laptop computer.

Two had a hard time not reacting with incredulity to the price tags on the clothing she was looking at. Eight hundred dollars for a pair of blue jeans seemed outlandish even in this new world where she could afford the extravagance. Two owned a cashmere sweater that had cost her half as much, and had been convinced when she bought it that she would never spend more on an article of clothing.

She modeled outfits for Stephen while Naomi stood in the corner, murmuring into her cell phone.

"I like the pants, but not the sweater," Stephen was saying. "You need something tighter. It will look good with that jacket ... which, by the way, may be the only thing you own that you shouldn't immediately burn."

"I have some other nice stuff, but not much," Two admitted. She stepped back into the dressing room, removed the sweater, and pulled on a simple, long-sleeved black top.

Stephen nodded when she emerged. "Better. You're a little thin. Less cigarettes, more burritos."

Two laughed. "I guess. I'm hoping not to need the burritos for too long."

"Aye, but it's always best to prepare for anything. Now try on that shirt that Naomi pointed out, the green one that goes with your eyes. That might work for the council meeting."

"You know what they say about men with fashion sense, Stephen?"

"That they've lived for three centuries, deeply appreciate the female body, have seen dozens of fashions come and go, and are comfortable enough with their masculinity to admit that they know what looks good?"

Two laughed. "Yeah, something like that."

She shopped for forty minutes in total, amassing a pile of clothing that she estimated was going to cost at least ten thousand dollars. As she was finishing up, Naomi wandered over, her cell phone in her purse, and casually glanced through Two's selections.

"These are nice," she said. "You need underwear."

"Yeah. What did your friends on the phone have to say?"

"While we were chatting last night, three Burilgi broke into your home. Jakob, an Ay'Araf council member, took care of them. He escorted two humans that the Burilgi had attacked to the hospital and, as of this evening, has them under guard at their house."

"Two humans? Who?"

"A blind woman and her boyfriend, I was told."

Two's eyes widened. "Jesus Christ! Are they OK?"

"The woman is fine. The man suffered some injuries, but nothing terrible. Bruises, some stitches, a few broken—"

"Oh my God ..."

"They are safe now."

"I need to go see them!"

"I'd advise against it. The council feels that you should be kept with me until our meeting. The Burilgi are very aware of you, and while Stephen and I are more than a match for a few of them, if they come in numbers it could be problematic. There are things which the Burilgi are unhappy about, and some would not hesitate to take the opportunity for violence."

"Things like what?"

"Like what happened with Abraham," said Stephen. "A lot of them looked to him as something of a god."

"Oh. Great. So it's my fault, and I'm a danger to anyone I'm around."

"That's the gist of it!" Stephen gave Two a cheerful grin.

"Story of my life. OK, I'll leave Rhes and Sarah alone until this gets straightened out, as long as you're sure they're safe."

"As safe as anyone can be in New York. Jakob has them guarded during the nights. His men are very loyal."

"Jakob is a good man," said Stephen.

"Fine," Two said. She quickly selected several sets of bras and panties. "I think we can call this done. I can't believe I'm about to pay a hundred and fifty bucks a pop for bras."

"They're very comfortable," Naomi said.

"And easily removed," Stephen commented. Naomi shot him a look.

"From me or from her?" Two asked.

"I don't know you well enough to answer half of that question," Stephen replied.

"Something you're not telling me, Naomi?" Two asked, grinning.

Naomi shrugged, rolled her eyes, shook her head. With an air of deliberate indifference, she picked up the pile of clothing and made her way toward the front of the store. At the counter, the owner of the shop went through the pile of clothing, ringing the items up and making comments as she went, all of them positive. Two supposed this was good business; the compliments were probably designed to ease the sting of paying thousands for perhaps three hundred dollars' worth of fabric.

There seemed to be little sting for Naomi regardless. She pulled out a black credit card without even checking to see what the total was and within minutes they were out on the sidewalk, each carrying bags filled with clothes.

"What now?" Two asked.

"Home to change," Naomi said. "Then I believe I will go out to the club for a while, have some wine, get some dinner. Are either of you interested?"

"Sure," said Two.

"Good sweet Christ, no," Stephen said. "Every time you drag me there, I swear to every god I've ever heard of that I'll never go back. I've no idea how you stand it."

"I like to watch people," Naomi said.

Stephen shook his head in disbelief. "I like to watch basketball. I'll do that instead."

"Far be it from me to stop you," said Naomi. "You stay home. Two and I will go out and have fun."

* * *

When they arrived at *L'Obscurité,* Thomas gave them a wide smile and set them up with drinks. Naomi took her customary glass of red wine, and Two again ordered a bourbon with one ice cube. Naomi paid, though Two offered. Naomi only smiled. Money was not something she had to worry about, she explained. Her investments had accumulated over centuries and were more than self-sustaining. Naomi, like many vampires in New York, was extremely wealthy.

"And I thought I did pretty well, looting the mansion and setting myself up for life," Two said.

Naomi shrugged. "My life never ends."

"Don't rub it in."

"You'll get it back."

"We'll see."

They were quiet for a time, observing the bar.

"She's cute," Naomi said, flicking her eyes toward the edge of the dance floor. The woman dancing there had straight black hair cropped in a pixie cut and held back with bright pink barrettes. She was wearing an outfit that could only be described as a cross between a school girl uniform and a fetish costume, a sort of latex-and-leather skirt and blouse combination. She was dancing by herself, undulating to the music.

"Dinner?" Two asked, watching the girl.

"With any luck, if she's not too drunk." Naomi took a sip of her wine, smiling a small smile.

"Why can you drink that? I mean ... how are you able to?"

"That is a gift, one that is fairly common amongst Ashayt and Ay'Araf vampires and almost entirely unheard of in the others. Older Eresh vampires like Abraham or perhaps Theroen could force themselves to drink a bit, but not much. I will, well, regurgitate anything solid after a few minutes, but my body will tolerate most liquids. I can also walk under the sun without any major discomfort, though it does rapidly exhaust me."

"What about Stephen?"

"Ay'Araf can drink if they choose, but sunlight is very painful for them. We have scientists studying it. Given today's technology, I doubt it will be too much longer before we understand why the different strains of blood do this, and possibly even fix the problems. Like all discovery, it's really just a matter of time, study, and effort ... and money."

"Money always helps," Two said. "Are there a lot of scientists?"

"Not among our people, no. Few of us are particularly interested. For my part, I enjoy the romance of my existence. I enjoy the magic. I live forever, never get sick, don't have to deal with the betrayals and indignities that age wreaks upon the body. I take young men or women to bed, or just to the bathroom, and I charm them, and I bite them. Instead of screaming or dying, they typically have an orgasm and then forget me ten minutes after I've gone. I bring immediate, easy pleasure to someone every night. That's pretty magical."

"It's always someone new? Why not pick one person?"

Naomi tried to smile, but the expression looked weary, as if this was not the first time she had answered the question. "I try not to form such attachments. I ... what happened to Lisette, I think, was partially responsible for that. Still, I have what you might call repeat customers."

Not exactly the same thing, Two thought, but kept her mouth shut. She understood what Naomi was saying. Hadn't she withdrawn from her own friends, these past months, and chosen to pursue a solitary life? Was it the same sort of thing? Two wasn't sure. She *wanted* attachment. She wanted the joy of loving another and receiving that person's love. She wanted to need and to be needed. The problem was that the man she wanted these things from was dead.

"Theroen said that before the end, you had already distanced yourself a bit, even from him and Lisette."

Naomi nodded, sipped her wine, glanced again at the girl in the pink barrettes. "Yes, that's true, particularly in the matter of sexual relations. I was excited by my own sexuality – something very few women were able to learn much about in those times – and wanted to explore. I also knew that Lisette and Theroen loved each other very much. I loved them both as well, but in a different sort of way. They needed time together without interruption, especially Lisette. She suffered from depression. Theroen was her anchor."

"Do you suppose he's with her now?" Two asked.

"It's beyond me to guess what happens to us when we die. Would you begrudge him it, if he was?"

Naomi was looking back at her, and Two could read simple curiosity, devoid of any malice, in her expression. She considered the question carefully before shaking her head.

"No, I don't think so. Wherever Theroen is, I hope he's happy. He lived for hundreds of years trapped under Abraham, punishing himself for the sins he thought he had committed. He felt like it was his fault that Lisette died and you disappeared, and his fault that he didn't stop Abraham from making Tori and Melissa into vampires. He knew that he would probably have to kill them someday, and that Abraham would probably murder him for it ..."

Two was surprised to find herself on the verge of tears. She took a large drink from her glass of bourbon and closed her eyes.

"He was hard on himself," Naomi said.

"Yes, and then he met me, and all I really did was set everything in motion that got him killed."

Naomi frowned. "I doubt that very much. I knew Theroen when he was in love with Lisette. She was the reason for his existence, the beginning and the end to everything he was. If he loved you like that, Two – and I don't doubt that he did – then he must have died a happy man."

"Gonna start crying if we don't stop talking about this," Two said. She was holding very still, breathing deeply, trying to keep her emotions in check.

"Would that be so bad?"

"I did a lot of crying when I was still a vampire, and it didn't get me anywhere. I don't cry anymore if I can help it. It's pointless, and weak, and stupid."

"And therapeutic, and healthy, and natural ..."

"Whatever."

"It's not good to keep all of that emotion bottled up inside you," Naomi said, her brows pulled tight in an expression of concern. Two shrugged.

"Don't really want to talk about it," she said. "Please."

"Very well. I'll change the subject."

"Go for it."

Naomi was quiet for a moment before turning to Two, leaning in and speaking in a conspirator's voice. "That man at the bar, there. Thomas. He has been observing me for nearly three years now, reporting my actions to his superiors."

"His ... what, like the bar manager?"

Naomi grinned. "Not exactly. He is a member of a cult that calls itself the Children of the Sun. We have known about them for decades but did not consider them a threat. They would occasionally catch and kill a Burilgi that was terrorizing a neighborhood somewhere, but we viewed this as a good thing. It helped us keep a low profile, and they did the same. Then, all of a sudden, something woke them up."

"What are they doing?"

"Since May of this year, the Children of the Sun have been actively recruiting at a rapid pace. We can only assume that they intend to begin murdering vampires on a much larger scale."

Two looked at her, eyebrows raised in surprise. "I'm confused," she said finally.

Naomi looked at her, head tilted, waiting for Two to elaborate.

"You know what he is and what he's doing ... and you let him do it?"

Naomi gave her a gentle smile. "What would you have me do? Kill him?"

"I don't know. Yes? Or at least put him in prison or something. Can't your council do that?"

"Eliminating a single human is not difficult for us, but what would be the value? Thomas is no danger to me or anyone I associate with. His cult has only ever busied itself with Burilgi who live in low-population areas and act in ways that break our laws anyway. Thomas does not know that he is suspected. Why tip our hand? Why tell our enemies that we are aware of them when he presents an opportunity for study?"

Two finished her drink, thinking this over. A pretty young woman with long, purple hair swooped over and removed the glass almost immediately. She asked if Two would like another drink, and Two said that she would.

"Her blood is fantastic," Naomi said when the girl had left. "She's healthy, in good shape, and doesn't poison herself with anything except a few cocktails now and then. I drink from her every couple of months. She never remembers me until I've bitten her, and then it's 'Oh, I missed you' over and over."

Two laughed. She glanced over at Thomas, who caught her looking and smiled at her. Two smiled back and gave him a small wave.

"He seems so nice," she said.

"He's a fine young man who is simply misguided. You did a good job there, not showing any concern."

"My previous ... career ... involved a lot of acting." Two rolled her eyes.

"I don't doubt it."

"So what are you guys gonna do about this cult?"

"We'd like to determine where they operate from, and why they're so intent on killing vampires. They're very secretive. What little we know has all come from following operatives like Thomas, and as soon as they realize they've been compromised, they disappear."

"So the council is investigating things? What happens when you find out who's running things?"

Naomi's eyes were full of dark mirth. "I believe we will have a little chat with those in charge."

"And if that goes badly?"

"Stephen and the other Ay'Araf would like very much for it to go badly. They can certainly handle any unpleasantness that might arise."

Two nodded. "And it doesn't bother you that they're killing Burilgi?"

"I don't know of any better way to deal with the rogues, but I detest killing of any sort. It's not solely my decision to wait. You must understand, Two ... most of my people don't live much more than a normal human lifetime, if that. We don't die from sickness or age, but those aren't the only things that kill people. It takes a great deal of caution, and no small amount of luck, to live for the amount of time I and many of the council members have. We approach every action with caution and scrutiny."

"So you're pretty conservative ..."

"When it comes to things like starting wars with cults we barely know about? Yes. The Burilgi are well aware of the Children, I am sure. It is up to them to stay safe. The council is more concerned with those vampires that opt to follow its laws, and that rules out nearly all Burilgi."

"Fair enough." Two glanced up as the cocktail waitress arrived with her drink. She paid, gestured the waitress to keep the change, and returned the girl's smile. The waitress paused momentarily, giving Naomi a confused look, and then moved on.

"That looked like a 'where do I know you from?' moment," Two said.

Naomi gave a small laugh. "I wonder what she'd think if I complimented her on her Hello Kitty bed sheets."

"Classy ..."

"She is a very sweet girl. She'll make some nice young man or woman very happy, someday." Naomi sounded wistful, her voice far away.

"Can I ask you something kind of personal?"

"So long as I have permission not to answer, certainly."

"Do you sleep with people often? It seems like Theroen and Melissa did, and earlier, what Stephen was saying about the bras ..."

Naomi shrugged. "I can't get pregnant and won't get sick. There's no risk and the reward is pleasurable enough. I pursue it frequently, yes. That's what Stephen meant."

Two pondered this for a moment. "All that sex, but no love?"

"There have been a few, but not all loves last forever. I try not to get that attached to humans, and it has been some time since I met a vampire that I ... a vampire who I could be able to love."

"Are you lonely?"

"As I said, I am a solitary person. I suppose it makes me lonely at times, but this has been my life for centuries now. I am used to it."

"Being used to it and being happy aren't the same thing. Doesn't it ever bother you?"

"I ... yes, sometimes. There are times when I wish greatly for a companion, someone like Stephen whose company – exasperating though it often is – I enjoy, but with whom I could share more. It is unfortunate that I have no one like that, I suppose, and I do sometimes feel unhappy. I can never tell if it's real depression or just my Ashayt nature asserting itself."

"Don't think that'd make it any less real," Two said.

Naomi toyed with her glass, not making eye contact, saying nothing.

"Why not make a fledgling, or at least take someone in like Lisette did for you?"

Naomi grimaced, as if her wine had suddenly gone bitter. "Where did that get Lisette?"

"Sorry, Naomi. I didn't mean to upset you."

The vampire girl shook her head. "No, it's not your fault. We've both had our fair share of loss, Two. You would think that after hundreds of years it would fade, and I sometimes think it has ... but you and your stories have brought up some long-buried hurt. I don't blame you – it's just the way things are. I miss them both. I thought we had forever."

Two nodded and took a sip of her bourbon. Forever, yes. That sounded familiar. Two found that getting drunk suddenly seemed very appealing.

"Let us talk of something more positive," Naomi said.

"Kind of low on positivity right now. I could tell you some stories from the good times in my life, I guess. I spent a lot of time hanging out with Rhes and Sarah, before I got into drugs."

"I would love to hear them."

"OK, but I get to hear some stories, fun ones, about your life, too."

Naomi signaled for another glass of wine, rested her chin on her palms, and looked at Two. "That seems fair."

* * *

"I love nights like this," Naomi told her as they returned to the apartment. "I feel wonderful. *Je dévorerai le monde!*"

"We should probably be quiet," Two said. "It's four-thirty in the morning. People will be asleep."

"To hell with people," Naomi said, leaning against the wall and pulling at her leather boots.

Two had lost track of her drinks somewhere around the fourth, and Naomi had compounded the effects of her wine by feeding in the ladies' room on the young woman with the barrettes. Both Two and Naomi were quite drunk.

"I always wanted to be a ballerina," Naomi said, twirling in a circle, her stockings gliding easily on the hardwood floors. She made her way to the living room, and Two followed, weaving a bit.

"Where's Stephen?"

"Out at his club, no doubt," Naomi said. "He won't be back until just before dawn."

She flopped down on the couch, rolled on her side, and curled up in something resembling a fetal position. Two sat down on the same couch and laid her head back. The world spun, but in the gentle way that told her she'd had just enough and not too much. She felt giddy and giggly and happy for the first time in months.

"I never finished telling you about the play," Naomi said from beside her.

"Oh, right. There was a fight?"

"Yes! The woman had this awful feather boa, this huge thing which stuck up above her head like a hat, and she wouldn't remove it. Lisette couldn't see a thing, and she just kept complaining and complaining no matter how much Theroen and I tried to shush her. Finally, the woman turned around and told Lisette to behave like a lady."

"Oh, wow ..."

"Lisette punched her right in the teeth! Oh, Two, it was the most incredible thing I've ever seen." Naomi covered her mouth with a hand, breaking into pretty laughter, her eyes squinting closed.

Two grinned. "That doesn't sound much like the Lisette that Theroen described."

"We were so shocked we couldn't move! I don't know what came over her. There was this *huge* scene, and Lisette had to be forcefully ejected from the theater. I remember standing in the street, utterly mortified, and Lisette was raving ... Theroen was holding her, keeping her from rushing back inside, only he could barely keep her with him because he was laughing so hard. Tears were just rolling down his face."

"That doesn't sound much like Theroen, either!"

"No, but ... he could barely breathe, Two. It was truly absurd."

"I punched a girl in the teeth once."

Naomi sat up and leaned in closer, curious. "Really?"

"Sure. I didn't want to, but she was coming at me. It cut my knuckles up pretty bad, and she lost two teeth. I feel bad about it, but ... no, wait, I guess I don't really feel that bad about it."

Naomi laughed and rested her head briefly on Two's shoulder. "Oh, you're funny. *Je comprends ce qu'il voyait eu toi.*"

"Thanks, but sorry, I don't speak French." Two could feel waves of warmth, not entirely physical, emanating from the vampire. They seemed to mix with the alcohol in her brain, softening the edges of the world. The sensation was not unpleasant.

"None at all?" Naomi asked.

"Not a word. Just English and a couple of Spanish swears."

Naomi put her lips close to Two's ear, whispering. "*Je veux t'embrasser et partager le sang avec toi.*"

"Naomi, I don't understand ..."

Naomi sighed, shifted, said, "I was checking to see if you were lying."

"Nope, sorry."

"It was nothing, Two. Just a test."

They were silent for a time. Two wanted to ask about the waves of feeling Naomi seemed to be throwing off, but she couldn't find the right way to phrase it. She was not entirely sure that it was anything more than her imagination.

"I'm sleepy. So much wine," Naomi said at last.

"Yeah." Two was nodding, feeling the same way herself. The warm pulses were lulling her to sleep.

"Curtains are open. Shouldn't stay here." Naomi rubbed her eyes and stood up. Two felt a sense of regret as the warmth seemed to drain away.

"It was nice going out with you," Two said. "Thanks."

"You're very welcome. It was a wonderful evening."

There was a long, awkward pause as each seemed to wait for the other to say something. Two knew this moment, had felt it before after nights of flirting with some boy in a pool hall. *She wants to ask me to—* her brain began, but Naomi interrupted it.

"Goodnight, Two. I'll see you tomorrow."

"OK Naomi. Goodnight. Or ... morning ... or whatever."

Naomi laughed and disappeared down the hallway. Two heard the door to the vampire's bedroom open and close. Shortly after, she stood up and went to her own room, where she pulled off her clothes and slid into bed. The sheets were cold, and Two thought again of those pulses of warmth, and of the expression on Naomi's face during that last extended silence.

Forget it, she thought to herself. She turned over on her stomach, closed her eyes, and was soon asleep.

CHAPTER XI

Living Under Guard

Rhes Thompson felt like a walking bruise. It seemed that every muscle, from toes to head, ached from his beating the night before. He was propped up on the couch with three pillows, watching television and waiting until he could take his next dose of painkillers. Sarah was in the kitchen making a late lunch.

He had been dismissed from the hospital at nine in the morning, and they had taken a cab home in near-silence, happy to be alive and, if not safe, at least in no immediate danger. The sun was out and no vampires would trouble them until the evening when Jakob was scheduled to arrive.

Sarah had called Molly from the hospital early in the morning, told her that they were fine, and instructed her to go ahead and go to school. Molly had begun attending a private institution in early September, the tuition paid by a trust that Two had established. The school dealt specifically with juvenile addicts, and Molly seemed to be doing well there. By the time Rhes and Sarah got home, she had already gone.

Jake, Sarah's guide dog, had been ecstatic to see them. Sarah had said hello and let him out into their tiny backyard. Rhes, still dazed from pain and painkillers, had limped into the living room, collapsed on the couch, and promptly fallen back asleep.

He had awoken a few hours later to find that Sarah had brought him pillows and a blanket, and was sitting next to him, reading one of her books. Her fingers moved across the page with startling speed, and Rhes had watched for a moment before she stopped, turned her head toward him, and smiled.

"You awake?" she had asked.

"Yeah. How'd you know?"

"Breathing changed. Want some lunch?"

"That'd be great, hon, thanks. I'm starved."

And so she'd gone to prepare it. Now Sarah was emerging from the kitchen with a tray. On it were two bowls of what looked like minestrone soup, a roast-beef sandwich, and two glasses of water. She set the tray on the coffee table.

"Can you reach this?"

"Think so. Not totally crippled, just hurting. When am I due for more meds?"

"Another thirty minutes or so. The doctor said we can bend the rules if you really need it, though."

"No, I'm all right. Thirty minutes is fine. This looks great, Sarah." Rhes leaned forward, wincing, and picked up one of the bowls. Sarah took the other and sat back down.

They were quiet for a time, eating, and then Rhes said, "I wouldn't believe last night really happened if I didn't feel like this."

"It's pretty surreal," Sarah agreed.

"Where do you suppose Two is?"

"Could be dead."

"She's not dead." Rhes set down the bowl of soup, already empty, and picked up the plate with the sandwich. He was ravenous. "You want any of this?"

"It's all yours. I just wanted the soup."

"Thanks. Two's not dead, Sarah."

Sarah ate a spoonful of soup, sipped at her water, said nothing.

"If she were dead," Rhes continued, "there'd be no reason for those things to have broken into her apartment, right? They'd have her keys."

"Maybe."

"Sarah, come on. Two might need our help."

"Our help with *what?*" Sarah snarled. She slammed her bowl down on the end table, sloshing a bit of soup over the edge, and turned to face him. "What can we possibly help her with? She's told us *nothing* for months, and when we finally go and try and help, it nearly gets us both killed. Fuck her, Rhes. Fuck Two, and fuck her stupid vampires."

Rhes said nothing, unsure of how to respond. Sarah pressed her palms against her forehead for a moment and then sighed.

"I'm sorry, baby. I didn't get a lot of sleep and I ... I'm sorry. I'm so angry."

"It's OK," Rhes said. He stood up, ignoring the pain, and knelt down beside her, reaching out to take off her glasses. Sarah's hazel eyes still remembered how to track, from before she had lost her sight, and it was hard sometimes to remember that she couldn't see him. Rhes leaned forward and kissed the bridge of her nose.

"I'm too dumb and doped up on painkillers to figure it out," he said. "What can I do to make you stop feeling bad?"

Sarah shrugged, shook her head. "Probably nothing."

"I don't understand why you're so upset. Is it the blindness thing? I told you, it wouldn't have changed anything."

"It's not that. It's ... I've never been that scared. Not ever. Even when I woke up blind, after the car accident, I wasn't that scared. I was just a kid then, too young to understand that my whole life had changed, so I wasn't *that* scared. I just couldn't stop thinking about you, and about Molly, and about how I want to get married and have a baby with you, and I *hated* Two. I hated her so much. I wished she had been killed by Abraham, or overdosed on heroin, or got hit by a fucking bus ... anything that would have gotten her out of our life before last night. I hated her for not even being there. We were going to *die* for her and she wasn't even there!"

Sarah took in a shuddery breath. Rhes smoothed her hair away from her forehead and said nothing. He wanted Sarah to talk, wanted her to get this out before it could be bottled up somewhere secret to grow and fester.

"All I wanted was a normal life," she continued. "That's all I've wanted since I was eight and that drunk *bastard* hit me and took my eyes away. I never thought I'd feel normal again, not until I met you, and then finally here I was having a normal life, and Two came along and fucked it up. And all I could do, because of my stupid eyes, was lie there and wait for it to be over."

"Sarah ..."

"I told you I hate being blind, and I do, but what I really hate is being powerless. I have never felt more powerless – more *disabled* – than I felt last night."

"So you were scared and confused, and didn't feel in control of the situation, and you're upset not only because you didn't like that but also because of how it made you feel about Two," Rhes said.

Sarah nodded.

Rhes kissed the back of her hand and the tips of her fingers. "Would it make you feel better if I told you that when I see Two again, I'm not sure if I'm going to hug her or punch her right in the damn face?"

"A little," Sarah admitted.

"Look, last night was the best night of my life. I got the shit kicked out of me, but I asked the woman I love to marry me and she said yes. I'd do it again."

This time Sarah smiled at him. She moved her head forward and kissed him, still being careful of his split lip. Rhes kissed her back and then stood up.

"I'm going to go take some painkillers. Then I'm going back to sleep on the couch. There's room for two if you're interested. I think we could both use it."

"Sounds wonderful. You're sure it won't hurt you?"

"Positive." Rhes wandered into the kitchen to refill his glass of water. When he returned, he swallowed the two pills that the bottle told him to take and lay back against the pillows. Sarah sat down beside him and leaned into his chest. Rhes put his arms around her, and minutes later, both were asleep.

* * *

"Holy fuck!"

Sarah stirred, shook her head to clear it, and said, "Molly ... language."

"Oh, sorry. I just ... what happened to Rhes?"

"It's a long story," said Rhes, not bothering to moves. "A long, rich story, filled with kings and queens ... fairies, dragons ... a young girl with golden hair and green eyes and an incredible penchant for getting herself in trouble."

"You mean Two?" Molly asked. She set her backpack down on the coffee table and took a step closer to inspect Rhes's injuries.

"Yes, I definitely mea—oh, ouch, baby, don't use my ribs for leverage, please."

Sarah had been trying to sit up but stopped immediately. "Sorry, didn't mean to hurt you."

"Don't listen to her," Rhes told Molly. "She's a sadist. First the beating, and now the torture. It's too late for me ... save yourself!"

Molly giggled. Sarah shook her head. "Molly, help me up, would you?"

"Sure." Sarah felt Molly's hands take hers and pull her to a sitting position.

"Thanks. How was school?"

"Fine. I have an English test on Wednesday and a math quiz on Friday."

"OK. We can help you study for those. Did you have group today?"

'Group' was short for 'Group Discussion and Therapy,' an activity in which the students were broken into small clusters, each with an instructor, and given projects to work on relating to addiction and recovery.

"Yeah," Molly said. "It was OK. I got paired with Jen and Theresa and Bill, and Mr. Peterson. We had to make a list of things we liked to do for fun, but he wanted more interesting stuff than like, basketball or reading or whatever."

"What did you come up with?"

"I told him about how you take me with you sometimes to your school and I get to help the blind kids learn Braille. He said that was good, and then we talked about focusing on constructive things like that."

"You're doing fantastic, Molly. We're very proud of you," Sarah said.

"Thanks. But anyway, what happened? Did you see Two? How come she never comes over anymore?"

"We didn't get to see Two, unfortunately," Sarah said. "We went to try and find her and got mugged instead."

Sarah hadn't rehearsed this story with Rhes, but she hoped he would be able to back her up without too much effort. He didn't disappoint her.

"These three guys came at us with a baseball bat. I managed to hold them off while Sarah called for help. And by 'hold them off' I mean 'absorb the blows with my face and body.' And arms. And legs. And my groin, but don't worry, no permanent damage there. The groin is safe, ladies, and will be back in action soon!"

"Rhes ... gross," Molly said.

"I'd smack him, but he'll just start crying like a baby," Sarah told her.

"It's true," Rhes said, his voice filled with mock seriousness.

"You guys are weird. Can I watch TV?"

"Do you have any homework?" Sarah asked.

"No, I already did my French in study hall."

"OK. I'm going to need your help later though, to clean this place up. We're going to have a visitor late tonight, after you go to bed, and I want the house to look neat. Rhes can't really move, so it's up to us."

"No problem." Molly replied.

"Sarah, can you help me stand up?" Rhes asked. She did, and he shuffled toward the hallway that led to the downstairs bathroom.

"Is he OK?" Molly asked.

"Doctor says he'll be fine."

"Cool. Who's coming over tonight?"

"A friend of Two's who might be able to help her. I don't want you staying up, Molly. You've got school in the morning. I don't think he'll be here long anyway."

"I promise I'll go right to bed ... *if* we can have pizza for dinner."

Sarah stuck her tongue out at Molly. "You'll go right to bed whether we have pizza or not, but I've got no objections. Ask Rhes when he gets back, but you know he'll say yes."

"Yay!" Molly cried, an excitement in her voice that only teenagers, and occasionally full-grown men, could muster over pizza.

Sarah heard Molly turn on the television and begin flipping through the channels. She smiled, stretched, and headed for the kitchen to get a drink. She knew it must still be light out, if Molly was just getting home, but that sunset would come shortly, and with it would come danger. She hoped Jakob's guards were as good as he'd claimed, and she hoped that all of this nonsense would be over with soon; she had a wedding to plan.

* * *

"I don't think we should tell him about Tori," Sarah said. They were sitting in the living room, waiting for Jakob to arrive. The house was clean, the pizza leftovers put away, and Molly was in bed. Jake was out in the yard, happily gnawing on a piece of rawhide. Neither Rhes nor Sarah were sure how he would react to Jakob's presence, and they had felt it best to keep him away from the vampire entirely.

"Why not?" Rhes asked.

"Do you remember what he said? He was investigating Two's house to see 'if she needed to be hurt or not' when he ran into us. Tori's clearly got enough problems of her own already. I don't want to set someone on her who'll willingly murder three other vampires without the slightest hesitation."

Rhes thought this over. "He might be able to help her more than we can, though."

"He might. Or he might chop her up. I'm pretty sure Tori can take care of herself, and I'd rather we tell Two before we tell anyone else. She knows these people better than we do."

"You think she'll know what to do?"

"She'll do *something*, anyway, whether it's the right thing or not. You know Two. I just don't want to go making decisions for her."

Rhes shrugged. "OK, hon. Your call. Right now we have to worry about ourselves anyway. Supposedly, we're still in danger."

"Do you think they're watching us right now?" Sarah asked.

"Yes. Watching the house, anyway. I doubt they're peering in through the windows or anything."

"What time is it?"

"Almost eleven. He'll be here soon."

They lapsed into a nervous silence. Sarah was attempting to read. Rhes was watching baseball at a low volume, but not really paying it any attention. Both were waiting for a sign of the vampire's arrival. It came as a small knock on the front door.

Rhes took a deep breath and said, "I'll get it."

Jakob was wearing a maroon button-down shirt made of silk, a pair of grey slacks, and a grey sport coat. The clothes were exquisitely tailored and looked surprisingly casual and comfortable. His dark hair was pulled back into a ponytail. He smiled as Rhes opened the door.

"It is good to see you standing, my friend," Jakob said.

Rhes laughed. "It's good to be *able* to stand. I was a little worried about it last night. Come in."

Jakob stepped inside. "Thank you. This is a lovely home. Hello, Sarah."

"Hi, Jakob. Your cell phone's on the table by the door."

"Ah, thank you." Jakob slid the phone into an interior pocket.

"Can I take your coat?" Rhes asked.

"No, thank you. I don't think I'll be staying long, as I don't want to keep you awake. Also, I make you nervous. Not that I blame you ... it's unusual for humans to enjoy company of my type."

"It depends on the company, I suppose, but you don't need to rush on our behalf. Have a seat."

Rhes sat down on the couch. Sarah remained in her easy chair. Jakob took the other recliner, which faced both of them, and got down to business.

"Your friend did not return to her apartment last night," he said. "Until we find out what has happened to her, I would like to keep you under guard."

"Are we really still in danger?" Sarah asked.

"I do not know, which makes it prudent to assume that you are."

"Not to look a gift horse in the mouth," Rhes said, "but why are you protecting us, anyway? Aren't we basically ... food?"

Jakob laughed. "No, not exactly. I know, like, and respect many humans. Few of them are aware of what I am, of course, but that doesn't change anything. You are under protection because I choose to protect you. Your friend is responsible for some very significant events in the past year, and there is a great deal of action happening amongst my people."

"How do we fit in?"

"To the best of my knowledge, you don't. I think you're innocent and well-intentioned bystanders who've been swept up in something that you can't control and don't deserve to be punished for. The Burilgi may not even know who you are, which would be the best-case scenario. Unfortunately, until I can determine your status with them, I can't guarantee your safety without keeping you under guard."

"Where are your people?"

"On the rooftops, mostly, watching the entrances to this building. They will not miss anything, and they will not disturb you in any way unless it is necessary."

"What will you do with Two, when you find her?" Sarah asked.

"I will take her before the council. She is wanted for questioning but not necessarily punishment. There are many who feel that, if anything, she deserves to be rewarded for her actions."

"When will you have news?"

"The next council meeting is on the fourth of October. With any luck, we will have located Two by then."

"Can you call us? I mean, you don't have to tell us any details if you don't want to. We just want to know if Two's OK."

"I will have someone call you as soon as we know for sure that your friend is alive, and what the council's judgment is. In the interim, it's safer for all involved if you have as little contact as possible with Two and the rest of us."

Rhes said, "I guess that's all we can ask. Thank you."

"When does this end?" Sarah asked. "When do we get to go back to normal life?"

"I cannot imagine that it will take more than a week to determine whether the Burilgi harbor any ill intentions. If your friend has been kidnapped, it may take longer to obtain information on her, but I believe you will be able to return to your normal routine within a few days."

Sarah nodded. "OK, Jakob. Thank you. Was there anything else?"

"I have nothing more, except to offer my apologies that you had to become involved in this at all."

Rhes smiled. "Not your fault. Our friend dragged us in. You saved our lives."

Jakob nodded and rose from his chair. Rhes and Sarah both stood as well and escorted him to the front door, where he said, "Take care, stay inside during the evenings, and I will be in touch as soon as I can."

"Do you believe him?" Rhes asked when the vampire had gone.

"That we're safe and that he'll get us out of this mess? Yeah. Why protect us now if he intends to kill us later? As far as Two goes, I have no idea. It could be he's lying, and they're just looking to find her and murder her so she'll shut up and stop bothering them."

"You know, it's your sense of optimism that I love," Rhes said, his voice dry.

"I thought it was my perky tits," Sarah replied.

"Those, too."

"I'm tired, Rhes. Think you can handle the stairs?"

"Sleeping on the couch means waking up next to the dog, and sleeping in the bed means waking up next to you. I'll brave the stairs."

"I'm touched," Sarah said. "You get a head start. I'll let Jake in, shut off the lights, and meet you upstairs."

"Sounds good," Rhes said. He watched as Sarah headed for the rear of the house, and then turned and began the ascent to their room, grimacing at the pain in his legs and ribs. Eventually he made it to the master bedroom, which faced the rear of the brownstone, its windows looking down on the garden below.

He heard Sarah come in behind him and he said, "Sit down on the edge of the bed for a minute, hon."

"OK ..." Sarah's voice was questioning, but she did what Rhes asked.

"I wanted to do this right," Rhes said, walking over to her and dropping to one knee. Sarah realized what was happening and gave him a radiant smile.

"Sarah Victoria Taylor, I love you and I want to spend my life with you. Will you marry me?" Rhes asked as he took her left hand.

"I will," Sarah said. Rhes slid the ring onto her finger, and let her hand go. He watched as Sarah traced the ring with the fingers of her right hand, feeling the circular center diamond and the two oval stones that flanked it. He understood that she was admiring it – seeing it – in the best way that she could.

"They're diamonds in a gold band," Rhes said.

"I'm sure it's beautiful, baby. I wish I could see it, instead of having to imagine."

Rhes sat down on the bed next to her, still holding her hand, and Sarah leaned her head against his shoulder.

"You think we'll ever have a normal life again?" she asked him.

"Yes," he replied without a trace of doubt in his voice.

"How can you be sure?"

"Because it's all we really want. We'll get there. We just have to deal with a few ... bumps in the road, first."

Sarah laughed. "They're big bumps."

"No kidding. Sarah, do you remember how last year Sid offered to make me a partner if I'd help him open a second bar, and I turned him down, and you got pissed about it?"

"Yes. I told you I was sorry. I just—"

"No, you were right. I'm ready to run a place, and avoiding the responsibility just because it's easy to keep living on our salaries and letting Two cover the expensive stuff is the wrong thing to do."

Sarah was quiet. Rhes knew she agreed with what he was saying, but also understood that she wanted him to express it himself. He continued.

"We're going to get married, and start ... well, we've already started a family, I guess, but there's going to be a baby eventually too, and I have no idea what's going to happen to Two. I can't count on her money, and even if I could, it's not what I want to do. I want to know that my family can depend on me. I'm not expecting you to quit your job or anything, but I have the opportunity to go into business with a guy who's already shown he can make a shitload of money in the industry. I want to take it, for us."

Sarah put her arms around him, squeezed gently, kissed him on the cheek. "I'm so glad! You'll be great, and I'll have to worry less about some drunk jackass stabbing you, or something."

"Yeah, now you can just worry about me having a heart attack or something from the stress."

"You'll be fine. Rhes, seriously, I think this is great and you'll be terrific at it. But if it's not what you really want ..."

"It's what I really want. Promise. I've been thinking about it for a long time. I already told Sid I was going to talk to you about it."

Sarah kissed him again, this time on the lips, and said, "You know ... they say the best sex you'll ever get is on the night you propose."

"What about the people who save it for marriage?"

"Guess they're missing out."

Rhes took the edges of Sarah's T-shirt and pulled it up over her head, tossing it on the ground. She wasn't wearing anything underneath, and he cupped her breasts as he kissed the place where her neck met her shoulder. Sarah shivered and put her hands in his hair.

"So you're saying that broken ribs or not, this is totally going to be worth it," he said.

"I'll be gentle," Sarah told him.

Rhes laughed, pushed her softly onto her back, held her hands in his, crossed above her head, and kissed her.

"I'd rather you didn't," he said.

* * *

It took three days for the vampires to contact them again. Living under guard was surprisingly stressful; Rhes and Sarah never saw any of Jakob's people, but they could sense being watched during the night. Attempting to go about their normal lives was more difficult than it sounded.

In the end, they realized there was little they could do but wait. Rhes's boss, Sid, had been thrilled to hear that Rhes was ready to take on an increased role in the business and told him to take as much time as needed to heal. Sarah had returned to work, teaching her kids three days a week. Molly, largely oblivious to what was going on, had continued to live the life of a thirteen-year-old girl, or as near to it as one who had been through so much could live.

The phone call came shortly after dusk on the fourth night after the incident at Two's apartment. Sarah answered. "Hello?"

"Is this Sarah Taylor?"

"Yes, it is."

"I am a friend of Jakob's. He asked me to call you." The voice on the phone was female, and Sarah wondered if it might be the same woman who had driven them to the hospital.

"Oh, OK."

"Your friend Two is alive and well. She has come under the care of one of our council members and shouldn't be in further danger. She has been informed that you are safe as well, and understands that it is not in your best interests to see her at this time. She may contact you at some later date, after her issues with the council have been resolved."

"When will she—"

"I can't speak for your friend or for the council. I can only relay the information given me. We are working with the Burilgi to exonerate you of any guilt related to the incident in her apartment on Monday. When this is accomplished, and Jakob thinks it will be very soon, you will be notified and your guards removed."

"OK, but what about—"

"I'm very sorry, but I don't have any other information at this time. The council hasn't met, so there's been no judgment."

"Listen, we went looking for Two for a reason. She has a friend in Ohio, a girl who used to be a vampire, and—"

"The council is well aware of Ms. Perrault and is investigating her situation. Please do not trouble yourselves with it any further. We will call again when we know more. Goodbye."

There was a click, and Sarah was left holding a dead receiver. She returned it to its cradle and sat for a moment on the couch, processing what she had been told.

"Who was that?" Rhes asked from the kitchen.

"Friend of Jakob's."

He came into the room, curious. "What'd he say?"

"She. And ... not much. Two is OK, and has been told not to contact us because it might endanger us, I guess. They're working on the other thing, so we can stop being watched. And they already know about Tori."

"Ah. Well, great." Rhes sat down next to her and took her hand. She leaned against his shoulder.

"She wouldn't let me ask any questions. I tried, but she just cut me off."

"Was she rude?"

"Not really, just businesslike. I think it might've been the woman who drove us to the hospital. That would make sense, if she works for Jakob."

"Could be a girlfriend."

Sarah shrugged. "Could be. Dinner almost ready?"

"Ten more minutes."

"Need any help?"

"Got it covered. Put pot pie in oven, set table, sit and wait for pot pie to become golden and delicious."

Sarah smiled. "OK. Molly keeps asking if we've picked a date yet. She's very excited. She wants to be in the wedding party."

"So that'd be your sister, and Molly, and Jill from school. Anyone else?"

Sarah was quiet for a moment and then said, "You know I'd ask Two if I could."

"You don't have to."

"I *want* to. I just don't know if we'll ever see her again, or – if we do – whether she'll be able to go out in the sunlight anymore."

"Ouch, yeah, I hadn't even thought about that. Well ... that's Two's choice. It's *way* out of our hands at this point."

"Yeah. Rhes, I want to ask Molly about the other thing. Adopting her. She's never asked about it ... maybe she's scared to, but I think it's what she wants. We should find out for sure."

"OK. You sure you want a teenage daughter? You're young enough to be her sister."

"I'm positive. What about you?"

"Can't imagine life without her at this point. I love the kid."

"Me, too."

"All right. Then we'll ask her at dinner ... which should be just about ready. So if you'll kindly remove your head from my shoulder, I'll go finish things up."

Sarah smiled, doing as he asked. As Rhes headed for the kitchen, she stood and went to tell Molly that dinner was ready.

* * *

"Ohmigod ... YES!"

Molly's eyes were wide and sparkling with joy. Sarah had expected a positive response, but it was gratifying to hear the girl's feelings expressed so emphatically. They hadn't beaten around the bush at dinner. After talking for a few minutes about the events of the day, Sarah had simply turned to Molly and said, "When Rhes and I get married, we'd like to adopt you. Would that be OK?"

After a momentary pause to process this question, Molly's excited shout had followed. Now she was glancing back and forth between Rhes and Sarah, looking happy but unsure, as if she doubted the reality of what they were saying.

"You're serious, right?" she asked.

"Very serious," Rhes said.

"Absolutely," Sarah agreed.

"So, like, I'd be your real daughter and I can call you Mom and Dad and everything?"

Sarah nodded. "If that's what you want, Molly. We'd love to be Mom and Dad."

"It is! Totally! Oh, this is so ... cool ..." Molly's voice wavered. Sarah took her hand just as the girl burst into tears. Molly stood and Sarah stood with her, embracing her. Molly wrapped her arms around Sarah, crying into her shoulder.

"You OK, kiddo?" Rhes asked.

"She's all right," Sarah said. She felt Molly nod against her, still crying. "I think she's just a little overwhelmed."

They both knew Molly's story; she had been shuffled from foster home to foster home for most of her life, and had never been lucky enough before now to find a caring set of guardians. Instead she had found apathy and neglect, which had allowed her to come into contact with drugs, sex, and violence. Molly had been eleven years old, living in a Queens housing project and already smoking crack cocaine, when a friend had first introduced her to heroin. Within six months she had run away from home in pursuit of money to afford the drug. Life at Darren's had followed, a waking nightmare from which there had seemed no escape.

Then Two had brought her salvation. Molly's body still ached for the drug sometimes, but as badly as she wanted it, there was something she wanted more, something that kept her from turning back to that life, something that she had spent her entire young life searching for without ever knowing it.

"All I want is a mom and dad," she cried into Sarah's shoulder.

Sarah hugged her and said, "I know, sweetheart. We're here. We love you."

Rhes stood up, crossed the room, and put a hand on Molly's shoulder, "We can't wait for you to be our daughter."

Molly sobbed, her hands wrapped tight into the fabric of Sarah's sweater. Rhes and Sarah waited, letting her cry, until she had at last regained some control. She loosened her grip on Sarah and stood back, sniffling and rubbing her hands against her eyes.

"Sorry," she said finally.

Rhes laughed. "Nothing to be sorry about. Couldn't have asked for a more enthusiastic reception."

"I can't wait to tell my friends! Do I get to change my name and stuff?" New York State had assigned her a last name, Smith, and Molly hated it.

"Of course," Sarah said. "You can be Molly Thompson. Or maybe Molly Taylor-Thompson, if we go that route."

"Or you can pick a random last name and we can all change to that," Rhes said. "I've always liked Santiago, myself. Listen to the majesty: *Rhes Santiago!*"

He rolled his "R," and Molly and Sarah laughed.

"I think Thompson will do," Sarah said. "Mr. and Mrs. Thompson, and their daughter Molly Thompson. Sounds good to me."

"Me, too!" said Molly.

"Motion passed," said Rhes. "Let's celebrate this historic decision by finishing dinner. There's ice cream in the freezer and I've been waiting all day to break it out."

CHAPTER XII

The American council

"God, I'm bad at this shit," Two said, pulling at her skirt to adjust the position of the waistband. It seemed like no matter what she did, the fabric didn't want to hang on her hips in a way that she approved of. Behind her, Stephen laughed.

"Those panties are lovely, but you might want to pull the skirt up in the back," he said.

Two growled and hiked the skirt back up an inch. "Am I still exposed?"

"No, that will do." Stephen's lips were set in a subtle, sarcastic grin.

Naomi laughed. "Honestly, Two, you'd think we were putting you through some kind of torture. Have you never worn a skirt before?"

"I'm ... more of a jeans person."

"Well, you look wonderful. You needn't worry."

Two shrugged. "I'm not worried, just annoyed."

She understood the necessity for the professional attire. This was, after all, a meeting of the most powerful vampires in the United States. It wasn't even that the skirt was uncomfortable – it was, in fact, so soft and smooth that she almost understood why it had cost hundreds of dollars – but rather that she was unable to make herself look the way she wanted. This skirt, like virtually every other piece of clothing in existence, would sit better on Naomi's curvy hips and emphasize her longer legs. Next to the vampire, Two felt like she looked short, dumpy, and unattractive no matter how she dressed.

Naomi was wearing a long black gown that hugged her body and complemented her figure very well. She also had on a pair of black gloves that stretched nearly to her shoulders, and her honey-colored hair was pulled up into a bun. Emeralds sparkled at her ears and around her neck. She smelled of exotic flowers and was wearing makeup that accented her cheekbones and eyes.

Stephen was dressed in a manner that, Two thought, was consciously set just a bit below the obviously formal standards of the council. He was wearing dark khaki pants and a cream-colored button-down shirt, loose at the collar, its sleeves rolled up. His reddish-brown hair was pulled into its customary ponytail. Still, Two noted, he had put on an obviously expensive pair of leather shoes, and a Louis Vuitton wristwatch that she doubted was fake.

Two's outfit was assembled from the best of the items that she had purchased at the boutique a few weeks before. Her long black skirt, made up of multiple, shifting, translucent layers, was complemented by a green silk blouse that matched her eyes. Naomi had helped her pick out jewelry that worked well with the outfit, and had applied Two's makeup while chatting gaily about events of the week. For a brief moment, Two had been reminded of her first meeting with Melissa. Would this friendship turn out like that one had, in the end?

These were phantom worries, Two thought. Naomi was in full possession of her body, was not threatened by anybody, and was a member in good standing of the American council. There was no Abraham lurking in the darkness, no madness or death around the corner. There was only the council, and the fear that they might deny her request. If that happened, Two was truly unsure of what she would do next. She hoped it would not be necessary to find out.

They had spent the better part of the past week in relative peace, sleeping during the day and spending their nights keeping a low profile. For the most part, this had meant staying in the apartment, chatting quietly or reading while Stephen watched sports or went out for his fights. A few times, Two had accompanied Naomi to the club across the street.

On most nights, Two felt that calming, pulsing warmth whenever she was near Naomi. She suspected that there was a meaning behind this sensation but was not yet sure how she felt about it. Probably, she thought, she should be concerned, but there was so much to worry about already. Two didn't want to push Naomi away or make the vampire uncomfortable by asking about it, not while she was learning so much.

Naomi enjoyed teaching what she had learned of vampire history, and in Two she found a willing pupil. She explained that the first strain of vampires, the Eresh, had by all indications arisen around 3100 BC in Mesopotamia. Eresh-Kigal, the Mesopotamian goddess of death and consort to the lord of the underworld, was thought to be the first true vampire, though how this came to be was unknown.

The second strain arose when a woman named Ashayt, sometimes referred to in older vampire writings as *The Girl from the Desert*, was infected by an Eresh vampire in ancient Egypt. The blood had mutated within her, altering the effects of vampirism. Of the four source vampires, the *Vamper Ovras,* Ashayt was the last to have been seen alive. She had disappeared more than six hundred years ago, however, and was presumed to have gone at last to her death.

"Given the depression that most Ashayt vampires are prone to," Naomi had said, "I find it unlikely that she yet lives. So many years alone ... surely she would have had some sort of contact with the councils, if she were still alive."

Ay'Araf, the third *Vamper Ovras*, was a poet and a priest whose work had been revered in Persia for its complexity and beauty. How his progeny had come to be warriors no one was quite sure, but the strain seemed to reward those who sought conflict and confrontation. Ay'Araf vampires were, like Ashayt vampires, dissimilar in many ways from the Eresh. What exactly had become of the *Ovras* himself was a matter of some debate, though it was generally agreed upon that he had been dead for many centuries.

The final group of vampires, by far the most common, was the Burilgi. Their origins were lost to history, but it was believed that the strain had originated in the lower Russian lands near the

Mongolian border. It was also suspected that Burilgi vampires were really nothing more than a bastardized strain of the Ay'Araf, created over a period of centuries by young, weak vampires making younger, weaker fledglings. The Burilgi had lost most of the gifts of vampirism, and were left predominantly with the less enjoyable aspects of the blood.

Sunlight would kill them outright in a matter of minutes. Their victims were most often paralyzed not by lust or love, but by an overwhelming terror that locked their limbs and kept them from fleeing. Their blood was not strong enough to fight off high-level toxins, and they could be killed by venomous bites or by poison. Contact with silver, ash wood, fire and the chemical alliin, most commonly found in garlic, would burn them. Many Burilgi were severely altered physically and could not pass for human, and insanity ran rampant among their ranks.

"They live like vermin," Stephen had said. "They hide in sewers and abandoned buildings, drinking the blood of animals and the homeless and anyone else who stumbles upon them. There are few among them that haven't been driven mad by the change. In those cases, one only feels sorrow that these good people were not gifted with the blood of another strain. Burilgi blood is a curse, not a blessing. I wouldn't wish it upon anyone."

During the dark ages, an increase in the number of Burilgi vampires had led to many of the myths that still informed modern vampire lore. The European council had been established, in the years after the fall of Rome, as a direct response to the increased scrutiny and danger that vampires had come to face. The council, following codes supposedly laid down by Eresh-Kigal herself, had established a body of laws by which all vampires were held accountable. These rules – the Code of Eresh-Kigal – had been altered and added to over the centuries, but were still in effect.

"The American council is both an extension of the European council and a separate entity," Naomi had explained. "We are born of the same laws, but typically govern ourselves and rarely defer to the European council. Abraham made sure of that."

"What about vampires on the other continents?" Two had asked.

"South America has its own council. I have met with them on occasion in the past two centuries. They, like us, operate independently but will sometimes contact the European council for help in interpreting the codes. The vampires in Africa, Asia, and Australia have remained largely untouched by our rules and laws. Most Japanese vampires, for example, will murder a vampire from another clan on sight."

"Couldn't I hypothetically go to one of those places and find someone willing to make me a vampire?" Two had asked.

"You would have to be prepared to never again leave those countries," Naomi had told her. "If the American council rules against you, you will be an outcast for breaking the laws under which you were originally bound. Theroen was a part of those rules, even if he didn't know it, and returning to council-dominated lands as a rogue vampire would earn punishment ... perhaps death."

"In other words," Stephen had said, "if there's any real chance of you finding what it is that you really want, you're already in the best place to do it."

Left with little option but to accept this as fact, Two had spent her time waiting, trying not to dwell on things that might or might not be, until her time with the council arrived. At last that time was upon her, and she would stand before them and be judged.

* * *

The American council of vampires met in a building that had been a cathedral, before the Roman Catholic Church had been forced by financial need to sell the property. Abraham and the other senior members of the council had bought the building through intermediaries and renovated it, and it now held offices for many of the council members in addition to a central meeting area.

Two wondered if it was appropriate to find humor in the irony that such traditional creatures of the night were meeting in this place. She supposed it made sense, in a way. Even those in the mortal world who followed the mythology would be unlikely to guess that the most powerful vampires in the country met monthly under stained glass portraits of Jesus and the Apostles.

Naomi had arranged travel with a car service, and they pulled up in front of the cathedral at quarter to ten in the evening. Standing in front of the building were a man and a woman, both vampires. The man was wearing a dark red suit that, Two thought, would have looked ridiculous on nearly anyone else. With his dark complexion and long black hair, coupled with a general aura of calm confidence, the man had the air of Mephistopheles: charming and debonair and deadly.

The woman was tall, nearly six feet, and also had dark hair. Her skin was very pale, even for a vampire, and her eyes were a light and watery shade of blue. She was dressed in a gown patterned in black and red that matched the man's suit. The red-suited man stepped forward with a wide smile.

"*Stephen, vate se posir!*" the vampire said, extending his hand. Stephen grabbed it without hesitation and shook it, grinning.

"Far too long, Jakob," he said. "I trust those Burilgi last week weren't too much for you?"

Jakob laughed. "Hardly enough exercise to work up an appetite."

"I've no doubt." Stephen turned slightly and addressed the woman standing behind Jakob. "Sasha, you look lovely."

The woman nodded and, in an accent that Two thought was eastern European, or perhaps Russian, said, "Thank you. Perhaps one day someone will teach you how to dress, and I shall return the compliment."

Stephen laughed, stepping backward and to the side, allowing Naomi to move to the front. Jakob took her hand and kissed it. Sasha gave her a brief embrace.

"You both look stunning as always," Naomi said. Jakob and Sasha thanked her, complimented her outfit, and looked at Two, who tried to return their glances without showing any discomfort or concern.

"Introductions?" Jakob asked after a moment.

"This is Two," Naomi said. "Two, this is Jakob and Sasha. They are Ay'Araf warriors and members of the council. Sasha is Jakob's fledgling."

"Pleased to meet you both," Two told them, shaking their hands.

"The pleasure is ours," Jakob said. "We've been eagerly waiting to meet Naomi's human."

"She's *Theroen's* human," Naomi corrected. "Though I suspect she belonged no more to him than Sasha belongs to you."

"Theroen was never interested in owning anyone," Two said.

"Not much like his father, was he?" Jakob asked.

"No, not at all."

"That is for the best."

"It was until the end," Two said, glancing up at the dark sky and thinking of her days at the mansion. "At the end, he could have used a bit more of Abraham in him."

"Oh?" Jakob asked. "And why is that?"

Two returned from her reverie and looked into his eyes. "Because then he'd be standing here with me right now, and that murdering piece of shit would still be just as dead."

Jakob tilted his head, glanced at Naomi, and said, "I believe this will be a very interesting evening."

"Of that I've no doubt," Naomi said.

"Shall we?" Stephen asked and, opening the door for them, he beckoned them inside.

* * *

The American council consisted of nineteen vampires. Of these, the majority were Ay'Araf. There were two Eresh, two Burilgi, and three Ashayt vampires. There should have been four of the latter, Naomi explained, but she had not yet selected an apprentice.

Two felt like an intruder and, beyond that, like an animal in a zoo. While most of the council members were careful not to gape, Two could still feel their eyes examining her. She could feel smoldering disapproval from some, and thought it likely that she was the first human ever brought through these doors during a full meeting.

Only Stephen and Naomi seemed unconcerned with her presence. During the period of general mingling that preceded the actual meeting, Stephen wandered with Two, spending most of his time on the sidelines, murmuring explanations to her.

"These meetings are usually brief," he said. They stood at one end of the room, which had once been the rear of the cathedral. The altar at the other end had been converted to a podium and, down below, where once there had been pews, there was now a loose gathering of overstuffed leather chairs.

"I think this one might run a little longer than normal," Two said.

Stephen nodded. Two glanced around at the group and her gaze fell on two men who seemed different from the others. She realized after a moment that this was because they were, while not ugly, not beautiful either. The other vampires all seemed to be amazing physical specimens, perfectly shaped and without blemishes. These two looked much more like average human beings.

"Those are the Burilgi, aren't they?" Two whispered, making a small gesture toward the men.

"Yes. Good eye."

"They look normal."

"Indeed. Burilgi vampires are rarely gifted with any cosmetic enhancements – if anything, they are cursed with deformities. The rest of us are slowly sculpted by the blood."

"I never thought I was pretty enough to be a vampire," Two said.

Stephen shrugged. "You have a beautiful face, and I think you'd be well-shaped if you weren't so scrawny. You're short, and you're not going to win any wet t-shirt contests, but I don't think Theroen cared about that."

As was common with Stephen, Two was unsure whether she wanted to laugh at him or hit him. She settled for rolling her eyes and said, "Thank you for the warm evaluation of my appearance, Stephen."

Thank you for the warm evaluation of my work, Melissa, Theroen's voice said in her head, and Two had to turn away for a moment, blinking back tears. When she looked again at Stephen, he did her the favor of not asking what was wrong, instead moving toward a table in the back. There were wine glasses and various bottles there. Some were labeled, others – resting on warmers – were not, and when Stephen poured from one of these, Two understood why. The liquid in these bottles was not wine.

"This doesn't offend you, does it?" Stephen asked, sipping at his glass full of blood.

Two shook her head. "Nope. Would it stop you, if it did?"

"Nope."

"You can drink things other than blood, though, right?"

"Yes, if I choose to. I think the only ones here who can't are the two Eresh, and Lewis and Richard over there ... the Burilgi."

"So why are you drinking blood?" Two asked. She poured herself a glass of merlot.

"Because I *like* blood," Stephen replied. "By the way, that bottle you're holding is worth about seven hundred dollars. Try not to spill."

"Jesus," Two hissed, setting it down hastily. "I don't know enough about wine to appreciate it at a hundred bucks a glass!"

"Don't worry about it. To be honest, it's one of the cheaper bottles on the table. The discerning palate would have chosen the burgundy."

"Well la-dee-da," Two said. She sipped at the wine. It was very good, but what might have made it worth the price she couldn't say.

"It's all just rotten grapes anyway," Stephen said, "but if there's anything vampires enjoy, it's being pretentious, and it doesn't get much more pretentious than oenology ... that is, the science of wine snobbery."

"What ... you just assume I don't know the word?"

Stephen raised an eyebrow. "Did you?"

"Course not. That's not the point."

Stephen gave her a sideways grin and drank from his glass of blood. A member of the council made his way to the podium. This seemed to be the signal that the meeting was starting, as the others began taking their seats.

"Over here," Stephen said, gesturing toward a bench on the right side of the cathedral. "We get to sit to one side and wait our turn, like good little children."

"I'll try not to fidget too much, but church always did bore the shit out of me," Two said.

"And I as well, which is why I don't often attend these meetings. Too much flowery bullshit. Tonight's important though, for you and for Naomi."

"Why Naomi?"

Stephen glanced down at Two and smiled.

"I may be wrong," he said. "It happens on rare occasions. But I do believe she has her eye on a potential fledgling."

* * *

"If you would, please begin by telling us your name."

Two glanced around. She was standing at the podium next to an Ay'Araf vampire of Middle Eastern descent. His name was Malik, and at nine hundred years old, he was the eldest of the vampires assembled here, and also the current head of the council. The rest of the vampires were sitting in the plush chairs arranged around the podium, looking up at her. Stephen was leaning against the wall off to her left, looking disinterested. He caught her glance, gave her a sarcastic smile, and made a shooing gesture with his hand. *Go on and get this done with.*

"My name is Two, like the number," she told the members of the council. "Two Ashley Majors."

"Do you know why we've brought you before us today?" Malik asked her.

Two glanced now at Naomi, unsure how best to respond. Naomi also smiled at her, the expression a good deal more reassuring than Stephen's had been, and spread her hands as if telling Two she had no advice.

"Yes, I know why I'm here. I think ... I may have accidentally broken some of your laws."

"Several of them," said a vampire in the crowd, and Two could hear distaste dripping from the woman's voice.

Two shrugged. "They're not my laws."

"Not until you're found guilty, anyway," the woman snapped.

"That's quite enough, Leonore," Naomi said, unperturbed. She threw a casual glance at the woman who had spoken. "It is not your turn to speak, particularly since, as is so often the case, you've little idea what you're talking about."

There were murmurs and chuckles around the room. Leonore's upper lip raised for a moment in an unconscious sneer and she glared at Naomi, who answered the look with a cool smile. After a moment, Leonore's eyes dropped and she settled back into her chair, crossing her arms and turning her gaze back to Two.

"If I'd known the law, I might have done things differently," Two said. "Things happened the way they did because Abraham kept Theroen in the dark. He never learned your laws, so he never passed them on to me. I didn't know there was a council, or a book of rules, or whatever it is you have. I just ... I just want to be a vampire again."

There was more murmuring at this statement, and Malik, still standing beside her, tapped on the podium.

"Perhaps we should let Two tell her story. Does anyone object?" he asked.

It seemed that even those in the room who had already made up their minds regarding Two's guilt, or lack thereof, were curious to hear the details of what had happened. There were no objections.

"The floor is yours, then," Malik said. He stepped away from the podium and made his way down to one of the chairs, sitting down and watching her intently.

Two put her hands on the podium and took a deep breath. The things that were at stake this evening made her knees weak, made her feel like throwing up, but there was no choice before her but to press on.

"I'm not a great public speaker," she told them. "I can only tell you what I know. I can't tell you why the people involved did the things they did, other than me. I don't know. I didn't have time to understand ... not even Theroen, let alone the rest of the people in that house. I didn't totally understand him, but I loved him. I loved him so much that when he was taken from me, I ... there was nothing else I could do. I went back to the house expecting to die. I assumed that Abraham would kill me, because that's how it should have happened. I never expected to wake up the next day, but I ..."

Two looked away for a moment, trying to decide how to go on, trying to decide how to start. As if reading these thoughts, Naomi spoke up.

"Start at the beginning, Two. Tell us everything, without fear or shame."

Two nodded, paused a moment longer to gather her thoughts. Here she was in a situation not so different from that night in the forest, facing death at Abraham's hands. Either she would win, or she would lose. It was too late now for fear. There was nothing to do but what Naomi had told her to do.

"I've told this story before," she said. "I hate telling it, and I'll probably have to stop a few times to cry. I usually do. Here it is: when Theroen first started watching me, I was a heroin addict, living in a building owned by an awful man named Darren."

She looked out at the group and felt the last of her concern evaporating. Naomi had told her to tell the truth, and Two would be damned if she was going to sugar-coat it. Screw this group of rich, arrogant, out-of-touch immortals. Let them understand exactly what she had been through.

"Darren made me fuck strange men in exchange for my drugs, and I did what I was told. Sometimes two or three in a single night. Sometimes groups of them at a time. Sometimes the men would beat me, or kick me, or ... or hurt me in other ways. Some of them wanted to call me by their mother's name, or their sister's, or their daughter's. I came home every night wishing I was dead, and I'd shoot up half hoping to overdose, and once the rush hit I'd be happy. I'd still wish I was dead, but in the same way that people wish they would win the lottery; it was something nice that might happen eventually. I assumed death was one of two things: either it was unending, unfeeling blackness, or it was heaven.

"And heaven ... I thought heaven must be a lot like heroin."

* * *

"The last time I saw Tori was at the airport in Ohio, right before I went through the security gate. We send emails sometimes, and we've called each other once or twice, but, to be honest, I've been ... I've neglected all of my friends for months. All I cared about was finding vampires, and after a while I didn't really even care about that anymore. I was just searching because it was what I'd trained myself to do. Go out. Walk. Look for vampires that I thought I'd never find. I was waiting to die again, but I didn't even know it this time."

Two found that her hands were clamped to the sides of the podium, her knuckles white, and she forced herself to breathe deeply and relax. She looked up at the members of her audience, who were regarding her with a silence that might have been shocked, fascinated, or disgusted. It was impossible to tell.

"Then I met Naomi and Stephen," she said. "You know the rest."

The vampires were silent for what seemed to Two a long while – long enough, at any rate, for her to become tremendously uncomfortable standing at the podium, looking down at them all. At last, Malik stood. He looked composed, as most of these vampires did, but he took a moment to contemplate before speaking.

"Two, I thank you for what I believe was an honest recount of what happened to you. There is unfortunately no way to prove that you are telling the truth, but between our heightened senses and long years of experience, most vampires are fairly sensitive to lies, and I do not believe you have told any. I believe we can absolve you immediately of at least one of the crimes you stand accused of committing. It is quite obvious that by 'abducting' Tori Perrault, you were acting in her best interests and probably saved her life."

"Thank you," Two said.

"I'm afraid there are still two matters which require further debate amongst the council, so we must keep you here a while longer."

"What are they?"

"First, you've killed an elder vampire. Not just an elder, but an *Eresh-Chen*, the head of the American council, and one of the oldest vampires left on the planet. Whether or not this action should be punished is one of the topics up for debate."

"What's the punishment?"

"There is only one punishment for most of our laws, Two. Surely you can guess what it is," Malik said.

"Surely I can," Two said, rolling her eyes. She was tired and unimpressed with all of this formality. If they meant to kill her, she thought about saying, then why not just fucking do it?

"The second matter is your stated wish to return to vampirism. This *is* still your desire, is it not?"

"Yes, definitely. I ... think I might have a potential patron."

Two glanced at Naomi for a moment, feeling oddly nervous. A faint color rose in the vampire girl's cheeks, but she smiled.

"If it comes to that, I would be happy to stand as her patron," Naomi said. "We have not known each other long, but I trust Theroen's judgment and my own."

"You've gotten ahead of yourself," the woman from earlier, Leonore, said. "There is much still to debate, and not all of us share the Ashayt line's natural sympathies."

Malik nodded. "We must discuss this. Two is *Eresh-Chen*, and that makes an already delicate matter even more difficult. It would be easier if any previous *Eresh-Chen* survived and could give their permission, but to our knowledge there are none. Most of us had not yet been born when Abraham was turned, and his matron killed herself not long after. It will not be an easy choice to allow Naomi to make Two an Ashayt, and so end the *Eresh-Chen* bloodline."

Stephen stirred, muttering something under his breath.

"What was that, Stephen?" Malik asked, not trying to hide his distaste.

"The *Eresh-Chen* bloodline is dead already," Stephen said. "Can you not see that? If you kill her, it's dead. If she becomes fledgling to another vampire, even another Eresh, it's dead. Even if you turn her away and force her to live out her life as a human, it's *still* dead. Theroen's blood was in her, yes, but not for long enough. She is not *Eresh-Chen*. Not anymore. Theroen was the last of that line."

"And he's dead," Two said. "Dead and buried. Was it ... did the council burn the mansion? You did, didn't you?"

Malik nodded. "We left his body where it lay and burned the mansion. Whether the flames reached him or not, I cannot say. The land has not been redeveloped, and never will be. It will be owned by the council forever and never disturbed."

"Good," Two said.

Stephen stepped forward and looked at the council members. "There are some on this council who do not like me, and I certainly return the feeling. I make no secret of that, and to be honest, care very little. Yet there is no one here who can accuse me of disloyalty to the council, its laws, or my fellow vampires. I say this now: Two is guilty of no crime, and to convict her would be a travesty. She's earned the right to become Naomi's fledgling, if that is what she wishes. She's done us a *favor*, eliminating one of the greatest evils our kind has ever seen. It seems to me the very least of repayment that we do her one back."

"You exaggerate, Stephen," Leonore said. Her voice held an unimpressed, don't-be-so-dramatic tone that made Two want to reach out and smack her.

Stephen whirled to face her. "It will do you no good, you power-hungry bitch, to continue kissing Abraham's arse. He's dead and burned."

"How dare—" Leonore began. She was halfway to her feet when Naomi's voice overrode her.

"Kindly respect the council members, Stephen," she said. "All of them."

"No, but I'll not antagonize them further, at least," Stephen replied. "You have my opinion, which is why you asked me to come here. Go and have your debate. Get it over with, so that I might salvage something of this night."

"Reasonable advice if, as always, poorly presented," Malik said. "Two, we thank you for the information you have provided. We ask that you wait out here with Stephen while the council deliberates."

Two resisted the urge to make a sarcastic remark and instead nodded, smiled, turned, and made her way from the podium.

"The rest of you," Malik said, "should take a few minutes to freshen your drinks, and then make your way to the west meeting room."

The council left their seats and began to mill around the drink table near the rear of the cathedral. Naomi stopped for a moment by Two and Stephen before joining them.

"You did well," she said to Two. "It is a hard story to tell, and you gave as much detail as you could have. You handled yourself very well, and I have little doubt that a majority of the council will find you innocent. Abraham was not loved."

"Is a majority enough?" Two asked.

"Oh, yes. The vote need not be unanimous."

"What if you're wrong?"

Naomi bit her lower lip, considering this.

"There's no way out now, right? Not even if you wanted to help me, and go against them."

Naomi shook her head, glanced at Stephen, and said, "No. But I ... I would try. If they find you guilty, then they're wrong. I knew Theroen. I *know* you're not lying. I've spent all of these years believing that any evil the council may have performed was due to Abraham's influence. If they make the decision to kill you, then they have failed my trust. I will try to take you from here, and to stop me they ... they will have to kill me, too."

"This could be an interesting night indeed," said Stephen.

"What about you?" Two asked him.

"I'd fight just to fight, so I'll certainly fight for Naomi. She knows that. We might even convince a few others to join us but likely not enough. If it comes to combat, we will die ... but it will be entertaining, and I promise you I'll take Leonore with me."

"You will not lose this trial," Naomi said.

"Good," Two said. "Go make sure I don't. I think we have a lot of things to talk about after you clear my name."

Naomi smiled, nodded, and left.

* * *

"Two Ashley Majors, you stand before this council accused of breaking one of our oldest laws. The punishment for this offense, should you be found guilty, is death."

Malik looked around the room, and Two had time to wonder whom all of this drama was supposed to benefit. If they thought it would impress her, they were wrong. She could barely summon the energy to be concerned. She was exhausted. Shellshocked. Weak and tired from months of malnutrition, days of hope, and hours of nervous waiting. The emotional pain from having to relive her experiences with Theroen had not helped.

Two had tried to read Naomi's expression when the council members had, after nearly two hours of deliberation, returned to the room. Naomi had given her a smile, but her eyes had been sad. Two didn't know how to interpret that.

She had spent the time during the debate talking with Stephen, learning as much as she could about the various council members. Malik had moved to North America centuries ago, only a short time after the Europeans had begun colonizing the continent. When Abraham had approached him about establishing an American council, he had been receptive, though Abraham's reputation for cruelty and power-mongering had been known for more than a millennium. Malik had believed that the good of an organized vampire society would outweigh any evil that Abraham might perpetrate. For the most part, even Stephen had to admit, this had been true.

Leonore was an Eresh vampire, and considered herself to be above most of the rest of the council despite her relative youth. At one hundred and twenty-six years, she was older only than her apprentice and the two Burilgi, who had fought in World War II before being attacked and turned by a Polish vampire. Leonore had been Abraham's apprentice in the last few years of his life, and she had openly approved of his methods and philosophies. Abraham scared her – he scared everyone on the council – but Stephen knew that Abraham also excited her.

Two could understand that feeling, as horrible as it was to admit. When Abraham had touched her, that first night, she had felt a raw lust that was overwhelming, dwarfing even what she had felt for Theroen. When his teeth had actually pierced her neck, she had nearly blacked out both from pain and from the orgasm that had seemed to run, twisting and clenching, through her entire body. She could only imagine how exciting Abraham's presence might be to a person who didn't thoroughly and instinctively revile him.

Two was looking at Leonore now, trying to judge her expression. Was the vampire angry? That would indicate good things for Two. Before she had time to make a determination, however, the council had taken their seats and Malik had begun making his pronouncement.

"Is there anything else you wish to speak of before I deliver our verdict on this charge?" Malik asked her.

Two shook her head. "You know everything. If there's anything else, I've forgotten it. It was ... it was a chaotic few weeks."

Malik nodded and then, to Two's surprise, smiled.

"Two Ashley Majors, the council has voted, and we have found you not guilty. We believe that though you took the life of an elder vampire, and though you admit to doing so with full malicious intent, that you were acting to the benefit of vampires everywhere. Abraham's destruction is believed by most to be a boon to the entire world, and we have no intention of destroying the person who did us this service. You may go from this place in peace."

Two felt her legs go weak and, for a moment, feared she might collapse. She bit down on her tongue, nearly hard enough to draw blood, and drew in a great breath of air. Her entire body seemed to be unwinding, though she had not felt it tensing up. She hadn't known her own fear until she had seen that smile. In that moment, she had not been able to tell if he was about to release her, or condemn her to death.

"Thank you," she said finally. "I ... I don't ... thank you."

"Let her sit down," Stephen said from somewhere to her left. "For Christ's sake, are you people idiots? She's going to pass out. Look at her."

"I'm OK," Two croaked, but even as she said it, she realized that it was a lie, and without embarrassment she sat down on the floor, put her head in her hands, and began to take deep breaths. After perhaps half a minute she felt better, and looked up at Malik.

"Can I be a vampire again? Is ... is that OK?"

At this, Malik frowned. He looked frustrated and concerned but, to Two's relief, not angry.

"We were ... unable to come to a conclusion," he said.

"What the fuck does *that* mean?" Stephen snarled.

"Stephen, please ..." Naomi's voice was sad, but Two heard in it both resignation and hope. "Just let him finish."

Malik continued. "We do not feel that it is within the rights of the American council to grant your wish, Two. We cannot say that it is acceptable for a vampire, even one so esteemed as Naomi, to take you as a fledgling. It is a decision we do not feel equipped to make."

Two felt the old, familiar touches of despair at the back of her mind. She tried to shake them off, and asked, "So ... what now?"

"If you are sure that you truly wish to become a vampire again, then we recommend that you travel to Europe and petition the council there. They have more experience with interpreting our laws, and we feel confident that they will be able to come to a conclusion in this matter."

It took Two a moment to process this. At last, she said, "You want me to go to Europe?"

Malik nodded. "London, specifically."

"But ... I've only ever been to one other *state*. I don't know anything about London. How will I know where to go?"

"You will not be alone," Naomi said, her voice gentle.

"Oh, for Jesus's sake ... I ... this is ..." Stephen seemed nearly apoplectic. He struggled to bring himself under control and finally succeeded, sighing.

"Fine," he said. "Add me to the list of companions. I'm seeing this through, now, if for no other reason than to alert the European council that their American counterpart is made up of indecisive ninnies."

"Your opinion has been duly noted, Stephen," Malik said, his voice dry.

Two coughed out a small laugh and pulled herself to her feet, turning to face the council.

"I, uh … I know that some of you would rather I was dead. I can only apologize for breaking your laws and thank those of you who voted to let me live. I was only doing what I had to do. I'll go now. I don't want to bother anyone, anymore. I don't want to cause trouble, or hurt anyone, or … or …" Two held her hands open in a gesture of apology. "I don't have the words."

Naomi stirred, seemed about to stand up, then said to Malik, "Can we adjourn this meeting, please? I'd like to take Two home now. I think she's been through enough."

Malik nodded. "This council meeting has come to a conclusion. Thank you all for attending on this most important night, and thank you, Two, for sharing your story with us. We have learned a great deal."

The vampires stood and began to file out, murmuring among themselves. Two made her way over to Stephen, who favored her with a look that was both sympathetic and enraged at the same time. She nodded, gave him a wan smile, leaned against the wall. Eventually, all of the vampires had left except Stephen, Naomi, Jakob and Sasha.

"We both voted for you," Jakob told her as they made their way toward the front of the building. "That is no small thing. Sasha in particular is not fond of humans."

"She is not truly a human," Sasha said. "She is, or was, *Eresh-Chen*. In either case, her actions against Abraham have more than proven her worth."

"Thank you both," Two said, the first words she had spoken since the council's dismissal.

"What would you like to do now, Two?" Naomi asked. There was deep concern in her voice. Two looked up at the vampire girl and gave her a tired, sad smile.

"I want to go home," she said. "To your home, I mean. I … want to lie down in bed, and think about Theroen, and probably cry for a while. I don't want to do that here."

Naomi seemed about to say something, stopped herself, and instead said only, "Yes, we'll take you home."

Two did not want to weep in front of the others, and so she settled for a kind of mute despair, walking with her companions to the waiting car in silence. She sat, leaning against the door with her eyes wide, and stared out at the city in which she had lived her entire life as it flashed by her. She wondered when, if ever, this quest would end.

CHAPTER XIII

Last News

"Oh, don't!" Sarah snarled beneath him. "Not yet. Fuck me!"

The need in her voice was bringing Rhes perilously close to disobeying her command, and he thrust hard against her, enveloped by liquid warmth, trying to hold on. She bit into the skin of his shoulder, and the pain of it helped bring him back from the edge.

Pleasant and quiet and composed most of the time, Sarah became someone else in bed. He didn't mind; both women appealed to him. He loved the sweet, rational, erudite Sarah who liked to discuss Tolstoy and listen to National Public Radio. He also loved the writhing, sweating woman below him, her fingers hooked into his back, legs wrapped around him, growling profanity into his ear.

Rhes managed to last long enough to feel her arms tighten, to hear her gasp "come with me" into his ear. The shaky tone of her voice excited him, sent him over the edge. He strained against her, moaned into the pillow, bit lightly into the muscles between her neck and shoulder as his own orgasm ran its course.

When they were done, they rolled, still joined together, lying on their sides and kissing. Sarah ran her fingers along his chest, shifted her hips slightly, and laughed as Rhes gasped. She enjoyed him like this, he thought, in these last few moments of hypersensitivity, still half-erect and not yet wanting to leave that warmth and wet.

Sarah reached into the nightstand behind her, found a cloth, used it to keep things clean as she slid herself apart from Rhes. She nestled against him, her skin hot and slick, and gave a contented sigh. Rhes ran his fingers along the skin of her back, drifting toward sleep.

"Did you talk to Sid?" Sarah asked after a time.

"Yeah. He knew what it was about as soon as I asked for the meeting. Said he'd been waiting for me to come around. Actually, he was surprised you hadn't made me do it sooner."

Sarah laughed, and said, "Good. Things will be back to normal soon."

"Yup."

"Then we'll get married."

"Yup."

"And adopt Molly."

"Yup." Rhes was falling asleep.

Sarah giggled. "Then we can make dozens of babies!"

"Dozens, huh?" Rhes mumbled.

"Dozens. Do you think we'll hear about Two soon?"

At this, Rhes seemed to wake up a bit. "Not sure, baby. I suppose Jakob will contact us. Or maybe Two. Who knows? I'm half-convinced she'll show up as a vampire and try to takes us with her. Make us one of them."

"Would you go with her?"

"No way. Not a chance."

"Why?"

Rhes contemplated this question, unsure how to put his feelings into words. Finally he said, "I think you know the path your life is supposed to take, once you find it. I'm not saying that Two's on the wrong path. I think she's probably doing what's right for her."

"But it's not for you," Sarah said.

"No. It's not for me. I want to be here, with you and Molly … and our dozens of babies."

"You're not interested in living forever?"

Rhes propped himself up on one arm, smoothed a lock of hair away from Sarah's forehead, and said, "How many vampires did Two meet that lived forever?"

"None," Sarah conceded.

"How many does she know that spent their last days surrounded by people they loved, able to reflect on their lives, proud of who they were and what they'd accomplished?"

"None."

"Yeah. I'm a simple person, hon. I want what my father has. What my grandfather had. A wife, a family, kids I can be proud of. It's not like my grandfather *wanted* to go ... no one does. But when he went, he knew exactly what he was leaving behind. That's what I want. I have no interest in getting stabbed with a table leg, killed by my own father, burned alive, or decapitated."

Sarah grinned, kissed his shoulder, wrapped his arm up in hers. "I love you, Rhes. Goodnight."

"'Night, baby. I love you, too."

While he slept, Rhes dreamt of his family. He dreamt of the house they would have, the rooms they would gather in, the things they would do together. Inside that house, it was happy and warm. Outside, though, dark things fluttered just beyond the edge of the light.

* * *

Sarah answered the phone on the third ring, trying not to curse at the pain running through the toe that she had just stubbed on the edge of the couch. Instead, she gritted her teeth and, keeping most of the exasperation out of her voice, said, "Hello?"

"Sarah Thompson?"

"Sarah Taylor ... but close enough." Sarah smiled, tracing the pad of her thumb over the band that now encircled her left ring finger.

"Ah, Taylor, that's right. This is Jakob."

"I know. Your accent is pretty unique."

"The country I was born in no longer exists. I hope you are well. We have made headway with your issues."

"We're fine here, thanks. What's the news?"

"The Burilgi have agreed that the attack on you and your boyfriend was simply poor timing and are willing to let bygones be bygones. They are less than thrilled, of course, that I was forced to kill three of their number, but they understand that you were not at fault."

"Well, that's good. So we can go back to living our lives, now?"

"Yes, I believe you can. I will be removing my guards slowly over the next few days, but I don't anticipate that you will be troubled any further."

"Good. Thank you."

"I am sorry that you had to become involved in this nonsense. I trust that you and Rhes will practice an appropriate level of discretion."

"We won't tell anyone that we were attacked by vampires, no. We'd just end up locked up in a psych ward somewhere, anyway."

Jakob chuckled. "Good. Discretion is always wise. You may be contacted at some point in the future, but so long as you've told no one of this matter, you can expect any such contact to be friendly. I would imagine you will want to know, for example, of your friend Two's activities."

"Yes, very much so. Have you heard from her?"

"I have. I spoke with her last night, in fact."

"How is she?"

Jakob paused, and then said, "Less happy than she would have liked, but things went well over all. She is still alive, at any rate."

Sarah gave an incredulous laugh. "Well, that's good."

"Two has been fully exonerated and is preparing to go to Europe."

"What for?"

"She is ... not satisfied with her present life."

Well, duh, Sarah thought. Out loud, she said, "Yes ... we noticed."

"She has petitioned to be allowed to join our ranks again."

"No surprise there."

"Unfortunately, the council is uncomfortable granting this request. It's complicated. The European council is more equipped to make a decision."

"Oh. Well ... when will she know?"

Jakob sighed. "I am afraid I do not know. The European council meets infrequently, and I'm not entirely sure when the next meeting will be. It could be a year, perhaps more."

"A year? Can she at least call us?"

"We've asked her not to. It's ... we don't want to give the Burilgi any excuse to trouble you further."

"Oh. Fantastic ..." Sarah bit her lower lip. "Jakob, are we ever going to see Two again?"

"I'm afraid I have no idea. I apologize. Even if she is granted her wish, you may not *want* to see her. It is often difficult for humans to accept our kind."

"She's our friend. We'll deal with it."

"I am sure you would try your best. For the time being, all I can do is leave you in peace, and promise to be in touch when I know more."

"I guess that's all I can really ask for," Sarah said. "Thank you for your help, Jakob. Rhes and I know we owe you our lives."

Jakob laughed. "There is no debt. It was an honor to defend you and an enjoyable battle. I haven't had the chance to fight to the death in some time."

I'm never going to understand these people, Sarah thought. *Blood and death and chopping each other up with machetes? I want this to be over.*

And so she decided to end it. "OK, then. Is there anything else?"

"Nothing at all. Goodbye, Sarah. Give my regards to Rhes."

"I will. Thanks again, and goodbye."

Sarah hung up the phone and, after a moment of consideration, went to tell Rhes the news.

CHAPTER XIV

Travel Plans

"Two? Two ... we're here."

The car had stopped but Two, still staring out the window without really paying attention, hadn't noticed. She felt Naomi's gentle touch on her shoulder and stirred, nodding.

"OK, Naomi. Thanks."

"Are you all right?"

"She looks fantastic," Stephen said, his voice laced with sarcasm. He opened the door and slid out of the car.

"I'm alive," Two said. She knew it would be hard to tell from her tone if that was a positive or a negative, but wasn't sure herself which was the case.

"Yes, you are," Naomi said. She stepped from the cab, handed the driver a bill, and said, "Keep the change."

"You sure?" the driver asked, surprised.

"Yes. Come on, Two."

The driver made a low, impressed whistle and said, "Take your time, sweetheart. No rush."

Two opened the door, got out of the car, and stood next to Naomi and Stephen. The car rolled away, reached the corner, and turned left, disappearing out of sight. Two could hear the thudding of electronic music coming from *L'Obscurité* across the street. The air was cold and damp and spoke of rain.

No one spoke as they waited for the elevator, or as they rode up to Naomi's apartment. Finally, as the doors were sliding open, Two said, "It's OK guys. I'm not made of glass."

Naomi shrugged. "Everyone has moments in their life when they are fragile. It's been a long night."

They entered the apartment, and Two went first to the bathroom, a room that her companions had little use for. When she finished, she returned to the living room. Stephen was sitting on one couch, watching highlights from a football game. Naomi was sitting on the other, her head back, eyes closed. Two wandered into the kitchen, tossed a frozen dinner into the microwave, and turned it on. The machine hummed to life, and Two went to sit down.

Naomi opened her eyes and rolled her head to glance at Two, who had positioned herself at the opposite end of the couch, legs pulled up underneath her.

"Hungry?" she asked.

"Yeah. Did you ... eat?"

"Stephen and I went out earlier, while you were showering."

"Oh."

"Two, do you want ... is there anything you'd like to discuss?"

Two glanced at Stephen for a moment, and then said, "Not now."

"I will be gone as soon as this program ends," Stephen said without looking away from the television. "I wouldn't want to spoil your personal time, ladies."

"I'm sorry, Stephen," Two said. "No offense. It's just ..."

"That my brand of contribution is not what you're looking for at this time," Stephen finished for her. "I know. I do many things well, but sensitivity is not one of them. The way I make up for it is by knowing when not to stick around. No offense is taken."

Two nodded. The microwave beeped, and she stood to retrieve her dinner. She returned with it, sat down again, and began to eat, staring at the television without really watching it.

"This tastes like fucking cardboard," she remarked after a few bites.

Stephen laughed. "Perhaps you should try a different brand of frozen 'meal' ... and I use that term in the loosest possible sense."

"Your advice on food is somewhat suspect, Stephen, considering you've had naught but blood for three hundred years," Naomi told him.

"Yet, somehow, I have a hard time believing that any dinner one can purchase frozen, in a four-compartment plastic dish, is going to qualify as fine cuisine."

"He's got a point," Two said.

"Thank you."

"But I'm too lazy to bother with anything else."

"That I cannot help you with," Stephen said. He used the remote to shut off the television, and then stood. "Ladies, I have acquired tonight's football scores. My work here is done, and I'll bid you a good evening."

"Goodnight, Stephen," Naomi said. She had her eyes closed again, still leaning back against the couch.

"Later," Two said.

"Later indeed," Stephen replied, and made his way out of the apartment.

Two finished her meal, not talking, and Naomi didn't seem in a hurry to speak. After perhaps ten minutes of silence, the vampire glanced over at her.

"Is it too soon?"

Two shrugged. "Too soon for what, Naomi? To talk about the bullshit that went on tonight? No, now is fine."

"I'm sorry that the council couldn't grant you what it is that you want, Two. I argued your case as strongly as I could. Please believe me."

"I know. I believe you. I'm not angry at you, Naomi. It's just ..." Two sighed, stood, and looked out the window at the city, arms crossed.

"Just?" Naomi prompted.

"I feel like this is never going to end. It's so frustrating to finally find the place you belong and have it yanked away from you."

"I understand."

Two continued. "And now I can't even manage to get some new version of it. I don't know what being an Ashayt is going to be like, but it has to be better than this. It has to be better than waiting, and wondering, and getting my hopes up. Christ, what if they say 'no?' I almost wish I'd never run into you. At least before, I just didn't *care* anymore."

Naomi was quiet for a time, and when she spoke, her voice was subdued. "Do you mean that?"

Naomi's tone seemed to cut through Two's frustration. She turned to look at the vampire and, after a moment, made her way back to the couch, shaking her head.

"No, I don't mean that. I'm sorry, Naomi. I wasn't being very fair. I'm glad I met you. I'm even glad I met Stephen, believe it or not."

Naomi smiled. "He grows on you."

"I miss Theroen. I miss being with him, and seeing him smile, and hearing him talk, and listening to him breathe. I just miss *all* of it. Theroen ... what he gave me, it made me warm and happy and comfortable. Being with him made those feelings even stronger. Now it's all gone and I'm just tired and cold and empty. I hate it."

Naomi nodded.

"And now I'm going to have to go to London, where I thoroughly do not want to go, in order to petition a bunch of ancient people about being allowed back into their club. I'm sure *that's* going to go perfectly ... it's not like old, rich, powerful people are usually set in their ways or anything."

"It may not be like that," Naomi said. "The European council is ... not like the American council."

"Sorry if I don't get my hopes up."

"You're forgiven."

"Anyway, what happens when this is done?" Two asked, running a hand through her hair.

"I imagine that depends on the council's conclusion," Naomi said.

"Right, but if they say I can be a vampire again?"

"Then I'll gladly fulfill that request. Two, I ... you are someone that I think I could teach. Someone I could spend decades with. Someone that I ..." Naomi's voice trailed away.

"Someone you could what?" Two asked.

It was Naomi who stood this time, pacing back and forth, looking agitated. "Someone I feel should be a vampire! You are worthy, if you'll excuse my arrogance. So many people are brought in, especially amongst the Burilgi, who are so very *useless*. You are *Eresh-Chen*! You were chosen by Theroen, and it would be unlike him to make a mistake. I do not believe that he did."

"Dunno what you all see in me," Two said. "I'm just a junkie hooker. When Theroen met me, I was nothing. Garbage."

"I guarantee that you have never been garbage," Naomi said. "You don't understand, Two; it is because of where you've been and what you've done that Theroen chose you. You have remained strong in such terrible conditions. Think, Two, in every situation you've been in, what was the end result?"

"That I wind up miserable?" Two asked. She heard a shakiness in her voice, and was angry at it. *You're not allowed to start crying,* she told herself.

"That you triumph. You moved out of your house as nothing more than a child, and you survived for years. If not for random bad luck, you would be surviving still. You triumphed over Darren, over the heroin ..."

"Only because of Theroen."

"But *you* attracted him in the first place. Do you see?"

Two shrugged. "I guess."

"You triumphed over Abraham. You triumphed in your goal of bringing Tori home. You triumphed in your search for more vampires. Do you not think you will triumph in this latest quest?"

"I have no idea. Suppose I don't. Suppose the council says 'nope, sorry, ain't gonna happen' and forces me out the door. What then?"

Naomi looked out the window. "Then you adapt. You find another way to accomplish your goals. There are other vampires, in other lands. You could go to Australia, or even Asia. If it comes to that, there is nothing to stop you from going to these places."

"I'd have to leave everyone I know and love behind."

Naomi turned to look at her, a sad smile on her face. "When you make the change, you will leave those people behind regardless.

Your friends will age. They will die. You will not. It is unwise to stay too attached to humans."

"I don't generally worry about what's wise," Two said.

"I know. It's ... one of the things I like about you," Naomi conceded. She sat down on the couch again, next to Two, the warm feeling that she sometimes projected rolling off of her in waves. It was stronger now, perhaps, than it had ever been before. It was comforting, lulling.

Two sighed and said, "Are you doing this on purpose? Hypnotizing me? Filling me with happy vibes so I'll stop being depressed?"

Naomi looked surprised. She shook her head. "No, I ... what you're feeling isn't under my control. It happens to some Ashayt vampires. Lisette was able to control it, but she never had time to teach me. It is a manifestation of the fact that I care about you."

"It's nice. Warm. I've felt it before, but never this strong."

"I ... care about you very much."

Two opened her eyes, glanced over at Naomi. "Do you?"

When Naomi leaned forward and kissed her, it was not exactly unexpected, but Two was unable to prevent herself from going rigid for a moment. Naomi took this as a sign of displeasure and broke quickly away.

"I'm sorry, Two. I shouldn't have done that. I'm sorry."

"It's OK. I'm not angry," Two said.

"No?"

"No."

"You're sure?"

Two leaned her head back against the couch again, closed her eyes, sighed. "Naomi, I have no idea what I want. I know what you want. I already kinda guessed it, and now it's ... well, it's pretty much on the record. I just don't know what I want. I don't know how to feel. I'm numb."

"Your life has been very cold," Naomi said.

Two nodded. "Freezing."

Naomi leaned her head against Two's shoulder and spoke in a voice that was just above a whisper. "I would very much like to help make you warm."

Two put her hands over her face. "Oh, God, what's wrong with me?" she asked, her throat aching.

"There is nothing wrong with you." Naomi wrapped her arms around Two and pulled gently sideways, sliding into a reclining position against the arm of the couch. Two turned with the vampire girl, nestling against her. Naomi held her, saying nothing. Eventually the urge to weep passed, and Two took a deep and shuddering breath.

"Are you all right?" Naomi asked her.

"Yes. No. I don't … can we just …"

"Whatever you would like."

"Just stay like this. I'm tired and confused and sad, and I don't want to make a dumb mistake."

Naomi was playing with a lock of Two's hair. "Of course," she said.

"Thanks. I … I'll figure out what I'm feeling soon, I promise."

"There is no rush. We have plenty of time."

All the time in the world, Two's mind whispered, and she thought again of Theroen. For the first time in her life, she made a conscious effort to push his face from her mind. Closing her eyes, Two let herself drift, floating along the warm currents that Naomi was providing.

* * *

"I've booked three tickets to London," Naomi said, looking up from her laptop. She and Stephen were sitting on one couch, Two on the other.

Nearly twenty-four hours had passed since she and Two had lain together on the couch, and Naomi had made no further efforts to advance their relationship, had put no further pressure on Two. The previous night had ended with Two eventually getting up, thanking Naomi, and going to bed. She was no closer to determining how she felt, but at least Naomi didn't seem to be expecting any immediate answer.

"How do you guys deal with stuff like traveling?" Two asked. "I mean, what if it's light out when we arrive?"

"It's a bit of a pain in the arse," Stephen admitted. "Not so much for Naomi, since she handles the sunlight relatively well. If I absolutely *must* go out during the day, I can do it, but it's rather painful and it doesn't do wonders for my otherwise charming personality. Most of the time, I stop in Iceland and spend the day there, flying out again at night. Unlike most people, I rarely have to look for the cheapest or fastest option."

"That's exactly what I did," Naomi said. "We leave JFK airport at ten in the evening, and reach Reykjavik in the middle of the night. We stay in a hotel there, and then fly out of Iceland at night, and arrive in London before the sun rises."

"Nice," Two said.

"It's much better than the old days," Stephen agreed. "Booking passage on a ship, breaking into cabins at night to feed or just surviving on rats. Now the hardest thing is explaining to the flight attendants that even though you're flying in business class, you don't need or want the free meal."

"It's so weird to think that you guys were alive before airplanes."

"When I was born, America was still a vast, unexplored land filled with natives, save for a smattering of European settlements," Naomi said. "Reflecting on it does sometimes make one feel old."

"You look fucking spectacular for four hundred," Two said dryly. Stephen made a snorting sound.

"I came to the States in nineteen fifty-two," Naomi continued, ignoring them. "I had spent World War II moving from town to town in France, trying to kill as many Germans as I could without arousing too much suspicion. Once the war ended, I decided it was time for a change of scenery and came here. I met Stephen in nineteen sixty-eight. He used to wander around the city by himself, late at night, in dress clothes, hoping to get mugged so that he could beat the offending party half to death."

"Those were good times," Stephen said, smiling. "This city is so boring, now."

"You should spend some time where I grew up," Two said. "Still plenty of bad shit going down there."

"Yes, but then I'd have to go to Brooklyn."

Two laughed. "Typical Manhattan asshole. All right, so when do we go?"

"Friday night," Naomi said. "Two days."

"How long until we can see the council?" Two asked.

"That ... is a fine question," Stephen said. "They don't hold themselves to quite as rigid a schedule as the American council does, so it may be a while."

"OK, but how long are we talking?"

Stephen glanced at Naomi, who shrugged. He turned back to Two.

"I think they try to meet every year, if they can," he said.

"Oh my God," Two moaned, putting her head in her hands. "Are you fucking serious?"

"This is why I was none too pleased with the American council's decision," Stephen told her.

"It won't be so bad," Naomi said. "London is a wonderful city, and perhaps we can take some trips to other parts of Europe while we're there. I will have to spend some time making inroads with the council, but I don't think it will be difficult to gain a meeting with them."

"Do you know any of them?" Two asked.

"Not well. I have been before the European council before, but it was centuries ago. I think two of the members have since been replaced."

"One of them for certain ... unless his ashes stood up and started talking," Stephen said.

Two rolled her eyes. "You guys have such peaceful lives."

"Faegan went by choice," Naomi said. "He was tired and in pain."

"Emotional pain," Stephen elaborated. "Not real pain."

"That is the most ridiculous thing you've said in some time," Naomi said, a touch of disgust in her voice. "The woman he loved wouldn't let him turn her. He spent seventy years living with her, begging her to reconsider. When she finally died ... I've never seen a man so devastated. He was like a shell. You don't think that's pain?"

Stephen shrugged. "Aye, terrible, I'm sure. I once saw a man get his arm crushed by a morning star. Took the whole bottom half

... he was left with this jagged nub of bone jutting out of a pile of ground meat, a big flap of skin swaying below it, blood spraying everywhere. He was begging for someone to kill him."

Naomi sighed, shaking her head and turning back to her laptop. "You're an idiot."

Stephen grinned, leaning back on the couch and putting his feet on the coffee table. Naomi glanced with distaste at this, but chose not to say anything. Two watched without comment, amused. Stephen seemed to know all of Naomi's buttons, and took no small amount of pleasure in pushing them. Two wasn't sure yet what it was Naomi got out of their relationship, but she suspected that below the refined, political façade there was a part of Naomi that deeply appreciated Stephen's irreverence and disdain for protocol.

"I'm booking a hotel for us in London," Naomi said, glancing at Two. "We'll get a flat eventually, but it'll take a week or two. Do you mind sharing a room with me? There are two beds."

"No, that's fine. I don't mind."

"Good. We can just get a two-bedroom suite."

"You mean I'm not invited to share the room, too?" Stephen asked in mock surprise.

Naomi rolled her eyes. "Don't you have a fight to attend?"

"Not just yet," Stephen said. "Another hour and I head for the Upper West Side. Then you ladies can get to your knitting, or ... whatever it is you do when I'm not around."

Two glanced at Naomi, but the vampire girl appeared to be intently involved in whatever was on her laptop screen. Two didn't think Naomi had told Stephen about the previous night, or about her feelings for Two, but she wondered if Stephen had not perhaps guessed some of it for himself.

Naomi closed her laptop, stretched, looked at Two.

"Flights are booked, hotels in Reykjavik and London are booked, and I've sent out an initial email to the council requesting their attention. I'm afraid that is all I can do for tonight."

"That's plenty, Naomi, thanks," Two said. "Is there anything I can do to help?"

Naomi shook her head. "Just promise you won't go running off to Australia until we hear their decision."

Two blew air upward, shaking her head slightly, but after a moment she sighed and said, "OK, I guess that's reasonable."

"Is there anything you would like to do in New York before we leave?" Naomi asked. "We will likely be in Europe for some time."

Two shrugged. "My house got busted up by vampires, I'm not allowed to see my friends, and there aren't any movies playing that I care about. I think I'm good."

Naomi smiled, nodded, glanced at Stephen. He gave her a dismissive wave.

"We're fine," he said. "No need to mother us. Besides, we all know you'll want to go to your club a last few times, say goodbye to all of your little friends. If you would, try not to alert the cultist to the fact that we're harboring an *Eresh-Chen*?"

"I have never given Thomas any information on our activities," Naomi said.

"Then all is well."

Naomi looked over at Two. "Would you like to go to *L'Obscurité?*" she asked.

"Sure, I could use a drink."

As they prepared to leave, Two thought of London, and what it would be like to live there for a year. Would she love it? Hate it? Not care? She had no idea, knew only that she was glad to be going with Naomi and Stephen. Two had spent too many long months alone. She was happy, now, to be with friends who would help her along this journey.

She wished that she could see Rhes and Sarah one last time, to apologize for the way she'd treated them, but that couldn't happen. She would have to hope that they understood and didn't hate her for it. When this was over, when she was a vampire again, then she would go to see them and make things right. Until then, it would be best if she remained focused on the European council and the things she might be able to say to them that would sway their decision.

Thinking of this, and of her impending return to vampire life, Two stood at the door waiting for Naomi. When the vampire girl was ready, she led the way, and as had been the case for some weeks now, Two followed.

INTERLUDE

"What is your name?"

She hears the voice, but does not open her eyes. There is a hint of smoke in the air. Incense. It has been burned here within the past two days. This detail is unimportant, but she notices it anyway. She notices everything.

If she had a name once, she no longer remembers it, and so she gives the answer that she knows the owner of the voice wishes to hear.

"I have no name."

The air in the room is cool against her skin but not cold. She has knelt here in this room before, naked, eyes closed, for hours at a time in conditions of every type. Sometimes the ceiling is opened and rain pours in on her. Sometimes the vents at the base of the wall blow freezing air in around her. Sometimes the room is heated to such levels that the floor singes her knees and the small pads of her toes. She has endured all of this without complaint.

"Why are you here?" the voice asks her, and this she remembers.

"I am here to learn."

She doesn't flinch when the needle enters her skin where her neck meets her shoulder, nor at the sudden burning as the liquid is injected. The sensation spreads out, becomes less acute, runs hot through her entire body. Colors swirl behind her eyelids. Her nipples grow tight and hard for a moment, the digits of her hands and feet going numb. There is a taste like heated copper at the back of her mouth. This is the only absolute during her daily visits to this room: the questions and the needle.

This is not something she must endure. She knows this because she has been told, and slowly she is coming to understand. This is something she must accept. This is something she must embrace.

"Who are your enemies?"

She takes a breath, and the air flows cool inside her burning body. "The enemies of my master are my enemies."

Her heart is pounding now, her breathing ragged. The injection makes the edges of her mind fuzzy, makes it difficult to think but easier to sense. She feels a bead of sweat roll down her forehead, pausing at her eyebrow and falling to land on her thigh. It is difficult to concentrate on anything else, but still the voice persists.

"Who is your master?"

Her hands move as if on their own, fingers interlocking to form a symbol, the gesture already ingrained within her. It is the symbol of all that they are. She can no longer remember how to form words but knows she must answer. When she speaks, it is as if someone else is controlling her lips and tongue.

"The Emperor of the Sun is my master," she says. "The Emperor brings light to scour the world of darkness. The Emperor brings power to his children and death to his enemies. With the sword in his right hand, the Emperor cleaves through the darkness. With the staff in his left hand, he sweeps away those who stand before him. All those who would oppose him are vanquished. All those that give him their allegiance are rewarded. Those who do his work will bask forever in his light."

"Will you swear to serve your Emperor and do his work?"

"I am his to command, always and forever. I am the right hand of the Emperor. I am the blade with which he will strike down his enemies."

"Name these enemies."

Even the drug is not enough to dull the ache in her soul, though she cannot remember the reason for this pain. It throbs within her like a decaying tooth, and she knows that only blood and death will satisfy it.

"Vampires," her mouth says, and she knows that it is the truth. "Those who walk by night and drink the blood of the Emperor's children. Those who would destroy us all. Vampires are my Emperor's enemies, and there can be no rest while any still live."

There is a pause, and when the voice comes again, it is pleased.

"Good. Meditate on this."

"As you command."

She leans back on the balls of her feet and lets the drug take over at last, a red haze settling behind her eyelids. The red reminds her of blood, and blood reminds her of vengeance. Somewhere, in the furthest and dimmest recesses of her mind, there is a brief flash of memory. Blood on the floor ... not red, but black in the early morning light. Her jaw tightens, and then the vision is gone.

All that remains is her hate.

Christopher Buecheler

PART III

CHAPTER XV

Disquieting News

"They're tired of waiting. If the council isn't going to take action on this, then the Burilgi are going to take matters into their own hands."

Jakob rested his fingers against his brow. Vampires did not get headaches (or at least he never had), but it seemed to him that one was brewing nonetheless.

He was tired. This came as something of a surprise to Jakob, who was quite capable of spending an entire evening in athletic competition without reaching the point of exhaustion. This fatigue was mental. Abraham had kept the council running during his many long years at its head, but Malik was proving incapable of doing the same. As a result, Jakob had become more and more involved in the past months, trying to help maintain order amidst an increasing swell of grudges, petty vendettas, and legitimate concerns.

Naomi would have been better at it than he was. Much better, most likely, and though there were older members of the council, Jakob would gladly have supported her in an attempt to seize control. The problem was that Naomi had been out of the country for more than a year.

Just now he was sitting with Malik in a private room at the back of the council's cathedral, meeting with Lewis, one of the two Burilgi representatives. The bi-weekly council meeting was still two hours away, but Lewis had requested an early, private session.

Now he was waiting for an answer to his ultimatum, and Jakob didn't have one. Malik looked shocked by Lewis's statement and, Jakob had to admit, more than a little frightened. Jakob pitied the man. Malik had spent all of his time on the council serving under Abraham, who had ruled with an iron fist. Many complaints could be made about Abraham's time as leader, and Jakob had made more than a few of his own, but outbursts like Lewis's never would have happened before; the young Burilgi would never even have considered it. Threatening Abraham in even the most minor of ways would have led only to a swift and inexorable death.

"Lewis," Jakob said. "I don't know what it is you want me to tell you ..."

"You could start by telling me that you're going to do something. *Anything*. My people are being abducted. There's no point in denying it anymore."

Jakob, who had seen the reports himself, nodded.

"This is the beginning of the war," Lewis said. "Don't ask me to sit here and debate with you while the Children are out there kidnapping vampires."

"You don't know for sure that it's the Children ..."

Lewis made an exasperated noise and rolled his eyes, but otherwise refused to respond to that. He sat, staring at Jakob, not speaking. At last, Jakob continued.

"The latest reports are confused. We're not sure what to make of them."

"Quit fucking playing dumb with me!" Lewis snarled. "I'm not an idiot. I know what you all think of me. You're the nobles, I'm the commoner. That's never going to change, so whatever, I'll be a fucking commoner and tell things like they are instead of hiding behind formality and façade. That work for you, *Jake?*"

"By all means," Jakob said, trying and mostly succeeding to keep the sarcasm out of his voice. "Enlighten us."

"Something has mobilized the Children," Lewis continued. "Some spark has lit a fire under their asses, and they're rolling through Burilgi like a thresher in a field. Twenty-five missing so far, and twelve of those happened just in the last week. There was a series of coordinated strikes across three different time zones within fifteen minutes of each other. There was one witness ..."

"I had not heard about this," Jakob said, tilting his head.

"Why am I not surprised? I left the report with Malik. Maybe he can explain why he didn't get around to telling you."

Malik coughed. "Yes, the witness ... a little boy who should never have been turned in the first place."

"I'm not making excuses for his sire," Lewis said. "I can't control every Burilgi, particularly not neurotic pedophiles who insist on making slaves out of children. If it's any consolation, the sire is one of the missing."

"I take no consolation in what may be happening to your people," Malik said. "Just don't ask me to take the ramblings of an abused child seriously."

"Malik," Jakob said, his voice pitched low and respectful, "I would like to hear what Lewis has to say. Please let him continue."

Malik glanced at Jakob with disapproval, but nodded silently.

"The kid was half-delirious when we found him," Lewis said. "He'd been hiding behind the furnace in the basement for *three days*, starving but too scared to leave. He said that a group of at least five humans had broken into the house and used silver and garlic to round up the people who lived there. Said that one of them was a female, blonde hair, who 'moved like a vampire' as she rounded them up. That sound familiar to anyone?"

There was silence now in the office as even Jakob found himself at a loss for words. The conclusion was obvious and, in a way, beautiful in both its simplicity and its irony.

"Right," Lewis continued. "I thought so. It's the daughter. The one you pretended not to know anything about when the *Eresh-Chen* came through here last year. You guys left a dangerous weapon lying around, lost track of it, and now it's being used against us. The Children have her, and they're using her to murder my people."

"You have no proof of that," Malik said, but his voice was wavering, and he refused to meet Lewis's gaze.

"Oh, for God's sake, think about it!" Lewis shouted. "What else would they be doing with their prisoners? Storing them up to trade in for a better model of vampire? They are training for war!"

"Lewis, are you sure of this?" Jakob asked.

"Her parents are dead. She's been missing for months. All the trackers you sent came up empty-handed. Now, all of a sudden, there's some blonde chick, super-fast and super-strong, out there rounding up Burilgi. Put the fucking pieces together."

Jakob had already done so, had done it as soon as Lewis had recounted the child witness's story, and come to the same conclusion. It didn't matter; he couldn't act without the permission of the council.

"What do you suggest we do?" he asked.

"Wipe them out. Do it now, and do it completely. We've known about this cult for decades ... maybe centuries. We've allowed them to persist because they didn't seem to pose any real threat. Now they have a weapon, and she's leading their troops. These are just preliminary strikes, to gauge our reaction and thin the herd a bit. They expect you to sit on your ass and do nothing, because who gives a shit about a few Burilgi?"

"Unless someone on this council is a spy, and I doubt that very much, they have no idea how we might be reacting," Malik said.

"It doesn't matter. All they know is what they can see, and so far I'm sure they've been thrilled. They took *twelve people* and we're doing nothing. I can't even get you guys to take me seriously."

"The council must debate," Malik said. "This is how things are done."

"We should've called an emergency meeting last week," Jakob muttered, half to himself. Malik glared at him.

"Thank you," Lewis said. "Finally."

"Don't misunderstand me," Jakob said. "I support the council completely and will abide by whatever decision it makes. I may not agree with every conclusion, but I've lived for over four hundred years under our laws, and they've served me well."

"I understand that," Lewis said. "But things have changed. This isn't the old days."

"No doubt you'd prefer to have Abraham back?" Malik asked, his voice laced with disgust.

"At least then something might get *done* around here," Lewis shot back.

"Gentlemen," Jakob said, cutting off whatever retort Malik had been preparing. "Let's not resort to sniping at each other. What is different from the 'old days,' Lewis?"

"In the old days, for one thing, Richard would be here talking with me. You might have noticed that he's not around."

"I must admit some curiosity in that matter," Jakob said.

"He's with Aros."

Malik made a snarling noise and said, "I don't ever want to hear that name spoken in this building again."

Lewis gave him an angry grin. "Yeah ... ignore it and it'll go away, right, Malik? It doesn't work like that. You can't hide the past by not talking about it. God knows you've been trying, but all that's doing is allowing him to grow stronger every year."

"Aros has done nothing in direct violation of any major laws," Jakob said. "He's done nothing to challenge us, and Abraham seemed ... surprisingly reticent to simply wipe him and his followers out."

Lewis shrugged. "Maybe they had an arrangement. It doesn't matter. Do you know how many Burilgi have gone over to his side now? His people dwarf your numbers. I know we're not as strong as the Ay'Araf, or even Ashayt, but you haven't seen what I've seen. You don't know what he's doing."

Jakob leaned over the desk, looking carefully at Lewis. "What do you know?"

"Not much. Not everything, anyway ... he doesn't share much with Richard and me. He knows that we're still council members. The reason Richard's with him right now is to try and calm him down, to keep him from using his army to attack the Children."

"You exaggerate," Malik said. "I'm certain he has many Burilgi supporters, but really, Lewis ... I would think a veteran of World War II would know not to throw around the term 'army' so lightly."

Lewis turned toward Malik, a grim smile on his face. "You're right. I'm a military man, and I know my terms. He doesn't have an army, not by human standards. What he has is something between a battalion and a brigade. Do you know what that means, Malik? It means that if he wants to, Aros can point more than a two thousand Burilgi at whatever enemy he chooses. If he decides to go after the Children, how exactly are you going to stop him?"

Jakob felt his eyes widening, and tried to keep from looking too obviously shocked. "Two thousand?"

"At an absolute minimum. How many of you are there, Jakob? If you combine all of the Ay'Araf, Ashayt, and Eresh in this country, what number do you get?"

"Not two thousand," Jakob replied.

"No. There's what … twenty Eresh, a hundred Ashayt, and maybe five hundred Ay'Araf?"

Jakob, who thought those numbers might actually be optimistic, said nothing. Malik did the same.

"Yeah," Lewis said. "We know *you* can kill Burilgi, Jakob. I don't blame you for that … those assholes had it coming. But that was three of them. Can you kill ten at a time? Twenty? What about Sasha?"

"Are you threatening us?" Malik asked in a voice that was trying to sound unimpressed.

"I'm explaining that you should feel threatened. If you don't do something about the Children of the Sun, Aros is going to bring his army down on them. If you try to stop him, he'll bring them down on *you*. For all I know, he's planning on doing that anyway, at some point."

"Why did you not tell us of this sooner?" Malik asked.

"You didn't ask."

"Lewis …" Jakob began, and the Burilgi vampire whirled on him.

"I'm not a spy, Jakob, for either side! I'm not going to report to my 'superiors' every time Aros takes a piss, and I'm not going to sit here and be interrogated by you, or Malik, or anyone else about it."

Jakob held up his hands in a gesture of peace. "Lewis, please stay calm."

"When the Children send Abraham's daughter for Sasha, and Naomi, and Stephen, will you stay calm? When she takes them off somewhere to be murdered, will you just sit back and relax?"

"I ..." Jakob paused, unsure of how to respond, and found himself wishing not for the first time that Naomi would return from the errand that had taken her and Stephen to Europe.

"You won't be calm, but it'll be too late. I'm asking again, and this is really the last time ... if you value the status quo, then you need to do something. Richard and I can't hold Aros back for much longer. Quite frankly, every time another Burilgi disappears, we're that much less inclined to even try. I don't care who you have to convince, just do it quickly. Get your shit together and do something about this. Please."

With that, he gave them each a curt nod, turned, and walked out of the office.

* * *

Jakob was pacing up and down the Cathedral's central aisle, his feet making no sound on the heavy carpet of red and gold, pondering the meeting with Lewis and subsequent discussion with Malik. It was obvious that Malik did not really want the responsibility of sitting at the council's head, but it was equally obvious that he had no intention of giving up the prestige that came with the position.

The American council of vampires had grown arrogant and apathetic. They hated the Burilgi, for the most part, and Jakob suspected that most would secretly be pleased to hear about these abductions. The idea of raising a large group to go fight the Children of the Sun seemed improbable. The thought of obtaining enough support to take on Aros's growing ranks directly seemed completely absurd. Jakob supposed he could rally some of the Ay'Araf to the cause, if for no other reason than the promise of a fight, but would it be enough?

If the Children had really recruited Abraham's youngest daughter and were training her to be a killing machine, as Lewis claimed, then they were all in great danger. Malik was barely a competent leader in times of peace. In a time of war – Jakob shuddered to think about it. Malik was likely to bury his head in the sand and insist nothing was wrong until it was far too late.

What could be done? Jakob paced and thought, but no solution came to him. After a time the thud of the building's heavy front doors closing broke his reverie. He glanced up and saw Richard, the other Burilgi council member, rounding the corner. The look on the man's face said that whatever news he carried, it was something far from good.

Wonderful, Jakob thought. *There must have been more abductions.*

"Jakob! Hey, Jakob ... you've got to listen to me." Richard rushed up and stopped in front of him, visibly agitated.

"Certainly. Calm down, Richard, and tell me what's causing you such distress."

"There's not a lot of time. Look, you've gotta go. Now."

"Go where? To see the site of the abductions myself?"

Richard looked shocked. "Have more people been taken?"

Jakob paused, eyes narrowing. "I assumed that was your news. Apparently, I was wrong. What troubles you, Richard?"

"It's Aros. He ... I ... did Lewis explain where I was this evening?"

"Yes. Has Aros mobilized his fighters?"

"No. I mean, not yet. He's going after someone though. Two people. You know them. He ... I wasn't supposed to hear this, and normally Lewis and I have a 'no spying' policy ..."

"I'd heard," Jakob muttered.

"This time, though, it's too big. I can't protect him on this. He wants the girl. Two. He wants her."

"He's going to have a hard time even locating her, let alone taking her from Naomi and Stephen," Jakob said.

"No, you don't understand. He's not going after *her*. He's going after the other two ... the ones you rescued at her apartment."

Jakob felt a jolt of surprise run through him. The man and the woman that he had saved, yes. He fished in his mind for their names and came up with them. "Rhes and Sarah."

"Yes."

"What in God's name does Aros want with them?"

"He's going to take them and hold them. He knows when the other one – Two – when she hears about it, she'll come to him. He's heard all about how impetuous she is."

"Richard, where did you hear this?" Jakob was already forming a plan of action in his head, but he wanted as much information as Richard could give him.

"We were in his office, and I was trying to calm him down over the last set of abductions, and his cell phone went off. He left the room to speak, but he didn't close the door all the way, and I could still hear what he was saying. It was someone alerting him that they'd found the two humans."

"Did he specifically say it was Rhes and Sarah?"

"He said they were friends of the fallen *Eresh-Chen*, and the ones who were at her apartment. Seems like a pretty safe bet." Richard ran a hand through his hair, concerned and frustrated. "I got out of there as soon as I could. This is the last thing we need. He's going to go fucking around with an *Eresh-Chen* while we're trying to deal with the Children? He's crazy."

"Indeed," Jakob said. "Do you know when he was planning on doing this?"

"I don't know, but considering how happy he was, I doubt it's going to be a long wait. For all I know, he's already sent people."

Jakob nodded. He needed to get to Rhes and Sarah immediately. He could organize protection for them again, but not on such short notice. He would need to get there first, make sure they were safe, and then call in his men.

"Richard, I must go. I ... thank you. You and Lewis have every right to be unhappy with the council at the moment. We've let you down, and I apologize. I will do my best to make amends."

"I know. That's why we wanted you in the meeting with Malik," Richard said. He clapped Jakob on the shoulder. "You're a good man. Go take care of those guys and keep them the hell away from Aros. I'll be here when you get back."

Jakob nodded, and he headed for the door.

* * *

"This is Sasha. I'm not here. Leave a message."

Jakob was simultaneously annoyed and amused. Sasha's businesslike, no-nonsense manner never failed to impress him, but he needed her to answer the phone.

"Sasha. Contact me as soon as you possibly can. I'm *en route* to the home of Rhes and Sarah ... Thomas? ... whatever. The human couple that I saved from the Burilgi last year. They are in danger again and I am trying to keep them safe. I need your help. Call me."

Jakob hung up, still striding down the street toward the garage in which he'd left his car. It was dark out, had been for hours, and the December air was brisk but not quite freezing. Jakob barely felt it.

He had the utmost confidence in Sasha; that was why he had made her his fledgling. Unlike many vampires, Jakob had made neither a lover nor a daughter of his fledgling. Sasha was a very good friend, a very good fighter, and a most capable business associate. She had been serving as a sort of personal assistant for more than two hundred years. Jakob would need her aid.

Aros was planning to abduct Rhes and Sarah. Once the rogue Burilgi had them, Jakob did not know whether he would kill them or simply detain them. Either way, he was planning to use them as bait in the hopes of bringing Two to him. That she was presently out of the country likely didn't concern him. Vampires, particularly those clever enough to have survived for more than seven hundred years as Aros had, usually planned for the long term.

"Why would he want Two?" Jakob muttered to himself, opening the door to his car and sliding in. The engine purred to life as he turned the key. "What value is she to him?"

A bargaining chip? A hostage? An example to be made? Jakob had no idea. He hoped to find out quickly, in time to head off any plans Aros might be making.

Jakob drove impatiently, frustrated that he had not been able to reach Sasha. She would be able to get to a computer, find Rhes and Sarah's phone number, contact them to alert them to the danger. Jakob had long since deleted the number from his phone, and could not call information unless he could remember their last name.

"Johnson?" he asked himself. No, that wasn't right.

Jakob navigated his car through the Manhattan streets as quickly as he could, but the evening was still young, and the traffic was only just beginning to thin. The city had moved past the gridlock of rush-hour, but he was still surrounded by a mass of cabs, cars, and delivery trucks. Fifteen minutes into the drive, his phone lit up and began to ring.

"Sasha?" he asked as he picked it up.

"No, Jakob. Naomi."

"Naomi! Jesus, woman ... where have you been?"

"It's ..." there was murmuring, and when Naomi's voice returned, she sounded rushed and distracted. "It's a long story. I am sorry for not contacting you, but things became very complicated."

"Is everything all right now?"

Naomi gave an odd laugh and said, "I have no answer to that question. Ask me again when we see each other in person."

"What happened?"

"No time. I need a favor."

"Certainly."

"I need you to rent an apartment for me. Furnished, please. Two bedrooms. I need it now, or within the next few days."

"What happened to your apartment?" Jakob asked.

"Nothing. We won't all fit."

"Naomi, what—"

"Really, Jakob, I can't explain right now. We have a plane to catch. I will see you very soon."

"Good. Naomi, before you go, I have news. I do not advise sharing it with your friend Two."

"That won't be a problem," Naomi said, her voice wavering a bit. Jakob considered asking another question, thought better of it, and pressed on.

"It seems that her friends are in danger again. Rhes and Sarah. I am on my way to their home now."

"Who is threatening them?"

"Aros."

"The ... the Burilgi rebel? But why?"

"He wants to use them as bait."

"Bait for what?"

"For your blonde-haired friend with the Eresh blood. Naomi, things are ... happening here."

"So it seems. I wish I could help. I really have to go. I'll keep quiet about your news and try to get home as soon as I can. Get me that apartment?"

"I will take care of it."

"Thank you. Jakob ... take care of yourself."

There was a click, and the line went dead. Jakob pondered the conversation for a moment, but decided that there had been too few clues to come to any real conclusions. He tried to put it out of his mind and instead focused on maneuvering through the traffic, making his way towards Rhes and Sarah.

* * *

The knock on the door was hard and urgent, and Sarah turned to Rhes with her head cocked. "Uh ... you expecting anyone?"

"No," said Rhes, standing up and setting aside his newspaper. "No, I'm not. Particularly not at ten thirty at night."

Jake, their guide dog, was lying on the floor next to Sarah. He looked up at the door and growled once, briefly, but this was a standard reaction, and not indicative of anything out of the norm. Rhes crossed to the door, went to open it, then thought better of it and glanced out through the peephole first.

"Jakob?" he said.

"Jakob?" Sarah echoed.

"Looks like it."

"Probably should let him in," she said.

Jakob's voice came through the door. "Yes, you should let me in."

Rhes rolled his eyes and opened the door. "Good ears."

"A gift from my ... father," Jakob said, stepping in. "Your dog is very calm. We don't usually induce fits of barking, the way the movies claim, but he's still quite exceptional."

"He's very well trained. What brings you here, Jakob?" Sarah asked.

She and Rhes had spent the past fourteen months barely thinking about vampires, other than to occasionally wonder whether they would ever see, hear from, or even hear *about* Two again. There had been a wedding to plan and execute, a daughter to adopt, and a normal life to reestablish. All of these had been accomplished, and Sarah was less than enthusiastic about letting the supernatural world encroach upon her life again.

Jakob seemed to pick up this concern in her voice. He frowned, shaking his head. "I am only interrupting your lives because I must. You are in danger."

"We are? Why?" Rhes asked.

"It is complicated ..." Jakob pondered for a moment, trying to determine how best to sum it up. Finally, he continued. "The leader of the Burilgi – the creatures that attacked you – has decided that he wants your friend Two. He feels the best way to bring her to him is to use her friends as bait."

"Fucking *Christ*," Sarah snarled. "We don't even know where she is!"

"Baby, relax," Rhes said, though he sounded no happier than she did. "Jakob's just trying to help us."

Jakob nodded. "I would much prefer to stay out of your lives."

Sarah sighed. "I know. I'm not angry at you. I just ... can't you guys just *handle* this? What does he need us for? Don't you know where Two is? Why doesn't he just call her and be like 'hey, stop on by?'"

Jakob grinned at this. "To be honest, we are not entirely sure where is. I only heard from Naomi earlier this evening, for the first time in months. They are safe, I think, and returning soon, but I don't know where they are right now. Even if I did, Aros – the leader of the Burilgi – he's not the type that one visits voluntarily."

"Wonderful," Sarah said. "So we get to go back under guard, right?"

"That is the plan."

"For how long?" Rhes asked.

Jakob shrugged, looking apologetic. "I don't know yet."

Sarah muttered another curse.

"When is this going to happen?" Rhes asked.

"Now," Jakob said. "That is ... I don't know exactly when Aros intends to move, but it will be soon, and I want you well under guard before he does it."

"You and us both," Sarah said.

Jakob's phone began to ring and he pulled it from his jacket pocket, glancing at the screen.

"Ah, good," he said. "It's Sasha."

Before he could answer the phone, however, the front door to Rhes and Sarah's house was driven inward by some exterior force. Jakob was standing only inches in front of it and the door hit him, throwing him forward into Rhes, the phone flying from his hand. Windows in the front and back of their brownstone shattered, the protective exterior bars torn from their bolts. A moment later, the power went out. Jake, quiet earlier, was now barking furiously.

Lying on the floor beneath Jakob, who was still struggling to get to his feet, Rhes could only watch in horror as black silhouettes began to pour into the house from every entrance.

CHAPTER XVI

Foster Care

Panicking was not in her nature and so when Jakob did not answer his phone, Sasha simply left him a short message, delivered in her cool, businesslike tone, asking him to call her back. When he had not done so ten minutes later, she tried again, and again got no response. As Jakob's voicemail came on for the second time, Sasha sighed in frustration.

"Jakob, this is Sasha, returning your phone call. Given the level of urgency in your message, I'm concerned that you're not answering. I think it would be best if I made my way to the apartment where Rhes and Sarah Thompson live. I will have my laptop with me and my mobile wireless connection. If you'd prefer I take a different course of action, please call me."

She hung up and glanced around her home office, trying to decide if leaving was indeed the best course of action. Jakob would likely need her to help him organize defenses for the humans, and she could best do that from home, but she was growing deeply concerned about what might have happened to him.

Sasha decided to trust her instincts, which were telling her to go. She would have access to their data no matter where she might end up. Packing up her gear, she tossed it in a carrying case and left. She rode the building's elevator down into a subterranean parking garage without interruption, and was soon behind the wheel of her Cadillac, heading toward Brooklyn.

Sasha cursed herself as she drove. She had been listening to Beethoven at a volume that had completely drowned out Jakob's original call. If she had answered then, she would know the details and be able to do something to help. Instead she was trapped in her car, driving and worrying, until Jakob called back or she arrived at the apartment in Brooklyn.

Fortunately, it wouldn't be a long drive even though she lived in Carnegie Hill, further north than the cathedral from which Jakob had left. It had been nearly an hour since Jakob's original call, and traffic had thinned substantially. She took FDR Drive down the eastern side of Manhattan, crossed the Manhattan Bridge, and made her way towards Park Slope. In all, the drive took just over thirty minutes.

She was halfway up the staircase before realizing that what at first appeared to be the normal face of a Brooklyn brownstone was, in fact, nothing more than camouflage. The front windows were shattered, their ornamental wrought-iron bars hastily replaced after having clearly been torn down. The door was broken and slightly ajar. All of the lights in the house were off.

Sasha immediately slowed, crouching slightly, scanning the area. She could neither see nor sense anyone else in the vicinity. It might be hours before anyone noticed the condition of the house and called the police, or it might only be minutes. If there was anyone else inside, she would need to deal with them quickly, though she had her doubts that she would make any such encounters.

Sasha pressed the palm of one hand against the door, opening it slowly and quietly, sliding inside. There was light in here after all, though too weak for her to have noticed it from the outside. It was a single flashlight, resting in the lap of the young girl sitting on the stair landing. She had brown hair pulled back in a ponytail, and was clothed in a blue cotton nightgown. Her head was bent, and she stared at her hands, her face miserable.

"Child … are you all right?" Sasha asked.

The girl did not start, did not even lift her head, just shook it and said, "They killed Jake."

"Who?" Sasha asked, fearing for a moment that the girl might mean Jakob.

"Jake. Our dog. They killed him. He was barking, and then he made this ... this noise. He's down there somewhere. Don't step on him."

"I won't," Sasha said. She was struggling to remain calm and not bombard this girl, who was obviously in a state of shock, with countless questions. She settled at first for one that was both easy and obvious.

"What is your name?"

"Molly. Are you going to kill me?"

"No. Why would you think that?"

"Because you're one of them."

"One of what?"

Molly looked up at her, and the expression of disgust and exasperation on her face was so extreme as to be almost comical.

"One of the *vampires* ... Jesus."

"Oh. I ... I'm not sure what you mean," Sasha said.

"Cut the shit," Molly muttered, looking back down at her hands. "Adults are always like this. You think kids are stupid, or blind, or deaf. You think I don't hear things and see things. Two met some vampires, and then some shit went wrong, and now she's gone and they came here. You're one of them. So I'm asking: are you going to kill me, like you killed Jake?"

"No, Molly," Sasha said, furiously organizing questions in her head. "You are right, and I won't pretend anymore. I am what you think I am, but I am *not* like the things that did this."

"OK," Molly said.

"Can you tell me what happened?"

"Someone came to the door. I was supposed to be asleep but I was reading, and I heard them knock. There was some talking for a while, and then this huge crashing noise and all this shouting. That's when I got out of bed ... but I heard my mom screaming, and my dad was shouting too and then ... then ..." Molly's voice wavered.

"It's all right," Sasha said, trying to sound comforting. It was not a natural tone of voice for her, and she doubted that she had done a particularly convincing job.

"It is *not* all right!" Molly cried. "They *took* them! They took my mom and dad and they've only even *been* my mom and dad for like two months and they took them and they *killed my fucking dog!*"

The flashlight dropped from her lap as Molly brought her hands up to her face, voicing a series of harsh sobs. It fell clattering down the stairs and spun on the hardwood floor, casting deranged shadows across the living room. Sasha took a moment to look around. She saw signs of a struggle: broken furniture, a large hole in one wall and, behind an overturned easy chair, the corpse of the dog. Its neck was bent in an impossible direction.

Not wanting Molly to see this, Sasha took two quick steps forward, leaned down, and returned the dog's head to an appropriate position. There was no noise, but Sasha could feel the shattered bones grinding against each other. *Animals,* she thought.

Above her, Molly's loud sobbing had become something more gentle, but the girl's face was still buried in her hands. Sasha picked up the flashlight and climbed up to the landing, sitting down next to the girl. She didn't put her arm around Molly, nor did she think Molly would have wanted her to.

"It only hurt him for a moment," Sasha said. "The dog, I mean. It didn't last long."

Molly took a hitching breath, made another sobbing noise, and spoke into her hands. "Don't tell me he's gone to a better place. I don't w—want to hear it."

Sasha, having no intention of telling Molly any such thing, said nothing. She was thinking. Jakob was not here, nor were the girl's parents. She would have to search the rest of the house, of course, but knew she would find nothing. Jakob would not have been killed without a fight, and if there had been a fight, there would have been at least *some* blood spilled. Sasha could smell none. Clearly, he had been abducted along with Molly's parents.

"I have to go," Sasha said out loud.

Molly looked up at her, rubbing the back of her arm across her eyes, and said, "I'm coming with you."

"That's not possible."

"I want to help find my mom and dad."

"I know, Molly, but—"

"But *what?* What am I supposed to do, lady? Two's gone. My parents are gone. Where do you want me to go?"

That's not my problem, Sasha thought to herself, and yet she couldn't bring herself to abandon the girl here.

"I can take you somewhere safe," she offered.

"I don't want to go somewhere safe. I want to go with you and find them."

"I want to find them, too, and my friend Jakob, but that's not going to be easy. I don't know where they've been taken. I have to go and talk with my people."

"So take me with you."

"I can't. It's … you're not one of us."

"Shoulda thought about that before you busted up into our house and killed our dog," Molly spat.

"That was not my people."

"Don't care. You owe me! I'm not staying here. You're not leaving me here. I'll do whatever you want … help you, or whatever, but you're not leaving me here."

Sasha blew air through pursed lips and bit her tongue for a moment, thinking. Then she handed the flashlight to Molly.

"Fine," she said. "Until we find your parents, you do whatever I tell you to do, whenever I tell you to do it. If you don't like that, I will happily drop you on a curb somewhere and you can decide your own path from there. I am a woman of very little patience. Is that clear?"

Molly nodded. "OK. What do you want me to do?"

"First? Go upstairs and get dressed. We cannot stay here."

"All right. What's your name?"

"Sasha."

Molly opened her mouth to ask another question, but Sasha interrupted her.

"There will be time in the car. Go get dressed."

Molly shut her mouth and did as she was told.

* * *

She stopped for a moment to kneel next to Jake's body, fresh tears squeezing from her puffy red eyes and rolling down her cheeks. They fell on the dog's muzzle and soaked into his fur.

"Goodbye, Jake," Molly said. She scratched the spot between his eyes, as he'd always loved, and then kissed him there. After a moment more she stood and, wiping her tears away, nodded to Sasha.

"I'm sorry," Sasha said, indicating toward the dog's inert form. "After we leave, I will call some people to take care of him."

Molly tried a smile, couldn't manage it, and shrugged instead. "OK."

"Will you be all right?"

"I'll live. Been through worse. Could really use a fix, though."

"A what?"

"Forget it. Let's just go."

A thought occurred to Sasha, and she paused. "Do you have school tomorrow?"

Molly made a noise that Sasha supposed held some relation to a laugh and said, "I wouldn't worry about it."

"No, but—"

"Look, I spent the last couple years fucking people for smack, OK? It doesn't matter if I make honor roll."

"If you would let me finish, I was going to say: 'but it is a good idea to take care of loose ends.' I can have someone from the police contact your school and take care of the situation."

"Oh," Molly said. "Sorry. I—"

"Your past does not matter to me, nor does your academic standing. To use your terminology: I don't care how many people you've fucked, and I don't care how much smack you've taken, as long as you're not taking it anymore. It's irrelevant."

Molly said nothing. Sasha continued.

"I do not like children. I'm going to treat you as an adult. It's up to you to behave like one. Do so, and I'll let you stay with me while I search for Jakob and your parents, at least for now. Don't, and I leave you behind."

"OK," Molly said.

Sasha nodded, satisfied. "I know you're hurting. I am trying to help you."

"I know. Sorry."

"Apology accepted," Sasha said, starting for the door. "Now, you're going to do something that very, very few humans have ever done ... though your friend Two is one of them."

"What is it?" Molly asked, following her.

"You're going to walk in on a vampire council meeting."

* * *

"Oh, this is just *brilliant!*"

Leonore's voice was caustic in its disgust. She was standing up, staring at Sasha, who was making her way down the aisle and toward the front of the converted church with Molly in tow.

"Kindly lower your voice," Malik said, his voice haggard.

"She's late ... Jakob is still *nowhere* to be seen ... and she has a *human child* with her!"

"And knowing Sasha, I have little doubt that she has explanations for all of those things," Malik replied.

"Well, I think—"

"No one cares what you think!" Sasha snapped as she came down the aisle. "Sit down, hold your tongue, and extend some respect to your elders."

Leonore looked none too pleased by this verbal slap, but she did as she was told. Sasha stepped up in front of the assembled council. Molly was looking around, wide-eyed and curious, but thus far adhering to Sasha's command that she was to say nothing.

"Something has gone very wrong," Malik said.

"Oh, yes," Sasha replied.

"What can you tell us?"

"Not enough. This is Molly Thompson. She is the adopted daughter of the two humans that Jakob saved from the Burilgi last year. The two who were in the *Eresh-Chen*'s apartment."

"*Former Eresh-Chen*," Leonore said. Sasha whirled on her.

"Speak another word," she snarled. "Go ahead. I dare you to. I *want* you to."

Leonore chose to ignore this request. After a moment, Sasha turned back to Malik.

"Where is your sire?" he asked.

"The Burilgi took him, along with the girl's parents."

"Fuck!" Lewis shouted from somewhere behind her.

"This is ... not good," Malik agreed. "We had hoped that Jakob would arrive in time to protect them from Aros's forces."

"Apparently,, they were attacked by numerous Burilgi just after Jakob arrived," Sasha said. "The girl was upstairs, and they missed her. As far as I can tell, there was a struggle but no one was killed."

"Except my dog," Molly exclaimed and then, remembering that she was not supposed to speak, said, "Oh, sorry."

"Dog?" Malik asked.

Sasha rolled her eyes. "The woman, Sarah Thompson, is blind. She had a guide dog. It must have attacked one of the Burilgi, and they broke its neck."

"Ah," Malik was paying only cursory attention, pondering the situation.

"We need Jakob," Sasha said. "The council needs him, and he's not safe with Aros."

"Yes, but we can't be hasty."

"Hasty?" Sasha was taken aback. "Malik, they've abducted a council member. We need to get him back!"

"If we move too quickly, we risk bringing harm to Jakob or the humans. Aros is not known for patience and tolerance."

"Of course I am concerned for his safety," Sasha said, "but I ... I believe we must act quickly and decisively to show that the council will not tolerate this sort of action."

"I understand. Still, it will be difficult for a variety of reasons."

"Such as?" Sasha prompted.

Lewis spoke up again. "Such as, none of us know where Aros is, let alone where he's keeping Jakob and the girl's parents."

* * *

"Well, that was an *exquisite* waste of time," Sasha growled. She and Molly were back in the Cadillac, driving toward Sasha's apartment.

"No kidding," Molly said, and yawned. She looked exhausted, and Sasha supposed that made sense. The girl was supposed to be asleep right now.

"I'm not going to sit around and wait while the council hems and haws," Sasha said. "I need to figure out where Aros is hiding. This is a dangerous time for the council, and we need Jakob alive."

"Didn't that Lewis guy say he met with Aros?"

"Yes, but apparently not at Aros's main base of operations."

"Oh."

"It's ridiculous that we have allowed him to do these things without punishment. Ridiculous," Sasha said. During the meeting, Lewis had given the rest of the council the same information that he had earlier given to Malik and Jakob: Aros was building an army.

Molly didn't say anything. These issues were beyond her. She just wanted Rhes and Sarah back, wanted to see that they were OK. She wanted to feel their arms around her, hear them tell her everything was going to be fine. It wasn't fair. Things had just *finally* started to seem normal.

Sasha chewed on her lip, watching the road and also not saying anything. Molly glanced over at her. "You're worried about your friend."

"Jakob can take care of himself," Sasha said.

Molly yawned again. "Doesn't mean you're not worried about him."

"I don't worry."

Molly gave her a surprisingly adult smile. "Sure. Where are we going?"

"My apartment."

"Oh. Is it as nice as your car?"

Sasha smiled. "You'll have to decide for yourself."

"Mm. Hey ... Sasha?"

"Yes?"

"Thanks for, you know ... not leaving me."

Sasha shrugged.

"No, seriously," Molly continued. "I know you could have. What was I gonna do, right? I mean, I'm like ... dinner to you guys. I understand that."

Sasha gave a small laugh. "No, it's not like that. Not exactly."

"But you don't really like humans, right?"

"I don't. That's true."

"So ..." Molly paused, thinking.

"Yes?"

"So why'd you take me with you?"

Sasha considered this for a time and then said, "When I was eighteen, Napoleon's armies invaded my land. A group of his men murdered my parents and were pursuing me as I ran from our farm. I imagine they would have raped me first and then killed me. Jakob appeared out of nowhere and slaughtered them all. Six of them, and he was finished with them almost before they knew what was happening. I watched in awe and, at the end, when he bowed to me and turned to leave, I begged him to take me with him. I didn't know what he was, only that he had saved my life.

"I told him I would do anything for him, would serve him in any way he asked, if only he would not abandon me. I had nothing else. My parents were dead, the young man I would have married had been killed fighting in Sweden two years earlier, even my home was in flames. There was *nothing* left ... except Jakob.

"He took me with him. I was alone and had no one else to turn to, and Jakob took me in. He taught me to fight, showed me what I could be, and gave me my chance at immortality."

Sasha looked over at Molly, who was listening intently.

"Your situation is not the same as mine, but I felt the echo of the past. I remembered Jakob's kindness, and felt that I could do no less."

Molly smiled, then laughed a bit.

"What is it?" Sasha asked.

"Nothing."

Sasha looked over at Molly again, tilting her head. Molly grinned.

"You're just not as much of a bitch as you try to be."

CHAPTER XVII

The Burilgi King

Sarah Thompson had been hearing the voices for some time now, although time would have been difficult enough to gauge even if she could see. At least then there might have been some hint – the progression of sunlight on a wall, perhaps. Sarah was trapped in a world of darkness, lying on a cold steel floor, unsure of anything except that she had been taken forcibly from her home, separated from her husband, and thrown into what must undoubtedly be a cell. Judging time was essentially impossible.

Though she could not see her surroundings, she had managed to struggle to a sitting position, leaning against the wall. She sat, wondering what fate held in store for her. She had finished crying, had finished screaming, and had spent the past – whatever – simply breathing, trying not to let her fear overwhelm her again, and listening to the voices.

"*Ki epile kom Aros fite? Na chole,*" said the hissing voice that Sarah had come to think of as The Rat.

"*Sa mokoste kel, vi tao chareson sata imrati jal,*" said the other, a slow and dopey voice that seemed to struggle with the foreign language it was speaking. Sarah had nicknamed this one The Dunce.

"*Na vose taravas a ker,*" The Rat replied.

"*Sa lur se. Na vateto kom tao majeto a Nikki. Tao paceto kel kuessa pha chesas essi morteto kel javin.*"

"*Fan? Ghaso?*"

"*Tao se fusto. Ghaso fusto. Nan loraden empas fam nan loraden fusto.*"

"*Na osame. Sa prise kel teo se progos?*"

"*Na vobreve. Setra vort fiteto tao nifleto kel* ... damn, how do you say 'screaming'?" The Dunce asked.

"*Quovre.*"

"Right ... *quovre vilmon, munta tao praveto ae karecomar.*"

"*Nan lur praven vi puosten cheo kel. Na nifle teo se enposto.*" The Rat made an ugly chuckling noise.

"*Nan lur ustalon omrinen rotan. Na se lostro.*"

"That's why I want to stop!" The Rat exclaimed. There was laughter, and then the voices trailed off a bit, other than an occasional curse in English or murmur that she couldn't catch.

Sarah tried, as best she could, to determine what exactly had happened earlier in the evening. Jakob had told them that they were in danger, and almost immediately his words had been proven true. There had been a crash, and the sound of glass breaking, and then the rapid shuffling noise of a group of people entering the brownstone. Jake had started barking, and then he'd made a noise that Sarah had understood, instantly, was the last he would ever make. Thinking back on this now, she felt a wave of heart-wrenching sadness. Jake had been a constant companion for almost eight years of her life and had been responsible for her meeting Rhes. He'd deserved better.

During the commotion, Sarah had been grabbed by both of her arms, and a rough hand had slapped over her mouth after only a couple of screams. Rhes had barely had time to begin shouting before he'd made a strangled noise, and a young voice had said, "Make any more noise and we'll kill blind-o over there. We only need one of you."

"This one here is Ay'Araf," another voice had said. "What's your name, pig?"

Jakob hadn't deigned to answer, and Sarah had heard the sound of blows landing.

"I asked you a question, you elitist piece of shit," the voice had snarled. Jakob had laughed at it.

"By all means, keep hitting me," he'd said.

Sarah had thought that Jakob was trying to stall their assailants, waiting for reinforcements of some kind. One of the Burilgi in the room must have had the same thought.

"Fuck it," a female voice had said. "Take him with us. Let's go."

There had been pain then, a sharp jab in her arm, just below the edge of her sleeve, and the last thing Sarah had heard before waking up in this cell was the woman's voice saying, "Cooperate with us or we'll pick one of them to kill, got it?"

After that there was not blackness, but rather a startling loss of time. She did not remember passing out, did not remember dreaming. It had seemed merely seconds between those words and waking up on the floor of her cell, disoriented and nauseated from the drugs. She had sat up, leaned sideways and vomited, and then had begun calling for help. When that hadn't worked, the tears had started, prompted by fear, anger, and an overwhelming sense of helplessness.

Sarah had been without her sight for twenty years and still so often felt crippled. In her present situation, abducted and imprisoned, she felt completely useless. Rhes was not here, and there was nothing left to do but sit, and listen to the voices, and wait.

* * *

Rhes Thompson could see, but when he woke from his own drug-induced sleep, he found himself in no better a position to do anything than Sarah had. The cell he was in measured perhaps twenty-five square feet, small enough that he could only have lain flat by spreading out on the diagonal. The walls and door were metal, and there was a small vent near the top of one wall. The ceiling, some sixteen feet above him, was made of concrete. The floor was some kind of industrial linoleum, a minty green color, scraped and scuffed. A single bare light bulb hung high above him, and there was a small plexiglass window in the door.

Rhes had gone there first, once the drugs had worn off enough that he was able to stand, and looked through the window. It had offered little in the way of a view. It appeared that his cell was positioned at the end of a long cinderblock hallway. Across from him was another door with a window looking in on what appeared to be another cell. To the left, the hall ended in a bare wall. To the right, it disappeared out of view.

Rhes tried banging on the door. He tried shouting. Neither accomplished anything. In the end, Rhes sat down on the floor, his back to the wall, and waited. If the creatures that had abducted him had meant to kill him, surely they would have already done so. He was here for a purpose: to lure Two to someone named Aros for some unknown reason that, Rhes thought, even if explained to him would make no sense.

"What it is that motivates these motherfuckers, other than making my life difficult, I have no idea," he muttered to himself.

He checked his watch, noting that it was three in the morning. He wondered if Molly was all right, and how Sarah might be handling her imprisonment if she was awake. Time passed. Rhes sat and thought, dozing occasionally, and eventually came to the conclusion that if he ever saw Two again, his best course of action would be to run screaming in the opposite direction.

Footsteps sounded in the hall. Rhes resisted the urge to leap to his feet and press his face against the window like a kid. Instead, he tried to remain as calm and casual as possible. When the door opened, he glanced up and said, "If you wanted an autograph, you could've just asked."

The man standing in the door was blonde and strikingly handsome. To Rhes, he looked like James Dean, in a way, sensitive and almost delicate. He gave Rhes a polite smile and said, "This is not how I would have preferred to meet you. I did not think you'd be receptive to my people if they simply knocked on your door."

"Jakob would probably have started slashing them up. That's what he did with the last three that bothered us."

"Yes. A regrettable situation, that. I am not a … vindictive man – or perhaps it's just that those fools were of no real value. Regardless, I've allowed him to live for now."

"You're Aros?"

"That is my name, yes. Aros Kreskas, at your service."

244

"'At my service' ... right. Where's my wife, Mr. Kreskas?"

"Here and safe. You'll see her shortly."

"And my daughter?"

Aros tilted his head and narrowed his eyes. "Daughter?"

Rhes rolled his eyes. "That's a hell of a research team you've got there, Kreskas."

"You seem a bit hostile, Mr. Thompson."

"Your people fucked up my house, killed my dog, threatened to kill my wife, then drugged us both and locked us up. I'd say, under the circumstances, that it's a small miracle I'm just sitting here and not trying to punch your teeth in."

Aros considered this, and he nodded. "I was unaware of the dog. My apologies."

"So, apologies for the dog, but nothing else ..."

"I'm not accustomed to apologizing for much of anything, so you'll have to be satisfied with that."

Rhes said nothing – just sat there, arms crossed, looking up at Aros.

Finally, the vampire said, "They've taught you already not to respect my kind."

"No," Rhes said. "It has nothing to do with that. I don't know anything about you, or your people, and I don't care. I just want this shit to be done. I want you to do whatever it is you need to do and let my wife and I go home and try, once again, to return to our lives."

"A reasonable desire. I have a simple question for you, Mr. Thompson."

"Go for it."

"Can I trust you not to make a pointless, foolish attempt at escape if I provide you and your wife with some freedom during your stay here?"

"You mean like waiting for daylight and then just walking out?"

"The human guard I employ might have something to say about that."

"Right. Look, I'm not interested in putting Sarah's life in danger – or my own, for that matter. So, whatever. It's your dungeon, do what you want. Long as I can see my wife. When Two shows up, are you going to let us go?"

"That is my current plan, yes."

"Fine, then."

"And you're not concerned about *why* I might want your friend?"

"Buddy, I don't even give a shit. Two can take care of herself. The last time a vampire fucked with her, she chopped his head off and burned him to ashes."

"Yes, I know. That's part of the problem. She has something I want."

"What's that?"

Aros paused, and then gave Rhes a grin that seemed ill-fit for his handsome face. He no longer looked sensitive to Rhes, nor delicate. He no longer looked human. Rhes understood in that moment that despite the civility Aros was displaying, there was something very dangerous about this man.

"What I want," Aros told him, "is her blood."

* * *

"Hon?"

Sarah sat bolt upright. She had been leaning against the wall and had fallen into a doze, but that was *his* voice, and she knew it even half asleep.

"Rhes?"

"I'm here, Sarah." She felt him touch her face and then take her hand. Sarah wrapped her arms around him, clutching at him. Rhes hugged her back.

"You OK?" Rhes asked her, and she nodded, not letting him go.

"Yes. I just ... you know."

"I know."

Sarah heard the rustle of fabric as Aros came through the door and said, "Who else is here?"

"This is Aros Kreskas. He's ... in charge. Mr. Kreskas, this is my wife, Sarah."

"It's a pleasure, Mrs. Thompson," Aros said. "My guards say you were shouting earlier. Are you all right?"

"I was scared. And sick ... sorry about that."

"Not a problem. It was not my intention to scare either of you."

Sarah paused, apparently consider a response to this. At last she said, "OK ..."

Rhes spoke up. "Aros is going to move us to some nicer rooms while we wait for Two to show up. As long as we don't try to escape, he says we don't need to be locked up."

"That would be fine," Sarah said. "As ... as long as we're together."

Rhes took her hand. "That's the plan."

"Think of it as ... an extended vacation," Aros said. "You will have a suite, your needs will be taken care of, and you won't even have to cook if you don't want to."

Sarah bit back a sarcastic comment and instead asked, "Where *are* we, anyway?"

"You're in a decommissioned military base two hours outside of New York, on sub-level B, approximately forty feet below the surface. I house many of my fellow Burilgi, not to mention a handful of humans and rebel Ay'Araf."

"What about the other kinds?" Rhes asked.

"We don't have any of the 'other kinds' here," Aros said, his distaste evident in his voice. "The aristocracy has no reason to want change. Even most of the Ay'Araf are quite comfortable feeding off of their table scraps."

"The ones we've met seem all right," Rhes said, and immediately regretted it as he saw Aros's expression darken.

"I'll keep that in mind," the vampire told him.

"I'm sure you're right. We've only met a few of them," Sarah said, and Rhes could tell by her tone that she understood his mistake. Something about Aros had clearly spooked her.

Don't blame ya, hon, he thought. *Guy makes me nervous, too.*

"What should we do now?" he asked aloud.

"I have things to do," Aros said, his voice still brusque. "I will take you to more comfortable quarters, and then I will leave you in the care of my associates."

Sarah, who had not long ago been listening to the ugly laughter of some of Aros's associates, shuddered, but said nothing. She had not yet released her grip on Rhes's hand and didn't intend to for the foreseeable future.

"That's fine, thanks," Rhes said.

"Follow me."

Aros lead them through a series of undecorated hallways and into a concrete stairwell. They climbed the twisting staircase for three stories before coming to a halt in front of a heavy metal security door. Aros used a key to open this, and they exited out into a set of dark, mostly empty rooms that must once have been offices.

"This office is mine. The rest are rarely occupied," Aros said. He walked over to his desk, glanced at his laptop, opened a desk drawer, and checked something on a notepad. Apparently satisfied, he looked up.

"There is no reason you should need to be here again."

He led them outside. Rhes could see that there were guards patrolling under the large arc-sodium lights that illuminated the walkways between buildings. Rhes couldn't get a feel for the size of the complex in the few brief moments they spent outside before Aros led them into another building.

"This was an officer's townhouse, at one point," the vampire told them. "I'm sure you'll find it to your liking. It's been aired out, and the linens are fresh. There is food in the kitchen. A young woman named Janet will be by tomorrow to find out if you need anything."

"I'm sure it'll be fine. Thank you," Rhes said.

"There are guards at all entrances and exits to the compound, twenty-four hours a day. It's not that I don't trust you, precisely, but at this stage I must take all precautions."

"We're not going anywhere until you tell us we can," Sarah said.

"Very good. I hope you have a lovely night."

Aros took two steps down the walkway and then turned, looked up at Sarah, and said, "By the way, Mrs. Thompson ... if you'd like to do something about those eyes, we really should sit down and talk sometime."

With that, he turned and walked briskly away.

* * *

"What do you suppose he meant by that?"

Rhes and Sarah were sitting in the living room of their quarters, and had been doing so for nearly fifteen minutes, trying to wrap their minds around their new situation. Rhes knew that for quite some time, Sarah was going to be relying very heavily on him. She didn't know her way around this house, and Jake was gone. Until they could get her a cane, Rhes would have to serve as her eyes.

"Meant by what?" Rhes asked, knowing full well what she meant.

"Don't. Don't play dumb, Rhes," Sarah said, and there was an odd note in her voice that Rhes didn't find particularly pleasant.

"Sarah, you don't really think this guy has a miracle cure for blindness, do you?"

Sarah was quiet for a moment, then said, "I don't know. I mean, I don't know anything about vampires. The stuff Two told us ..."

"Two was dealing with vampires who didn't feel the need to break into her house, kill her dog, and drug her."

"Yeah, no, Two's vampires were awesome," Sarah said, her voice acerbic. "They only wanted to torture and kill her."

Rhes sighed. "OK, true."

"I don't like Aros," Sarah said. "He's ... the politeness is a put-on. I'm sure of it. But Rhes, what if he can fix my eyes?"

"Even if he's not lying, and he probably is, you know what his solution's going to be."

"Well ..."

"He's going to want to turn you into a vampire."

"Maybe he could just give me blood, like Theroen did for Two. You have to be *drained* to be turned. Otherwise the blood just ... just does things for you."

"Aros is a completely different type of vampire than Theroen was. Do you remember everything we've been told about these guys?"

Sarah bit her lower lip, sitting in silence for a time. Finally she said, "You're probably right. Sorry, I just ... it's just ... why would he *say* something like that?"

"To fuck with you? Not to jump to conclusions, but I think our new friend might be a bit of an asshole."

"Yeah, I guess. Sorry."

Rhes pulled her close and hugged her. "I'm not mad at you. I just don't want you getting full of false hope and being disappointed. I don't want you to let him hurt you."

Sarah hugged back. "I know. God ... I want all of this shit to be over. When is it going to end?"

"Don't know. I'm going to kill Two, if she's not already dead. She's traipsing around Europe, and we're stuck here with some lunatic. They took our phones, and the lines in here don't work. Jakob's gone. Molly's all by herself. I'm supposed to be opening a new bar in eight weeks. Hell, I haven't even finished my Christmas shopping. I have shit to do, and the list doesn't include being held prisoner by some crazy vampire."

"We don't even know if he's really going to let us go. He might just kill us."

"Yes, that's absolutely true, and it's why we need to get out of here."

"How?"

Rhes sighed. "I have no idea. No idea at all. Right now, I'm too tired and sick from that stupid drug to even think about it. It's gotta be four in the morning. Maybe tomorrow I'll think of something."

"At least they don't have Molly," Sarah said.

"Right, not yet anyway. I made the mistake of asking Aros about her. He didn't even know we *had* a daughter, so now he's probably sending someone to get her."

"That's not your fault, baby. Don't be angry at yourself."

"No, it's probably not my fault, but it's still a problem. 'Course, I have no idea what Molly's going to do without us."

Sarah nestled in against him, obviously exhausted. Rhes shifted position, helped her recline with him, not wanting even to make the effort of going upstairs to go to a strange bed. He was tired, still somewhat dizzy from the drug, and just wanted this night to end. He leaned back and closed his eyes.

"Molly's a smart kid," Sarah said, her voice fuzzy with approaching sleep. "She'll figure something out."

CHAPTER XVIII

The Fixer

"I'm tired of just sitting here. We gotta do something!"

Sasha looked up from her computer, glanced over at Molly, and said, "I am doing something."

"What, surfing porn?" Molly asked.

"I'm searching for information on Aros. Why must you be so sarcastic all of the time?"

"Picked it up from a friend," Molly replied. She left Sasha's leather couch and moved to stand behind the vampire, peering at the computer screen.

"This is impossible," Sasha said after a moment. "Even if I knew enough about him to search efficiently, Aros has likely covered his tracks. Searching his name brings up nothing of value. I doubt he's used his real name on official documents in hundreds of years."

"You're never gonna find him like this," Molly agreed. She sat down in a short-backed armchair that had been positioned next to the desk. "Come on, you're just going to get nine million Goth sites or whatever. You need to be outside, talking to vampires."

"The type of vampires I would need to question won't take very kindly to my presence," Sasha commented.

"Fuck 'em ..."

"Yes, that's all well and good from the perspective of a thirteen-year-old human girl, but when I'm swarmed by Burilgi and torn into pieces, it's going to make rescuing Jakob rather difficult."

"Don't forget my parents."

"Yes, your parents, too."

"You don't really give a shit about them, do you?" Molly asked, her voice angry. Sasha turned and raised her eyebrows.

"Should I?" she asked without malice. "Try to see it from my perspective: they came stumbling into our world, as humans typically do, getting involved in things they should have left alone. They are paying the price for that. If your parents hadn't gone to Two's apartment last year, Jakob would not be in this situation."

"Yeah, but—"

"Even putting that aside, I've met your parents exactly once. They seem like reasonably intelligent, decent people, and I didn't mind helping them. That doesn't mean we're friends. If you think my concern for them is going to equal my concern for Jakob, you're mistaken."

Molly chewed her lower lip, looking at Sasha for a moment, and then said, "OK, fine. But guess what, if you don't start worrying about my parents the way you're worrying about Jakob, you won't get my help."

"And I need your help ... why?"

"These vampires you're looking for ... they hang in crappy areas, right? With addicts and muggers and hookers and shit?"

"Not all of them, but ... some, yes. I imagine so."

"Ever been to East New York?"

Sasha tilted her head. "This is beginning to sound like you may have an idea."

"I think I can help. Are you in, or should we just watch TV and wait for those fuckheads at the council to get off their asses?"

Sasha leaned back in her chair, crossed her legs, regarded Molly with cool interest. At last she said, "Tell me your plan. You have my attention."

* * *

"This ... you lived here?" Sasha asked, her disgust evident. She had visited worse slums in her life, but the idea that Molly had ever spent time here seemed absurd. The girl beside her gave a cynical laugh.

"You see?" she asked. "I told you taking the Caddy was a bad idea."

Sasha nodded. Molly had convinced her to take a cab, something Sasha rarely did, and she was thankful for it. The area was filled with chop shops and auto yards, and Sasha doubted that all of their parts were acquired by legitimate means.

More than a match for half a dozen humans at a time, Sasha felt no inherent fear of the place, but she was both disturbed and saddened by what she was seeing. Litter was piled in drifts against dilapidated buildings covered in graffiti, their foundations slowly sinking, giving them drunken, leaning appearances. A block down the street was a large group of men who appeared to be gathered around a fistfight. They were laughing, shouting profanity, occasionally throwing garbage from the street into the center of the ring their bodies had formed.

"Lived here. Worked here. Once in a while I had to pick someone up on the corner but not usually. Darren mostly arranged stuff. I uh ... I cost too much for most of the guys you find on the street."

"Why is that?" Sasha asked, more out of instinct than real interest. A moment later her brain caught up with what Molly had said and filled in the blanks. She glanced at Molly, who suddenly looked miserable.

"Rather not talk about it," Molly said.

"Never mind. I understand," Sasha said.

They walked down the street in the opposite direction from the fight, and Molly began rattling away, barely pausing for breath, pointing out landmarks.

"Some guys tried to rape me under that bridge. Two and Janice started screaming for Darren and one of the guys pulled a knife and I was like 'oh shit I'm dead' but he got up off me and started chasing Two, who I guess he sort of knew, and then Darren came out of the building with this *huge* gun and he just started shooting, right in the middle of the street. All the guys ran away and when the cops came later, me and Two had to go with them to a motel and do a group job. She'd never done it before and after she just kept crying and apologizing and I had to give her some of my smack so she could calm down."

Molly's voice had a rough, almost frantic edge to it, and after a time Sasha put her hand on the girl's shoulder.

"You do not need to tell me these things, Molly, if it's hurting you."

"I ..." Molly paused, shut her eyes, visibly struggling against tears. After a moment, she looked up, her eyes red-rimmed and bloodshot. "If I talk about it, I don't have time to th—think about it."

"Then by all means, continue, if it helps you." In truth, Sasha found the stories fascinating, in their own gruesome way. She tried to imagine herself living in this place, selling her body to feed a ravenous addiction, and found it impossible.

"It doesn't matter," Molly said. "We're almost there anyway."

"I must admit, I'm curious to meet this person that you think can help us."

"Jerry's a fixer. He's ... you know ... one time I needed some handcuffs with pink fuzz on them. Took Jerry about ten minutes to get them. Or like if Darren needed info on a guy who'd beaten up a girl, or skipped out on paying, Jerry could get that for him."

"A fixer," Sasha said. "Yes, I understand the concept."

"You bring him a problem, he takes care of it. I bet you could bring him a body, and Jerry would know what to do with it. He was always good for free smokes, too. Once in a while maybe he'd ask for a handjob or something, but not always."

Sasha grimaced, but said nothing.

"That's his place there," Molly said. "The one with the neon."

Sasha glanced up the road. The only visible neon sign was for an adult bookstore.

"This trip just improves with each passing moment," she said. Molly made a kind of sick laughing sound and nodded. They passed a basketball court, dimly illuminated by a single streetlight. A man was standing, staring at them, holding a ball. Two others knelt in the far corner of the court, passing a glass pipe back and forth. Sasha could smell an acrimonious odor in the air, not tobacco, not marijuana.

"'Sup, ladies?" the man with the basketball asked.

"Goin' to see Jerry," Molly mumbled, not looking at him. She didn't speed her pace, as Sasha might have expected, simply continued on.

"Yeah? 'Choo want with that fatass anyway? Should come chill with us. You smoke rocks?"

"Not anymore," Molly said, shivering a little.

"Shorty goin' clean," the man said to his friends. They laughed and returned to their pipe. "Come back if you need something. We got dust, chronic, chiba ..."

Molly took in a deep breath, held it. Tears were leaking from the corners of her eyes. Sasha looked down, frowning.

"Chiba's heroin," Molly croaked.

"If it will make you feel better, I can ensure that none of those three sell anything, to anyone, ever again," Sasha told her.

Molly shook her head, wiped her arm roughly across her eyes, gritted her teeth.

"It doesn't matter," she said. "You can't kill it. You get rid of those guys, some other guys take their place, and they have everything, and people keep on buying. Girls like me keep on smoking crack and shooting up and dropping pills. It doesn't matter."

They walked in silence for a moment, and then Molly slammed a fist into her own thigh. "*Fuck,* I want a fix so bad! Just a taste. Just ..."

Sasha, who understood very well what it was like to need a particular substance more than anything else on earth, put her hand on the girl's shoulder.

"Take me to Jerry," she said. "After that, we leave, and we're never coming back. Either of us."

Molly nodded, still shivering. "OK. I ... yeah, OK."

"I understand that this is hard for you," Sasha said.

"No, it's easy. It's easy when you're here, or when I'm with my mom and dad, or my teachers. It's not like I have a fucking choice. You're not going to let me go buy a nickel bag and a needle. You're not going to let me trade a blowjob for a couple of hits off the crack pipe. This isn't hard. It's when I wake up at, like, three in the morning, and I'm lying in my bed staring up at the ceiling, and all I can do is say to myself, over and over, 'go one more minute, see if you can just do that.' So I just lie there knowing that I could go outside and get on a train, and I could score before my parents ever found me, and I want it. I want it so bad! That's when it's hard."

"What keeps you from doing it?"

Molly shrugged, gave a harsh little laugh, stopped in front of the entrance to Jerry's building.

"Two coulda left me here," she said. "Left me to rot and die, living at Darren's place until I was all used up and worthless to him, or until I OD'd. Either way. She could've, and it would've been easier for her ... but she didn't."

* * *

"Sweet Mary-n-Baby-Jesus! Is that Molly?"

The back room of the shop looked as if it had gone without cleaning since opening day. Papers, video cassettes and DVDs, fast food wrappers, cigarette butts; all were scattered around the office, piled high in the corners. Cheap bookshelves lined the walls, double- and triple-stacked with items, sagging under the weight. There was a path cleared through the debris, leading from the door to an easy chair set in front of an ancient console television, and from the television to a desk in the corner.

"Hi, Jerry," Molly said, her tone less than enthusiastic. Sasha couldn't blame her.

Jerry seemed to be in his early sixties, was grossly overweight, and must not have bathed for several days. Sasha could smell him from across the room, and she found the idea of this man enjoying any sort of ministrations from a girl Molly's age to be nearly blasphemous.

"Figured you was long gone after what happened to poor Darren," Jerry said.

"I won't be back long," Molly replied.

Jerry reached into the pocket of his jeans, which were old and threadbare, warped and distended by time and the pressure of the man's enormous thighs. He brought forth a battered pack of

Camel cigarettes, removed one, lit it and dragged. His gaze ran up and down first Molly's body, and then Sasha's.

"Who's your friend?" he asked.

"My name is Sasha. We need information. Molly says you might be able to provide it."

"Well, Sasha, I don't know you, and normally this conversation would already be over. Molly's done me a few … favors, in her time, so I'm listening, but information has a price. How're you paying?"

He glanced again at Molly, and for a moment a look of ravenous desire was more than evident upon his face.

"Not with that," Sasha snapped.

Molly gave her a grateful look and said to Jerry, "I don't pay like that anymore."

"Shame," Jerry replied, not the least bit embarrassed. "Darren never would let me hire you."

"How much is information in cash?" Sasha asked.

"Kinda depends on the info, don't it?"

"I need anything you can find on a man named Aros Kreskas."

"Shit, name like that, you can't just look him up in a phonebook?"

"Don't be an idiot," Molly said.

Jerry chortled. "All right, all right. You wouldn't be here if it was easy. I gotcha. One more question, and I need the truth. You lie to me on this one, and I'll throw everything I have at you."

"Ask," Sasha said.

"You gonna kill him?"

"Unlikely, but not out of the question. Can we do business or not?"

"'Course!" Jerry cried. "Just means the rates go up. Six grand, and you get everything I can find on the guy. Might be a page, might be ten. Ain't my problem. You in?"

"I'm in. How is the information delivered?"

"Anonymous drop-off at a mailbox, or encrypted email. Your call."

Sasha was impressed despite herself. "How do you want your payment?"

"Cash. We don't take MasterCard in my line of work. Half up front, and you get a week to deliver the other half after delivery. You hold out on me, and I use my network to find you and take it from you."

"I have no intention of holding out on you."

"Wish more ladies would say that." Jerry grinned, gave a wheezing laugh that turned into violent coughing, and finally recovered, his face beet red. He stood, his chair groaning as its joints readjusted, and waddled over to his desk. He pulled a notepad and a pen from beneath a promotional box of bright green condoms and said, "Spell it."

Sasha did, and also gave him an email address to send the information to. Jerry wrote the information down. "Kreskas, huh? Whassat ... Russian?"

"It's Greek," Sasha said.

"I like Greek," Jerry mused. "Shit, maybe I'll go down the street, get me some gyros ..."

"When will we hear from you?" Sasha asked.

"Four days from when you give me the first half of the money."

"I can do that now."

Jerry laughed. "You got three grand on you?"

Sasha reached into a hidden pocket in her jacket and pulled out a wad of bills. She stepped over to Jerry and flipped six of them onto the desk. Jerry made a choking, coughing noise.

"Jeeeeesus, lady!" he cried. "You can't walk around with that kind of cash on you. You'll get jumped. Hell, *I'm* thinkin' about it now."

"I would *love* to see you try," Sasha said, "but I doubt you could catch me."

Jerry shrugged and laughed again. "Probably right. I was gonna close up shop and go upstairs, but since you ladies are so good lookin', I'll do you a favor and get started tonight."

"Fine. Are we done?"

"Far as I'm concerned, the both of ya can stick around as long as you want. Nice eye candy. But unless you need something else, I got what I want."

"Let's get the fuck out of here," Molly said.

"Indeed," Sasha said. She turned and, without another word to Jerry, followed Molly out the door. She could feel the man's eyes on her posterior the entire way.

Outside, Sasha turned to Molly and said, "That man deserves to die."

Molly shrugged and made a sweeping gesture. "Pick a building, you'll find someone who does. There are good people here. Really. But they get stomped underneath all the shit."

Sasha nodded. "How are you?"

"Better. Kinda hungry though. I know this isn't the best neighborhood, but there's a killer diner two blocks down that's open all night. S'OK if I get some food?"

"Certainly," Sasha said, and they began to walk in that direction.

Molly continued with the previous conversation. "Some of the people here get out. Some don't. Some do OK even if they stick around. I only got out thanks to Two."

"Your friend's story is a remarkable one," Sasha said.

"I haven't heard it. Not all of it anyway, just enough to figure some stuff out. I eavesdropped a little. I had to know ... I didn't get at first how she could have just quit. You know, taking smack. She, like, never thinks about it."

"And you do."

"Yeah. All the time. When it's bad, I can still ... when you shoot up, it makes your mouth taste like heroin. I taste that sometimes, when I really want a fix."

"How did you get over it?"

"I didn't. You never get over it. You just stop taking it. I heard somewhere that the relapse rate is like a hundred percent. I'm practically guaranteed to go back to it someday."

"That sounds improbable," Sasha said. "Surely some people quit and don't go back."

Molly shrugged. "Dunno."

"How did you stop?"

"Rhes and Sarah, my mom and dad now, but back then they were just some people I'd never met. Two sent me to them. They locked me in a room and wouldn't let me come out. Not for like a week, and then only with supervision for months. It sucked."

"Was it painful?"

"I thought I was going to die. I ... I said some horrible things. All kinds of stuff. Threats and begging and offering to fuck Rhes if he'd just let me go. I was so mad at them for so long. They just dealt with it. I don't even know why."

"They're good people."

"They're the *best* people," Molly said, and a moment later she was crying again. "They're my mom and my dad, and they saved me."

"You're returning the favor."

"Yeah ... in *four days!*" Molly said. "What if they're dead by then?"

"It will take the council four months to move. Would you prefer that?" Sasha asked.

"No."

"Then this is the best we can do. Molly, I don't want to sound like a condescending adult doling out life lessons ..."

"I'm fourteen. You all sound like that."

Sasha gave a small laugh and said, "Fine. Something that I think you should learn, then: if you are doing all that is in your power to do, then you must learn to be satisfied with that."

"I know. I just feel like ... so ..." Molly clenched and unclenched her fingers. Her tears had come to a stop, but there were still tracks on her cheeks.

"Helpless?" Sasha asked.

"Yeah."

"Thus far, you've been very useful. You brought us here."

"Well, you're the one who put up the three grand."

"Yes, and I'm rather curious to see whether it will buy me any information I can use, but my point is that you're not helpless. You're actively doing something. That is better than most people would do, including the other – how did you put it? – 'fuckheads' on the council."

"I get your point," Molly said. They turned a corner, and she stopped in front of a small diner. "This is it."

"Very well. I need to eat, too."

"Oh," Molly said. "I ... how do you ... I mean ..."

"Relax. I'm not going to kill anyone."

"OK."

"I'd have fed on Jerry, but I need him to be working."

"Yeah," Molly said, and gave Sasha a sad smile. "That, and you don't want to put your lips on his neck. Trust me."

* * *

"Whoah ... awesome! You're doing it right here?!"

Sasha, attached as she was to the neck of the diner's single waitress, was unable to answer Molly's excited question. Instead she made a waving gesture with her hand, indicating that Molly should be quiet. After a few more swallows, Sasha pulled away.

"It defeats the purpose," she said, "of waiting for the cook to use the bathroom, if you start shouting about it."

"Oh," Molly replied, her eyes wide and fascinated. "You have blood on your chin."

"Yes, I know, thank you," Sasha said, wiping her face with a napkin. "Now, no more talk about this until we've left, OK?"

Molly nodded. She was watching in wonder as the two bite marks on the woman's neck faded and disappeared. The cook returned from the bathroom and made his way to the kitchen, not paying any attention to them.

Sasha turned to the waitress, who was standing and staring out through the window, her eyes far away. "Miss? Miss!"

The waitress's eyes cleared, and she shook her head once, then laughed to herself. "I'm sorry, hon ... zoning out. What was it you needed, again?"

"Just the check, please."

"Oh, that's right. Here you go."

The waitress wandered off, rubbing her neck and calling out to the cook, asking if he had any aspirin.

"That was the coolest shit *ever!*" Molly whispered.

"Let's go," Sasha said, standing up. She set a twenty down on the table, more than enough to cover Molly's meal. The girl followed, leaving the remains of her hamburger and fries behind, and the two were shortly outside.

Sasha made a noise of vague distaste and said, "That woman's been drinking cough syrup when no one's watching."

"You can taste that?"

"Yes. I can't tell you what flavor, but I'm willing to bet that's what I'm tasting."

"Funny."

Sasha shrugged. "I'm going to call a car now, unless you have some desire to stay here longer."

"Nah, I don't ever want to come here again," Molly said.

"A reasonable wish. You did well tonight, Molly. It is often hard to be confronted with one's past. The first time I returned to the site of my parents' farm in Russia, I fell to my knees and wept."

Molly, who had a hard time picturing Sasha crying for any reason, shrugged. "Nothing about my life was good until I met Two, and I met her here ... so I guess that's something."

"She's causing you a lot of trouble now."

Molly shook her head. "No, she was trying to keep us away from all of this. We just wouldn't let her go."

Sasha made a noise of understanding. She pulled out her cell phone, dialed a number, and asked to be connected to a taxi service. Within minutes, their cab arrived.

"Don't normally get a lot of business out here at this time of night," the cabbie commented as they got in. "Especially not two ladies. Rough neighborhood."

"That is exactly why we're leaving," Sasha replied.

"Where to?"

"Manhattan. 75th and Lex."

The driver grunted an acknowledgment, put the cab in gear, and began the drive home. Molly didn't seem to have anything to say, sitting curled up against the door, staring out the window.

Sasha didn't press her, and spent the ride thinking of Jakob, wondering if he was all right. In four days, she hoped, they would find out.

CHAPTER XIX

A Matter of Vision

"Aros, this is absurd," Jakob said. He was standing at a window looking out at the grounds of the military base, illuminated under its giant lights. "You can't keep us here."

"So escape," Aros said. "Surely a mighty Ay'Araf such as yourself should have no problem."

"I'm a fighter, but I'm not suicidal," Jakob said. "You have too many men with too many guns."

"A wise choice."

"It won't be long before somebody comes for me."

"Am I facing the wrath of the council, Jakob? Forgive me if I'm not shaking in my boots."

Jakob turned to look at him. "You've not properly thought this through."

"*Au contraire.* I've thought it through quite well. It's quite simple: I hold your friends here until *their* friend comes and gives me what I need."

"You have no idea how long that will take."

"And who will come for you in the meantime? Malik? He can barely hold the council together, let alone mount an attack."

"Sasha will come."

"By herself? How very effective that will no doubt prove."

Jakob frowned. "Even if you are able to hold me here, when Two comes she will bring Naomi and Stephen."

Aros slapped his hands to his cheeks in mock surprise. "A single warrior and an *Ashayt politician?!* However will we defeat them?"

Jakob said nothing, and Aros grinned at him.

"You see? There is no one. Abraham's death has left the country empty and weak. You are perhaps the most dangerous vampire in the United States at the moment, other than myself of course, and I already have you here."

"You consider yourself more dangerous than I am?"

"I do have four hundred years on you."

"Four hundred years with swill in your veins."

Aros's lip curled, but he maintained his composure. "That was impolite. Must I remind you, Jakob, that you live only because I've had no particular reason to kill you? It's the humans I need."

"If you're expecting me to cower or beg for my life, you're in for a long wait."

"That remains to be seen. For now, I am content. You are correct: the blood in my veins is not of the same quality that yours is. That will soon change."

"Yes ... I believe this is where your plans move from ill-conceived to outright madness."

"It's a simple matter of vision, and you lack any."

"You truly believe the things that you claim Abraham promised you?"

"I do. We had an arrangement, and I delivered my part of it. That he managed to get himself killed by some human whore is not my fault. He owed me blood. I want it."

"Abraham is dead. His *son* is dead. His son's daughter is a human with only the slightest trace of Eresh in her blood. By the time she returns, she may well be an Ashayt fledgling. Even if Abraham wasn't lying to you, and he almost assuredly was, you can't really believe that her blood can do anything for you."

"You don't understand the research Abraham has done on our blood, and on his own most particularly. You have no idea what strength still lies dormant in the human girl's blood. I have known for many decades now that Abraham's research held the key to ending the misery of the Burilgi."

"And when you left the council, you struck a deal with him. Build him an army, and he would make you an Eresh."

"Not an Eresh. Something else."

"Indeed. And now you have an army, but no blood."

"Yes."

"What, pray tell, are you going to do with all of these poor creatures you've tricked into following you? What will happen when you fail to lead them to the promised land?"

"There is no trick. That is what you fail to understand. They will be delivered. We will *all* be delivered. The Ay'Araf, the Ashayt, the Eresh ... they will be wiped out."

"You plan to wage war against the other races?"

Aros again flashed his disquieting grin. "Why make war when all I need is the blood from a single girl?"

* * *

"I'd like to know what you meant, before."

Sarah was sitting on the couch, where she had spent most of the past two days. Rhes had been more active, taking advantage of the compound's indoor pool and weight room, but Sarah had not been able to find the motivation. At this moment, her husband was taking an after-dinner walk around the grounds, enjoying the unexpectedly warm weather for December.

"What I meant about what?" Aros asked.

He had arrived unannounced at the house just after Rhes had left, and Sarah doubted this timing was a coincidence. He had rung the bell and waited outside, apparently not minding that it took her a couple of minutes to make her way through the unfamiliar surroundings and open the door. Sarah had asked him why he hadn't simply entered. After all, it *was* his base.

"It would be impolite," Aros had said as he stepped through the door.

"So is abducting people," Sarah had pointed out.

"Sometimes it is necessary to be impolite. This isn't one of those times."

"Why are you here, Mr. Kreskas?"

"I thought I would stop by, check in on the two of you, see how you're getting along."

"Rhes isn't here."

"Perhaps we could talk, then? I was hoping to find out a bit more about you."

Sarah had agreed to speak with him. Why not? It wasn't as if she had anything better to do, and though she had tried, she had not been able to dismiss his comment about her eyes from her thoughts. Now, after some small talk, she had worked up the courage to ask, and he was toying with her.

"You know what I mean," she said.

"Your eyes." There was a smile in Aros's voice.

"Yes, my eyes. Tell me what you meant."

"I don't imagine you enjoy being blind."

"No, I don't. Can you fix me?"

"That is an interesting question. I have seen many remarkable things in my time. Some have even seemed miraculous. I have seen the blind restored to sight more than once."

"In humans?"

"No, Sarah. Vampire blood – and there's no sense pretending that's not what we're discussing – can perform small feats of healing in human beings, but it is not going to fix your eyesight."

"Well ... shit."

"In order to truly take hold of the body and begin to restore complex functionality, the blood needs complete control. You would need to embrace the gift of vampirism."

"Not interested," Sarah told him.

"Ah. A shame, though, spending your life in darkness."

"Science has come a long way in twenty years," Sarah said.

"Indeed it has."

"Maybe in another twenty, they'll be able to give me my eyes back."

"Anything is possible, I suppose," Aros replied. His voice was serene, but Sarah thought she could hear an unpleasant undertone to it. She had the sense that Aros was mocking her, and enjoying it.

"Rhes ... he thinks you're just saying this stuff to, you know, fuck with me."

"Rhes is paranoid, and his impression of me has been stained by talking with Jakob. He says he doesn't care about vampire politics, but the influence is clear."

"That doesn't mean he's wrong."

Aros chuckled. "I've not lied to either of you since you've arrived, nor have I made any attempt to 'fuck with' you."

This was true, at least as far as Sarah could tell, but she didn't want to discuss it any further.

"Let's change the subject, huh?" she said.

"Whatever you'd prefer," Aros said.

"Well, you're the one who showed up at our door ..."

"I was merely curious about how you and Rhes were finding it here."

"It's fine. Comfortable. We'd like to go home ... we're worried about our daughter."

"My sources tell me that she's been taken in by Jakob's fledgling, Sasha."

Sarah didn't respond to this, but Aros must have read something of her shock and dismay on her face.

"Not fond of that idea? Can't say I blame you."

Sarah sighed, shrugged, said, "Not much I can do about it now."

"That is true."

"Do you have any idea how long we're going to be kept here?"

"I have some idea, yes. Your friend is no longer in London, and no one seems quite sure where it is that she's gone, but Jakob himself informed me that he has heard from one of her escorts, and that they will be back in the United States 'soon.' I have no doubt that your friend will come for you, when she hears that you've been taken."

"When you have her, what are you going to do with her?"

"Vampire things," Aros said, and made a little giggling noise that Sarah didn't like at all. When he made no further elaboration, she debated pushing him and decided against it.

"OK. I was just curious. We have lives to get back to. If Rhes hadn't taken a bunch of vacation time this month, you'd probably be costing him his job."

"I am aware that this is inconvenient. Unfortunately, it is also essential. I assure you, all of your worries will soon be over."

Not liking the sound of that, Sarah chose to say nothing. After a moment, Aros continued.

"I will go now, Sarah. Do not feel the need to escort me out."

"OK. I ... well, thank you for telling me about Molly."

"Certainly. I am sure we will speak again. Perhaps you can think some more about my offer."

"We'll see."

She heard Aros stand up and say, "Goodbye for now."

"Bye."

She heard him cross the room and exit through the front door. His footsteps on the concrete sidewalk dwindled away. Sarah sat back on the couch, took off her glasses, and put her hands over her broken eyes.

* * *

In her dreams, Sarah could see.

The world of her dreams was oversaturated, radiant with light and color, and Sarah found herself moving wildly, trying to take it all in at once. She would weep at the beauty of it all, spinning in circles, arms outstretched, laughing and crying all at once.

Rhes would be there, and she would run to him, and he would kiss the tears from her cheeks, and smile at her, and look into her eyes. They would stay like that, communicating without speech, talking with their eyes, until at last the dream would begin to fade.

Usually, she woke from these dreams filled with melancholy, wondering if her mental image of what Rhes looked like was even correct. Did she have it right, or had her brain turned him into something he wasn't? Sarah hadn't seen anything but darkness in twenty years. She only knew what her fingers had told her about Rhes's face.

This time, though, when he appeared before her, she felt no joy. With every step he took, a curtain of darkness descended further and further upon her. Sarah cried out to him to stop, to wait, but he didn't seem to understand her words, and by the time he had reached her there was only an unending black, darker even than an empty ocean in the dead of night.

Sarah woke, weeping in the dark. She tried to stop herself but felt overwhelmed, unable to gain control. Here she was, lying in this strange bed, trapped in this strange house, captive of a creature she could never truly understand. Now he was taunting her even in her dreams. Aros held the key to that which she had wanted most for twenty years and was dangling it now just out of her reach. It wasn't fair.

Rhes stirred beside her but did not wake. Sarah stared upwards with her sightless eyes and wept.

I don't even know what he looks like, she thought, and sobbed again. *I only know his eyes are brown because he told me. I only know his hair is black because he told me. How can he stand that?*

Rhes moved again beside her, twisting onto his side, and said, "Hon?"

Sarah rolled onto her side as well, turning away from him. "Don't," she said through her tears.

"Don't what?" Rhes asked, his voice groggy and perplexed.

"Don't look at me."

"Why not?"

"I can't look back!" Sarah cried. She covered her face with her hands.

She could hear Rhes sitting up. God damn her ears and how they had adapted to her lack of sight. God damn her sense of smell, and touch, and taste for doing the same. God damn *everything* about her blindness.

Rhes touched her shoulder and said, "It's never bothered me that you can't look back. I'm sorry it hurts you so much."

"Oh, Rhes, I just want to *see* you," Sarah said. "I just ... I dream that I can see you. I dream about it all the time."

"I didn't know that," Rhes said.

"I never wanted to tell you," Sarah replied. She shifted to her back, sniffling. "I don't like you to think about me being blind. It scares me."

Rhes ran his fingers through her hair. "Scares you?"

"I'm fucking defective. I'm broken. I'm afraid you'll realize that and won't want to be with me anymore."

She felt the pad of his thumb smooth tears away from first one cheek, and then the other.

"I'm with you because I'm in love with you. Baby, I don't give a shit if you can see or not. When we're living our normal lives and things aren't crazy like this, I don't even think about it anymore."

"I don't want you to stop loving me."

"There is no way that's going to happen."

Sarah managed some semblance of a smile at this. Rhes slid back down next to her and put an arm around her waist. She curled up against him.

"This is because of Aros, right? You talked to him again."

"I had to. He came by and I ... I couldn't help it. I'm sorry."

"You don't have to be sorry, but he's lying to you."

Sarah shook her head. "I don't think so, baby. Not about that. He really *can* fix my eyes, or at least he believes it."

"I guess."

"I told him no. I told him I wasn't interested."

"Good," Rhes said. He paused for a moment, long enough that Sarah thought he might be falling back asleep, before continuing. "Sarah ... did you tell him that for you? Or for me?"

Sarah considered this and couldn't locate the answer. Finally, she gave Rhes the truth.

"I don't know."

* * *

Jakob showed up at their door the next night, escorted by four of Aros's guards. The guards left Jakob at the front door, saying they had been told to surround the house. One of them advised Jakob that if he wasn't back out in thirty minutes, they would come in after him.

"Glad to know you're not dead," Rhes said once they'd taken a seat in the living room.

Jakob nodded. "I think Aros enjoys lording his control over me. At any rate, he has no reason to kill me yet, or either of you."

"Why would he kill us?" Rhes asked.

"Once he has your friend, you are expendable. He might let you go, or he might murder you both. I am quite sure he'll have me killed."

"You seem ... pretty calm about that," Sarah said.

"I will go out fighting," Jakob replied. "In the end, that's my primary concern. He's going to have to use up more of his Burilgi on me than he thinks."

"What the hell does he even want with Two, anyway?" Rhes asked. "He mentioned something about her blood."

"He believes he can use her blood to somehow change himself into some new type of vampire."

"Can he?" Sarah asked.

"I highly doubt it."

Rhes rolled his eyes. "Awesome ... so what's the point?"

"Aros has been a vampire for seven hundred years. That's exceptional for a Burilgi, and as far as I'm aware, he's the oldest living member of the race. Most of them die much earlier, usually within their first century or so. Aros has spent all of that time in envy of the other vampires around them, jealous of their blood. It's driven him more than a little mad, I fear."

"You can hear that in the way he laughs," Rhes said.

Jakob nodded. "Yes, and you can see it in his eyes at times."

Sarah bit her lower lip, thinking, and said, "So if he gets Two and takes her blood, that will kill her?"

"Draining someone's blood typically has that effect," Jakob said.

"I didn't know how much he needed," Sarah said, her voice dry. "Why would he kill us, if he gets what he wants?"

"As I said, I've no idea if that's what he'll do. In my case, it would be a test of whatever newfound power it is he thinks he's going to acquire. Or, if it turns out that I'm right and all he ends up with is a dead girl and nothing to show for it, then he'll probably just kill me out of spite."

"Jakob ..." Sarah began, and then stopped.

"Yes?"

"I ... I spoke with ... you know what? Never mind. Forget it."

Jakob raised an eyebrow and glanced at Rhes, who sighed.

"Tell him, hon."

"Aros told me he could cure my blindness," Sarah said. "Can he?"

Jakob considered this for a moment and said, "It's not out of the realm of possibility."

Sarah leaned forward in her chair, resting her elbows on her crossed legs. "You're sure?"

"Vampire blood works to perfect the host," Jakob explained. "It's a slow process, and the final result depends on the blood. If Aros were an Eresh, he could guarantee it. The blood would go to work, repairing your eyes. You might begin to see again within a few weeks."

"That fast?" Sarah asked, and Rhes frowned a bit at the breathless quality of her voice.

"Aros is not an Eresh," Jakob reminded her.

"Yeah, but still ..."

"Indeed. He is a Burilgi. That means there is a *chance* your sight will return. A relatively good chance, actually; even Burilgi blood is not always without its benefits. There's the strength increase, for example."

"Familiar with that one," Rhes commented.

"You must understand the risks, though," Jakob continued. "With another type of blood, you would be almost assured of regaining your sight. With Burilgi blood ... Who knows? It could just as well leave you blind *and* curse you with deformities."

Sarah bit her lip, saying nothing.

"Sarah ... hon—" Rhes began.

"I don't need a lecture!"

"Wasn't planning on giving one," Rhes muttered, frowning. Jakob glanced at him, and then back at Sarah.

"Aros is most definitely toying with you, but he is not lying to you," the vampire said. "Unfortunately, that is not the greatest of our concerns at this time."

"It isn't?" Sarah asked, sounding mildly insulted.

"Aros has, in the best tradition of all lunatics, decided to fill me in on some of his plans. He means to steal Two's blood, and we know that once he does he will kill me, and kill Naomi and Stephen if they come here with her. Further, he plans to use the blood to create some sort of serum that will 'level the playing field' by unifying all vampires under a single strain."

"What if they don't want to be unified?" Sarah asked, and Jakob glanced at her.

"I don't think he plans on giving them a choice. And given what I've learned tonight, that is what concerns me the most. I didn't know for sure until this evening that the army he's built for himself now stands at well over two thousand vampires."

Rhes stared at Jakob in astonishment. "What the hell does he need that many men for?"

"It began at Abraham's request, God only knows why. Now? A cult organization called the Children of the Sun, an anti-vampire group, have begun abducting Burilgi. Many Burilgi have come to him for protection because they have no faith in the council. I ... can't say that I blame them, though I wish they'd chosen a more stable leader."

"What are they doing with the vampires they kidnap?" Sarah asked.

"We don't know, but it's probably not good. Aros has reached a point where he no longer cares what they're doing with the abductees. He plans on wiping the cult out entirely. Once that's done, there's nothing to stop him from sending his people out across this country, and further. He will attempt to usher in this new age he desires."

"Would it be such a bad thing if all vampires were the same? I mean ... it does seem kind of unfair that some of you get to be superheroes, and others are stuck living in sewers."

"It's highly unfair, and I'm not entirely against taking steps to attempt to improve the Burilgi strain, or to unify all four races.

The problem is that I don't believe Aros is going to get what he wants from your friend's blood."

"And when he doesn't ..." Rhes began.

"You're afraid he's going to crack," Sarah finished for him.

Jakob massaged the back of his neck, frowning. "Yes. I'm afraid it will be the last straw that sends him from envy to murderous rage. If he can't be on the same level as us, he may decide to simply wipe us out entirely, and if he comes at the council with two thousand vampires, he stands a good chance of accomplishing that. His chances are further improved if he kills Naomi, Stephen, and me, the three vampires most capable of actually galvanizing the council members into action."

"And if Two comes here, so will they," Rhes said, "because they're the ones protecting her."

"It's a very pretty little package," Jakob said. "I really don't think it could have worked out this well if he'd planned it. My being at your townhouse, Naomi and Stephen on their way back to America, the council in complete disarray ..."

"So what's the plan?" Sarah asked, and Jakob glanced up at her, amused.

"Americans. There must *always* be a plan."

"I think if we try to wing it, we're going to get shot to death."

"I think you're correct. There are several issues with an escape attempt, not the least of which being that Aros does not even allow me above ground without a detachment of guards, all of them carrying guns. I'm not fast enough to outrun a hail of bullets, and even if I managed to fight through them, you would both die. I'm not fond of that idea."

"Hey, me neither," Rhes said, his tone unusually sarcastic. Sarah gave him a wan smile.

"Nobody's dying," she said.

"I think we wait," said Jakob. "We wait, and we try to keep Aros in a good mood. At least for now, it seems to be serving us well."

"I don't like counting on Aros's goodwill," Sarah told him.

"Nor do I. If you have suggestions, Sarah, I am open to them. I'm rather tired of living off of bagged blood. It tastes like plastic."

"Gross," Sarah said. She bit her lower lip for a moment, thinking, and then sighed and shook her head.

"Got nothin'."

Someone banged on the door and snarled, "Time's up! Fucking *Bourgeoisie*, get out here!"

"Oh, for God's sake ... I grew up a goat farmer," Jakob muttered. He stood, and started for the door.

"Try not to get killed before we see you again," Sarah told him as he passed her. Jakob laughed.

"Yes. I will do exactly that. You do the same."

CHAPTER XX

Reunion

"Malik, I'm telling you that I have the information we need right now. I know where Aros is. Will you not at *least* call an emergency meeting to discuss it?"

Sasha was leaning back in her chair, staring at the ceiling, clearly furious. Molly was watching from the couch, no happier than the vampire about what was obviously being said on the other end of the connection. The email from Jerry had arrived that evening, containing not only information on Aros's whereabouts, but blueprints of the decommissioned base and even information on some of his known associates, most of whom Sasha had never heard of, though Lewis and Richard's names had been among those listed. Jerry was many things, and most of those were bad, but he took his work very seriously.

"No," Sasha was saying, "I don't think I'm overreacting. I think you're afraid of confrontation and unwilling to do what's necessary."

Sasha was expressing more emotion than she had at any time since Molly had met her. As well as the vampire woman had hidden it, Jakob's absence was eating her up. Molly could sense ragged edges growing in Sasha's composure, and knew she must be terrified of what Aros might decide to do with Jakob.

"I will *not* take it back!" Sasha snarled. "Mark my words, Malik, when this is over, there will be changes."

Sasha's voice had grown tight, her left hand wrapped around the chair's arm, knuckles white with the pressure.

"We will see. No. No! No, I will not promise you anything. Ah … *yebat' tvoyu mat'!*" This last was a shout, and Sasha hurled the phone across the room. It made a dent in the sheetrock and clattered to the floor in three different pieces. Molly doubted it would ever work again. Sasha sat forward and put her head in her hands.

"*Govnyuk*," she muttered, her voice tired.

"What?" Molly asked. Sasha glanced over at her. The sofa folded out into a bed, and Molly had been using it as such for several days. It was almost two in the morning, and Molly was propped up against her pillows, wearing a pink nightgown.

"Nothing. Russian. Go to sleep."

"Can't," Molly said. "Hanging with you is totally fucking up my schedule."

"We won't be 'hanging' for much longer," Sasha said.

"Why not?"

Sasha ignored her and instead turned to the computer. She read the email again, looked over the attached documents again, went to the Web and checked on a few things.

"Two hours," she muttered.

"Until what?" Molly asked.

"No, I mean that is how long it would take to get there, give or take. Two hours. I could go tonight. I could …"

"Get killed," Molly finished for her.

"I have to try something," Sasha replied. "He's going to kill Jakob. He *has* to. If Aros leaves him alive through all of this, there's going to be a reckoning. Such blatant disregard for council law won't be tolerated. Aros knows that Jakob can stir the council where Malik cannot. The only way this works is if Jakob never comes back alive. He might be dead already."

"What could you do for him?" Molly asked.

"I'll do whatever's necessary for him," Sasha said.

Molly tilted her head, resting it against her palm, studying the vampire. At last, Sasha made a sound of frustration, tired of this silent appraisal.

"What?" she asked. "What is it?"

"Do you love him?" Molly asked.

"Love is a waste of time," Sasha said. "He is my boss."

"Didn't ask what you *thought* about love."

Sasha bit her lip, but she wouldn't meet Molly's eyes.

"I love my mom and dad, too," Molly said. "Not like *that*, of course, but I mean ... I love them."

"I didn't say I loved him."

Molly smiled, another of those adult expressions she sometimes wore that had no business being on the face of a young teenage girl.

"Sure you did."

Sasha sighed. "It's not like that. Not exactly. Yes, very well, I love Jakob. Not quite the way I loved my fiancé before he died, but not quite the way I loved my father, either. It's ... somewhere between the two, and is difficult to explain. I would die for Jakob if he needed me to, but I am not upset that in two hundred years he has never kissed me. Why does it matter?"

"I dunno, maybe he wants to but—"

"No, I'm not asking about that. Molly ... he doesn't want to. Jakob has never fancied women."

"Oh. OH!" Molly's brain caught up with this information, and her cheeks went pink. "I get it. Sorry."

"It's all right. It's no secret. What I meant was, why does it matter now whether I love him or not? How does it impact the present situation?"

"Well, I have an idea, but it's not gonna make you popular. I thought, you know, if you loved him enough ..."

Sasha glanced over at her. "What's your idea?"

"Just call the meeting without Malik."

Sasha laughed at this, a pretty, sparkling sound that Molly thought the vampire's friends probably would have liked to hear more often than they did.

"You are insane," Sasha said. "I probably just cost myself a council seat with that phone call. Attempting a *coup d'état*? I would be killed."

"You'll be killed going after Jakob by yourself, too."

"Yes, that's why I'm not going to."

"Not tonight anyway," Molly muttered.

"What?" Sasha asked.

"Oh, come on. You can hear whispers through walls. I know you know what I said."

Sasha looked exasperated. "I wasn't asking you to repeat yourself, but to explain yourself."

"You've gotten worse every night. What's it gonna be? Two more days? Three?"

"Until what?"

"Until you fucking go by yourself and try to save him!" Molly sounded annoyed, and Sasha supposed that was within the girl's right. It was a bit unnerving, having her motivations so easily and accurately read by a child.

"You may have a point," she admitted.

"The vampires on the council don't like Malik, right?"

"Not particularly."

"So who do they like?"

"Naomi. Jakob. Stephen is highly respected, but he wouldn't accept a position of leadership even were anyone so insane as to offer it to him. There is no one who ..." Sasha's eyes grew suddenly wide.

"What?" Molly asked.

"Good God, I've been a fool," Sasha said, already turning back to her computer. "William! They would listen to William."

"Who's William?"

"Naomi's council seat once belonged to William. He retired after ... you remember what I told you of Abraham and your friend Two's actions? He retired after that. I believe he needed some time away from politics."

"Will he help you?"

"Me? Probably not. We were on good terms but not friends. But he might help Jakob, if for no other reason than because Naomi would. He is nearly as old as Malik, and he is an Ashayt, and he is ... Lord, Molly, thank you. I should have thought of this already."

"No prob."

Sasha clicked through a few screens, scanned one briefly, and said, "I have his number."

"Awesome," Molly said, dryly amused. "Now if only you had a phone …"

* * *

"I agreed to meet with you because I know that you and Jakob are very close with Naomi, Sasha, and because I respect your sire very much," William said. "I am not sure, though, that I can do these things you are asking of me."

They were sitting in William's apartment, a penthouse in lower Manhattan that offered extraordinary views of the Brooklyn skyline. Two entire walls of the room they occupied were made of glass, and Molly was standing in front of one, staring rapt out at the city below.

"I would not ask you for this help if there was anyone else," Sasha said. "Malik is … he is weak. Forgive me – he is my elder, but it is true. Aros is going to kill Jakob and bring his army down upon us. We must strike now."

William sighed and laid his head back against his couch, staring up at the ceiling. He was an older man, as vampires went, having reached his early forties before undergoing the change. He had short, immaculately cut brown hair and the polished look of a corporate VIP, a vice president, perhaps. He was wearing what Sasha could only assume was his idea of a casual outfit: a button-down shirt, tie, and sport coat. Every time she had seen William in the past, he had been outfitted in a full, exquisitely tailored three-piece suit.

"I thought I had escaped all this," William said at last, to no one in particular.

"Sasha, you should check this out!" Molly was pressing herself against the window, arms spread wide. "It's like you're flying!"

Sasha, who in nearly two hundred years had never fully conquered a fear of heights, said only, "There is more important business at hand."

"Your loss," Molly said, glancing over her shoulder before returning her attention to the view.

"William ..." Sasha began, but he held up his hand.

"I knew when I left the council that Malik was weak," William said. "Are you sure I am any better? Stephen had unpleasant things to say about me when I announced my retirement."

"Stephen was frustrated because he cares about the council. He knew that leaving Malik in charge would cause problems. He was ... disappointed."

William shrugged. "Stephen did not have to spend three hundred years dealing with Abraham. Attempting to counter that maniac's machinations was exhausting. If there had only been Malik to hold him back, the vampires of this country would be living as his slaves."

"We know. That was why we assumed you would succeed Abraham ... but few of us would deny that you've earned some peace."

"There must be others who are capable. Naomi is ready."

"Naomi is *gone*," Sasha said. "She left us to take care of the *Eresh-Chen*, and no one has any idea where she is. Calls are going unanswered. The European council could keep her for years, if they choose to."

"I am sure if she could have predicted the current crisis ..."

"But she couldn't."

"And now she's gone. Yes, very well, I understand."

"All you have to do is call them. You know they will come, if it's you. Tell them it is an emergency, that we must meet tomorrow and decide our course of action. There is no more time."

"You are sure that this army of Aros's is a real thing?"

"As sure as I can be without having seen it with my own eyes. Lewis and Richard swear to it, and the data we acquired from Molly's ... acquaintance ... backs them up. He's building an army. He may aim his people at the Children of the Sun first, but eventually he will come for us."

William closed his eyes. Sasha continued, trying to keep the note of pleading desperation from her voice.

"You spent three hundred years fighting to protect the vampires of this country, William. Abraham is dead now, and you deserve your peace, but there is danger still and ... and I cannot face it alone. I am not strong enough."

This was as hard an admission as she had ever made. Sasha was Ay'Araf; she was a warrior. She was not supposed to be so powerless, so dependent upon others for help. The tone in her voice seemed to convey something of her misery at this situation to William. He looked at her, smiled, and nodded.

"Very well, Sasha. I cannot promise you that the council will decide in your favor, but I can promise that you will have your meeting. I will help you."

"Yeah!" exclaimed Molly, turning again to look at them. "Kickass!"

Sasha took William's hands in hers and said, "Thank you. Jakob would thank you too, I'm sure, as would Molly's parents."

William gave her a thin smile. "Wait to thank me," he said, "until we are sure that they are still alive."

Sasha, who didn't want to think about any other possibility, nodded her head. She collected Molly, shook William's hand, and took her leave. Soon they were in her car, driving north along First Avenue, heading for her apartment.

"So what now?" Molly asked.

"Now? Molly, I ..." Sasha shook her head, focused on the road ahead of her for a moment, thinking.

"What?"

"If the council decides to act, there is going to be fighting. I think your part in this is done," Sasha said.

"Fuck *you!*" Molly cried. "I've been helping! Haven't I been helping?"

"Yes, of course. Very much! But things are going to get complicated."

"I've done complicated."

"And dangerous."

"Done that, too."

"Not like this."

Molly crossed her arms, her lower lip jutting out, and stared ahead. "This isn't fair. I want to help."

Sasha glanced at her and smiled. "I know, but—"

"I'm not a kid! I'm not a normal kid, anyway. I know how to hold a gun, and I know how to ... how to ... I can do *something*, anyway!" Molly's voice wavered and Sasha realized the girl was fighting off tears. She reached across the seat and took Molly's hand.

"You've already done much."

"Not enough."

Sasha smiled a little and said, "Your parents ... do you love them?"

"Yes!"

"Do they love you?"

"I ... I think so? I mean, they say they do."

"I am absolutely sure you know the answer to this question," Sasha said.

Molly nodded. "Yes, they do. I ... when I'm with them, I can feel it."

"Think of how you would feel if they died."

"Been thinking about that for days," Molly croaked.

"Now think of how they would feel if you died."

"But ..."

"Do it. Take the time and actually think about it. If your parents live through this and come back to find you dead, what will it do to them?"

Molly thought and, at last, took in a deep, hitching breath. She blew it outwards, head down, in a weary sigh.

"It would ruin their lives," Sasha said.

Molly nodded.

"I cannot protect you from what may happen at Aros's base. I am not sure I will come through this alive, and I will not let that uncertainty extend to you. I ... this may not mean much to you, but it would be fair to say that, at present, you are absolutely my favorite human in the world."

Molly turned a shade of pink at this but said nothing.

"I don't want to see you hurt, or killed, and I would never put your parents through such a thing. You've all been through too much as it is."

"I want to help them," Molly said.

"You've given them so much help already, but it will all be worthless if they come home to a murdered daughter."

Molly opened her mouth to protest this but couldn't seem to find the words. Finally, she shut her mouth and stared out the window. Sasha gave her the time she needed, not speaking.

"OK," Molly said at last. "OK, fine ... but I'm coming to the meeting. No one's going to try to kill me there. Once you know what's going on, I'll stay out of it, but I want to be there."

Sasha thought that was fair. "You won't try to stow away or anything else equally foolish?"

"No, I won't. I'm ... you're right. I can't fight vampires."

"Do you have somewhere to go in the event that ... I mean, should your parents be ..."

"If they're dead, I'll go see Sid," Molly said. "They're not dead. I don't want to talk about that."

Sasha couldn't blame her.

"Thank you, Molly," she said. "Thank you for your help, and for accepting this. I ... you've changed my view on humans quite a bit."

Molly glanced over at her and said, "Good. We're not *all* assholes ... just most of us."

Sasha was feeling in substantially better spirits now that William had agreed to help her. She produced her pretty laugh again and said, "Most vampires, too."

* * *

There were ten, so far, who had arrived at the cathedral. William, Sasha, Lewis and Richard had been the first to arrive, followed by the two remaining Ashayt council members, Samuel and his apprentice Wilson. Leonore was sitting in the back of the church, looking simultaneously annoyed and curious. Her apprentice, a dimwitted vampire named James, looked dumbfounded as usual.

Sasha had expected these two to arrive early, and they had not disappointed her. Leonore desperately wished to be involved in anything of significance that was happening in the vampire world.

The last two vampires in the cathedral were both Ay'Araf. The elder, who was standing near William and glancing around with interest, originally came from England and was named Peter Markham. Of the Ay'Araf in the country, he was younger only than Malik and Jakob, nearly three hundred years old. His apprentice Kanene, a strikingly beautiful woman with jet-black skin who had become a vampire on board a slave ship bound for the Caribbean, stood at his side.

"This is highly unorthodox, William," Markham commented.

"I understand your concern, Peter. I assure you, if there were any other choice ..." William let the sentence trail off, shrugging. The vampires of this country knew that he, of all people, would not break protocol without a reason.

"Do you think more will show?" Sasha asked. She had barely left William's side since arriving at the cathedral, understanding that if she did so, she and Molly would only be ostracized. The other vampires would avoid them both, Molly for her humanity and Sasha for her role in this seeming *coup d'état*. William was protection, and not only of a political sort; as the single most physically powerful vampire in the new world, with Abraham and Theroen dead, he could offer support that no other could give.

"Malik will show, certainly," William said. "I assume he will bring Theresa with him."

Theresa was Malik's apprentice, only recently elected. When Abraham had still lived, neither he nor Malik had taken an apprentice. Malik had served the subordinate role, despite being older than any other vampire on the council, because Abraham had not wanted to involve Theroen in vampire politics. Naomi claimed that this was because Abraham both detested and feared Theroen's nature. The other vampires, having had no contact with the *Eresh-Chen*, could only take her word for it.

Theresa was a sycophant, able only to parrot Malik's views on the rare occasions when she spoke to anyone. Her own sire had been killed by the Comanche in the years just following the Civil

War, and she had spent the time since latching on to vampires in various positions of power. She worked diligently for whomever she served but seemed incapable of surviving on her own. Malik had chosen her not because he wished for a weak apprentice to control, but because there were no other Ay'Araf interested in the job.

"Will he be angry?" Sasha asked.

"I should think so," William replied. "Don't concern yourself. I will handle Malik."

"I will be concerned with all of this, until a decision is made," Sasha said. William nodded at this, smiling slightly to himself.

"You were wise to bring the girl," he said. Molly was sitting on a church pew not far from them, playing a video game on her cell phone. She glanced up at this but said nothing.

"It was her idea," Sasha conceded. "Why do you think so?"

"Although it sometimes seems like all those on the council – save perhaps Lewis and Richard – have lost touch with their humanity, we are all still at our cores the people that we once were. Molly can touch that. Her youth, her exuberance, her comfort with her more basic emotions ... these things may be useful. They could help perhaps to reawaken the council members from what has become decades of complacency and apathy."

Sasha considered this. "She has certainly had some impact on me. I've become quite fond of her. It hadn't occurred to me that she might have a similar effect on the others."

William turned toward her, eyebrows raised. "If you're going to be successful in politics, you must learn how to manipulate people. You must do it consciously, without shame, no matter how distasteful you may sometimes find it."

"I've no interest in playing political games," Sasha said.

"Yet you serve as apprentice to a man who is quite adept at it. You must learn to connect with people, the way Jakob does, and use that to your advantage."

"Why?"

"Do you believe the current structure will exist forever? People, even vampires, get old and tired. Sometimes they die. Jakob and Naomi will inherit this council soon enough, and you will find yourself even more deeply enmeshed than you already are in what goes on here."

Sasha frowned, trying to keep from betraying the concern that welled up within her at this statement. William put a hand on her shoulder.

"There are many years yet before all of this comes to pass. Jakob has taught you well thus far, and will continue to do so, once we've found him."

"If he's not dead," Sasha said.

William shrugged. "We're working to prevent that, if it can still be prevented."

Sasha sighed and nodded. It was as she had told Molly on the night when they had visited her fixer, Jerry, they were doing all that they could. That would have to be good enough.

A few more Ay'Araf vampires entered the cathedral, greeting those who had already arrived, and more came after that. Sasha waited, observed, glancing occasionally at her watch. They were ten minutes past when the meeting was supposed to start and there were still six council members missing, including Malik and Theresa. Sasha was surprised by this last, having expected Malik to be one of the first to show up.

Eventually, two more council members strolled in, and William turned to her.

"I don't believe the Janssen twins will show up," he said. "They're notoriously unconcerned with this sort of thing. That leaves only Malik and ..."

As if waiting for his name to be spoken, Malik banged through the cathedral doors, Theresa in tow, eyes ablaze. Sasha wondered if he had been sitting outside, waiting for the last vampires to show up before making his entrance. He made his way down the aisle and stood in the center of the arc of council members, glowering. William, standing at the podium, regarded him with a calm that impressed Sasha.

"This is against every law, every policy, every—" Malik began. William interrupted him.

"Then step up here, Malik, and lead. Your council needs you. Your *people* need you, and you have done nothing."

"Jakob—" Malik began again.

"It is not up to Jakob to do these things, and would not be even had he not been abducted."

Malik paused, frowned, his eyes narrowing.

"I am not here to take your council from you," William told him, and then he smiled. "Though when Naomi gets back …"

Malik's lip curled. "Taunt me as much as you like, William. You *left* your responsibility, and I had no choice but to pick up the load. If Naomi wants this council, she may come and try to take it. I doubt very much she will."

"Oh, no?"

"Your apprentice has run away with her *Eresh-Chen* friend and that idiot Stephen. She's been gone for months, impossible to contact. We've heard nothing from her, but I've heard from the European council. They passed their judgment weeks ago. Where is she, William? Where do you suppose she's gone?"

William was about to respond to this when he was interrupted.

"Think what you will of me, Malik, but Naomi is very much alive," Stephen said, walking toward the front of the cathedral with a sarcastic grin on his face. He and another guest, who was trailing behind him, her face obscured by shadows, had slipped through the doors unnoticed.

"Stephen?" Sasha asked, and she saw his grin widen at the shock clearly visible on her face.

"So surprised to see me, Sasha?" he asked. "Naomi called Jakob and told him we were on our way home. Did he not communicate the news to you?"

"Jakob has been abducted by the Burilgi," William said. "It's good to see you, Stephen. There is much to talk about."

"Finally standing where you belong," Stephen said to him with an approving nod. "Good. Yes, there is much to talk about. More than you know … but there must be more than I know as well, because this information about Jakob is new to me. I suppose this means he hasn't rented the apartment Naomi requested."

"Where *is* Naomi?" William asked.

"She's here ... but not *here*, clearly. There was another matter that she and Two had to attend to."

"The *Eresh-Chen*?" William asked. "Is she a vampire again?"

Stephen grinned again at this but didn't answer.

"The *Eresh-Chen* is not a concern right now," Malik said. Stephen gave him an amused glance and looked back at William.

"Stephen, please, where is Naomi?" William asked.

"She and Two had an errand to run. They'll be back in the city later tonight."

"What errand?"

"One that's going to wait for her to tell. Never fear, though, I've my own surprise for you. Why don't you say hello, dear?"

Stephen's guest stepped out of the shadows and glanced around at the other vampires, a small, serene smile on her face. She was short, thin but well-muscled, her skin dark and her hair black. She had straightened it and pulled it tight into a high ponytail, banded with gold. She was wearing a jade-colored sleeveless gown and every exposed inch of her brown skin, including her face, was covered with interweaving blue-black tattoos. These markings seemed almost to move on their own, as if forming words in some ancient, forgotten language.

"Greetings, children," the woman said, and her accent was unlike anything the vampires assembled in the room had ever heard before. She bowed her head momentarily to William, still standing at the podium. "It is good to see that even in this modern age, you attempt to hold to the codes laid down by Eresh herself, so long ago."

William tilted his head, inspecting this newcomer, unable to take his eyes away from her. "Madame ... I'm sorry, but I must ask, who *are* you?"

The woman's smile grew broad, her white teeth contrasting against her dark, inked skin. She looked up at William and spoke in that same calm, even voice.

"But child ... surely you know who I am?"

There was a momentary pause, and then William's body actually jerked with the force of his recognition, and he grabbed the sides of the podium tightly. His eyes grew wide, his jaw dropped, and when he spoke it was with a breathless tone that none in the audience had ever before heard from him.

"Oh," he said, and then, after another moment, "oh my dear God ..."

CHAPTER XXI

The Offer

"Something is happening amongst the vampire council," Jakob said. He was sitting with Rhes and Sarah in the living room of their temporary home, fingers tented and pressed against his chin.

"About time," Sarah commented, and Jakob nodded.

"Yes, it could have been faster if there had been someone left in charge other than Malik, but something is happening nonetheless. Aros seemed quite agitated when he came to speak with me earlier. He didn't explain much, only that my council was preparing to do something stupid and that he would be ready for it."

Rhes sat forward, then back, shifted his legs, perplexed. "And then he let you come over here? No offense, Jakob, but I don't get why he's keeping you around."

"He may have considered me a bargaining chip, but if that was the case, it no longer seems that he values me. He told me that if I had anything left to say to 'the humans' that now would be a good time. If the council is indeed planning something, I don't think he intends that I be alive to see it."

"So basically, when you leave here, he's going to kill you," Sarah said.

"That does seem likely," Jakob said. His voice was calm, but he could not keep a note of distaste at his impending death from creeping into it.

"Can you ... I mean, will you try to escape?" Sarah asked.

"Yes, and I'll come for you if I can. I would prefer not to leave you here."

Rhes coughed. "We'd prefer that, too."

"There's not much hope in an attack on the front gates, and I'm not sure I could climb a thirty-foot wall lined at the top with razor wire."

"Pretty sure we couldn't anyway," Sarah said.

"Indeed. When we arrived, we came in below ground. We didn't pass through the gates."

"How do you know that?" Rhes asked.

"The drugs they used to knock you out won't work on me. The best that Aros's soldiers could do was blindfold me. Trust me: we entered a tunnel outside the grounds that led directly to the prisons in which we were initially kept."

Rhes glanced around. "What if he has this place bugged? He might be listening right now."

Jakob shrugged. "It's a risk, but any escape attempt is a risk likely to end in our deaths. I'm not going to hide that fact from you. He will have all exits guarded. My hope is that there will be fewer guards below ground than above."

"Worth a shot," Rhes said. Sarah seemed about to speak, but abruptly changed her mind and closed her mouth.

Jakob continued. "I believe we passed through at least four security doors in the process, which are made of metal and require a key. I won't be able to break them down."

"Don't need to," Sarah told him.

"No?"

"Aros has a key."

"I ... don't think he is likely to part with it," Jakob said.

Sarah blew air upwards through her pursed lips. "You can take that patronizing bullshit tone elsewhere, Jakob. I'm not an idiot. He leaves the keys in his desk."

"You sure, hon?" Rhes asked.

"I heard him drop his keys into the drawer the night he got us out of there. Remember when we stopped in his office? Left side, top drawer. Heard him open it, heard the keys drop, heard him close it."

"Did you hear anything?" Jakob asked Rhes.

"No, but I was probably distracted, and anyway I don't hear like she does. I'm not sure *you* hear like she does."

"I assure you—" Jakob began, and Sarah interrupted him.

"I assure *you* that you don't need to use your ears like I do. Whether they're better or not doesn't matter. Look, I know what we're planning here. I know the stakes, and I'll put our lives on what I heard. That's where he put his keys."

"What if he moved them?" Rhes asked.

Sarah shrugged. "What if we open the first door and he's standing behind it with an army of guys, waiting for us? We're trying to escape from a lunatic vampire who's probably going to murder us all. I don't think there's any safe plan."

"Good point," Jakob said. He was smiling slightly, amused and impressed by Sarah's decisive manner. "My apologies for the 'patronizing, bullshit tone' in my voice."

Sarah made a shooing gesture with her hand. "Whatever, forget it. Help us get out of here and get somewhere safe, and all is forgiven. I just want this shit *done* with. I want to go home, find my daughter, bury my dog, put new locks on my door, and never deal with another vampire again."

"A reasonable list of desires," Jakob said. "Very well, then I will—"

He was interrupted by the sound of the front door opening, and footsteps in the hallway. Aros emerged from the front foyer into the living room.

"It's impolite to enter without knocking," Jakob told him.

"It's my house," Aros replied, and the tone of his voice told them that he was in no mood for frivolity. Jakob looked unimpressed but made no reply.

"Can we help you with something, Aros?" Sarah asked after a moment, and Aros turned to look at her.

"I thought perhaps we should finish our earlier discussion," he replied. "The time of change is coming. We are in the final hours, now. Soon, there will be no more Eresh, no more Ashayt, no more Ay'Araf. They will convert or die and we, the Burilgi, the *horde*, will be transformed. It has been told to me, and I have foreseen it. The

Lady Eresh herself has come to me as I sleep. She speaks into my ear and tells me of her blood and its powers. *One will arise.* That is what she says to me."

Jakob stirred but said nothing. Aros glanced at him, giving him an ugly grin.

"The humans will continue to move through their days and sleep through their nights, unaware, providing my people with the services we desire, just as they've done for you and your aristocrats for centuries. They will be what they have always been: unwitting fools whose only purpose is to toil, to serve, and, when their usefulness is at an end … to die."

"Enough, Aros," Jakob said.

Aros turned fully to face him and pointed toward the door. "Get out. Your guards are waiting to take you back to your room, but I wouldn't worry about spending much time there. I do hope you've made the most of your last moments on earth."

Jakob shrugged, stood, looked at Rhes and Sarah. "May we meet again," he said.

"Hopefully soon," Sarah replied. To her left, Aros snickered.

"Good luck, Jakob," Rhes said.

Jakob nodded, and to Rhes's surprise, left the house smiling. Aros waited until he was gone, and then spoke Sarah's name. She turned toward him, head slightly cocked, listening.

"Let me make you more than what you are," Aros said.

"I like what I am," Sarah replied, but Rhes could hear the doubt in her voice. So could Aros, and he laughed.

"Don't lie to me. You hate what you are. I can make you something better, and you know it."

"I … you're the one who's lying," Sarah said, but her heart wasn't in it.

"You know I'm not. I'm sure you've asked Jakob, and I'm sure he's confirmed the power of the blood. I can give you your sight back, make you whole again."

"She's already whole," Rhes said. He was resting his hand lightly on Sarah's leg and could feel the tension in her body.

"Is she? Think of how *he* would look, Sarah. Think of how it would feel to see him for the first time, to see his smile, to look into his eyes with your own."

"Don't you fucking use me against her like that!" Rhes snarled.

Aros glanced at him, then back at Sarah, unperturbed. "He is angry with himself because he can't sacrifice his own happiness for yours, even though he knows that he should."

Sarah's jaw was clenched tight, her head tilted down.

"Baby, that's not true. I'm trying to keep you from making a mistake," Rhes said.

Sarah took a harsh, shuddering breath, suppressing a sob, and said, "I want to *see* you!"

Aros gave Rhes a savage grin and said to Sarah, "I can give that to you."

Sarah drew in another hard breath. She was visibly shaking now, and Rhes realized that in another minute at most, he was going to lose her. Sarah was going to give up, give in, accept the offer. He had underestimated just how thoroughly she hated her blindness and how desperate she was to be rid of it. He was going to lose her unless he did something, and so he did the only thing that he could think of, leaning in next to her and putting his lips to her ear.

"He's not telling you something," he said. He kept his voice low and even, not trying to keep his words from Aros, but simply trying to help calm Sarah.

"What?" she asked, her voice miserable.

"There's nothing at the end of his road but the dark."

"You know nothing abou—" Aros began, and Rhes whirled to face him.

"Shut up!" he shouted. "Shut the fuck up and let me talk, or kill me now and see if she goes with you after that."

Aros glowered at him, and in that moment Rhes understood that there was no longer any possibility that the vampire would let them go. Unless Sarah chose to take his offer, Aros would have them killed as soon as he had Two in his grasp. This was certain, and their only chance for escape had just walked through the door and out to his seeming death.

Well, fuck it then, Rhes thought, and turned back to Sarah.

"I'm going to finish whether he likes it or not," he said. "I love you. I love you more than anything else in the whole world, but I can't follow you if you choose to go with him. I won't. That road doesn't go to our house. It doesn't go to Molly or to raising a family. There's no baby at the end of Aros's road and no normal life. There's just years and years of looking out into the dark."

"A prospect you're faced with in either case," Aros said. The black humor had left his voice, and he seemed to be growing tired of the game. "This is the last time I will offer, Sarah. I can fix you. He cannot."

Sarah sighed and leaned the side of her head against Rhes's shoulder. When she spoke, her voice was tired and hoarse, filled with a terrible resignation.

"Go away," she said to Aros. "Just ... go away. I don't want to be fixed. I want to spend whatever time I have left with my husband, even if I'll never get to see him. Go away and leave me alone."

It was Rhes's turn to give Aros a savage, triumphant smile. The vampire's eyes narrowed, but after a moment any emotion seemed to leave his face, and he shrugged.

"Your loss," he said with an air of supreme indifference and, with that, he turned and left the house.

"Baby, I—" Rhes began, and Sarah turned and pressed a hand to his mouth, her jaw clenched tightly shut.

Rhes wanted to tell her that he understood: she had done this for him. She had chosen him over the very thing that she wanted most in the world. He wanted to tell her that he knew what it meant, this thing she had given up, and that he was thankful, but Sarah didn't want to hear it. Couldn't hear it, he realized, not right now.

Without another word, he put his arms around his wife and held her. Sarah pressed her face into his chest and stood like that for a long time, her breathing slow and deep.

* * *

The building in which Jakob had been housed had once served as a dormitory for soldiers, and it was approximately a sixty-yard walk from the row of townhouses where Rhes and Sarah had been stationed. Jakob made the walk from their house to his building with four of Aros's soldiers surrounding him. Each carried a pistol, and two of them also had automatic weapons.

He knew from experience that when they reached the building, the two guards with assault rifles would break off, heading back to positions along the outer wall. The two guards with pistols would bring him to his room, a small space that had once been an officer's bedroom but now, with the addition of sturdy bars outside the single window, had been converted into an effective cell. Jakob did not know if any other people, prisoners or soldiers, were currently stationed in the building. If they were, he had not heard them.

The entrance did not go as expected. When they reached the building, instead of unlocking the door the group swerved to the right, indicating to Jakob where he was to go by waving their guns. The two guards who normally left the group instead continued with them, and Jakob realized that he was likely in the presence of his execution squad. He felt mildly insulted that Aros could not even be bothered to oversee the event.

"Have you ever killed an Ay'Araf before?" Jakob asked the nearest guard, a short, squat vampire with brown hair and dark eyes who walked with a limp.

"Shut up," the guard said.

"But surely this must be exciting for you, no? The chance to off an aristocratic pig?"

"I said shut up. You're not talking your way out of this. We've got our orders."

"Orders. Yes, of course," Jakob said. They reached the end of the building and turned again, walking along its side. Jakob could see a dirt patch behind it, and a section of the outer wall that was pockmarked with bullet holes.

"Do I at least get a blindfold and a cigarette?" he said to no one in particular, and one of the guards behind him nudged him in the back with the muzzle of his gun.

"When we tell you to shut up, it means shut up."

"I'm just asking for a little kindness in my final minutes," Jakob said.

The guard behind him drew up close, shoving the barrel of his gun against the place where Jakob's spine met the back of his head, and growled. "You're lucky I don't just shoot you here and leave the body for the crows."

"We have differing ideas of luck," Jakob said, and he spun sideways. He grabbed the guard's left arm in both hands and twisted, snapping the humerus so violently that one jagged end of it pierced the skin. The guard shrieked in pain and lost his grip on his rifle.

The Burilgi were quick to react, but not as quick as Jakob. He shoved the screaming guard into the other vampire who held a rifle, and the two fell to the ground in a heap. Jakob leapt forward, grabbed one of the remaining Burilgi, and spun him around just as the last was raising his pistol.

"Oh, Jesus, *don't!*" the guard cried, but it was too late. His companion pulled the trigger, and there was a sharp crack as the gun fired. Jakob heard the vampire he held make a gasping noise as the bullet hit him in the chest. The slug passed through the Burilgi's body and embedded itself in Jakob's side, but was slowed enough in the passing to prevent a deep wound.

"Fuck!" Jakob snarled. He shoved forward, barreling toward the vampire who had fired, using the guard as a shield. Before the remaining guard could get off another shot, Jakob was upon him. With his right hand buried deep in the hair of the vampire he was using as a shield, Jakob rammed his arm forward and the two soldiers' heads collided with a sickening crunch. Blood sprayed, and as Jakob let go, both bodies slumped to the ground. He reached down, picked up a pistol, and spun back to the first two guards.

The one with the broken arm was still writhing on the ground, but the other had managed to free himself and was raising his rifle to take aim. Jakob shot him in the face. He knelt again, and quickly put one bullet each into the heads of the unconscious vampires next to him.

The remaining guard was now dragging himself toward his rifle, snarling profanities in pain and exertion. Jakob took a few quick steps over toward the prone figure and brought his foot down on the vampire's broken arm. The guard howled in pain, and without further hesitation, Jakob put a bullet into his forehead.

It would not be long before he was discovered. The firing would probably not immediately attract attention, as surely the Burilgi on the base knew that Jakob was to be executed, but the screams might have been heard. At any rate, someone, perhaps Aros himself, would be along to check in on things shortly. Jakob glanced down at his side and grimaced. His shirt and pants were stained with blood and there was a bullet wedged somewhere against one of his ribs, but removal would have to wait. At least the flow of blood seemed to be stopping.

Jakob turned and, taking a deep breath against the pain, began to run back toward the row of townhomes on the other side of the compound.

* * *

"It has to be now," Jakob said as Rhes opened the door.

"Jesus Christ, are you all right?" Rhes asked.

"Yes. No ... I was shot, but it was a weak hit. It's not going to kill me. Rhes, we have to go. Right now."

"OK, I ... Sarah, we have to go. Jakob's here and—"

"I'm blind, not deaf," Sarah said from the living room. "Come get me, and let's do this."

"She sounds upset," Jakob said.

"We'll talk about it some other time," Rhes replied. "Stay here. Shit, should I get ... I don't know, Band-Aids or something?"

Jakob grunted out something like a laugh and shook his head. "Get your wife and let's go."

They crossed the grounds as quickly as they could, Jakob leading, Rhes and Sarah trailing close behind. The grass was flat and even, making things easier for Sarah, but she nonetheless kept a tight grip on Rhes's hand. Shortly, they had made it to the building that housed Aros's offices. As of yet, it seemed, Jakob's escape from execution had not been discovered.

"There will not be time for pulling punches, so to speak," Jakob said as they reached the door. "If we meet any Burilgi, I am going to dispatch them. Quickly."

"Jakob, hon," Sarah said, keeping her voice low, "If we were going to get upset about you killing these people, we probably would've stopped letting you into our house a long time ago."

Jakob made another low laugh and said, "Just warning you."

"Do what you have to do," Rhes said, and Jakob nodded. He grabbed the door handle and, finding it locked, leaned against the door to muffle the noise and twisted his wrist in a harsh, jerking motion. The knob splintered away and the door swung inward.

"That's handy," Rhes commented as they slipped inside.

"That's why I'm only worried about the metal doors," Jakob replied. He shut the door behind them and propped a chair against it. Close inspection would certainly reveal the damage, but at least any passing Burilgi soldier wouldn't see the door hanging wide open.

They made their way upstairs to Aros's office slowly, trying to stay quiet, expecting at any moment that the lights would be thrown on as soldiers invaded the building. It didn't happen.

Aros's office was dark and empty. Jakob went to the desk, opened the top-left drawer, and a moment later they heard a jingling sound as he picked up the keys. Sarah smiled a little, but didn't speak.

"You're entitled to tell me that you told me so," Jakob said as he returned.

"Yeah, but I'm way too polite for that," Sarah replied. "Let's find out what's behind door number two."

The third key that Jakob tried unlocked the door. Behind it there was only an empty stairwell, with no sign of Aros or his guards.

"Is it too early to worry that this is way too easy?" Rhes asked.

Jakob shook his head. "No. This won't last."

They descended to the second sub-basement and exited quietly into a hallway that held a bank of cells, identical to the ones in which they had awoken four days ago.

"There's a guard post down the hall," Sarah whispered. "Be careful."

They crept forward to find that Sarah was right, the hallway emptied out into a central room that contained, among other things, a table covered with scattered playing cards. The room appeared to be empty, and Jakob stepped into the middle of it, looking around and frowning.

"Yes," he began. "This definitely qualifies as too—"

With a roar, two vampires leapt from the shadows of one of the other hallways and charged at Jakob. Sarah had no way of knowing it, and never would, but these were the same guards whose conversation she had overheard when she had first awoken in this place.

The Rat and The Dunce came into the room howling, racing toward Jakob, moving at an alarming rate that Rhes had difficulty reconciling with forms that looked so human. He felt sure that Jakob would be torn limb from limb, and realized even as he began to shout a warning that it would surely come too late.

Jakob turned almost casually to meet his aggressors. He reached his hand out, palmed The Rat's face, and with a flick of his shoulders threw the diminutive vampire across the room. The Rat's head punched through the plasterboard and his body embedded itself deeply in the wall, pinning his arms against his sides. Rhes had no doubt that The Rat's head had come through the other side. The vampire's legs kicked in the air, and the effect was so comical that Rhes's warning shout became a burst of surprised laughter instead.

The Dunce, not as quick as The Rat but substantially larger, skidded to a halt, looking confused and nervous. He and Jakob circled each other. The Rat was shouting, still kicking his legs, the words muffled and impossible to understand. It would not be long before he did enough damage to the wall to free himself.

"You could run," Jakob told The Dunce.

"You're gonna die," The Dunce replied.

"Surely you're not *that* stupid," Jakob replied.

"Don't call me stupid!" The Dunce roared. He charged at Jakob, swinging his fists, and Jakob easily avoided the blows. His expression of detached amusement never changing, he spun to the side, grabbed one of The Dunce's hands in mid-swing, and pulled it up behind the Burilgi's back. There was a loud cracking noise and The Dunce howled, dropping to his knees.

"If not stupid, then at least uneducated," Jakob muttered. He put his foot against The Dunce's back and shoved. The Dunce went sprawling, sliding across the floor and crashing into the table. Jakob picked up a chair and, with a jerking motion, snapped off one of its legs, leaving him holding a hollow metal tube, jagged at one end, some eighteen inches long.

The Rat had managed to remove himself from the wall just in time to see his friend go sprawling. He shouted something in a language Rhes couldn't understand, and moved toward Jakob, who regarded him with an expression that was almost disappointed.

"There is no challenge in this," Jakob said to no one in particular.

"I'll show you cha—" The Rat had time to begin, and then the metal tube, turned from chair leg to deadly projectile with a single swing of Jakob's arm, caught him in the throat. The Rat's words became a spraying gurgle, and he clutched at the foreign object now protruding from his neck, blood pouring from his wounds.

Jakob stepped forward, grabbed The Rat by his shoulders, and looked into his eyes.

"Is this really the best that Aros has to offer?" he snarled. "You are the army that's going to crush the council and wipe out my kind?"

The Rat clawed ineffectively at Jakob's shirt. Jakob made a noise of disgust and reached up, took The Rat's head in his hands, and twisted. There was a crunching, shattering noise, and The Rat dropped to the floor.

"Ah, Jesus, that was disgusting," Rhes commented.

"Did he kill him?" Sarah asked.

"Uh ... yeah. Yes."

"What about the other one?"

"He's getting back up, but I ... I don't think Jakob's going to let that happen."

Jakob had removed the chair leg from The Rat's throat and was crossing the room with determined strides. Just as The Dunce came to a kneeling position, babying his broken arm, Jakob drove the chair leg downward into the top of the vampire's skull. It made a sound like someone tapping a coconut for the milk inside, and Rhes covered his mouth and turned away, fighting the urge to be violently ill.

The Dunce's body fell to the ground, his seizing limbs thumping out a rapid, staccato beat on the floor for a few moments, and then lay silent. Jakob turned and glanced at Rhes, his expression slightly apologetic.

"Let's keep moving," he said.

* * *

It wasn't until they had passed the fourth security door that they reached any real resistance. They had met two other Burilgi guards, one at a time, each of whom Jakob had easily dispatched. Now the hallways they had been following emptied out into a large, warehouse-like room, bare save a few rusting barrels in one corner. At the far end there was a large vertical door on tracks, like one might find in a garage. There was no visible lock for Aros's keys to fit.

"I suspect that we are near the end," Jakob said.

"Great," Rhes replied. "How the hell do we open it?"

"I'm working on that."

Jakob was inspecting a bank of switches to the left side of the door. Most looked like ordinary light controls and, after some tests, proved to be exactly what they appeared. There was one panel, however, that held only a vertical slot.

"It's a keyhole," Jakob muttered, digging in his pocket for the set of keys they had taken from Aros's office.

"What, Jakob?" Sarah asked.

"One of these switches wants a key ... like in a public place where they don't want visitors to be able to adjust the lights. I believe it may control the door."

"Do you think it's the same key that we've been using?"

Jakob shook his head and then, realizing Sarah couldn't see that response, said, "No. It won't fit. There aren't many keys here. We'll know in short order whether any of them work."

There were just over a dozen keys on the ring. When Jakob attempted to insert the ninth, it slid easily in. He tilted it upward and there was a clicking noise, followed by a hum from above. The door began to rise.

"Hey, nice," Rhes said. "Maybe we'll get through this after—"

He was cut off by Jakob, who leapt toward them, shouting, "Get back!"

As soon as the door had risen to waist level, Burilgi soldiers had begun to make their way underneath it. Jakob could not guess how many were behind the door, but he could see a mass of legs. It looked like a full platoon.

The first Burilgi grabbed for Sarah, but Jakob managed to intercept him. He brought his hand down in a chopping motion, shattering the bones in the Burilgi's hand. The vampire wailed, Sarah shrieked, and Jakob used the moment's time he had bought to pull her and Rhes backward.

"This is more what I was expecting," he said as they backpedaled. "We can't fight them in this open space. We need to funnel them."

"How many are there?" Sarah asked.

"A lot," Rhes said. He turned, preparing to run back to the hallway, and stopped in his tracks. "More than a lot."

Even as the warehouse door continued to rise, the hallway behind them was rapidly filling with Burilgi soldiers. Jakob glanced in both directions, trying to determine the odds. It looked to him like there were at least a dozen soldiers for each of the three of them.

"I've always wondered how many Burilgi it would take to kill me," he muttered to himself.

"Think this is enough?" Rhes asked. They were standing together now with Sarah between them, watching as their aggressors closed the distance.

"It's enough," Sarah growled. "Can tell that just from the footsteps."

"I imagine so," Jakob said. "Stephen might be willing to bet on himself against these odds, but I am not."

"I don't know Stephen," Rhes said, "but I'll fight as many of them as I can. At least this time I won't be surprised by how strong they are."

"You take the chair leg then," Jakob said, and handed it to him.

"I'm not sure I can use this," Rhes replied.

"You can," Sarah told him.

"Sarah, I—"

"They're monsters and they're going to *kill* us, Rhes. You can use it. Either that or give *me* the fucking thing."

Rhes gave a stunned laugh, but said, "OK, you're right," and tightened his grip on the weapon. The Burilgi had come to a stop on either side of the group. One of them, with blonde hair and a large, tumorous growth bulging from one side of his face, took a step forward.

"Stand down!" he ordered. "Stand down, and Aros will be merciful."

Sarah laughed out loud at this. Jakob said, "We won't."

"Then you will die."

Jakob nodded, shrugged, said, "So will you. Some of you, at least. I'm at peace with my life … can you say the same?"

The Burilgi seemed momentarily taken aback by this. He glanced at his companions.

"I know, I know," Jakob said in a conciliatory voice. "I'm supposed to be a foppish aristocrat, too cowardly and hedonistic to put up a fight. Have you considered perhaps that Aros has been *lying to you?* No?"

"Aros does not lie to us," the Burilgi replied.

"Surely not. What could he possibly stand to gain?" Jakob asked, his voice now laced with sarcasm.

"Enough. Shut your mouth, Ay'Araf. You may be strong, but there are too many of us for you. Stand down or die."

Jakob made an extended bowing gesture, hands held out at his sides, one leg crossed. He looked up at the Burilgi officer and gave him a malicious grin.

"*En garde,* then," he said, but before anyone from either group could move, the fight was taken out of their hands.

Later, Rhes would be forced to reconstruct the following few moments from jumbled fragments in his memory. There was a huge crashing sound from somewhere behind the large garage door, followed swiftly by the sound of running feet and snarling words in both English and the vampire language he was coming to recognize. These were followed rapidly by shrieks and wet tearing noises.

The Burilgi on both sides of the group were thrown into chaos as fast-moving forms infiltrated their ranks, tearing at them with claws, hacking at them with blades, and otherwise decimating their numbers. There were screams, splashing noises, the clanging sounds of metal on metal. Rhes lost track of Jakob, who seemed to have joined the fight. He grabbed Sarah and pulled her toward the far wall, trying to stay out of the way. Eventually they reached it, panting, pressing into the corner and hoping to avoid any attack.

It seemed to Rhes that a very small but skilled group of vampires was rapidly working their way through the troop of Burilgi. He thought he could make out Jakob, now armed with a machete, within the ranks. He tried to count the number of new vampires, but they were moving so fast that it was impossible to pick out any distinguishing features.

The battle raged for perhaps ten minutes, but it seemed to Rhes that the outcome was in little doubt. Burilgi soldiers were falling like wheat before the thresher, and as far as he could tell none of the other vampires had even been hurt. The advantage of surprise and the pure ferocity of the attack had splintered the Burilgi, thrown them into confusion and chaos, and was leading swiftly to their wholesale slaughter.

A few moments more and it was done. Their vampire saviors had met at the center of the room and were talking with Jakob. The floor of the warehouse was slick and shiny with blood, piled with bodies, and Rhes reflected that he had never in his life expected to witness such a scene.

Just when he thought that the night's events could not possibly get any more bizarre or unpredictable, Rhes heard a voice speak up from beside him. It was a voice he had not heard in more than a year, but one he recognized instantly nonetheless. Chipper, slightly amused, as if they had run into each other in the park, the girl spoke with the happy tone of someone without a care in the world.

"Hi guys!" Two exclaimed. "How's it going?"

Christopher Buecheler

PART IV

CHAPTER XXII

Kensington Court

After they had flown to London, it had taken Naomi several weeks to find a townhouse that she liked, but neither Two nor Stephen could complain about the end result. A furnished, four-story dwelling in the ritzy Kensington district of city, the building had been fully restored and modernized in the recent past, and it was absolutely gorgeous inside and out. The neighborhood was scattered with chic hotels and pricey restaurants. Naomi hadn't told her what the monthly rent on the townhouse was, and Two wasn't sure she even wanted to know; it must have been exorbitant.

Naomi's bedroom and office were on the top floor, and the vampire had her own bathroom. Stephen and Two each had a room on the third floor, and shared a bath, which wasn't particularly an issue since Stephen barely used it. The second floor of the house was dedicated almost entirely to a massive living room, and the first floor housed the kitchen, dining room, and entry parlor. There was also a wine cellar, but Two had never ventured into it. Naomi kept a few bottles of wine there, but did most of her drinking at a club not far away.

They had been in the country for little more than a month, and Two was still frequently surprised by the differences between London and New York. She wasn't homesick, not yet, but she thought that it would come eventually. Naomi's early investigation into the activities of the European council had made it obvious that it would be some time before their next meeting, and Two had spent the past few weeks trying to prepare herself mentally for what was likely to be an extended stay in Europe. She had bought several books dealing with the UK, and with London specifically, and a couple of titles about life as an expat. So far, she had spent much of her time there reading.

Naomi and Stephen, more accustomed to traveling, had an easy time of adapting. There were many Ay'Araf in London, and Stephen arrived already knowing where the best fighting locations were. Naomi had a few friends in the city as well, and had visited London enough in the past to have favorite bars and clubs. She and Two had made a few tourist excursions in the late afternoons so that Naomi wouldn't have to spend too much time in the sun, and so far Two was enjoying her time in the city. Or at least, she had been, until she realized upon waking up one afternoon that it was November twenty-third, and that it had been one year to the day since Theroen's death.

She hadn't said anything about it to Naomi, but Two had been powerless to prevent herself from spending the day thinking about him. She had tried to keep herself to positive memories, but it hadn't been easy. When Naomi had left to visit a club with two friends and Stephen had gone to his fights, Two had starting drinking bourbon, and this hadn't helped either. That had been four hours ago, and Two had long since given up trying to think happy thoughts. She was instead sitting in the living room, staring out of its large windows at the unfamiliar city around her, weeping and trying to drink the memories away.

She had just poured herself another glass and returned to the couch when she heard the front door opening downstairs. The sound of heels on the stairs told her that it was Naomi, not Stephen, which was probably for the best. She wasn't sure that she could deal with Stephen right now.

"Two, are you still awa—what's wrong?!" Naomi asked as she came into the living room. Two was rubbing at her eyes, trying to stop crying but not having much luck with it. She looked up at Naomi for a moment, felt herself losing control again, and covered her eyes.

"S'been a year," she sobbed.

Naomi crossed to the couch and sat down next to Two. She kicked off her heels and put a hand on Two's shoulder.

"A year since what?"

"Since he … Since Theroen …" Two didn't want to say it out loud. She paused for a moment, sobbing, and Naomi figured it out on her own.

"Oh, since he passed. I didn't know. I … did you drink all of this?" Naomi held up the bottle of bourbon, which was almost half empty.

"No. Was open."

"But you've had a lot of it tonight."

"Maybe …" Two picked up her glass and tried to raise it to her lips, but she was crying too hard to complete the act. Naomi took it from her hand and set it back on the coffee table.

"Two, don't."

"Why not?"

"You're going to hurt yourself."

Two could feel Naomi's aura pressing against her, warming her, eating at the edges of her despair. She felt herself growing frustrated with this strange sensation, this artificial comfort, and her emotions whipped suddenly from sorrow to rage. She pushed Naomi's hand off her shoulder. "Who cares? Who fuckin' cares?! He's gone!"

"Yes, he is, but you're still here."

"Wish I was dead. I should just … let me go!"

Naomi had taken Two's hand in hers, and now tightened her grip as Two tried to pull away.

"I'm not going to let you drink yourself to death in our living room. I know you miss Theroen. I understand. I miss him, too, and I miss Lisette, but you have to be strong."

"Fuck being strong. Fuck … fuck *everything!*" Two began to weep again. She leaned forward, resting her forehead just above Naomi's breasts. Naomi sighed and put her arms around Two.

"I think you should be in bed," she said.

"Don' wanna."

"I know you don't want to, but it will be good for you."

"No it won't. It'll just be cold and dark and f—fucking empty."

"Stay in my room, then."

"Can't. Naomi, I'm not ready for … for that."

Naomi laughed a little. "Believe it or not, I wasn't planning on trying to seduce you while you're drunk and vulnerable. Two, I want to help you. If you're afraid to sleep alone, you can stay with me, and I assure you nothing will happen except sleeping."

"P—promise? No kisses or anything?"

"Have I pushed you at all, since that night in New York? I won't kiss you again unless you ask me to."

Two considered this, still leaning her head against Naomi, but slowly gaining control over her tears. Finally, she looked up.

"Are you OK?" Naomi asked her.

"I miss him so much," Two croaked. Her throat hurt, and her face felt hot, the skin raw from wiping at the tears.

"I know you do. I know it's hard. I want to help you, however I can." Naomi stood up, still holding Two's hand, pulling on it gently to encourage Two to follow.

"Walk slow," Two said, standing, unsteady. Naomi gave another small laugh.

"Do you need me to carry you?" she asked.

"Let's …" Two yawned. "Let's not be ridiculous."

"OK. Come on, Two."

With Naomi in the lead, the pair made their way up to her room. Two had not been in it since their initial tour, and she was glad for the light from the street coming in through the windows that Naomi had not yet shuttered. She followed Naomi over to the bed. The vampire girl turned on a small light that sat on the bedside table.

"Take off your clothes," Naomi said, turning toward her dresser.

"Wait, you said …"

Naomi glanced over her shoulder, shaking her head. "For God's sake, Two, I'm not going to rape you. If you want to sleep in your jeans, that's fine. I was going to offer something more comfortable."

"Oh, OK. Right." Two pulled off her T-shirt, unlatched her bra, slid down her pants. Naomi had not turned around, but was holding a man's flannel shirt out in one hand. Two took it, pulled it on, buttoned it up.

"I'm good," she said, and Naomi turned, smiling.

"I don't know whether to be offended or not by what you apparently think of me," she said.

"Don't. I'm retarded." Two sat down on the bed, tired and sad, dizzy, drunk. She took a deep breath and said, "Dunno why you don't hate me."

Naomi only looked at her, eyebrows raised, waiting for an explanation. Finally, Two continued.

"I know you ... you're interested in me. Can't be fun to listen to me bitch and whine about Theroen all the time."

Naomi shrugged. She reached down into her dresser, grabbed another flannel shirt, and moved to the side of the bed, stopping along the way to close the heavy curtains over the windows.

"You lost a true love," she said. "You bonded with Theroen in ways that most people can't even understand, and you lost him in a very traumatic manner. There's no time limit to grief and mourning, Two. Everyone is different. You can't help it, no more than I can help ... my feelings for you."

Two was lying on her side now, looking up at Naomi. The vampire girl did not bother to turn as she stripped down to her panties, and Two chose not to look away. Naomi was a nearly perfect physical specimen, lithe and shapely, taller than Two, with full breasts and small, pink nipples. Her skin was like porcelain, white and smooth and flawless. Two found herself feeling inadequate.

Naomi seemed to sense this, and she grinned as she pulled on the flannel and began buttoning it up.

"What you're seeing is the effect of the blood. It works on our bodies ... you know that. It makes us something more than we once were."

"I bet you were pretty hot to begin with," Two said, and Naomi laughed. She sat down on the bed next to Two, drew up her legs, and pulled the covers over them.

317

"Perhaps. That doesn't mean you should feel bad. You're a lovely woman, Two."

"Short, no boobs, no hips ..." Two began, and Naomi made a sound of perturbed amusement.

"Gorgeous eyes, pretty face, shapely legs, fantastic rear end ..." the vampire girl continued, and Two laughed.

"You been checking out my ass?" she asked.

"Every chance I get. Are you all right, Two? Do you need a glass of water?"

"I'll be fine. Sleepy." Two laid her head down on the pillow. "Thanks, Naomi."

Naomi reached over and turned off the bed-side light, enveloping them in darkness. Two lay on her side, listening to Naomi breathing, feeling the warmth of the vampire's aura. There was a tiny sliver of light coming into the room from a crack in the curtains, and eventually Two's eyes adjusted well enough to see Naomi's silhouette. She watched the vampire girl for a time, until Naomi opened her eyes.

"What is it?" she asked.

"Don't move," Two said. Naomi said nothing, only looked at her, questioning, unsure of what was happening.

Two reached out her left hand and touched Naomi's cheek. She moved her fingers up, into Naomi's hair, smoothing it back and tucking it behind Naomi's ear. Slowly she leaned her head forward, heart pounding, unsure of herself and of what she was doing but wanting to try.

When her lips touched Naomi's, the vampire gave a small gasp, opening her mouth instinctively. Two began with small kisses, tentative at first, but with growing confidence the individual kisses becoming longer, more connected. Naomi bit gently at her lowcr lip, and Two smiled, kissed for a few more moments, and then pulled away.

"Thank you for understanding me," Two said.

Naomi smiled, nodded, reached out and took Two's hand. Two let her do it, happy to have the contact. Exhausted, still far from sober, and wanting the day to be over with, she closed her eyes and surrendered to sleep.

* * *

Time passed, as it always does. Autumn gave way to winter and the temperature dropped. Two, Naomi, and Stephen settled into a routine; the vampires socialized with others among their kind, happy to enjoy the long hours of darkness, while Two had taken to waking up in the early afternoon and going out to a local pub for her evening meal. She was getting to be friendly with one or two of the employees, and happily answered their questions about life in New York. She also spent a great deal of time at the Kensington Central Library, just a few blocks away from their townhouse, and had made a point of visiting several of the museums in the neighborhood, rekindling her love of art that had lain dormant since before her time with Theroen.

Two's relationship with Naomi began to move slowly toward something more than friendship. After the night that Naomi had invited her to bed, there had been a period of several weeks where nothing further happened, but Two had nonetheless felt closer to the vampire girl than before, as if they had shared more than just a simple kiss.

Naomi's aura, too, seemed to have changed. Where before it had only been a source of warmth and comfort, there was now an intimate, nearly erotic tinge that sometimes left Two in a state of mild arousal. She was concerned by this, but also excited. She didn't know if she was falling in love with her vampire companion, but she was certainly becoming more physically attracted to Naomi.

Christmas came, and Naomi insisted that they celebrate despite Stephen and Two's lack of enthusiasm. Two had found a very pretty pair of earrings for Naomi and had managed after some effort to find a gift that she thought Stephen would like. Through careful searching on the Internet, she had been able to locate an autographed game ball from an Ireland Rugby Union match. Stephen, not normally one for sincere emotion, had been nearly speechless, then had apologized repeatedly for the inadequacy he felt for his own gift – an original work from a London street artist whom she had pointed out one evening – despite Two's obvious happiness with it. Naomi had given Two a book of poems authored by William Wordsworth and printed in 1807. She had also managed to find a more modern printing, sparing Two the agony of choosing between reading the book and causing it any physical harm.

Stephen spent New Year's Eve, and most of the month of January, in Ireland. Two and Naomi celebrated the transition of years by finishing more than a bottle of champagne apiece, an evening that ended in a lengthy session of kissing on the living room couch, and that might have gone further if Two had not forced herself to grab hold of Naomi's hands as they began to remove her shirt.

"Not yet," she had murmured around the vampire's lips. "I'm sorry ... please."

Naomi, to her credit, had stopped herself immediately, and the pair had spent the night on the couch until the early morning sun pouring through the living room's bay windows had irritated Naomi, forcing her to move to her bedroom. Two had not followed, still drunk and not trusting herself in the darkness and warmth of the room. When Naomi had awoken later, she had said nothing of the encounter, giving only a small smile when first she came back downstairs.

Two wondered sometimes whether Naomi had any real doubt about how this was all going to play out. Did the vampire already know what was going to happen? Was she just waiting for Two to figure it out? Or was Naomi just as confused and uncertain about her feelings as Two was, and simply better at hiding it? Sometimes Two wanted to ask, but whenever she began to do so, she grew flustered and uncomfortable, and would change the subject.

Naomi seemed to understand this, as she seemed to understand everything.

It was a bitterly cold night in late January when it happened. Two was sitting on the couch, channel surfing, nearly ready to go to sleep. Naomi had been out all night with three other vampire friends, though Two had no idea where. The sun would be coming up soon, so it was no particular surprise when Two heard keys jingling, the front door open and close, and Naomi's footsteps on the stairs.

"Hey, Naomi," Two said as the vampire came wandering into the living room. Naomi's face lit up when she saw Two.

"I thought you'd be in bed!" Naomi exclaimed. "I'm so happy to see you."

"Uh ... well, OK," Two said, laughing a little. "Glad to see you, too."

Naomi came over to the couch and flopped down next to Two, sighing in contentment.

"You've been out a long time. Good night?" Two asked.

"Oh, it was wonderful. First, we went to the theatre, and then we went dancing. Angeline met this lovely, beautiful boy and he invited us all back to his place ..."

"Cue the porn music," Two said, and Naomi laughed.

"It wasn't like that. We'd already fed, and he wasn't trying to get into our pants. At least, not all of them."

"Just Angeline's?"

"Yes. She was still there when I left. If she's not naked by now, she's a fool."

"Sounds like a good night," Two said, smiling a little. Naomi's lips were dark purple, stained from an excess of wine, and she was slurring her words.

"It was. I wish you would come out with us once in a while. Angeline and Penelope and Emma would love to meet you."

They had discussed this before, after Two had several times demurred when Naomi had asked her if she wanted to come out. Two had explained that she felt uncomfortable with the idea of spending time with other vampires. "It'll just make me jealous," she'd said, and Naomi had said she understood.

"I'd like to meet them, too," Two told her now. "Once we've been to see the council and I'm a vampire, I'll come out with you, I promise."

Naomi smiled, and rested her head on Two's shoulder. Two could feel the girl's aura now, stronger than usual, pushing on her like a physical force. Its warmth was spreading through her entire body.

"Once you're a vampire ..." Naomi said wistfully. "Oh, I can't wait."

"Me neither," Two said.

They were quiet for a time, and if not for the aura, Two would have thought Naomi had fallen asleep. The warm feeling still pulsed and throbbed within her, though, and it was becoming tinged again with desire, as it so often did these days. Two could feel her nipples hardening, and funny little bursts of adrenaline were running through her.

Finally, Naomi spoke, her voice a low, husky murmur. "I've been thinking about you all night. I couldn't stop myself."

"Good thoughts?" Two asked, trying to keep her own voice neutral.

The vampire girl put her lips to Two's ear. As she spoke, they brushed against the sensitive skin of Two's earlobe, sending shivers through her entire body.

"Warm thoughts," Naomi whispered. "Wet thoughts."

Two's heart was racing now, in a combination of fear and desperate excitement. She could feel Naomi's aura, more overtly sexual than at any time in the past, working on her, turning her on, making her hot. Part of her wanted to step away, to regain some sense of control. The rest of her wanted only to remain where she was and let this delicious warmth continue to run tingling through her body.

"Really?" she asked. "That sounds ... very interesting."

"I can tell you all about it, if you want," Naomi murmured into her ear. She reached a hand out, ran it lightly along Two's thigh, lifted it to cup Two's breast. "Or I could show you ..."

"Jesus Christ, Naomi," Two gasped, twisting, turning her head, searching for the vampire's lips. Naomi brought her head up and forward, kissing, biting. Her hand left Two's breast and went to Two's hair, fingers tangling there and pulling. As she did this, the last of Two's defenses seemed to give way, and the aura flooded through her, setting her on fire. She could feel, for the first time since Theroen's death, the lust for skin against skin, the desire to give pleasure, and the simple but overwhelming need for orgasm.

"I want you to be naked," Naomi was saying in between kisses. "Don't make me wait any longer. Let me make love to you. Please, Two!"

"OK," Two gasped. She pulled her lips from Naomi's, pressed them against the vampire's neck. She could feel the pulse pounding there, the skin hot. "Yes. OK, Naomi. Just ..."

Just what? Go slow? Be gentle? That wasn't what she wanted at all. Not anymore. In what seemed like seconds, she had gone from cautious attraction to white-hot desire. Were these feelings really her own, or were they simply a product of Naomi's aura raging out of control? Two didn't know. At the moment, it didn't seem to matter.

Naomi hadn't waited to find out "just" what, either. She was pulling Two's T-shirt up and off, kissing Two's abdomen while she did it. Two raised her arms up, then took Naomi's face in her hands, bringing it back up and kissing her again. Two wasn't wearing a bra, and Naomi cupped her naked breasts, running her thumbs over Two's erect nipples, making Two arch her back and draw in air through her teeth. Naomi responded to this by pressing her lips hard against Two's neck.

She didn't bite, though Two thought for a moment she would. She only pressed, and then began to kiss her way down Two's neck and shoulder. Two tilted her head back, eyes closed, enjoying the sensation of Naomi's lips on her skin, Naomi's hands on her breasts. The vampire was straddling her now, facing her. She brought her head up again and kissed Two deeply on the mouth. Two responded by bringing her own hands up to unbutton Naomi's blouse.

Naomi put her lips to Two's ear again, kissing and tugging at her earlobe. She shrugged off her blouse, and arched her back to help Two remove her bra. Two put her hands up, tentative despite her desire, and touched Naomi's breasts.

Naomi gasped, murmured Two's name, resumed kissing Two's neck and shoulders. Two could feel the vampire's nipples, hard little nubs pressing into her palms. She could smell Naomi's hair, her skin. She laid her head back again on the couch, lost in the aura and the waves of pleasure that seemed to spread through her from wherever Naomi kissed, like ripples in a pool of water.

Naomi was undoing her jeans now, and Two let the vampire slide them over her hips and along her legs, taking her panties with them. Naomi took a moment to remove Two's socks, and now she was naked, just as Naomi had wanted. Two shuddered a little, looking down as the vampire girl began to kiss her way back up Two's calves and shins.

Two was damp between her legs, throbbing, desperate. The anticipation as Naomi worked her way upward was murderous. Two's body tingled with it, her nipples standing up so hard that they ached. Had she wanted to wait? To take things slowly? It seemed like now it was all she could do not to beg, and she wondered again for a moment if this sudden need sprung entirely from her. It *felt* like it did, but ...

Naomi's fingers wouldn't allow her to finish her thought. They caressed the insides of Two's thighs, teasing their way upward into the soft, light brown curls of hair on her vulva. Two made a choked noise of desire, opened her legs wider, slid her hips forward.

Naomi said, "Oh," and kissed Two's thighs. Her thumbs pressed against Two's labia and parted them, opening Two up. Naomi moved her head slowly forward, looking up, eyes locked with Two's. She stopped just inches away, and Two could feel her breath, hot against her sensitive skin. The wait was excruciating. Interminable.

"Naomi," Two gasped. "Naomi ..."

She couldn't seem to move, couldn't close her eyes, couldn't do anything but wait and watch. Naomi favored her with a wicked smile that only seemed to make Two's need even more urgent.

"Please," Two said.

The vampire lunged forward, tongue teasing, running from bottom to top and then in a rough circle, around and around. Two made a sound that was more like anguish than pleasure and wrapped her hands in Naomi's hair. She had come very close to orgasm just from this initial contact, and knew she would not last long under Naomi's expert ministrations.

Naomi didn't seem to want her to try. After teasing Two with the slow progression up her legs and that last, agonizing wait, she seemed now intent on bringing Two to climax. She increased the pressure of her tongue, toying with Two, kneading at her sensitive flesh, and Two could do no more than lay back and pant. It seemed as if every nerve ending in her entire body was sending streams of pleasure down to the place that Naomi was attending to, and in only moments she cried out again as her body clenched, and clenched, and clenched.

When Naomi kissed her after, Two could taste herself on the vampire's lips. She was still tingling all over, still felt tremendous desire for the girl next to her, but the urgent, physical need had now passed. After a time, she broke away from Naomi and leaned her head back, eyes closed.

"Was that OK?" Naomi asked.

"Jesus, yes," Two said, this time with a shuddery laugh, still trying to catch her breath. She opened her eyes and saw that Naomi was grinning at her, watching her eagerly.

"I've been waiting to do that for months," the vampire said.

"Well, I ... God, that ... I don't ...." It seemed impossible to form a coherent sentence.

"I wanted to make you feel good."

"That was way beyond 'good,'" Two told her. She took a few deep breaths, and then sat forward. "Naomi, lie back."

"You don't have to—"

Two laughed. Kissed her. Pressed on her shoulder and made the girl lie down.

"Shut up," she said.

* * *

"What are we going to tell Stephen?" Two asked.

They had retired to Naomi's bedroom as the sun rose, carrying their clothes with them, racing up the stairs naked and giggling. Under the covers, Naomi had brought Two to orgasm again, this time with her fingers, and they were now lying in a sweaty jumble.

"Stephen won't care," Naomi responded, her voice fuzzy and near sleep.

"That doesn't mean he won't have something stupid to say," Two replied.

Naomi gave a small laugh. "True."

"He knows that you're into girls, right?"

Naomi made a *pfffft* noise and said, "I am into *people*. Some of those people are women. He knows that, yes."

"I'm just going to tell him to fuck off, I guess," Two said, yawning.

"That seems like a wise policy," Naomi replied. She turned over onto her belly and nestled her head into the pillow.

Two lay on her back, staring up at the ceiling, content for the moment to let sleep pluck at the edges of her consciousness without yet succumbing to it. She felt comfortably fatigued, exercised without being exhausted, too full of endorphins to worry about the repercussions of what she had just done. Still, one question lingered.

"Naomi?"

"Mmmh?"

"Did you make that happen?"

There was a lengthy period of silence. At last, Naomi propped herself up on one arm and looked at Two. Her hair was tousled, eyeliner smeared in dark smudges, lips still purple from the wine. She looked as if she wasn't sure whether or not to be offended by the question.

"Would you believe me if I said I didn't know?" she asked.

"Probably."

Naomi frowned. "What if I told you that I haven't slept with anyone, male or female, human or vampire, since I met you? Would you believe that?"

"Yes. Naomi, I'm not trying to start a fight."

"No. But I want you to understand. I've wanted to make love to you since the third night after we met, when we went to the club and talked about Thomas."

"I remember," Two said. "We came home and sat on the couch and then you were going to bed, but you stopped, and there was this ... this moment."

"I wanted to invite you, yes. If you'd shown any sign, I probably would have. That's, what ... three months? No, four. That's a long time to wait if I had magic powers that could make something like tonight happen."

"That's true."

Naomi sighed. "Lisette is the only other vampire I have ever known who did this ... this *thing* that I do. I've asked every Ashayt vampire that I've gotten to know on more than a cursory level, and it doesn't happen to any of them. Few of them have even *heard* of it. She was supposed to teach me, but ..."

"But Abraham happened."

"Yes. So now here we are. Did I make you do it? I don't know. Not intentionally, but that doesn't mean I didn't. Can you forgive me, if I did? Can we ... I mean, is it still happening now? Are you lying naked in my bed because I'm making you do it?"

Two gave Naomi a small smile, shook her head. "No."

"Good. I don't know about you, but I haven't had an orgasm in four months. I'm happy that I waited. I'm happy that I shared it with you. I don't want you to regret what happened tonight. I would very much like to pursue something more than friendship with you, but if that can't happen, I still don't want you to regret tonight."

Two rolled onto her back again, stared up at the ceiling again. "It's been more than a year for me. After Theroen ... after he died, I wasn't sure I would ever feel like I felt tonight again. I don't regret it. I don't think I'd regret it even if you'd made me do it. I just wanted to know."

Naomi smiled, nodded, and asked, "Do you ... are you interested in more?"

"Am I lying naked in your bed?"

"Yes."

"Are you making me do it?"

Naomi's smiled widened. "No."

Two turned her head and glanced at Naomi. "That's the best I can do right now. I don't know where this is going to go. I still don't know how I feel."

"Can I do anything to help?"

Two laughed. "Put up with my bullshit?"

Naomi put her head back down on the pillow and closed her eyes, still smiling. "Sleep well, Two," she said.

"Goodnight, Naomi."

The vampire girl who lay beside her was soon asleep. After a few more minutes of thought, Two rolled on her side, curled up, and closed her eyes.

* * *

"Am I to pretend that I'm not noticing you?"

Two glanced down from the top of the staircase. Stephen was looking up at her from the third-floor landing, an amused expression on his face.

"I guess not," she said, rolling her eyes, and walked down the staircase to join him.

Stephen had been home for twelve days, and in that time Two had spent four more nights in Naomi's bedroom. This was the first time that he had been both in the building and awake as Two had exited the room. Naturally, she had managed to time it exactly as he was leaving his own.

"I was wondering whether this would happen," Stephen said as she reached him.

"It's not—"

"Oh, good Lord ... You don't need to lie to me."

Two said nothing, simply favored Stephen with a look of annoyance.

"It's been painfully obvious for some time that she desired you. I just wasn't sure if the feeling was reciprocated."

"It took me a while to figure it out," Two said.

Stephen considered this for a time, looking at her, one eyebrow arched and his ever-present smirk as firm as ever on his face. Finally he said, "Treat her well," and turned to head down the stairs.

"That's it?" Two asked him. "No jokes? No sarcastic comments? Who are you, and what did you do with Stephen?"

"Oh, I could come up with something for you if you really want me to," Stephen replied, turning and grinning.

"No, that's OK. I'm sure you'll hit me when my back is turned."

"That's part of the fun," Stephen agreed, and began again to make his way down the stairs. Two watched him go, shaking her head. A moment later, she heard a small laugh from above her.

"I'm sorry, Two," Naomi said, leaning over the balcony. "I know you'd hoped to avoid him."

Two shrugged. "At least it's out of the way, right? That's probably for the best."

"Yes. I wanted to let you know that I just received an email from one of the council's representatives. Not a high-ranking one, unfortunately. Nonetheless, contact is good. They have no official date set for the next meeting, but the person who wrote said he'd do his best to communicate our situation to those who need to know."

"Uh ... woohoo?" Two was nonplussed.

Naomi smiled. "It's a start, Two. This is going to be a long process. The members of the European council are all very old. They value their time, and their privacy, and they are rarely quick to act."

"OK, Naomi. I'll try to be patient. Thanks for doing this."

"*Pas de problème*," Naomi said. "Perhaps we can work on teaching you French!"

"Yeah, or that vampire language you guys speak. Or do I have to wait for that until I get back into the club?"

Naomi considered this. "We're not supposed to teach it to humans, but you're a bit of a special case. It'd be fairly easy for you to learn. It's a constructed language with very rigid structure and rules."

"Why do you guys use it, anyway?"

"It was developed in the early twentieth century. The hope was that it'd make communication between vampires in different countries easier. Sometimes it does, but there are many who never learn it for one reason or another. It is still useful though, to be able to say things that one can be sure will be understood by no one other than fellow vampires."

"I'd like to learn it eventually," Two said. "That way no one can talk behind my back."

Naomi smiled at her. "Then we shall teach you. But right now, I'm going to take a shower."

"OK, see you downstairs."

Two made her way down to the kitchen, where she took a granola bar from the cupboard and an apple from the basket on the counter. She set about making a pot of coffee, eating the apple while she waited for it to brew. She could hear the television upstairs broadcasting sports scores, and water running through the townhouse's pipes as Naomi showered.

This is life, for a while, she thought to herself. *Guess you'd better get used to it.*

Two took her coffee and the rest of her breakfast, and went to find the book she had left, half-finished, in Naomi's bedroom.

CHAPTER XXIII

A Simple Request

"I want you to teach me to fight," Two said.

Stephen glanced over at her, one eyebrow raised, and studied her for a moment. Then he turned, smirking, back to the television.

"I know you did *not* just lay that patronizing look on me," Two muttered. She was standing by the hallway door, leaning against the wood paneling, looking at the vampire on the couch.

"And I know you didn't just ask me to teach you to fight," Stephen replied, still watching the rugby game that had been holding his attention for the past hour and a half.

"I'm serious, Stephen."

"You do not want to learn how to fight from someone like me."

"Why not?"

Stephen looked over at her again, and now the smirk that lived so often on his face was gone. "Because I'll make you work. Hard."

"That might not be a bad thing ..."

Stephen shrugged. "I like you. If you go into this with me and then cry off, I won't like you anymore. It's a part of who I am, part of who I was even before I made the change. We're warriors, the Ay'Araf, but part of that is because we pick warriors for fledglings. You are strong and have shown yourself to be remarkably capable, but I wonder if at your heart you are a fighter."

"What do you think I am?"

"Naomi sees something in you that calls to both the poet and the politician in her. Perhaps you are a lover?"

Two, who had seen a great deal of that particular side of Naomi over the past months, shook her head. "No ... I don't think so. Naomi – she'd admit this herself, so I don't feel bad saying it – but if it had been Naomi there staring down Abraham, she'd be dead right now."

Stephen considered this, and then nodded. "You are very likely correct."

"So ... teach me to fight."

"I could give you some pointers, if you'd like. That might be—"

"No, Stephen. Honestly, what else do I have to do right now? Nothing. Beat me up. Break me. I don't give a fuck. If you send me to bed every night so exhausted that I pass out before I'm even under the covers, that's fine."

A semblance of the smirk reappeared on Stephen's face. "Naomi might have something to say about that."

Two rolled her eyes. Stephen did not care that she and Naomi were sleeping together, but he was not above the occasional snarky comment. Two thought that part of this was because Stephen understood that while Naomi seemed thrilled, Two was still adjusting to this new reality. Stephen was incapable of *not* pushing so obvious a button.

"Naomi will deal with it," she said.

"No doubt."

"Are you going to teach me or not? I'm being serious, Stephen. I think I can learn *and* keep you as a friend." Two paused for a moment and then added, "An asshole of a friend, of course."

The smirk became a grin, and Stephen said, "Of course."

"Teach me?" Two asked again, for what she knew was the last time. If Stephen decided against it now, she would not push the matter further.

The vampire considered for a long moment, and at last shrugged. "Very well. I shall do what I can, given the fact that you're a weak, little human and will have a hard time keeping up with the big, bad vampire."

Two grinned and nodded. She had been on the receiving end of vampires' strength before and understood that the physical differences were substantial.

"Good," Stephen said. "First, go cut your hair. Three inches, no longer, until I tell you differently."

Two, whose hair had reached well past her shoulders since her twelfth birthday, began to tell him no, bit her tongue, and instead asked him why.

"Because I said to," Stephen replied. "Also, it's a liability in a fight."

"But ... your hair's almost as long as mine," Two told him.

"Which one of us is the three-hundred-year-old vampire who has forgotten more fighting styles than you will ever learn?"

Two rolled her eyes.

"That's right," Stephen continued. "My hair is not a liability for me. Yours will be, for you. Three inches is even a liability, but I'm trying to leave something for Naomi to hold on to when—"

"Stop," said Two. "I'll cut it."

"Good. By the way, that is the last time you get to ask me 'why' and expect an answer until further notice. Understood?"

I may have made a terrible mistake, Two thought. Aloud she said only, "Understood."

"Very well. Then go cut your hair, and don't bother me again until this game is finished."

With that, Stephen turned back to the television. Two stood where she was for a moment, looking at him, and then turned to go and do what he had instructed.

Two tried the bathroom that she shared with Naomi first. She wasn't sure whether Naomi would keep scissors there or not, but it was a good first guess. The vampire girl spent more time in the bathroom than Two did. This was mildly amusing, since Naomi could get away without showering for weeks on end. Despite this fact, and her nearly perfect skin, Naomi had a collection of makeup, perfume, lotions, soaps and creams that would rival any human woman.

It amused Two that Naomi owned such things. Vampire skin did not dry out so long as blood was in ready supply, yet Naomi used three separate moisturizers. They were there, she had told Two, in part because of the varying layers of scent they left, and in part simply because they made Naomi feel more human. Sometimes it was easy for a vampire of her age to feel disconnected from the world outside. These things, simple though they might be, helped her to stay in touch.

There were no scissors in the bathroom. Two assumed Naomi left her hair to professionals and didn't bother trimming on her own. She wondered if she would be forced to use the shears in the kitchen, most commonly used to clip the stalks from flowers that Naomi bought at the local market, but on more than one occasion called into service to cut a chicken into pieces that Two could freeze and cook at her leisure.

She found a pair of scissors in the top-center drawer of the desk in Naomi's office and returned with them to the bathroom. She stripped down to her panties to avoid getting hair all over her clothes and stood in the bathtub to help collect the falling locks. The porcelain was cold against her feet, and she felt mildly foolish, but disobeying the first command that Stephen had given her seemed a bad way to begin. Two took a deep breath, and she began to cut.

* * *

"You actually did it," Stephen said. There was an impressed note in his voice that Two knew from experience was a rarity.

"Yeah, I actually did," Two agreed. She had left her remaining hair in an unruly mop, unsure of what to do with it. She didn't particularly care; she wasn't trying to impress Stephen with her appearance.

Stephen glanced back at the television and said, "I can get involved in this football match ... soccer, that is, to you American idiots ... or we can start. Which would you prefer?"

"Didn't get all dolled up for nothing," Two said.

Stephen nodded and shut off the TV. He stood and moved around her, inspecting her.

"You've filled out a bit since I first met you," he said.

"I started actually eating again."

"Aye, and fortunately you don't typically eat crap, other than those horrific frozen burritos, but you spend a lot of time sitting."

Two nodded, not trying to deny it. She liked to spend her time reading, watching television, or hanging out at bars and clubs. If she was more of a dancer, that might have provided activity, but she rarely danced. At least she spent time walking around the city, exploring, going to museums and famous landmarks.

"You're fine, don't mistake me," Stephen said. "I don't think you'll ever be fat ... but you're not fit."

"No, I'm not." Two thought of the way that Theroen's blood had helped to make her fit, sculpting her body and making it noticeably stronger even on the first evening. Vampire muscles would still weaken with lack of use – one of the reasons why Stephen spent so much time training – but the blood was always working to perfect the body.

"Situps, pushups, and weights. And running. Once a day to start, then twice when you stop throwing up."

"I'm going to be throwing up?"

"If you follow the instructions I give you, yes. I'll have you drinking plenty of fluids to make up for it. You'll get used to it."

Two considered this, then said, "OK."

Stephen raised an eyebrow, given momentary pause by her lack of concern.

Two smiled. "I'm only twenty-one, but I've been through a lot of bad shit. Some throwing up isn't gonna kill me."

"Very well. You will likely feel better afterward, anyway."

"All the same, forgive me if I go a little light on breakfast ..."

Stephen nodded. "Not too light. At least 200 calories, one hour before you start exercising. You're going to need the energy."

"OK. Are we starting all of this tonight?"

He shook his head. "It's too late. Naomi will be home in an hour. She'll want her private time with you, and I'll want to go to my fights. Tonight, I think, we talk."

Stephen indicated a high-backed, upholstered chair that sat to the left of the couch. Two went to it and sat down. Stephen returned to his previous place, leaning back, crossing one leg, and spreading his arms across the back of the sofa.

"The first thing you need to learn about fighting is that there is nothing chaotic about it," he said. "Nothing at all."

"No?"

"Not if you're good at it. Consider …" Stephen thought for a moment, searching for an appropriate analogy. "Consider a car chase in a movie. To the viewer, it appears highly chaotic, dangerous, and unpredictable. To the stuntmen involved in its creation, it's simply a sequence of events, and reactions to those events. When car X moves right, car Y moves left, and so forth. It can still be dangerous, but only if mistakes are made. Just like fighting."

Two nodded.

"When an enemy comes at a trained fighter, that training allows them to gauge dozens of factors and come to a decision. Of course, this does not supplant instinct. If anything, it *relies* on instinct. The best fighters perform with a kind of pure grace that's impossible to describe. Each move flows from one to the other, the combination of training and instinct working together in perfect harmony. The training acts as a filter and allows the proper instincts to come through. When two of these fighters meet, the result is something beautiful, like a perfectly choreographed dance."

"Are you that kind of fighter?" Two asked.

Stephen smiled and shook his head. "I am better than many … my sire chose well, but I am not among the elite. Jakob is a more natural fighter than I am, and there are others, both here and in America. I make up for it by keeping my body finely honed, and with raw aggression."

"But you still use your training to filter your instincts?"

"Yes, absolutely."

"And you're going to teach me to do that?"

Stephen nodded. "Eventually. First you have to learn the basics of the tools. Then we can worry about technique."

"What are the tools?"

Stephen shrugged, looked out the window for a moment, turned back to Two.

"What can you use to kill a man?" he asked.

* * *

Stephen had spent another forty minutes or so discussing what he planned for Two's basic regimen. She typically woke up a few hours before the vampires did, and this time would continue to be hers, as would be the last few hours before dawn. The latter was Stephen's concession to Naomi. For the rest of the time, roughly six hours, Two belonged to Stephen. They would start with exercise and strength training, eventually moving on to hand-to-hand combat. Early on in the training he would also give her books to study, until her body was ready to stand up to more prolonged physical activity.

He didn't expect her to become a brilliant fighter overnight, but he expected her to work at it every single day. It didn't matter to him if she was tired, had a headache, was menstruating (it had taken six months for this particular sign of humanity to return to her), or whatever other excuse she might come up with. If Stephen felt Two wasn't giving him everything she had, he was going to make her life even more difficult.

Eventually, he had told her, the training would lighten up a bit. The initial intensity served a twofold purpose. First, it would help whip her body into shape in a quick and efficient manner. Second, and probably more importantly, it would allow him to gauge her commitment to the work. Two expected to be miserable for several weeks, but she also intended to give it her all.

"Oh, Lord, Two ... what did you do to your hair?!"

Two glanced up from her book and gave Naomi an apologetic smile. "I kind of asked Stephen to teach me to fight."

Naomi looked pained. "Please tell me you're kidding."

"Nope, sorry."

"Two, he's going to *kill* you!"

"Nah … but he's going to break me for a while."

Naomi sighed, flopped down on the couch next to Two, and put her head in Two's lap, looking upward. "You're going to get all muscle-y."

Two shrugged.

"I like you soft," Naomi continued, tracing a finger along one of Two's arm.

"It's something I need to do, Naomi," Two said. "I … it'd help me a lot if you were OK with it."

Naomi sighed again, but said, "I understand. I just … don't let him make you too hard. Not your muscles, but …"

Two smiled a little as Naomi's voice trailed off. "I get it. I won't. But I'm not always warm and fuzzy *now*, hon."

Naomi rolled her head sideways and kissed Two's navel where her shirt had pulled up. "I can think of a few places that are," she said. Two shivered, but didn't respond, running her fingers through Naomi's hair. The vampire sighed, shifted, drawing herself up so that she knelt, straddling and facing Two. The two of them regarded each other for a moment.

She is so pretty, Two thought to herself. Naomi, forever seventeen, fit, and toned, with her perfect face and body, was probably the most physically attractive person Two had ever met. There were times when Two wanted not to be with her, but to *be* her. Sometimes Two would wake in the afternoon and just watch Naomi lying naked and asleep on the bed, her body an ocean of curves, supernaturally devoid of blemishes. Two couldn't conceive of anyone, male or female, not wanting the vampire in those moments.

"Are you happy?" Naomi asked her, those big grey eyes wide and filled with concern. Two very nearly lied to Naomi in that moment, very nearly told her that everything was fine. Instead, she shrugged and gave Naomi a sad smile.

"I don't know," she said.

Naomi frowned, her eyebrows pulling tight. "I want you to be happy," she said. "I want … I want to make you happy."

"Naomi …" Two paused, trying to determine how best to explain the way she felt. "You do make me happy. This is all … it's strange and confusing, and I'm not always sure we should be together like this. We don't even know if I can be a vampire, and I'm still getting over Theroen, and I have so much *other* baggage ... but you do make me happy. But even though you make me happy, that doesn't mean I'm always, you know ... happy."

Naomi tilted her head, questioning, and Two sighed. "I don't have the words."

"Sometimes a sad person can laugh," Naomi said after a time.

"Yes."

"And they can still climax ..."

"That is *not* the only way you make me happy," Two said. In truth, there were times where even as her body was peaking, Two would think of Theroen and be filled not with joy but with an almost overwhelming sorrow. Sometimes even while lying in Naomi's arms after sex, Two felt as alone as she had ever felt since Theroen's death.

Naomi touched her face, searching with her eyes as if trying to look into Two and read her thoughts. "What can I do?" she whispered. "How can I help?"

Two looked away, suddenly near tears. "You can change the subject," she said.

She felt Naomi's eyes still searching, but couldn't meet the vampire's gaze. Finally, Naomi said, "Can I fix your hair?"

Two smiled, nodded, turned back to Naomi and gave her a quick kiss on the lips.

"I was waiting for you to ask."

* * *

I'm going to hurt her, Two thought.

She was sitting in bed, the sheets pooled around her waist, her body bare and exposed in the dim room. Outside the day was just dawning, its light held back by the heavy curtains on the windows. Two could hear pattering against the panes of glass and assumed that the cold rain that had been falling for the better part of four days was continuing to inundate London. March was nearly over, but the winter seemed not yet ready to loosen its grip on the city.

Naomi had brought a chair into the bathroom and worked on Two's hair for nearly an hour, styling it, washing it, restyling it, making small cuts here and there and chattering away. She had told Two stories of early America, of vampires that Two would never meet and events that Two knew of only through watching the History Channel. Naomi's aura had washed over Two, strong and sensual, and Two had welcomed the respite from the melancholy she had been feeling. By the end of it, she had been warm and wet and waiting for Naomi to finish so that they could go to bed.

"There," the vampire had said at last, and Two, who had been resting with her eyes shut, looked into the mirror. The haircut was controlled chaos, urban and trendy, and Two had thought that yes, it looked very good. In a way, it suited her more than the long hair had. She had wondered if she would be able to style it without Naomi's help and thought that probably with some practice she could manage.

"That looks great, Naomi. Like some of the girls at *L'Obscurité*. I just need a big pair of sunglasses and some of those jeans that only come halfway down my shins."

Naomi had laughed and clapped her hands. "You would look *adorable!*"

"Oh, God no ..."

Naomi had shrugged, bitten her lower lip, and favored Two with a wicked smile.

"Well, I think you're adorable anyway," the vampire had said, and then the two of them had been kissing, and standing, stumbling their way into the bedroom. In short order, Two's carefully sculpted hair had become a tousled mess.

Eventually, Naomi had fallen asleep and Two had sat up, the aura and the afterglow of sex gone, her mind ready again to fear and worry and think itself into knots.

Beside her, Naomi shifted, rolled from her side to her back in an unladylike sprawl. Two glanced at her and wondered, not for the first time, why it was that the vampire community hadn't made more of an effort to understand the blood that worked within them.

There were few scientists, Naomi had told her, and most vampires were content to merely accept things as they were.

Two supposed there was some logic at work there. Too much understanding might lead to a cure, though Two doubted that most of the vampires she knew would ever willingly return to humanity. Still, some would, and if a cure was made available, it seemed inevitable that it would fall into the hands of a zealot – or a group of them, like the cult that Naomi said Thomas was a part of: The Children of the Sun. If these zealots got hold of a cure, they would use it on vampires whether it was wanted or not.

Two couldn't understand that mentality. The vampires she had known were nothing like the parasitic, satanic creatures of legend. Very few vampires ever killed the humans they fed from, and those that were evil had not become so because of the change. They were simply evil the way men were evil. It was true that Eresh vampires had to kill, for a time. Two herself had done so, dropping at those times into a swoon breakable only by her chosen victim's death, but could she not have confined herself exclusively to those who deserved it? Could she not have fed only from people like the first man from whom she had ever drank? The wife-murderer, the child-killer. Hadn't he deserved it?

Or perhaps that was merely justification. Two had blood on her hands that could never be washed away. Little of it was innocent, but the blood was there just the same. Melissa's, Samantha's, Abraham's ... though this last she wouldn't have cleansed from herself even if she could. Abraham had taken her entire life from her, a life she was still struggling to get back. She was here in this foreign land, among foreign people, beholden to the whims of others, because of him. She was here with a lover, yes, but her *love* was dead and buried.

I'm going to hurt her, Two thought again, and felt hot tears sting at the corners of her eyes. It seemed inevitable, this hurt. Naomi was opening herself to Two at an alarming rate, exposing layers of herself that were normally kept well-hidden. She wanted the same from Two, but Two couldn't bring herself to reciprocate. Was she simply using Naomi? Would she, in the end, take the blood and run madly into the night? Part of her wanted just that: to make the change and then run as far as she could, away from the politics and the machinations of these ancient creatures. She wanted quiet, peace, and freedom. She wanted the time to let go of Theroen.

Part of her wanted this very much, but another part of her cared deeply for Naomi and didn't want to see the vampire hurt. Two was trying desperately to fall in love with Naomi, because she knew that was what Naomi wanted to happen. Naomi wanted Two to love her, so that when the European council agreed to allow Two to become a vampire again, Naomi could make her a fledgling, and the two of them could build a life together. Two understood the appeal in this, but she didn't love Naomi. She didn't know if she ever would.

Sitting in the dark, next to her lover but still so alone, Two lay back and put her hands over her face. She did not weep but simply lay there, breathing deeply and waiting for sleep to come.

CHAPTER XXIV

Learning the Dance

In her time with Darren, Two had learned humiliation, despair, and the blissful, numb apathy of a heroin high. Theroen had taught her love, joy, and the pulsing ecstasy of the blood.

Stephen gave her only pain, and pain, and pain.

In the end, though, he gave her strength, and as this was what she had asked him for, Two felt that she could not complain. It took nearly eight months, but Stephen reshaped her body. He did it in a way completely unlike how Theroen's blood had changed her. Stephen's way was gradual – grueling and slow.

For the first two weeks, Two cried herself to sleep, thankful that she had gone to bed each night, exhausted, before Naomi had arrived home to see her in this state. There were times, especially early on, when she wanted to give up, wanted to beg Stephen to call it off. *Please,* she imagined saying. *Please, it's too much and I can't stand it.* She was taking more than a dozen Advil each day, for God's sake, and couldn't he *please* just let her skip the running for once, or the weights?

During these times, with Stephen running next to her, or standing over her as she lifted, Two would bite her lips to keep from speaking. She bit them, sometimes, until they bled, and she tried to focus on that pain instead of the pain she was inflicting upon the rest of her body. Stephen would see her doing this, and the bastard would smile. Two would glare at him, hating him, hating herself for asking him to do this to her. Stephen never once dropped his gaze, never once apologized, never once did anything but stare back with calm, detached amusement.

Slowly, things changed. Two stopped throwing up at the end of her runs. She stopped biting her lips until they hurt so badly that she was unable to kiss Naomi, much to the vampire girl's relief. She stopped crying, and hating, and wishing it would end. Looking in the mirror one day, Two realized that she was in better shape even than she had been as an *Eresh-Chen*, though not so strong or fast. She was layered with muscle, toned in every way, not bulky but absolutely fit. She was stronger than she had ever been as a human. Faster. More agile. Even her reflexes and concentration had improved.

At last she mentioned all of this to Stephen one night, as he was spotting her while she lifted weights. His typical smirk had broken into a smile. He nodded.

"You're in shape, real shape, for the first time in your life."

"I was close when I was a vampire—" Two began.

Stephen snorted. "That's not the same. The blood did that to you. You did *this* to yourself."

"No, you did this to me."

"Oh? I don't recall taking your hands and making you lift. I don't believe I ever held a gun to your head and ordered you to run ..."

Two stuck her tongue out at him as she continued to bench press. Stephen laughed.

"Are you sorry, then, that you did this?" he asked.

"No."

"And what about Naomi?"

Two rolled her eyes. "She was at first. Now, uh ... not so much."

"Stamina *does* have its uses."

"Shut up."

Stephen motioned for her to stop lifting and sit down on the floor. Two did so, and he sat down across from her, on a weight bench. He had converted the basement of their townhouse into an exercise room, complete with a treadmill, multiple sets of weights, and a stationary bicycle. He looked at her for a time, and Two met his gaze, waiting to see what he had to say. Finally, he spoke.

"The first and most important weapon is *always* the body. Always. Do you understand?"

Two nodded. "I think so."

"Then tell me why."

This was not a lesson that he had taught her, not some saying to memorize by rote. What Stephen wanted from Two was an indication that she understood the meaning behind his words, and why he had pushed her so hard, changed her so much. Two thought for a moment before answering.

"Any other weapon is just an extension of the body, right?" she asked. "Even a gun."

She thought for a moment that she saw something in Stephen's eyes that looked like pride. He grinned. Nodded.

"Yes, even a gun. Speed and agility are key, but strength is important as well. You've all three now where before – let's be honest – you had none."

"Shoulda met me back when I was living on the streets, before Darren," Two said.

"I imagine you were fast then, yes, and agile. But strong?"

"No, not very strong. Had to be fast and agile, though. Not a lot of work for slow pickpockets and clumsy burglars."

"Were you ever caught?"

"Came close a couple of times. One guy on the L platform at Eighth Avenue had me for sure ... grabbed my arm and hauled me right around in front of him. When he saw how young I was, he just took his wallet out of my hand and let me go. I ran."

"Lucky," Stephen said.

"I was really lucky for a long, long time," Two mused. "Maybe all that shit with Darren was the payoff."

"Call it luck, call it karma ... call it random chance or probability shifts, it's all the same shite," Stephen said, and Two laughed. She leaned her back against the wall, still sitting on the floor, stretching her arms and legs.

"What now?" she asked.

"Your weapon, your body, needed sharpening. We've done that, so now it's time to train you how to use it."

"Ooh. Do I get to learn kung fu?" Two asked, grinning. Stephen merely nodded.

"If you'd like."

"Oh. Wow. I mean ... what are my options, I guess?"

"I can personally teach you kung fu, Brazilian ju jitsu, American boxing, Greco-Roman wrestling, jarate, tae kwon do, and both Thai- and American-style kickboxing. That's before we get to weaponry training."

"Jesus ... you're going to teach me all of that?!" Two asked, feigning wide-eyed innocence.

Stephen laughed. "No. At least, not this year. After the council meeting, assuming all goes well, we can evaluate our long-term plans."

"Well, if all goes well, there shouldn't be any real need to change what we've been doing, right? Other than going home?"

Stephen did not immediately answer this, but instead glanced away for a moment, up and to the left, toward the room Two shared with Naomi. Two sighed.

"You see a lot," she said.

"Training. Vampire eyes. Above-average interest when it comes to Naomi."

"Right. So what is it you see, when all of this is done?"

"Do you really want to get into this right now?"

Stephen's tone warned her that if she did, he would ... and Two knew from experience that he would pull no punches. She considered the question carefully before answering.

"No. No, I don't think so. Not now. Maybe not ever. You could tell me what you think will happen, to me and Naomi, to you, to all of us. You might even be right. But if you *are* right, then it doesn't matter, and if you're wrong, then I guess it doesn't matter either, right?"

"What I think will happen does not matter at all, Two."

"OK. Am I done for tonight?"

"Yes."

Two nodded, stood, and headed for the stairs. She was hot and sweaty and wanted a shower. She wanted to think.

"Tomorrow we'll start with boxing," Stephen said. He moved to the weight bench and began attaching more weights to the bar.

Two stopped for a moment, glancing over her shoulder. "Why boxing?"

Stephen glanced up, flashing her another brief glimpse of his grin. "I believe you've earned the right to punch something."

* * *

"Right. First off, please tell me that I don't need to remind you to keep your goddamned thumbs out from under your fingers."

Stephen was leaning against the basement wall, watching Two, who was standing before a simple, heavy punching bag. Two turned her head, gave him a cool glance, and turned back to the bag.

"Told you I knocked some girl's teeth out, didn't I?" she asked.

"Could've been a lucky shot," Stephen countered.

"Bullshit. I know how to punch without breaking my thumbs."

"Good, then punch. Let me see your form."

Two threw a few shots at the bag: stiff, short jabs.

"Stop trying to anticipate what I *want* you to look like and just punch like you would punch if this bag was 'some girl' whose teeth needed knocking out."

"OK."

Two threw punches, circling around a bit. She knew that it would be obvious to Stephen that she was not trained, but hoped she would be able to keep from making a fool out of herself. At least, as she had said, she knew how to keep from breaking her thumbs.

Stephen was right: she had earned the right to hit something, and Two found herself enjoying this exercise. Moving with the bag, timing her swings, not minding the scrapes on her knuckles as the heavy canvas bounced against them. She could feel a light sweat forming all over her body, but she felt good, not out of breath or overexerted, simply a well-honed machine performing in the manner that it should.

"I guess I should thank you for this," she said as she punched.

"I was curious if you would feel that way," Stephen replied.

"For a long time, I didn't. I thought you were pushing too hard, just enjoying being the asshole drill sergeant that I couldn't say 'no' to."

"Who says I wasn't?"

Two laughed. Punched. "Fine, but I'm still thanking you for it."

"Why?"

"Dunno. Passed the time? Gave me sexy abs? Made me cut down on the cigarettes?"

"You should quit those entirely."

"Sure. I should probably quit the bourbon, too, but that's not gonna happen either."

"Very well then, but I don't think any of those are the real reason that you're thanking me."

"Suppose not."

Stephen waited. Two punched. Finally, she said, "I was tired of not being in control of anything."

"That's very interesting," Stephen said.

"Why's that?"

"The way I see it, you've been in control of this entire situation from the moment Naomi tasted your blood and learned what it is you were. At the very least, you've been in control from the moment she stopped me from killing you."

"What the hell have I been in control of?"

Stephen tilted his head and answered her question with one of his own. "Do you know why the American council wasn't able to come to a decision?"

Two, who had no idea, shook her head.

"They're scared of you. Terrified. Centuries of order have come crashing down because you – little, tiny you, not even in shape at the time – killed the bogeyman. You didn't just kill him, you slaughtered him like a farm animal. You chopped his head off and set him on fire, and you didn't do it by accident. You did it by walking up to him with every intention of killing him."

"I ... hadn't thought of it like that," Two admitted.

"There's not a vampire in the New World who hadn't fantasized about doing what you did to Abraham, at some point. Not one. Just ... taking him on, and winning. But for them ... for *us* ... it was fantasy, until you actually went and did it. If you can kill Abraham as a weak, half-human fledgling, just think what you might be capable of down the road!"

Two shrugged. She knew what she wanted, and it had nothing to do with things that should scare the council.

Stephen laughed. "That says it all, Two. You don't even know what you did. Not really."

Two hit the bag, sidestepped, hit again. "Don't know, don't really care," she said.

"Exactly. That is exactly right. You are going to be a *fantastic* vampire. All instinct and action. The council is going to be horrified at first."

"And then what?" Two asked, smiling, enjoying this vision of herself as a raging agent of chaos.

"Then there will be changes. Many, many changes, most of which will involve you in some way or the other."

"Look, Stephen, I appreciate the confidence, but seriously ..."

"You don't have to believe me. Just call it a hunch. Now stop talking and keep hitting."

Two shrugged again and did what she was told.

"Good. Good enough," Stephen said after a time, and Two stopped, inspecting her knuckles. They were raw, but weren't completely destroyed.

"Did I look OK?" she asked.

"No, you looked terrible ... but not hopeless."

"Oh."

"You did very well, Two. It will not take long to teach you the basics."

"How long are we talking?"

Stephen made a noncommittal noise. "A week or so to get your jabs in the right place. We'll work on the other punches after that. If nothing else, you don't swing like a girl."

Two, who had seen too many street fights – some up close and personal – to still punch as if she were swinging a purse, laughed and nodded.

"It took me weeks to get Naomi out of that habit," Stephen said.

"You taught Naomi to fight?"

"I tried."

"Why'd you stop? Wasn't she up for the work?"

Stephen raised his eyebrows. "She put in the work ... though I might have been a bit softer in my youth than I am now. But I haven't seen Naomi fight in decades, and that's the crux of it. She doesn't have the heart for it. She's a lover, as you know. I have the suspicion she's as gifted in her craft as I am in mine."

"No comment," Two said, but she was unable to suppress a telling smile.

"Where is she tonight, anyway? It seems she's rarely home these days."

Two shrugged. "Naomi does her thing. We don't really go out much ... not since you started training me. I can't go out to the clubs because I'm busy training, and she gets bored sitting in front of the TV. She's got some vampire friends here, but I've never met them. I don't want to."

"When I first met you, all you wanted was to meet as many vampires as you could," Stephen said.

Two thought for a moment, trying to find the right words. "I want it too badly," she said at last. "I want what she has. I want what they have. It hurts sometimes just to be with her. Hanging out with her and a bunch of other beautiful, brilliant, perfect vampire girls? No thanks."

"It doesn't hurt to stay here and train with me?"

Two considered this, then shook her head. "You have what I want, but it's not the same. I don't understand you and your people. I want to learn to fight, but not because I love to fight. I'm not like that. I'm closer to what Naomi is."

Stephen shook his head, and Two glanced up at him. "What?"

"I don't think you're any closer to her than you are to me," he said. "I understand why I don't bother you, and why they would, but it doesn't mean you're like Naomi. I know exactly what you are, and so do you, and it's why every time I bring up your relationship with Naomi in any manner other than jest, you look like you're going to cry."

Two was unable to form a response to this at first. Finally she said, "Sometimes I hate your fucking honesty."

"You and the rest of the world," Stephen replied.

"What am I, then? Huh, Stephen? Not a fighter, not a lover ... what?"

Stephen looked her in the eyes, and he gave her a sad smile that she had never before seen on his face. She found herself wishing quite fervently that she would never see it again.

"You're an Eresh," he said.

* * *

"Two, they've set a date!" Naomi wasn't even through the front door yet, and she was already shouting. "The council has set a date!"

Two, who was sitting at the kitchen table and eating a late dinner, turned and raised her eyebrows. "Really?"

"Yes, really!" Naomi pulled her shoes off, walked down the hallway to the kitchen. "What are you eating?"

"Pork chop. Salad. Bread. Want some?"

Naomi wrinkled her nose and shook her head. Two laughed as the vampire sat down across from her.

"So when's the date?" she asked.

"Three weeks from today."

Two choked on her salad, coughed a few times, looked at Naomi in surprise. "Wait, seriously?"

"Yes ... why?"

"Well, that's ... I mean, we've been here for more than a year, Naomi. I kind of figured they'd be like 'OK, we'll have a meeting in six months' when you finally got through to them."

Naomi laughed. Two had opened a bottle of chardonnay to go with her meal, and now the vampire girl stood, found herself a glass, and poured the wine. She refilled Two's glass, and then held up her own.

"To not waiting another six months," she said.

Two grinned, touched her glass to Naomi's, and said, "Amen. Cheers!"

They were silent for a moment, drinking their wine and considering this information. Two spoke first, turning to Naomi with a wry smile that she couldn't help.

"So ... what do you think about my chances?"

Naomi shrugged, but she smiled back at Two. "I honestly have no idea. The European council members are all older than any living vampire in America, and there are only five of them. I can't guess at how they'll choose to interpret our laws."

Two blew air upward toward the short strands of hair that now spiked out above her forehead. "I think I hate your laws, Naomi."

Naomi made a noncommittal noise and asked, "How was your workout tonight?"

"It was OK," Two said.

After training, Two had made her way upstairs and taken a long, hot shower. She had thought about what Stephen had said and concluded that it was the truth. Theroen had chosen her for a reason. He had seen her on a random walk through Brooklyn and felt some spark, some kinship, and further observation had convinced him that she was the one. He had made her an *Eresh-Chen*, yes, but whatever it was he had seen in her had already been there, and was with her still.

There weren't enough Eresh vampires. Two didn't know any, other than Leonore and her apprentice James, and neither of them was old enough to make fledglings even if she'd wanted anything to do with them. According to Naomi, there might be as few as seventy

Eresh in the entire world, and of those only a scant few were within the right age range. Two wasn't about to go looking for them.

That left Ashayt or Ay'Araf. Lovers or fighters. There was only one route that made sense. She had an available patron, a high-ranking member of the American council and an Ashayt at the prime age to create a fledgling. There was no reason *not* to take Naomi's blood as soon as it was offered. No reason at all, except for the growing certainty within her that to do so would lead only to tragedy in the long run.

These thoughts ran through Two's mind in moments, their only outward expression a slight wrinkling of her brow. Naomi noticed this and tilted her head, giving Two a questioning look. Two waved her away.

"Nothing, don't worry about it," Two lied. "I was trying to remember if Stephen wanted me to do anything else tonight, but I think I'm good."

Naomi smiled, considering this. "So you're free tonight, hmm?"

Two felt Naomi's aura pulsing around her, and she gave the vampire a small smile. "Yes, but it's a little early to head for bed … still hours 'til dawn."

Naomi laughed. "I know. I thought perhaps we could go out, have a few drinks … relax, for once. You never come out with me anymore."

"I—" Two began, and Naomi held up a hand, stopping her.

"I'm not trying to make you feel guilty. I just miss you. I told you I understood, when we talked about it, and I really do. I know that it's not easy to stand on the outside, looking in."

"Yes."

"Tonight though, I promise, no long talks about vampire life, and no visits from any of my friends, and no worrying about the future. Just you, me, and some loud music. We'll go, and drink, and dance if you want, and then we'll come home."

"Before dawn?" Two asked.

Naomi smirked. "Oh, yes. *Well* before dawn."

"I'm sure you have some lovely ideas in mind for when we get home," Two said, heading for the hall closet where she had hung her jacket.

Behind her, Naomi laughed, a pretty sound not tinged by the sadness that Two so often heard in the other woman's voice. She was glad for this, glad that at least for tonight they were going to go out and focus on having fun, rather than worrying about the future.

"I think I *will* dance tonight," Two said, pulling on her jacket. "I want to get all close with you and make every guy in the place stare. Sound good?"

Naomi joined her in the hall, still smiling. "I cannot think of a single thing that I would like more."

* * *

Naomi pressed against her, soft and warm, expertly moving to the thudding music. Two could see that the exertion, the heat, the booze, and the excitement had combined to make even the vampire sweat, no easy feat. The club was packed with bodies, flooded with colored lighting, and had become something like an inferno. Throngs of people surrounded them, holding drinks and yet managing to undulate in time with the pulsing trance beats. Two normally hated this type of music but she was drunk and wanted to dance, and tonight she was happy to have it.

Naomi was six inches taller than Two and might have proven a difficult partner if not for her superhuman reflexes. She moved with Two, undulating, twisting, reacting perfectly in time with the beat and with Two's movements. Two, for her part, was in the best shape of her life and acutely aware of both her improved stamina and new agility. They had been drawing stares all night, their dance an open simulation of sex, liquid and sinuous, rhythmic, building and building, only to pull apart at what seemed the very last second.

Eleven men and four women had tried to cut in, break them apart, draw one of the two of them off. To Two's surprise and gratification, not all of them had targeted Naomi. Nonetheless, they had turned all of their suitors down. Two and Naomi weren't here to hook up with strangers. They were here to dance, and there was no better partner to be found for each than the other. Just as Two was thinking this to herself, Naomi seemed to reassert the fact by gleefully grabbing Two's rump. Two glanced up at her, eyebrows raised, and the vampire leaned in.

"I want you so badly I might strip you right here on the dance floor," Naomi said, her lips against Two's ear.

"I doubt anyone would complain," Two said, pressing against her lover, hands held above her head, hips moving.

"Don't tempt me!" Naomi laughed. She kissed Two on the cheek, moved her head away, continued dancing.

Two danced with her eyes closed, letting Naomi worry about adapting to her movements, knowing that the vampire girl would have no problem doing so. She thought about the life Naomi had lived, the people she might have loved who were no longer alive. There was Lisette, of course, but had there been others as well? Was Two the first human that Naomi had loved?

Naomi had begun biting Two during sex several months earlier, and as it had with Theroen, the act substantially enhanced Two's orgasm. While it worried Two, in a way, that they were becoming so close, it seemed impossible to ask Naomi to stop. Not only was the pleasure nearly indescribable, but she didn't want to hurt Naomi's feelings.

Then there had been the evening in June when, lying in each other's arms and at the very edge of sleep, Naomi had said "I love you" to Two for the first time. Naomi had fallen asleep within moments. Two had spent the next hour and a half staring up at the ceiling, unsure of how to react to the vampire's words. Love? Naomi was wonderful. Beautiful. Amazing. Yet, no, not love. Not quite. Love was for Theroen. Two would not, could not, say those words back to Naomi.

Three weeks ago, Naomi had proven her love in a way more intimate than all of the sex or words Two could ever have asked of her. After the apex of their lovemaking, with both women exhausted and near sleep, Naomi had bitten gently into her own arm and shared her blood with Two. Just a few drops before the wound had healed, just enough to coat Two's tongue, and yet it had set ablaze within her that old desire, a need that had gone unfulfilled for nearly two years. This was Naomi's promise, Two understood instinctively, that no matter what the council decided, they would find a way.

Am I the first since Lisette? Two wondered. It couldn't be possible. Lisette had died hundreds of years ago. There must have been others. Where were they now? What had happened? What could …

Naomi leaned in close again and said, "Whatever it is you're thinking about, I order you to stop right now!"

Two laughed, opened her eyes, smiled at Naomi. "Yes, ma'am."

"*Mademoiselle!*" Naomi corrected, feigning indignation. "I may be four hundred, but I'm not married. Good … now drink this."

Naomi thrust a glass into Two's hand, and Two did as she was told. Something sweet and strong burned within, a flavored liquor cut with cola. Vanilla vodka, perhaps, Two thought, but she was too drunk to be sure.

"Where did this come from?" she asked.

Naomi pointed toward a cocktail waitress making her way through the crowd with practiced expertise. "She stopped by while you were … lost in your reverie. Compliments of the bartender."

"What'd we do to earn that?" Two asked.

"He knows me, and he knows how I tip," Naomi said. "Also, there are at least a dozen boys who would have bailed on this place already if they weren't watching us. That's more money for him. The least he can do is a couple of free drinks, no?"

Naomi was holding a wine glass, cupping it so that her palm covered it. In a single fluid movement, still timed with the music, she switched hands, took it by the stem, brought it to her lips and drank.

"Ooh!" she exclaimed. "Bordeaux. Lovely. I was born near there."

"This is the last one for me, OK?" Two said. "I mean … unless you want to finish the night listening me to puke."

"I would truly rather die," Naomi said, looking grave. "You don't have to drink it!"

Two smiled at her, kept dancing. "I'm just fine," she said. "This should be perfect. We're working it off."

They were. The DJ had kept the music rolling for nearly two hours straight, blending smoothly from one song to another. Now he took the beat down, and down, ending his set. Two and Naomi cheered with the others in the club. The MC let them know that after a fifteen minute break, there would be yet another act. There was more applause at this announcement, and then the house stereo began blaring.

Two and Naomi turned and began to make their way from the dance floor. A few people applauded them as they left, and they laughed and waved. Eventually, they found a semi-circular couch in a dark corner where they could finish their drinks. Naomi curled up on the soft leather, resting her head on Two's thigh. Two, beyond caring if the entire world knew that she was sleeping with this woman, ran her fingers through Naomi's hair.

"Home after this?" she asked, and glanced down in time to catch Naomi trying awkwardly to drink her wine without raising her head. Two laughed, raising her knee in an attempt to aid in the vampire's endeavor.

"Thanks. Yes, I think I've had about enough."

"I'm going to want to take a shower when I get home," Two said.

"Can I join you?"

Before Two could make her reply, which would've been positive, a male patron leaned over the back of the couch and slurred something at Naomi. It took Two a moment to decipher his thick cockney accent, but she was pretty sure the man had told Naomi that he had a much more interesting lap to put her head in.

"I'll keep you in mind if I ever fancy getting syphilis, cunt," Naomi told him. The man sneered at her and turned back in the other direction.

"That wasn't very nice," Two commented. She finished her drink and set the glass on a small table at the edge of the couch.

"My first instinct was to punch him so hard in his 'lap' that it would be of no further use to him or anyone else. I thought I showed admirable restraint," Naomi said.

Two laughed. "Should I take you home before you beat someone up?"

357

Naomi finished the last of her wine in a gulp and sat up, grinning broadly at Two.

"Yes, please," she said.

* * *

They were lying in what was, for her, absolute darkness. There was no crack in the blinds tonight from which the light of the street might enter. It didn't matter; they hadn't needed any light, content to navigate each other's bodies with fingers, hands and lips.

Naomi had reached orgasm three times, and at the last she had gasped in a strained voice, "God. *Je vais mourir.*"

Two, who had learned a bit of French, had laughed. "You're not dying," she had said, yet only minutes later Naomi had brought her to a place that necessitated burying her face in the pillows and wailing, wondering for herself if she might not survive the night.

Both had lived, and soon they were lying tangled together, the blankets thrown aside, not yet cooled down and unwilling to disconnect. There was only the quiet rush of their breathing, the scent and taste of sex, the feel of each other's fingers tracing lines along each other's skin. Then Two had made her request.

"Tell me about the council."

Naomi took a moment to collect herself, then murmured her answer, her lips somewhere not far from Two's left ear. "I have been before the European council only twice. Both times were ... harrowing."

There was a pause, and Two supposed Naomi was waiting for the typical sarcastic, acerbic comment. Two had none prepared. She was in a state that precluded any such attitude, still drunk, half-asleep, floating on a cloud of post-orgasmic bliss. Right now, she thought, World War III could start and she would continue simply to lie there, at least until her legs stopped shaking.

After it became clear that Two had no response to her statement, Naomi went on. "I suppose it may be less difficult for you because you've not spent hundreds of years dealing with vampire politics. You don't generally care what's proper, and aren't as worried about offending people, so you may not be as scared of them as I was."

"Probably true," Two said. She moved her head, resting it between Naomi's breasts, listening to the vampire's heartbeat. This sound amused her, unexpected as it might be to people familiar with vampire myths and legends. Naomi wasn't dead. None of the vampires, regardless of their strain, were.

"Honestly, it's to your benefit," Naomi said. Her words were still somewhat slurred from alcohol, exertion, and the proximity of sleep. Two smiled.

"Probably true," she said again.

Naomi laughed a little, shifting her body, running a finger down Two's spine. "It will not be like the American council."

"No?"

"Some of it will be the same. They'll want your story, of course, and I think you should tell it just as you did before: pull no punches, and give as much detail as you can."

Two nodded, knowing that Naomi could feel the motion.

"Once you're done, they will ask questions. I don't know how many, and I don't know whether they'll be interested in anything Stephen or I have to say. It's possible. Once they have everything they need, they'll retire, deliberate, and pass judgment. They are all busy people, not much for dallying, and there are only five of them. It won't take long."

"Don't they ever disagree?"

"The youngest vampire on the council is approaching fifteen hundred, and they have all known each other for centuries. Even as you're telling your story, they will be anticipating each other's opinions. The American council sometimes needs to debate for weeks – lord knows, I've listened to Stephen complain about our 'pointless bickering' more than once – but the European council has no such need. They simply decide. Eadwyn understands Gaius, Gaius understands N'debe, and ... you get the point."

"Gauis, N'Debe, Eadwyn ... who are the others?" Two asked.

"The other two are Marian and Safeed. I do not know any of the five of them well. I am not even sure which type of vampire they all are, though I know Eadwyn is an Ashayt. He ... he hears voices and has a rather unusual manner of speaking. Many call him Eadwyn the Mad."

Two considered this without speaking. Naomi continued.

"I believe Marian is an Eresh, but she is not *Eresh-Chen*. Her line forked from that of Abraham and Theoren's sometime in the Bronze Age. The others I do not know, though there is a strong possibility that Safeed is Ay'Araf. That strain originated in the Middle East."

"Why do they have a crazy vampire on the council?" Two asked.

"There's no proof that Eadwyn is crazy, just eccentric," Naomi said. "He is the oldest living Ashayt vampire, has survived since well before the time of Christ, and fears nothing. He claims to speak with the voices of our ancestors, of all those vampires who have gone before us into death. I can't imagine this is so, but then, who am I to deny any claims of the supernatural? It doesn't matter – Eadwyn may be crazy, but his insight is always valuable."

"Oh," Two said. "Well, I suppose that's good, then."

"Yes, provided you can understand him."

Two sighed, long and deep, half in contentment, and half in concern.

"Don't worry about it now. It's late," Naomi said.

Two changed her position again, kissing Naomi's shoulder as she moved, resting her head on the pillow so that her lips were near the vampire's ear.

"I am too tired, too drunk, and way too full of hormones to get worked up about anything," she murmured.

"Did I ... was everything ... I mean, did you ..." Two could hear the concern in Naomi's voice. She laughed.

"Sweetheart, stop. Yes. I came twice, and it was amazing. Why do you *still* worry about this?"

Naomi shrugged. "I always worry about it."

"Why?"

Naomi was silent for a long time; so long, in fact, that Two was positive that the vampire girl had fallen asleep. At last, just as Two was beginning to doze, Naomi spoke. Her words came in a small voice that wavered with tension and, Two realized, terrible sadness.

"I worry because we have been together like this for ... for almost a year, now, and you have never said you love me."

Adrenaline coursed through Two at this statement, and it took an effort to keep her body from jerking, but she managed. When the feeling had passed, somewhat, she took a shaky breath, but did not immediately answer.

"I worry that I've failed to ... to satisfy you in some way," Naomi said.

"Naomi, no. It's not that. You're ... I wish I could say that. I wish *so much* that I could say those words to you. It's just that if I do say that, then that's it, right? All of your walls come down."

"I don't have many walls left," Naomi said.

"That still means you have some."

Naomi sighed. "Yes. And yes, if you say it, Two, then I won't be able to help myself. Whatever defenses I've still got left would disappear, and you could hurt me as badly as anyone ever has."

"Even Abraham," Two said.

Naomi nodded. Two waited, thinking, and then said, "Even Theroen."

When Naomi inhaled next, the sound was shuddery, and Two knew that she was on the verge of tears.

"He took her away from me," Naomi said.

Two nodded. She kissed Naomi's temple and put her hand on the vampire's waist.

"He hurt you," she said.

Naomi shook her head. "They. They did it together."

"He didn't know."

"I've forgiven him."

"What about her?"

There was another long pause, and when at last Naomi's words came, her tone was bitter. Angry. Resolute.

"I will never, ever forgive her. Not for leaving me, and not for leaving us both."

"Naomi, I don't know if that's—"

"Two, I can't. I can't!" Naomi's anger, as much at herself as at the woman who had made her a vampire, was obvious in her voice. "It's been *hundreds of years*, and still I can't. Oh, what is *wrong* with me?"

"There's nothing wrong with you."

"Then tell me you love me."

Two was silent, and Naomi gave a defeated little laugh.

"Indeed," she said. "I loved Lisette, and now I love you. I have loved others, through the years, and said those words that you can't say. I would know, even if you could make yourself say it, that you don't mean it. You'll never love me until you can let *him* go, and as hard as I've tried to make that happen ... here we are."

"I'm sorry," Two said. "Naomi, I'm sorry."

Naomi sighed, kissed Two's collarbone, turned over on her belly: a sure sign that she was preparing to sleep. When she spoke, her voice was tired, and sad, and empty.

"Goodnight, Two," the vampire girl said. "I love you."

CHAPTER XXV

The European council

The vampire elder did not look like a madman, but Two supposed that appearances could be deceiving. What Eadwyn looked like to her was a man in his late twenties, not tall, but broad through the shoulders. He was thin, almost painfully so, and had large hands that ended in long, delicate fingers. His hair was chestnut colored, and his light and watery blue eyes rested above a prominent nose. He looked to Two like a cleaned-up version of any number of British rockers she had seen on the covers of music magazines.

Eadwyn was standing at the door of a small, stone building that looked very old. It was nestled tightly between two more modern structures, both of which were several stories taller than it, making the meeting place look even tinier than it actually was. It seemed an odd place for the oldest and most powerful vampires in Europc to gathcr, but then perhaps its age gave it sentimental or historical value.

"Toothsome treacle twists from our lips, and with welcoming words we greet you," Eadwyn said. "We will be happy to take you inside to meet the others."

Two found herself glancing around in an attempt to determine who "we" meant. Eadwyn stood watching her, head tilted, an amused expression on his face. He gave her time, and Two quickly confirmed her initial impression: there was no one else there. After a moment more, it clicked: Eadwyn the Mad, the vampire who spoke to the dead.

"'Tis best never to travel alone," Eadwyn told her.

"Right," Two replied. "Yes. Uh … thanks. For the welcome."

Eadwyn nodded, and turned toward Naomi and Stephen. Two found it amusing that this – not the stately old gentlemen that she had imagined – was what a member of the European council looked like. It made sense, of course; vampires didn't grow old, and so despite Eadwyn's great age, he still appeared to be a young man. What surprised Two was that she heard none of Eadwyn's age in his voice, felt none of the imposing power that Abraham had seemed to give off.

Eadwyn had been about to speak to Naomi, but now he glanced back at Two with a small smirk. Without warning, Two was nearly overcome by the sudden onslaught of something that struck her as similar to Naomi's aura, though many times stronger. It was not sexual, not calming or warming, but rather filled her with fear, respect and awe. For a brief moment she could see in his eyes the ages that had gone by, that he had lived through unchanged in appearance but sculpted inside, mentally and physically, by the amazing blood that ran in his veins.

And then it was gone and he was just a young man again, gazing at her with that same amused expression.

"Flaunt, some fools do," Eadwyn said. "We have never felt the need."

Two, still trying to catch her breath, could only nod. Eadwyn returned his gaze to Naomi.

"Pray, pretty … picked any pockets of late?" he asked.

Naomi turned a shade of light pink and cast her eyes downward, but did not speak. Eadwyn chuckled.

"We are happy to see you again after so much time. You bring memories of your melancholy mistress."

"Thank you, Lord." Naomi said, her eyes still downcast. "She is with me still … I miss her every day."

"Whispers and words wander my head, but few from her I hear. Perhaps she has found peace."

"I hope so."

"You know the truth about her now, pickpocket?"

"About Abraham's involvement? Yes. Two told me."

Eadwyn gave her a look of sympathy, nodding. "We are older, but he was stronger. Eresh are pesky in that way. We could not stop him."

"I understand," Naomi said. "It is ... in the past now."

Eadwyn shrugged. Nodded. Turned to Stephen.

"*Fáilte*, fighter. We meet at last."

Stephen grinned, and Two understood that he was much more comfortable in front of this elder than Naomi was. She suspected that it was Stephen's lack of concern for the political ramifications of his interactions with the council that made it so.

"I was unaware that my reputation preceded me," he said, giving a small bow to Eadwyn.

"We hear many things," Eadwyn replied. "European escort is not a traditional toiling for one of the warrior class. From whom came your instructions?"

"It was my choice, lord."

"How unusual."

"I was unenthusiastic with the American council's inability to come to a decision. I wanted to register my thoughts with you personally."

"I see, and so you lead lovely ladies to light upon our doorstep."

"Naomi led. I followed."

"And will you follow further if so she must go?"

Stephen shrugged, held his hands apart, glanced briefly at his companions. Finally he said, "I don't make decisions until the time has come."

Eadwyn laughed at this and clapped Stephen on the shoulder. He turned slightly and addressed the group as a whole. "Shall we?"

He gestured at the door behind him, a sturdy thing of oak and iron the likes of which Two had rarely seen on anything other than cathedrals. Naomi and Stephen nodded, and Two said, "Yes, please."

"Very well, then." The elder vampire turned and unlatched the door, swinging it open to reveal a dimly lit stone hallway lined with other, similar doors. At its far end was a staircase that spiraled up and out of sight. Without further conversation, Eadwyn made his way inside, and the three companions followed.

* * *

The European council was made up of three women and two men, including Eadwyn. Two was struck again by how young they all looked, and how casual their demeanor. All were dressed in business attire, but there was no air of formality about them, no pretention of the type that had seemed to blanket the American council. These people were very comfortable, like long-time employees who had worked together for the same company, day in and day out, for many years. Two of the women were talking with the second man, while the third woman, a tall, black vampire with closely cropped hair, stood at the edge of the room, murmuring into her cell phone. When Eadwyn entered with their guests, she finished her conversation and snapped the phone shut, moving toward the others.

"Wanderers, we welcome you!" Eadwyn said, his voice taking on a theatrical air. "Behold: before you sit – or stand – these most powerful of vampires, eldest and greatest of their lines. We are beings so powerful that the simple sound of our voices may cause you to drop to your knees, weeping and begging for forgiveness from sins which you never committed. Tremble! Tremble before these mighty—"

He was cut off by a short, dark, severe-looking woman who Two thought must have been born in an area that was now India or Pakistan. "That'll do, Eadwyn."

Eadwyn, who had stopped in mid-flourish and was holding his arms apart in a gesture of showmanship, smirked again and clapped his hands together.

"As you wish, Safeed."

He made his way to one of a dozen large, tall-backed leather chairs that were gathered around the room's central oval table. The council members had grouped themselves in a semi-circle around one end of the table. Two, Naomi, and Stephen sat down across from them. Eadwyn leaned back in his chair, put his feet up on the table, and drawled at them in a John Wayne impression startling in its accuracy.

"Y'all make y'selves comfortable, now, pardners."

"You can feel free to ignore him," said a pale woman with red hair. Her accent sounded like a cross between Eadwyn's English intonation and Stephen's normal inflection. "That's what the rest of us do."

"Heartache!" Eadwyn cried, removing his feet from the table. "You wound me, Marian. I am aggrieved!"

"And you bore me, Eadwyn," Marian said, but Two thought that she saw the slightest hint of a smile on the elder vampire's face.

This is not what I expected, she thought.

Marian glanced at her and said, "You expected a bunch of powdered wigs and black robes, I imagine."

Two jerked, surprised, and asked, "Can ... can you all read my mind?"

"No, just me. Eadwyn sometimes gets flashes."

"The rest of us are not so blessed," the other male vampire said, "which is why Marian *usually* avoids responding to people's thoughts."

"I usually avoid reading them in the first place, as Gaius well knows," Marian said.

"It's easier for the rest of us if the conversation is held out loud," Gaius said. He was smiling slightly, and appeared relaxed and largely uninterested in the goings-on about him.

Two was almost put off by this display. She was here to plead her case on a matter which was, for her, of great importance. To these vampires though, she was nothing more than a minor speck in a world full of humans to whom they were superior in virtually every way. She had done them a favor, perhaps, by removing Abraham from the planet, but they seemed not in the least concerned with her fate. Two bit her lip and looked away for a moment.

"Is something wrong, child?" the Indian vampire, Safeed, asked her.

Two shook her head. "No ma'am."

"Not a good idea to lie to us, dear," Eadwyn told her. "Make a note of it."

367

Two shrugged, kept herself from sighing, said, "This is important to me."

"Would you have preferred the solemn formality of the American council, Miss Majors?" Marian asked her. There was no malice in her voice, but Two could find no sympathy there either.

"I don't—" Two began, but Safeed cut her off, frowning.

"Even Eadwyn is capable of being as serious as you would like."

"No, I—"

"We can be grim and grumbling ghouls if it gratifies you," Eadwyn said.

Two felt like throwing her hands in the air and screaming. Here she had said nothing, done nothing, and she was already offending these people and losing her chance at immortality. Naomi placed a hand on her shoulder and Two felt a calming warmth rush through her.

"Harrowing," the vampire girl murmured, and Two nodded, took a breath, looked up at Marian.

"You can run your council however you like, ma'am," she said. "I just want to tell you my story and see what you think."

"That seems reasonable," Gaius said. "If we're done intimidating the human, can we move on with this, please?"

Two had wondered if there was an official leader among this group, the way Malik lead the American council, but it seemed that was not the case. The vampires merely glanced at each other, seeming to confer without speaking. Two sat, trying to be patient, waiting to begin. It was not that she wanted to tell her story again. If anything, she was dreading it, but the sooner it was done, the sooner all of this could end.

It was Safeed who leaned forward in her chair, tapped her fingers on the table once, and said, "Very well. We know of you, *Eresh-Chen*, but we've not heard the full story. Would you prefer it if we asked questions, or would you rather tell us your tale in full?"

"It's ... it's your call," Two said.

"No, no, no," Eadwyn said. "That won't do. Don't defer duty. Make a choice."

Two looked over at him and felt a sudden anger burning within her, not focused at any individual before her but rather encompassing the entire situation. This anger took her nerves away and replaced them with something resembling strength. Eadwyn seemed to notice this change, and one side of his mouth rose in a smirk that was without malice.

"Just choose," he said.

"Fine," Two said. "I'll tell the story. It's easier, and I've got it down to a science at this point anyway. Everything I'm going to say is true ... but you know that. It's not like I can lie to you."

Marian smiled a little at this, and she nodded.

"I just wanna say ... I'm sorry, but I hate being here. I hate wasting your time, and Naomi's time, and Stephen's time."

"And *your* time," Gaius said pointedly. Two resisted the urge to roll her eyes at him.

"Yes," she said. "My time, too. The rest of you ... you *have* time. I have none, not compared to you, but even so, I feel bad about wasting your time on this ... this crap. It wasn't supposed to be like this. It wasn't supposed to go this way."

Two sat back, flexing her fingers in frustration, and repeated herself. "It wasn't supposed to go this way."

The black woman, who Two remembered from her earlier conversations with Naomi was named N'debe, spoke for the first time. Her voice was low and musical, the words rolling off her tongue in a rich accent. She radiated an aura of supreme calm, and Two had no doubt that this vampire was, like Eadwyn, an Ashayt.

"Things rarely go as they are supposed to, child. I am curious to hear the details, and I am sure my fellow council members feel the same. Please tell us your story."

"OK. Thank you," Two said. She sat back in her chair and put her head down for a moment, folding her hands and pressing the pads of her thumbs against her eyebrows. Finally, she spoke.

"I don't know when it was that Theroen first saw me, or how long he spent watching me before he decided to do what he did. I only know that when it happened, I was nineteen, addicted to heroin, and spending my days waiting to die."

She told them the story as she had told the American council, leaving out no detail, no matter how unseemly. How could it matter? These vampires would judge her in ways she would never understand. They might place no importance on her past, her addiction and the things she had done to support it, or they might find it the most important part of her story. It could matter to them that an *Eresh-Chen* had chosen her, or perhaps they would judge that fact meaningless.

Two had no idea what they would think, and by the time she was finished telling her story, she wasn't sure she cared. Here again was the pain, shoved to the back of her mind these past months, pulled forward again, bright and new. She fought against tears, fought against despair, and finally sat back in her chair with her eyes closed.

"That's it," she said, not opening her eyes. "That's all there is. We came to this country and spent a year in London while Naomi worked on setting up this meeting, and now we're here."

Naomi spoke up for the first time since they had entered the room. "If you have any questions for me, or for Stephen, we will be happy to answer them."

"Noted," Safeed said. She glanced around at the others, her expression still dark, still serious. Two wondered if the woman had ever smiled in her centuries of existence.

"We are quite, quite satisfied," Eadwyn said. "Such a stupendous story! Chair legs and machetes ... there is simply *not* enough excitement in our lives."

"You're welcome to some of mine," Two muttered, and Eadwyn grinned.

"You're not being very sympathetic," Marian said to her fellow council member, and Eadwyn shrugged.

"She's not here for sympathy," Gaius said, with an air of distaste that Two didn't understand. He seemed bored and frustrated, as if he had long since made up his mind.

Safeed glanced at Naomi. "You were able to taste the difference in her blood?"

Naomi sat forward, her body straightening, and took a deep breath. "Yes," she said. "I was, yes. It was faint, but I knew immediately that there was something wrong with her blood … something not human. It took me a few more seconds to understand what I was tasting. I have to admit that in my surprise and haste to stop drinking, I dropped her on the ground."

"Precipitate, perhaps, pickpocket," Eadwyn said. "Leaping from on high to attack without speaking?"

Naomi blushed again at Eadwyn's words and lowered her eyes for a moment. "I have only known a few humans who came looking for vampires, and in all of those cases, they were hunting, not looking to speak. It was a mistake to act so rashly."

"She's not the only one," Stephen said. "As Two mentioned, I tried to feed from her too, the next evening."

"We're not planning any disciplinary action for either of you," Marian said. "Regardless of your initial actions, you've both gone out of your way to help get Two to this point."

Naomi looked relieved. She glanced around at the council members and said, "The American council felt that you would have the authority to make a final ruling on interpreting the scrolls and determining how they should apply in this case."

"Of course we can," Safeed said.

"A few more questions first," Marian, the red-haired Eresh, said. "If you don't mind, Two."

"No problem," Two said. As far as she was concerned, they could ask questions of her all night if they needed to.

"I understand that much of the answer to this question is obvious, but indulge me: what is it that you want? Why do you seek to return to this life? Is it the power? The strength? The euphoria of the blood itself?"

Two considered this for a time before answering, trying to put her feelings into words. Finally, she spoke. "All of the above, and more. What I want is … the blood made me something better than what I am now. I didn't totally realize that until I lost it, but while I was with Theroen, I was complete. I was the best that I could be. When it was taken away from me, I felt broken, like parts of me had been removed and all that was left was a shell."

"Could that have been simply an illusion brought on by the blood ecstasy?" Safeed asked.

"I know what empty euphoria feels like," Two said. She looked down for a moment, then back up at the council members. "It feels really good while it's happening, the way drinking blood feels to a vampire, more or less ... but when it's gone, it's gone. Heroin never helped me understand poetry. It never made me run faster or see in the dark. It never made me able to sense someone's emotions, or hear someone's thoughts, or connect with anyone the way I did with Theroen. His blood *fixed* me. Heroin just made me forget that I was broken."

"Are all human beings broken?" N'debe asked in her soft, low voice.

"I don't know. If they are, I don't think most of them know it. I think people like my friends have no idea what they're missing, so it doesn't bother them."

"Would you try to convert your friends?" Eadwyn asked her.

Two shook her head. "No. They ... I don't think they would want it, and besides, I won't be ready to make a fledgling for a hundred years or more, right? They'll be ... I mean ..."

"Mort. Tot. Guasto. Inoperante. Muerto. Cacked off. Bit the bucket. Taking a dirt nap." Eadwyn was smiling at her, but there was a harsh note to his voice, a malicious glint in his eye. He spoke the last word with finality. "Dead."

"I know what I'm giving up," Two said. "Is that what you're trying to test? Do you want to know if I've thought this through? I know that Rhes and Sarah and Molly will be dust before I could ever offer them the blood. Even their kids and grandkids will probably be gone before I'm ready for that. Are you trying to make me feel bad, testing my resolve?"

"I'm not testing anything, child. I am merely stating the truth," Eadwyn said, and now the dark light was gone from his eyes. He smiled, spread his hands, leaned back in his chair. "I am without subtlety."

Two raised an eyebrow at this, but said nothing. Eadwyn smirked.

Marian turned to the others. "Is there anything else we need?"

"I have enough," Safeed said.

"Quite," Gaius agreed. N'debe nodded.

"Eadwyn?" Marian asked.

"Oh, I have *everything* I could possibly need," Eadwyn said. He stood, and the others followed suit.

"There is a small waiting room with couches, down the hall," Safeed said. "The three of you should relax there, and we will come for you shortly."

Two, Naomi, and Stephen shook hands with the council members and began to make their way toward the room's exit. Two got there first and stopped by the door, one hand on the heavy wooden frame. She turned and looked back at the European council.

"Thank you for listening," she said. "I hope ... I hope you understand why it is that I did what I did, and why I'm here today."

The council members nodded in acknowledgement, and N'debe smiled at her. Two waited a moment longer, then turned and made her way down the hall with her friends not far behind.

* * *

"What do you think?" Naomi asked.

Two glanced away from the window in front of her, looked over her shoulder at Naomi.

"Man," she said. "I have no fucking idea."

Stephen made a snorting, laughing noise from behind them both. He was sitting on a couch near the back of the room, watching a soccer game on a small television with the volume turned so far down that Two supposed only vampire ears could make out the announcer's words.

"Honesty. Good. They say it's the best policy," he said.

Naomi glanced over at him. "And you, Stephen? What do you think?"

Without taking his eyes from the television, Stephen said, "I think it's a swing vote. Three to two. Now ask me which direction I think the vote swings."

Naomi's hands twitched, as if she might be fighting off the urge to throttle her friend. "Which?"

"Man," Stephen said, now looking over at her and grinning, "I have no fucking idea."

"You're useless," Naomi growled. She was pacing back and forth near a set of shelves that held an orderly collection of leather-bound tomes.

"Yet you keep me around because I'm so good-looking," Stephen said, and he turned back to his game.

"Gaius doesn't like me," Two said. "He was bored the whole time, and he probably thinks I'm just some pain in the ass who should've died in the alley behind *L'Obscurité*. There's no way he votes for me."

"Agreed," Naomi said, "but his opinion is the only one of the group that I'm at all comfortable guessing about. Safeed is always so dire that she's impossible to read. N'debe rarely speaks and when she does, she is always very pleasant, but she wouldn't be on the council if she couldn't make hard choices. Marian is too ... too ..."

"Too Eresh," Stephen said.

"What does that mean?" Two asked.

"Eresh blood does things to the brain. You've experienced it yourself, you said so: you were able to understand poetry that eluded you as a human being. That doesn't happen to Ashayt or Ay'Araf or Burilgi. Poetry remains as dull and boring to me as it did three centuries ago."

"I like poetry," Naomi commented.

"You're a namby-pamby Ashayt," Stephen said. "Of course you like poetry. That's not the point. What I'm saying is, you liked and understood poetry as a human. The blood in you didn't change your brain, at least not like it did for Two. That's why Marian is hard to predict. Gaius had made his decision before he even got here, most likely. Marian has probably changed her mind fifteen times during the course of the evening."

"Long as she ends up on my side, she can change her mind as much as she wants," Two said.

Stephen shrugged, still watching his game. "Who knows? You might as well ask me to predict Eadwyn's response."

"I think he likes Two," Naomi said, and Two could hear the hope in the vampire girl's voice. It was touching. Two sometimes forgot that the council's decision was very important to Naomi as well.

"I hope he likes me. I think mostly he just likes being weird and confusing," Two said.

"It won't matter whether he likes you or not," Stephen said. "Eadwyn may be weird and confusing, but he is also as calculating as any vampire you can name. He will weigh many factors that we are not even aware of when making his decision."

"Doesn't mean it'll be the right decision," Two said.

"You don't need to convert me," Stephen told her. "I'm already on your side. As far as I can see, there is absolutely no question about the proper course of action. It's not my fault the American council members cannot – present company accepted – pull their heads from their arses."

Naomi frowned. "What you so often fail to realize is that people's actions may have unintended consequences."

"Those tend to follow me around," Two said. Stephen laughed.

"The problem with unintended consequences is that they happen no matter how hard you try to prevent them. That's life."

"So then we should all just give in to chaos and anarchy, right, Stephen?" Naomi asked. "Just do whatever we choose and to hell with what happens after that?"

"You have to admit that things would be interesting," Stephen replied.

Naomi sat down on a couch and rested her head in her hands. "Sometimes I have no idea why I spend time with you."

Eadwyn's voice startled them all as he spoke from the doorway. "A little contrast enhances one's life, we find. Now, we trust you three have dwelled long enough in this drab and dreary place?"

"You're finished?" Two asked.

"We're finished," Eadwyn replied.

"That was fast."

Eadwyn said nothing, merely smirked, stepped back into the hall, and beckoned with his hand. Two took a breath, turned from the window, and made her way toward the door.

The vampire council was seated once again around the table, and if anything was to be determined by their appearance, it was beyond Two's abilities to do so. They looked, to her, exactly the same as they had seemed to be before her story and their subsequent discussion. She felt some of the worry that she had experienced while standing before the American council but less outright fear. Her life, at least, was not in jeopardy this time.

Two took her seat near the end of the table, Naomi and Stephen on either side of her. The council members watched as they sat down.

"I trust we didn't keep you waiting too long?" Marian asked.

"No ma'am," Two replied.

"Are you nervous?" Eadwyn asked her. "Worried? Concerned? Succumbing to the vapors? Possessed of a most debilitating case of the heebie-jeebies?"

"Eadwyn ..." Gaius glanced over at his fellow council member, frowning. "Can we just conclude this business?"

Eadwyn nodded. "Certainly. But we have a request of the Lady *Deux*: we want a moment of her time, and that of her companions, after judgment has been rendered."

"Sure," said Two.

"Regardless of the perceived *quality* of such judgment."

Two shrugged. Did she have a choice? "Sure."

"Very well then," Safeed said. "Two, while many of us find your plight sympathetic, the council has decided against you by a vote of three to two. You will not be allowed to become a vampire."

Two felt her body deflate, as if someone had pulled a plug at the base of her spine, and it was only with a great effort that she kept herself from crumpling down on the table and weeping. She felt tears sting her eyes, but she clenched her jaw tight, and breathed deeply, and looked at the council members. She nodded.

Gaius gave her a look of faux sympathy, and Two felt a white-hot streak of rage run through her. *Gaius and Safeed,* she thought. *Those two for sure ... who else?*

Not N'Debe, whose own face was set in an expression of genuine sadness. No, not N'Debe, and not Marian. She couldn't imagine another Eresh voting against her. It had to be Eadwyn, who was looking at her with the same cool smirk that he had carried for most of the proceedings. But why? What had made him vote against her?

Safeed spoke again. "We understand your desire to return to vampire life, but that chance has passed you by. We are not prepared to allow Naomi, or any other vampire, to give you her blood. You are Theroen's fledgling, and so you must remain. To allow otherwise would go against policies and laws established thousands of years before you were born."

Gaius nodded. "We recommend you return to a life of humanity, and put this behind you."

Two wanted to scream at them, to wail that their recommendation was impossible, that when Theroen's gift was stolen from her it had damned her to some grey place between humanity and vampire kind for as long as she lived. Instead, she took a hitching breath and, in a croaking voice, said only, "Thank you for hearing my case."

"Is there anything further to be said?" Marian asked. "Naomi? Stephen?"

Two became aware of her friends for the first time since the judgment had been pronounced. Naomi's outward calm was betrayed only by the aura of pure despair rolling off her in waves. Surely everyone else at the table could feel it and were simply being too polite to comment on it. Naomi nonetheless gave the group a polite smile.

"No, thank you, I have no further business with the council."

Stephen was rigid with what Two guessed was fury. His hands were balled into fists, sitting atop his chair's armrests, and with a visible effort he uncurled them and tented his fingers, resting his palms on the table in front of him.

"I have nothing at all to say," he told them, his voice quiet but shaking with suppressed anger.

"Somehow we doubt that," Eadwyn said. "But see how he contains himself? Truly, the younger generation has been raised well."

"Can I please go?" Two asked him. She felt a bit like she was going to throw up.

"Absolutely not," Eadwyn told her. "You promised us a moment of your time, and we shall have it. Instead, we think it is time that our fellow council members took their leave."

There was a general murmur of assent, and the vampires stood to go. Gaius and Safeed moved immediately toward the door. Marian and N'Debe spoke together in low voices for a moment, and then the latter approached Two. She leaned in briefly and spoke quietly, next to Two's ear.

"Marian and I are sorry for your pain. You must listen to Eadwyn. For all his nonsense, he does not do anything, including what he did today, without purpose."

Two nodded. She tried to thank the vampire, but no words would come from her aching throat. N'Debe smiled and nodded as if she understood. She turned and left, and Marian followed her out.

"You may take a moment to cry now, ladies, if you need to," said Eadwyn. "If he'd like, your warrior can even rage. Perhaps break a few things ... threaten our life ... we won't take offense."

Naomi was shaking and had closed her eyes, but she remained stone faced. Two was proud of her. She fought her way through her own despair, found her voice, and said, "You're underestimating Stephen. He's probably going to break a *lot* of things."

Eadwyn, not expecting this, leaned back in his chair and laughed. Stephen gave Two a look of incredulity, but some of his tension seemed to fade, and Two was glad for it. Her eyes still shut, Naomi gave a small smile and murmured something.

"What, Naomi?" Two asked.

The vampire girl opened her eyes, wiped tears away from them, and smiled again. "That's why everyone loves you."

"Not enough to vote for me, I guess."

Eadwyn sat forward again in his chair and said, "My dear, we've only just *met* you. You have, we surmise, determined who provided tonight's swing vote?"

"Why did you do it?" Two asked. "Don't tell me you care about the letter of the law. You're older and wiser and stronger than me, but I'm not an idiot."

"We care about the law more than you might think," Eadwyn told her, "but we are not ... unmoved by your plight. We must admit, my dear, that our decision was motivated by entirely selfish ambitions. Quite simply, we want something from you, and we are willing to make a trade. Do what we ask of you, and we will happily change our vote."

It took a moment for this to sink in, and when it did, Two looked up at him in shock and anger.

"You complete bastard!" she exclaimed before she could help herself. She realized not a second later just who, exactly, it was that she was addressing, and opened her mouth to apologize, but Eadwyn waved it away, laughing again.

"Oh, yes," he said. "To be sure. Don't ever let anyone tell you otherwise."

"You voted against me just so you could control me."

"We are all pawns sometimes, my dear, kings and queens others. Right now, you are a pawn, and we are a king. We can send you on a journey at our whim, though perhaps by the time you reach the end, you will be royalty yourself. Or is that checkers?"

"If I do what you want me to do, you'll swing your vote?" Two asked.

"Indeed, but are you entirely sure you wish to rejoin our world?" Eadwyn asked. "We are a terrible group ... conniving, manipulative, uncaring."

"Not all of you," Two said. "Not me, either."

Eadwyn raised his eyebrows and grinned. "We shall see. But yes, Miss Majors, we will swing our vote in your favor if you perform this service we require."

"Fine. Tell me what I need to do, and I'll go do it. I don't care. Send me to China. Ask me to kill another two-thousand-year-old vampire. Tell me to find the Ark of the fucking Covenant. Whatever you need, Eddie."

"Two ..." Naomi began, but Eadwyn shushed her.

"Don't coddle her, Naomi. We're not going to kill her over a little sarcasm. We enjoy the spirit, though we suspect Two has absolutely no future in politics. Would you agree, Stephen?"

"I must admit, it seems an ill-fitting match," Stephen said. He was clearly less than enthusiastic about Eadwyn's manipulation, but the raw fury that Two had felt in him before was gone.

"An ill-fitting match indeed. Well put."

"Eadwyn, sir … please, what is it that you need me to do?" Two asked.

"Anxious to get underway? Very well, little *Eresh-Chen*. We do indeed require travel, but not all the way to China. Rather, we are sending you to Turkey."

"Turkey?"

"Yes – the country, not the bird."

Two chose to ignore the humor. "What's in Turkey?"

"An associate of ours resides there. We have something that she has been seeking for some time now, and we wish you to deliver it to her."

"That's it?"

"That is indeed it."

Two glanced at her friends, confused, and looked back at Eadwyn. "You ever hear of FedEx?"

Eadwyn laughed. "The object in question is priceless. In the wrong hands, it could easily be sold for enough money to purchase a small European country."

"Ohhh—kay? And you're giving it to me?"

"Can we not trust you? Would you, dear *human*, run off with it and live a life of wealth rather than become a vampire again?"

Two shook her head.

"Precisely. We trust you much more than we would trust any other mortal, or even most vampires. You are one of the few for whom that sort of money holds no real interest. You know what you want, and it can't be bought. All you have to do is bring this package to the one who requested it."

"You'll tell us where she lives?" Two asked.

"In order to do that, we would have to know where she lives, which we do not. We will, instead, tell you where to find her."

"Good enough," Two said. She stood up, glanced around. "Let's do it."

Eadwyn stood as well, as did Naomi and Stephen. Eadwyn held up his finger, indicating for them to wait, and disappeared into an adjacent room. He returned with a small wooden box.

"What is it?" Two asked. "Or ... should I not ask? If I'm about to unleash the plague or something on Turkey, I'd just as soon not know it."

Eadwyn held the box in his delicate hands for a moment, inspecting the intricate carvings on the wood, before shaking his head. "No, it's nothing like that. If you choose to open the box, and we won't stop you from doing so, all you will find is a rather nondescript metal cylinder with a tiny opening at one end. That tiny opening is a keyhole fit to a key that we do not possess."

"So you don't even know what I'm delivering?" Two asked.

"We didn't say that," Eadwyn replied. "We know *exactly* what it is, and how precious it is. You, however, would find little use for it."

"So what is it?" Two asked.

Eadwyn smiled, handed the box to her, regarded her for a moment before speaking.

"It's blood, of course," he said. "Delicious, nutritious, and incredibly rare blood. What else would it be?"

* * *

"So we're on a mission to bring some vampire a gourmet snack," Two said. "Fucking great."

She and her vampire friends were walking home, discussing the meeting they had just been a part of. It was past two in the morning. The London streets were covered in a heavy mist, and there was little activity. Somewhere, a bell was ringing; Two thought it might be a buoy in the Thames. The tiny vial of blood in its padded wooden box was in Naomi's purse.

"I doubt very much that it's a snack," Naomi said. She sounded tired, and Two couldn't blame her. It was still hours from dawn, but all she wanted was to go home and sleep.

"Then what is it?" Two asked.

"A relic, most likely. A keepsake. The blood of some powerful vampire, perhaps? Who knows, Two?"

"So it's basically a collector's-edition Star Trek plate. Even better."

Naomi sighed. "Must you be so consistently cynical?"

"Been a rough year," Two muttered. "Lots of bullshit, nothing to show for it."

"I would hope you could think of a *few* things to show for it," Naomi said, her voice tinged with annoyance. Two didn't respond.

Eadwyn hadn't kept them long. He had given them the wooden box and the name of a city in Turkey where his associate was located. While he knew no specific street address, he had suggested that they visit a ruined Islamic mosque on the outskirts of the city.

"She will find you," Eadwyn had assured them, and he had sent them on their way. "If you complete this task and return, then, as we have discussed, we shall give you what you want."

"I'll come back," Two had told him, and Eadwyn had only smirked again.

Stephen was speaking from behind her. "If we could avoid the lover's quarrel until after we've reached the house, it would make my night."

"Consider it done," Two said. "I'm too tired for it anyway."

"No desire to hit the heavy bag for a while when we get home?" Stephen asked her. "I'm not going to any fights tonight."

"You know ... maybe I'm not *that* tired," Two said. The idea of working out some of her frustration sounded very appealing.

"Oh, yes, by all *means,* let's spend the rest of the night *punching* something," Naomi growled. She was walking slightly ahead of them now, and her voice drifted back through the fog, unlovely in its acidity.

"I can't spend every night curled up on the couch with a bottle of wine," Two snapped back.

Naomi whirled, now walking backwards. "What exactly are you implying? I've been working constantly to get this whole thing set up, so don't you ..."

"Lover's quarrel laayyyy-ter!" Stephen cried, sing-songing the word.

"Shut up!" both women shouted in unison, and all three stopped moving for a moment. Stephen laughed.

"United, at least, in your annoyance at me," he said.

"That's because you're an ass," Two said. "It's been a shitty night. Just let us have our stupid fight."

"In what way has it been a shitty night?" Stephen asked. "You're closer by miles to getting what you want than you were twenty-four hours ago. You have a task – just a single task – to perform, and you've a guarantee that when you complete it, you'll get your reward. Eadwyn's a manipulating bastard, but he's not a liar."

Two considered this in silence. Naomi opened her mouth to retort, stopped herself, closed it. Stephen continued.

"If you're tense and need release, either go hit something or go have sex. I've offered one option. Perhaps Naomi can offer the other. I don't truly care, but standing in the middle of the London streets and shouting at each other after what has been, in my estimation, a victory ... that's an idiotic waste of time."

Two glanced at Naomi, who shrugged and, with a grudging smile, said, "I could probably wait until after you work out to go to bed."

"Yeah," Two said. "And I don't actually mind curling up on the couch with a bottle of wine. Still ... I hate it when he's right."

"I'm always right," Stephen said, and at this, both women could do little more than laugh.

* * *

Neither Two nor her vampire companions had ever been to Turkey, nor had they any particular knowledge of the country. For this reason, when they arrived at their townhouse, Two did not immediately pursue either the punching bag or her bed with Naomi. She instead sat down at the computer to look up information on the town to which Eadwyn was sending them.

She found it on the southern coast of Turkey, near its border with Syria. The town, called Silifke, was a small city of about sixty thousand people, nearly all of them Muslim. It was not a major Turkish city, which surprised Two. Vampires typically found it easier to live and feed in highly populated areas.

"It seems like a small place for a vampire to live," Two said to Naomi, who was sitting in a high-backed leather chair just to her left. Stephen had excused himself and gone to the living room to watch sports highlights.

Naomi nodded, holding her hands up in a 'who knows' gesture. "Whoever this person is – and God forbid Eadwyn tell us her name – she is likely an elder. Sometimes older vampires seek solace in low-population areas, away from the crowds of the big cities."

"I've never lived outside of a big city. I think I'd get bored and lonely," Two said. She was scanning through galleries of pictures, but had not yet located any from Silifke.

"I moved from Paris to London, back to Paris, and then to New York," Naomi said. "I travel sometimes to quiet places, but I've found that staying away from the cities allows one a bit *too* much time with one's thoughts."

Two turned and glanced at Naomi, but the vampire was not looking at her. Instead, Naomi was gazing up at the ceiling, her eyes distant.

"Don't like what your brain has to say?" Two asked.

Naomi shook her head slowly, still looking up. "Not usually."

"What does it ... I mean, what's wrong?" Two asked. Naomi looked over at her, gave her a small smile.

"I hear voices," she said. "Oh, not the way Eadwyn claims to hear them. Just my own thoughts, reflecting back at me in others' words and tones. I hear Lisette and Theroen. I hear people named Andrew, and Patricia, and Arenne ... people I've never told you about. These people have many things in common, and I loved them all, each in their own way."

Naomi was quiet for a moment, and Two held her own tongue, waiting for the vampire girl to say more. Naomi closed her eyes, tilted her head back, sighed. At last she spoke.

"I loved them all, and they're all gone," she said. "When I am alone, I hear them asking why. Why are they gone? What happened to make it so? When I am alone, I hear them. I ... try not to be alone."

There was another pause. Naomi gave a low, bitter laugh. "That, I suppose, is why between loves I so readily whore myself out to whichever pretty face in a bar catches my eye."

"Naomi, come on, that's not—"

"It is. It's the truth. We all have our demons, Two. We all silence them in our own ways. I use sex. It keeps the voices away, so I use it even though I know it hurts my political career."

"Can I ... Naomi, what can I do to help?"

Naomi looked over at her again, smiled, shrugged. "Once we've taken care of you, perhaps then we'll worry about me. For now? The voices are silent when I'm with you. That helps."

"I don't think that's enough," Two said.

"You know what I want from you," Naomi said, a trace of bitterness in her voice.

"You know why I can't give you that," Two replied.

"Yes. Don't worry about me, Two. I've outlasted many voices. I'm still here."

"You think that I'm going to become another voice?"

"It's beginning to feel inevitable."

"I'm not planning on dying."

Naomi sighed again. "Not all of my voices belong to the dead."

Two could think of no response to this, so she shut down the computer and stood up.

"Going to go punch things?" Naomi asked.

"No, I think I'm going to take a bath and then go to bed. I ... if you want, you could ..."

Naomi waited, listening. Two frowned at her own hesitance. Why was this so hard, after everything they had shared?

"You could come with me, if you want," she said.

"What do you want?" Naomi asked her.

Two really didn't know what she wanted, so she acted not in the interest of the vampire girl – whom she *did* love, just not in the way that Naomi wanted. She acted to still Naomi's voices, to what she could to help ease Naomi's pain, knowing that in the long run she could do little more than add to it.

"I want you with me," Two told her, and Naomi smiled and stood.

CHAPTER XXVI

The Girl from the Desert

When dusk came to Silifke on their second night there, it brought with it a respite from the heat of the day. There was no air conditioning in the hotel that Naomi had chosen for them, but the vampires didn't mind. Two had tossed and turned in her bed, waking up several times during the day, lying naked atop her covers. Naomi spent the day not only under the covers, but in a nightgown, oblivious to Two's discomfort. More than once during their daytime sleeping hours, Two had glanced over at her and felt waves of annoyance coupled with a deep envy.

Now, as the sun dipped below the horizon, Two was standing in the shower, shivering under a deluge of cold water. She had finally rolled out of bed, unable to sleep any longer, and done her exercises. Once finished, she found herself sweat, not the slick and enjoyable post-workout, post-sex sheen, but the sticky midsummer kind that made her want to crawl out of her own skin. She had hurried to the bathroom and stepped under the cool water with relief.

The bedroom's cooler temperature, when she emerged from the bathroom wrapped in a towel, was a pleasant surprise. The nerves she was feeling, also a surprise, were significantly less pleasant. Two didn't know where this feeling of nervous anticipation was coming from; it was only a meeting with yet another vampire, something that she had now done many times and should certainly be used to. It was not even as if, upon successfully completing their task, they would be able to make any immediate changes. It would be a few days at least before they would be able to return to London, and Naomi had taken special care to remind Two that there was no guarantee that they wouldn't have to wait for another council meeting before receiving Eadwyn's permission.

"That," Two muttered to herself, sitting down on the edge of the bed, "would thoroughly suck."

Naomi made an inarticulate noise, rolled, sat up squinting and blinking. Two watched, amused, saying nothing.

"Di'joo uhm … say something?" the vampire asked, still half asleep, and Two laughed at her.

"Nothing important, hon. Good evening."

Naomi rubbed her eyes and yawned, then crawled over on hands and knees until she was behind Two. She kissed Two's left shoulder blade and said, "Hi."

Two turned around and gave her a quick kiss on the lips, then stood and moved in front of the mirror, toweling her hair. She had kept it short, at Stephen's insistence, and was coming to quite like the look. She had played with Naomi's initial styling, finally deciding on something even more wild and chaotic. Stephen had said it suited her, and Two thought he was right.

"Wish I could sleep like you do," Two told Naomi, who was sitting cross-legged on the bed, stretching out her arms and back.

"Why?"

"Dude … it was a fucking *oven* in here!"

"Mmm. Yes, we don't feel it so much, one way or the other, icebox or oven. I … did you just call me 'dude'?"

"Maybe," Two said. She unhooked her towel and let it drop to the floor. Behind her, Naomi made a noise of approval.

"You are *really* tempting me now. That's not fair," the vampire said. "We have things we have to do tonight!"

Two caught Naomi's eyes in the mirror, grinned at her, wiggled her rump once, and then pulled a pair of panties from the drawer.

"Tease," Naomi said, heading for the bathroom. "I'm going to take a shower."

"Have fun. I'm going to go make sure Stephen's ready to go and not shouting at a friggin' dart match on TV or something."

Naomi laughed and closed the bathroom door. Two stared at it for a moment, wondering why it couldn't always be so easy and comfortable between them. After a moment longer she gave up on the question, and her attention returned to the nervous energy coiling in her belly.

She wondered what this mystery vampire would be like. Eadwyn had told them nothing, neither her name nor her age, no distinguishing features, no information other than her sex. He had told them to go to the ruined mosque that stood on a nearby hill, looking down on the town, and that the vampire they were supposed to meet with would somehow know they were there and arrive on her own. Two supposed they had little choice but to believe him.

She dressed casually but well, choosing light fabrics. Although the evening had brought some relief it was still quite warm outside, and Two didn't want to meet this new vampire while dripping with sweat. She put on a pair of stone-colored cargo pants and a slim, white button-down shirt, striped with thin pink lines. To these she added a simple pair of gold hoop earrings and the gold necklace that she had worn on the night when she first met Theroen.

When Two was satisfied with her appearance, she went across the hall and knocked on Stephen's door. He opened it shirtless, wearing a pair of jeans, his hair pulled roughly back and tied behind his head.

"You're interrupting my pushups," he told her, and he went back into the room, leaving the door open for Two.

"Boo hoo," Two said, following him in. "I already did mine."

Stephen had insisted that Two maintain what he called a maintenance schedule: a hundred and fifty situps, fifty pushups, and thirty minutes of running or other cardio each morning. Two usually did jumping jacks when the weather made running unappealing. She had also added some yoga to her exercises and Stephen hadn't objected, noting that it would help keep her limber.

Two enjoyed the calm that the yoga brought her, and she pursued it often in the evenings before the vampires awoke. It gave her time to relax and think, especially now that she was no longer focused on learning the movements. She had asked Stephen if the slow progression was similar to that of a martial art, and he had admitted it was.

"How many?" she asked him as he continued with his pushups, and he spoke his count out loud for her for a few moments.

"Two-twenty-one, two-twenty-two ..."

"What's your daily total?"

"Five hundred."

"Five hundred is your *maintenance* schedule? Jesus Christ!"

Stephen glanced over, noting her incredulous expression and grinning.

"Vampires are strong," he said and continued his workout.

"No kidding. Well, I just came over to make sure you'd be ready."

"Is Naomi out of the shower yet?" Stephen asked.

"No, at least not when I came over."

"Then I'll be ready ahead of her. She takes forever with her makeup."

Two, who had observed this fact for herself, smiled and nodded.

"Twenty minutes," Stephen told her. "If you'll leave me alone."

"You'll come over to our room?"

"Yes."

"OK. See you, Stephen."

Stephen grunted a response, not looking at her. Two rolled her eyes and headed for the door.

* * *

"This must have been beautiful, once," Naomi commented, and from up ahead of them they heard Stephen laugh.

"No doubt that was of great consolation to the people who were crushed to paste when it collapsed," he said.

Two and Naomi exchanged a glance of exasperated amusement. Hundreds of years ago, one of the mosque's supports had given out and the eastern wall had tumbled in upon the worshippers gathered there. Dozens had died, many more had been injured. The building had been subsequently abandoned and left to slowly fall to pieces until there was nothing left of any great monetary or architectural value. They were making their way now through the broken stones and dust, surrounded on three sides by the ruins of the other walls.

"What are we looking for?" Two asked.

"Nothing really," Stephen told her. He had stopped and hunched down to look at the faint carvings still visible on a fallen pillar. "We're just killing time until our mystery vampire arrives."

Two came up beside him, Naomi just behind her, and stopped.

"What if she doesn't show up?" she asked.

"She'll be here," Naomi said. "The blood is priceless. I'm quite sure she's anxious to acquire it."

"I still think it'd be funny if she just opened it and tossed it back, like a college kid doing tequila shots," Two said.

"We don't even know if it's still liquid," Naomi said. "If it's elder blood, it might be thousands of years old. I still believe it's a keepsake of some sort."

"It doesn't really matter what she's going to use it for," Stephen said.

"Suppose not," Two replied. "We're just here to drop it off."

"Exactly."

"Right, fine," Two said, and paused for a moment before adding, "... but what if she doesn't show up?"

Stephen laughed, shook his head, didn't answer. Naomi put a hand on her shoulder, and Two glanced over at the vampire girl.

"You're nervous," said Naomi.

Two nodded. "Not sure why. Felt this way since I got up."

"I'm sure that whoever we're meeting will be pleasant," Naomi said.

"Yeah, no ... it's not that. I'm not scared, and it's not like waiting for the council meetings or anything. It's hard to describe."

"Can I do anything to help?"

Two smiled at her. "Don't think so, hon. It's not actually a bad kind of nerves. I'll survive."

Naomi seemed to consider this and was about to say something when the presence descended upon them, a sensation that Two would have found impossible to describe even if she'd been able to speak. Naomi and Stephen both seemed paralyzed, eyes wide in surprise and what might have been fear. Two thought for a moment that she might now understand how it would feel to stand on a beach and watch as a great and devastating tidal wave swept toward her.

It was Naomi who found her voice first, squeaking out, "Oh … Stephen, what *is* it?"

Stephen's own voice was choked, and in it Two heard the same terror and awe that she could feel running through her own body. His complete inability to mask these things only unnerved her further.

"We must go. Naomi, Two, we must … we must go."

So it seemed they should, and yet none could move. When the voice came from behind them, each heard it in their mind as well as with their ears. The words it spoke were simple.

"Go?" it asked them, its tone amused. "Children, you've only just arrived."

Two felt herself turning slowly to greet this visitor whose presence now weighed down upon her like the depths of the sea. The movement was not precisely made against her will, but not by it, either. She saw from the corner of her eye that Naomi and Stephen were doing the same.

The woman stood perhaps five-foot-five and was well-built, thin and muscular. Her skin was dark, the shade of milk chocolate, but made darker by the fact that every visible inch of it was covered in snaking blue-black tattoos. The vampire blinked, and Two noted with detached amazement that even the woman's eyelids were tattooed. She was wearing a gauzy, multi-layered turquoise wrap and had sandals on her feet. Her hair was braided and pulled back in a high ponytail, decorated around the crown with a small ringlet of gemstones that caught the moonlight and sparkled like stars.

She spoke again, and again her voice reverberated in their minds.

"Hello, children of Eresh and Ay'Araf. Hello, daughter. It is good to see the three of you here tonight, together as companions."

Naomi was weeping openly now, though whether the tears reflected terror, or awe, or grief, Two could not say. Without words, Naomi went to her knees and bowed her head, her back still shaking with sobs. Stephen glanced over at Naomi, perplexed by her reaction, and then back at the tattooed vampire. A moment later, he was visibly shaken as a bolt of recognition ran through him. He dropped to one knee and bowed his head as well.

Two did not yet know who this vampire was, but it seemed obvious that the woman was to be treated with reverence, and so she went to do what her friends had done. The vampire's voice, still roaring inside of her head, stopped her before she could move.

"There is no need for all of that, children. I am a simple woman, glad to be once again in the company of my own kind. I would spend this time here with you as an equal."

Stephen glanced up, head still bowed, and spoke in a hoarse voice. "I don't believe that is possible, my Queen, but we will do our best to accommodate your wishes."

Naomi still could not raise her head, could not, in fact, seem to stop the sobs that were wracking her body. She covered her face with her hands, making whimpering noises, gasping for breath. The tattooed vampire smiled gently, stepped forward, put her hand on Naomi's head.

"Why do you weep, my daughter?" she asked, and after a few unsuccessful attempts, Naomi was able to answer the woman, voice muffled by her hands.

"I believed you dead. I truly did. Oh, forgive me, Mother."

"I have forgiven many for far worse, my child. You have done me no harm."

Naomi fought with her tears, slowly winning the battle. At last she looked up at the other vampire, her cheeks still wet, with something between awe and love.

"I know I should know who you are, uh ... ma'am," Two said. "But I'm afraid I haven't had much time to learn yet."

The vampire turned to her and smiled. When she spoke this time, her voice came to Two's ears, and no longer to her mind. It was the voice of a woman, nothing more, but as Two heard the name, she understood why her companions had reacted as they did.

"My name is Ashayt, Two Ashley Majors," the vampire told her. "I am the Girl from the Desert, last of the *Ovras*, author of the Second Doctrine, and I am *very* glad to meet you."

* * *

"This is ... most unexpected," Stephen said.

He was sitting on a collapsed pillar, still trying to regain his composure, seemingly unable to stop staring at Ashayt. Two couldn't blame him; the vampire elder was magnetic, seeming to draw all attention to her while doing nothing more than sitting, serene and unspeaking, gazing out at the moonlit village below them.

"Yes," Ashayt said. "Eadwyn felt it best to keep my identity a secret. He worried that you would be afraid of me or simply refuse to believe him."

Stephen nodded. "I would have thought him a liar."

"And you, daughter?" Ashayt asked.

Naomi jerked and looked up at Ashayt. She had been staring at the ground.

"I ... I would have been offended," she said, her brow creasing. "I would have been angry with him for teasing us with the name of a dead god."

"I am neither dead nor a god."

"I'm sorry," Naomi said, looking down again.

"You do not need my forgiveness. You must forgive yourself, my dear."

"For thinking you dead?"

Ashayt favored Naomi with a gentle smile. "For many things."

"I will try, Mother."

Ashayt nodded, sighed, looked again down at the buildings below. "On nights like this, I am reminded of Egypt, the home I left behind so long ago."

394

"Couldn't you go back?" Two asked, and Ashayt slowly shook her head.

"Not there," she said, an aching sadness in her voice. "Never there."

Two was going to ask for elaboration, but Stephen shot her a look that made her think better of it, and she closed her mouth. She wondered if she should feel patronized, like a child dismissed to the side while the adults talked, but Ashayt soon assuaged her of any such fear.

"I would like to hear your story, Two," the elder said. "I know some of it from Eadwyn but few of the details."

Two looked up, startled. She had not been prepared to tell her tale yet again.

"Everything?" she asked.

"If you would, yes. I know it is hard, and I know you are tired of telling it, but I must admit to harboring a great deal of curiosity."

Two took a deep breath. "OK," she said.

"Thank you."

"It's ... parts of it are ugly."

"I have seen many ugly things in my life," Ashayt assured her. Two nodded, then spoke.

"I was addicted to heroin and selling my body for it when Theroen found me," Two began, moving into the story with the smooth flow of an experienced teller. It still hurt, but she found it easier somehow to tell it to Ashayt than to any previous audience.

The elder vampire let Two tell the story without interruption for question or comment. In places, Stephen and Naomi made small additions, once the tale had reached the point at which they had become players. Finally, Two finished it and sat back.

"And, well ... here we are," she said. "We're delivering a vial of blood to an *Ovras* vampire that everyone thinks is dead, and I gotta say, ma'am, that every time I think that my life just *can't* get any weirder ... it does."

Ashayt smiled and nodded. "Thank you for telling me your story, Two. You have been through much pain and difficulty, and I am sorry. Thank you also for making this delivery. Do you have the box that Eadwyn asked you to bring?"

"I have it, Mother," Naomi said. She alone among them was still having a hard time looking at Ashayt, but she did so now, glancing up at the elder vampire and extending the wooden box toward her.

Ashayt took the box and opened it, taking the small silver cylinder and holding it in the palm of her hand. She smiled.

"When I left this in Pakistan, I thought that I was doing so forever," she said. "Now I am very glad indeed to see it again."

She took from some internal pocket a tiny silver key, and inserted it into the end of the cylinder. There was a clicking noise, nearly inaudible to Two, and with delicate movements Ashayt unscrewed one end of the container and slid its contents out into her hand. She held it up for them, a small crystal tube filled with deep red liquid.

"May I ask what it is, lady?" Stephen asked.

Ashayt looked up at him, smiling, and her eyes sparkled. "It is the very blood that runs in your veins, my brave warrior. This is the blood of Ay'Araf."

Stephen tilted his head. "Blood from Ay'Araf himself? Not from one of his line?"

Ashayt nodded. "Ay'Araf himself."

"Which you left in Pakistan ..."

"Yes."

"My lady, forgive me, but ... why would you have a vial of Ay'Araf's blood in the first place?"

Ashayt held the vial up to the moon and looked at the liquid within for a long moment before turning her gaze back to Stephen.

"He gave it to me," she said. "Long ago, on a night not unlike this, warm and pleasant, we sat with Eresh on a beach, hundreds of miles from any man, and she asked us to drink from her until she was dead and to burn her body to ash."

"You killed her?!" Two cried, before clapping her hands over her mouth. Ashayt looked over at her not with disapproval or anger, but with understanding.

"We killed her, yes. It brings me sorrow, even now, to think of it, but she was in pain. Torment. Her children were spreading. More and more of them were being uncovered and destroyed. She felt it, every time it happened, no matter the distance, and it brought her unspeakable agony ... physical pain and mental anguish. It finally became too much to stand. She begged us, the only other vampires old enough and strong enough to do it. She begged us to end her, to take her blood into ourselves and be strengthened by it."

Ashayt's eyes were far away now, remembering that night. "We sat on the beach in front of a great fire and we wept, and said our goodbyes. She was the mother of us all, and in the end we could do no more than give her what she asked. Ay'Araf and I took turns drinking from her until she was dead, and we put her on the fire. We made love while she burned, lost in the ecstasy of her blood. When it was over and we lay naked on the sand, Ay'Araf bit his wrist and filled this crystal with his blood, and told me to take it. It was to be a memory, a reminder of him, and of this night we had shared together, and of the thing that we had done."

Ashayt sighed, and she looked at them again. "I would never see him again, and I kept his gift with me until I traveled to Pakistan more than a thousand years later to see his tomb. I left it there with him, the only part of him that remained beyond ash and dust. Now Eadwyn has retrieved it, and you have returned it to me at last."

"Why did you have Eadwyn go get it?" Two asked.

Ashayt smiled at her, paused a moment as if considering her next words carefully. Finally, she said, "It is for you."

Naomi glanced up. "We are to keep it?"

"For now, yes."

"I don't understand, Mother," Naomi said. "Is it ... are we to use it as proof that you approve of Two's desire to be a vampire?"

Ashayt considered this but shook her head. "No, child, not precisely. It could be used as such, but Eadwyn sent you to me for another reason. There is a choice that Two must make, a choice that will change the rest of her days and shape the future of our people."

There was a momentary pause in the conversation, and then Stephen gave a small laugh.

"I'm rather curious to hear this one," he said.

"You and me both," Two told him. "Ma'am, could you ... elaborate on that a little?"

Ashayt smiled, but her eyes were set intently on the small vial of blood. She reached again into another hidden pocket of her gown and brought forth a second crystal vial, holding it up together with the first. From Two's vantage point, they looked identical.

Ashayt turned and held them both out to Two. "These are for you."

Two looked at them in surprise for a moment, and then took them from the elder vampire. She held one cupped in each hand, looking down at them, trying to determine what she was supposed to do with them.

"I'm confused," Two said at last, and Ashayt gave a small laugh.

"I would expect so."

Two looked up at the other vampires. Stephen was looking at Naomi, who was still staring at the ground. Ashayt was gazing out into the night again, her features still serene.

"This other one is yours, right? Your blood?" Two asked, and Ashayt nodded.

"What is she to do with them, Mother?" Naomi asked, looking up. "What choice is she to make?"

Ashayt gave Naomi an odd look of pity and then she turned back to Two.

"Before her death, Eresh revealed to us that she was not the first vampire. She was the source of all living vampires, but she was not the first. There was at least one who had come before her … and she was not like him."

Now it seemed Naomi could look at Ashayt, her reticence to do so lost in her astonishment. "We were always taught that Eresh was the first."

"The origins of our species are gone now," Ashayt said. "The one who turned Eresh told her nothing of his past, only that he was the last of his kind until her. You must understand: Eresh was thousands of years old by the time I became a vampire. To the Mesopotamian people, she was a goddess. The one who made her … who knows how old he might have been? Our origins may stretch back to the time of the Neanderthals or earlier. We don't know. We will never know.

"What I do know is that Eresh was not like her sire. Whatever it is that split our bloodlines, it began with her. Yet, some part of it seems to have lain dormant, because some of the traits of her sire reawakened in me, and others in Ay'Araf. Eresh had his strength and mental abilities, I have his aura and resistance to the sunlight, Ay'Araf had his near-immunity to poisons and his ability to go for days without blood."

"What about the Burilgi?" Stephen asked.

"I have never heard definitive word of their sire. Whether they represent a mutation like myself, or are simply a polluted version of one of the other clans is uncertain, but in either case I can think of no area in which they are the most blessed of the vampire races."

Stephen nodded, glanced at the blood vials in Two's hands, and looked back up, this time at Two.

"I can't ..." Two began, and then looked at Ashayt. "I mean ... I wasn't an Eresh long enough, was I?"

"No," Ashayt said. "The bloodlines cannot reunite within you."

"Even if I drank these, it wouldn't work. I'd have to be drained first, and this wouldn't be enough to bring me back. I'd have to take Naomi's blood, or Stephen's, and then I'd just end up like them."

"Yes."

"But you said I have a choice."

Ashayt nodded. Smiled. "Yes."

Naomi had been looking at the vials in Two's hands, but now made a sudden, startled gasping noise. She said only one word, and it came out as something near a whisper: "Oh."

"What, Naomi?" Two asked. "What is it?"

Naomi looked suddenly miserable. "You have a choice," she said. "You definitely have a choice ... although it's not really much of a choice, is it? And Eadwyn knew that when he sent us here."

Two pursed her lips in confusion. "I am totally lost."

"Aye, seconded," Stephen said.

"The blood can't combine in you because you're not a vampire, and I don't think it could combine in any other Eresh, because their own blood would simply overpower it."

"Correct," Ashayt said.

"Could the effect be reproduced with ... no, no, it's ... it'd be too weak." Naomi was mumbling to herself, staring at the ground. Ashayt was nodding.

"It has to be yours," Naomi said to Ashayt. "And his."

"Yes," Ashayt said again.

"But what the hell do we do with it?!" Two cried. She felt her hands clenching and forced them to loosen. She had been feeling left out for so long, and she was tired of it. "We don't have Eresh's blood. Even if we did, how do we make the combination?"

"You don't need her blood," Naomi said.

"Why NOT?"

Naomi turned and smiled her sad smile. When she spoke, it was in a voice both tired and defeated, and Two heard in it a note of resigned familiarity. It was a tone that said Naomi had been here before.

"You don't need the blood because you already have an Eresh husk, as pure as can be found, buried in New York, emptied of blood and just waiting to be filled."

"You don't mean ..." Two began, and Naomi's smile became something like a grimace.

"Of course I do," she said. "Of course."

"No wonder Eadwyn said no," Stephen said in a quiet voice.

A wave of extreme dizziness passed over Two, and her vision seemed to fade. She felt herself losing her balance, and bowed her head.

"I think I'm going to throw up," she said. The muscles in her arms and legs were jerking involuntarily, and her entire body was shaking. She kept drawing in breath to do something – Cry? Laugh? Scream? – but each time she instead had to suppress a rolling wave of nausea. Grey spots were dancing before her eyes.

"You're passing out," Stephen's voice said from somewhere far away, and there was a sudden, jarring blow to the right side of her face. Two's head whipped to the left and she lost her balance, falling to the dirt. The hit had proved effective, however; she was no longer passing out.

"Did you fucking slap me?" she snarled at Stephen, who was looking at her in amusement.

"No," he said. "That was Naomi. I was going to suggest biting your tongue."

"Sorry," Naomi said. She wasn't looking at Two but was staring again at the ground. "I forgot how hard I hit ... humans."

Two wanted to ask what was wrong, even though she knew. She wanted to give Naomi the chance to articulate it, to say it out loud and let the poison out of her, but she couldn't bring herself to do it. She turned instead to Ashayt, trying to keep her voice from shaking.

"Can I bring Theroen back with these?" she asked. "Is that ... is that what you're telling me? That I can use these to turn him into some new vampire, and bring him back to life?"

"It is only theory, Two," Ashayt said. "It has never been tried, and I have no way of knowing if it will work."

"How could it work? He's dead. I mean ... isn't he dead? His heart's not beating. He's not breathing. I saw him. I held him. I tried to give him blood."

Naomi spoke up, her voice strained. "Some vampires ... it's been hypothesized that the blood of powerful vampires may keep their bodies alive if they're not burnt or dismembered. Theoretically, they could be in some kind of suspended state. No one's ever been brought back, though, and it's been tried more than once."

"Not with source blood," Stephen said, and Naomi shook her head.

"No. The blood in those vials is orders of magnitude stronger than anything that would've been available."

"I don't understand," Two said. "This wasn't suspended animation. He's not frozen or ... or vacuum-sealed, or something. He's dead."

"He's almost dead," Naomi said. "For all intents and purposes, he *is* dead. Abraham drained Theroen dry enough that Theroen's body can't recreate the blood it needs to function. That doesn't mean that every last drop was removed. Theoretically, what little blood there is that's left might be sustaining the body's tissue. The older a vampire's corpse is, Two, the longer it takes to decay. We think that's because it's not really a corpse yet. Not entirely."

"Why didn't you tell me?!" Two was trying to control her excitement and agitation but wasn't doing a very good job. She wasn't angry with Naomi and didn't want to seem so; she was simply overwhelmed by all of this. Naomi, for her part, didn't seem offended. She shrugged.

"Until tonight, I never thought about it. Three hours ago, I would have told you it was impossible."

"It may still be impossible, Two," Ashayt said. "But now you understand why Eadwyn sent you to me. When he first heard of your story, it was before the three of you had even come to Europe. He contacted me immediately, and I sent him to find Ay'Araf's blood. It was not an easy feat, but he succeeded. By that time you had arrived, and it was nearly time for the council to meet. We felt it would be best if he discussed it with them all at that time."

"Why let me choose?" Two asked. "You could have just gone and dug Theroen up and tried it yourself."

"Yes. This is an experiment that goes well beyond your personal needs. Yet at the same time, you loved this man. You killed for him, and in so doing you freed the world from a great evil. How could we send you away, whether with a positive or negative verdict, without giving you the opportunity to choose?"

Naomi sighed, and Ashayt turned to her.

"I understand that this pains you, daughter. Would it have been good for anyone, though, to let you make this girl your fledgling, only to turn around and attempt to bring her original sire back to life? What if it works? How would that have been any better for you than this?"

Naomi said nothing, just continued to stare at the ground. Two walked over, knelt down in front of her, took her hands.

"I'm sorry," she said. "Naomi, you've given me so much, but I have to try this. I have to do this."

The vampire girl nodded and looked up at Two. Her eyes were shiny, but she was for the moment holding back her tears.

"I know," she said. "I understand. It's just hard."

"I won't be just another voice for you," Two said. "I won't leave you alone."

Naomi attempted a smile at this, but she couldn't seem to manage. She looked down at the ground again and said nothing. After a moment, Two let her go and went back to sit beside Stephen on the pillar.

"The choice is made," Ashayt said. "This night has been millennia in the making, and now at last it is finally here. I am glad to see it; my wait has been long and lonely."

"What will you do now, lady?" Stephen asked.

Ashayt looked at him, eyebrows furrowing, as if this question had never before occurred to her. After a moment, she smiled and looked out into the night, to the horizon, to the west.

"I believe I would like to see America," she said.

* * *

"I should thank you," Naomi told Two as they entered the hotel room that they were sharing, the pink light of dawn just beginning to show on the horizon. The vampire's voice held the same tired acceptance that it had since Ashayt's revelation.

"... the hell would you thank me for?" Two asked. She sat down on the edge of the bed, pulled off her shoes, looked up at Naomi. "I feel like you should hate me."

Naomi shook her head. She had her hands folded in front of her and was staring down at them. "No, I don't hate you, and I'm thanking you for not ever saying those words when you didn't mean them."

Two tasted a sudden bitterness in her mouth. "You're a better person than I am," she said.

Naomi sat down on the other side of the bed and began to undress. "I wish we'd made love last night instead of going right to bed," she said in a far-away voice.

"We didn't know," Two said.

"No."

"Naomi, I ... I don't know what to say."

403

"You don't have to say anything," Naomi told her. "Tomorrow morning I will book flights for the four of us, though it may be a few days before we can leave. Soon enough we'll be back in the United States, and then we'll go see what we can do about Theroen."

"Oh, hon, you don't have to do that. That's not fair to you at all."

Naomi shrugged. "He was my friend. More than my friend. I gave him my virginity, once upon a time, and I was happy to do it. We spent decades together with Lisette, and it was lovely. I have missed him very much these past centuries. Of course I'll go with you."

Two moved closer to the vampire. Naomi looked over, gave her a small smile, went back to gazing at her hands.

"It would mean a lot to have you there," Two said. "To me and I'm sure to Theroen. He missed you, too."

"Good. Then that's that. If … do you mind if I spend one more day in this bed? I will arrange for a different room in the evening."

"You can just stay here until we leave, if you want …"

Naomi smiled a little at this but did not look up. "No, I think it's best if we separate quickly. I just … I'm too tired to deal with the desk clerk right now. He barely speaks English, and I know exactly three words of Turkish."

"OK," Two said. "Naomi, I'm sorry it went like this."

"It had to end sometime, I think. You were never going to love me like you love him."

Two didn't respond to this. Her throat ached and she wanted to cry, but what was the point? Naomi was right: it had to end sometime, and now it was over. If there was crying to be done, she could do it in private and let the vampire do the same. She swallowed hard, pushed the tears away, sat in silence for a time.

"I'm going to take a shower before bed," Naomi said at last. "You should sleep."

Two said nothing, and after a moment Naomi stood. Two watched as the vampire stood and made her way toward the bathroom.

"Naomi," she said, and the vampire stopped, glancing over her shoulder at Two and waiting. Two tried to think of what to say, came up with nothing. It was over, and there was nothing more to talk about. Two shrugged, shook her head, looked away.

"Nothing," she said. "Never mind."

"Goodnight, Two," Naomi said, and in a moment more the bathroom door closed behind her.

"'Night, Naomi," Two said, and the words made her throat hurt again, so she turned off the light, lay down on the bed, and closed her eyes.

PART V

CHAPTER XXVII

The Last Source

The mansion where Abraham had lived with his small, strange family had been burned to the ground nearly two years ago, but the stone wall that surrounded the estate was still there and had been reinforced with razor wire. The vampire council had moved quickly to secure the land after Abraham's death to prevent prying eyes.

The wrought iron gate that served as an entrance to the grounds was padlocked shut, but Naomi had the key. The perimeter, she had said, was wired with motion sensors, heat detectors, and other devices that made trespassing nearly impossible, even for vampires. The security firms that monitored these systems were not directly owned by the vampire council, but they were well-trusted.

"That land is as secure as it gets, outside of the government," Naomi had told Two. "Only a few of us know the codes to disable the systems, and even so we have to call ahead of time and alert the security office that we're going to be doing it."

Most of the land had been allowed to grow untended, and was slowly being reabsorbed by the forest that surrounded the mansion. Where the building had once stood, however, there was still little more than a great expanse of ash, marked occasionally by the remains of a charred timber poking out at strange angles. Somewhere among those ashes there was a heavy concrete slab and, underneath it, a door of solid steel. That door, which faced straight upward, opened upon a stone staircase that spiraled deep into blackness. At its bottom, the body of Theroen Anders still lay upon its stone bier. In what state they might find that body, neither Two nor Naomi knew.

Two had thought her nerves under control, but when they pulled up in front of the gates, she felt her body jerk involuntarily in a series of spasms. Naomi noticed this, but made no attempt to calm her. In truth, Two and the vampire girl had barely spoken for the past six days. She had spent most of her time alone, and when she had been with the others they had been listening to Ashayt's stories of the past.

Their flight had arrived in New York's John F. Kennedy airport on December eighteenth, sometime just after dawn, much to Stephen's annoyance. The ride home in the sunlight had been painful and exhausting for him. They had gone directly to Naomi's apartment without announcing their arrival to anyone. Ashayt's presence complicated things; before anything else happened, Stephen wanted to take her to the cathedral at which the council met to introduce her to Malik and Jakob. The others had agreed that this was wise, not knowing that Jakob had been taken into captivity shortly after Naomi had spoken to him on the phone.

Ashayt was given the bedroom that had once been Two's, while Stephen and Naomi took their standard rooms. Two slept on the couch, not minding, just happy to be back in the United States and excited at the idea of being reunited with Theroen. There had been little talk once they arrived, the vampires preferring to go directly to sleep. The next evening they had separated; Stephen and Ashayt headed for the cathedral, while Naomi and Two went to Theroen.

Now they were here, and Two was fighting to keep her muscles under enough control to exit the car and walk. Just the sight of the mansion's grounds had brought up old, ugly memories that filled her with fear and pessimism.

"Christ," she said. "I thought I was done with this place. I never want to come back here again, especially not at night."

"One way or the other, this should be your last visit," Naomi told her. She shut off the car's ignition and opened her door, stepping out into the cold night air. Two sat for a moment longer, and the vampire came around to her side of the car and opened the door.

"Are you all right? Do you need help?" Naomi asked.

There was no malice in her voice, but Two bristled at the question anyway. "I'll be fine."

Naomi stepped back, and Two forced herself to get out of the car. Her legs were shaky, but they held her. Naomi had opened the car's trunk and was removing two hand-held electric lanterns.

"I wonder if he'll recognize me," Naomi mused, closing the trunk and turning on both lanterns. She handed one of them to Two.

"I wonder if this is all a bunch of bullshit," Two muttered. She stepped toward the gate, but Naomi held a hand out.

"Don't touch it."

"Is it electrified or something?"

"No. At least, not in the way you mean it. There is a mild current running through it, but you wouldn't feel it. Your touch would alter it enough to set off the alarms, though."

"We don't need security showing up while we're down there," Two said.

"Precisely." Naomi moved to a small metal plate attached to one of the stone columns that supported the gate. She inserted a key and the cover swung open, revealing a keypad. Naomi pressed several digits in rapid succession, pushed a large green button, and watched the tiny LCD screen. After a moment there was a single beep, and the screen flashed.

"Good?" Two asked.

"Yes. Here," Naomi said, and handed Two a key for the padlock on the gate. Two used it, the lock's action working smoothly, and in a moment she held the open padlock in her hand. She looped it through one link in the chain, leaving it open, and took a deep breath.

"Let's go," she said, and she pushed the gate open. They made their way up toward the mansion, Naomi taking the lead as they neared it. She brought Two to where the concrete slab lay, and they stood for a moment looking at it.

"Think we're strong enough to move that?" Two asked.

411

"Let's hope so, otherwise we've made a long trip for nothing," Naomi said. She bent down and wrapped her fingers under the slab, as Two did the same. Naomi counted to three and tensed her muscles, attempting to slide the block sideways. Two pushed as well, trying to help. After a moment, the concrete began to make a grinding noise as they slid it aside, revealing the door beneath – and a host of scrabbling black beetles, now hunting for cover.

"Gross," Two said.

Naomi made a noise of agreement and reached down, brushing a few of the beetles away from the door's lock and inserting the key. She twisted it counter-clockwise twice, clicks and ratcheting noises echoing from the lock mechanism, and then pulled on the large handle. The steel door creaked as it swung upward, revealing the stone stairway beneath.

Two stared into the receding darkness with some trepidation and glanced up at Naomi, who gestured for Two to go ahead.

"I feel like Abraham's going to be down there waiting for me," Two said.

"You cut off Abraham's head and burned him to ashes," Naomi replied.

"Yeah," Two said. "Still ..."

She began to descend down into the chamber, Naomi following. Two could hear nothing from below, only the sound of their footsteps, the faint rush of wind from above, the occasional skittering sound of some small creature behind the wall. The staircase smelled dusty and dry, and several times on her way down Two was forced to push her way through large cobwebs. At last they reached the bottom, exiting out into a large, dark chamber stuffed full of furniture and other objects that the vampire council had apparently deemed too precious to burn.

At the far end, Theroen's lifeless body lay on a stone table, covered by a white sheet lined with a thin layer of dust. Two stepped forward, heart pounding, and pulled the sheet from the body.

"Jesus, Naomi ... he looks exactly the same!" she exclaimed.

Theroen's body lay before them, pale and thin but otherwise spared from the ravages of time. He was still wearing the black suit in which Abraham had dressed him, preparing him for a cremation that had never come. If not for his lack of breath, he might have been taking a nap. Two felt her heart wrench at the sight of him, felt pain and grief spring forward, as fresh within her as the day she had lost him.

"We are lucky," Naomi said, and Two could hear a kind of breathlessness in her voice that sounded like awe. "His blood must be very strong."

"I don't know if I can do this ..." Two felt sick to her stomach with worry and excitement.

"You can. I know you can. Do you have the blood?"

Two had barely let go of the two vials in their slim silver casings since leaving Naomi's apartment. She reached now into the small interior pocket of her leather jacket and took them out, holding them up to the light, wondering if her hands were shaking too hard to spring the tiny locks. She dug in the pocket of her blue jeans with the other hand, fishing for the key.

Naomi was looking at Theroen, head slightly tilted. "He had longer hair when I knew him," she said at last.

"He told me he changed it to keep up with whatever a guy in his early twenties would probably look like, you know ... during whatever time period. Clothes, hair, all of it."

Naomi nodded. "I do the same – you have to. If I was still wandering around in the sort of clothing that was popular when Lisette first found me, it would look rather odd."

"Yeah," Two replied. Two had set the cylinders on the table next to Theroen and was looking at her hands now, willing them to steady. Naomi said nothing, waiting, and eventually Two was able to unlock the cases and remove the vials. The two women stood for another moment in silence.

"We can't make him swallow," Naomi said at last. "We'll need to inject it."

"I don't have anything—"

"I brought a syringe," Naomi said, digging in her purse. "Do you think we should mix the blood first or inject twice?"

Two shrugged. "It's going to mix in him anyway, right?"

"Yes." Naomi held out the syringe, which was much larger than the ones Two had used to shoot up with in a time that felt so long ago she thought of it almost as prehistory.

"Should I worry about air bubbles?" Two asked.

"I doubt we're going to give him a stroke," Naomi replied, her voice dry.

"All the same ..." Two filled the syringe with blood from one vial, and then from the other, holding it aloft and tapping it to clear the air from it. When she was done, she looked again at Theroen.

"My love, I'm so scared," she whispered to him. She touched his face, the skin icy cold. "What if it doesn't work?"

"There is no reason to delay," Naomi said. "It won't get any easier with time, and there is no other way to know."

Two nodded, took a deep breath, took her hand away from Theroen's face. Her heart was pounding, throbbing painfully in her chest, and she felt dizzy. Sick. Her muscles ached with tension and breathing seemed difficult.

"What do I do?" she asked, her voice somewhere between a whisper and a croak.

Naomi reached out and put her hand on Theroen's jaw, tilting his head and exposing the neck. The skin was clean and unblemished, no bite marks visible from Abraham's final, deadly attack. Whether this was a sign of healing from within or simply a factor of the minor healing properties in vampire saliva, Two didn't know. Naomi tapped against Theroen's skin.

"That's the jugular," she said. "It's as good a place as any ... we don't have the equipment necessary to go through his breastplate and into his heart. Frankly, I don't even know if that matters."

"I don't think I could stab him in the chest anyway," Two said. She felt sick just contemplating the idea of shoving the needle into Theroen's neck. Nonetheless, she brought the tip forward, pressing it to the point that Naomi had indicated.

"Push in first, then angle up a little," Naomi said, and Two could hear tension in the vampire girl's voice now. "Watch for blood. His skin won't have any ... there's not enough left, but the jugular itself might."

Two took a deep breath and did as she was told. After some resistance, the needle pierced Theroen's skin and slid forward into his flesh. Two angled upward a bit as Naomi had told her, and a single drop of blood welled up around the syringe's metal shaft.

"That's it," Naomi said. "Do it!"

Two pressed the plunger, injecting the mix of elder blood into Theroen's lifeless body. Once every bit had been pushed into him, she withdrew the needle.

"What should I do with this?" she asked.

Naomi took it from her and tossed it casually into a darkened corner. "We're done with that. Step back, Two. I have no idea what may happen now."

The two women took several steps backward and stood, watching and waiting for some sign from Theroen's prone form that the blood was working within him. Seconds passed, became minutes. Two felt frantic, her heart still pounding, her breath still coming too fast. Was it working? How could they know?

She was drawing in a breath, preparing to ask Naomi these questions, when Theroen's arm twitched. Two's chest locked, her heart seeming to redouble in its throbbing, her hands balling up into small, tight fists. She wanted to ask if Naomi had seen it, wanted to make sure she wasn't hallucinating, but she couldn't seem to find her voice.

Before she was able to do so, Theroen made the question irrelevant. His entire body heaved, curling from the slab at his midsection so that only his shoulders and heels touched the table. He drew in a ragged, gasping breath that seemed to go on and on, filling his lungs until Two felt sure they must burst.

And then he began to scream.

The noise rose, starting loud and growing into a horrific, ear-splitting wail of agony. Theroen's fingernails scraped audibly against the stone table as his hands clenched and unclenched, scrabbling for purchase. He drew in another breath with a horrible sound like tearing cloth and continued to scream. Two felt herself surging forward instinctively, screaming herself, terrified and wanting only to help him if she could. Naomi grabbed her shoulders and jerked her painfully backward.

"For God's *sake,* Two, stay back!" the vampire cried over the noise of Theroen's screaming. His body was convulsing now, arms flailing madly, legs kicking, beating his heels repeatedly against the stone table in a ghastly drum roll. The screaming went on and on, interrupted only by those harsh and terrible gasps for air, until Two felt sure the sound of it would drive her insane. She was still struggling against Naomi's grip, still trying to get to Theroen, to help him in some way.

It ended without warning, Theroen's voice suddenly cutting off in mid-scream. His muscles relaxed and he fell back onto the table, hands at his sides, motionless.

"Oh, Jesus ... God ... no!" Two cried. Had they brought him back from the dead only to kill him with the power of the blood? "Theroen!"

At the sound of her cries, Theroen's head turned to the side, the rest of his body still motionless. His eyes opened, and for a moment Two saw nothing behind them, no recognition, not even a spark of consciousness. Then they seemed to clear, focus, and Two felt her entire body clench in excitement at what she saw there. Not fear or pain, not madness or hate. She saw only calm and peace. There was a slight smile on his lips, that bemusing, mysterious smile that she so loved to kiss. She was looking at Theroen Anders, the man she loved, and he was unquestionably alive. Awake. Aware.

"Well," Theroen said after a moment's pause, still looking over at them. "*That* was unpleasant."

Two put her face in her hands and wept.

* * *

"Two ... look at me."

She had heard that voice countless times in her dreams these past two years. She had heard and woken weeping sometimes, as she was weeping now. She had never expected to hear it again outside of those dreams, and faced with it now she found she could not obey the command.

"I can't," she sobbed, and the voice came again.

"Why not?"

"Because this might not be real!"

Two felt hands, *his* hands, take hers and move them gently away from her face. She could see a male figure before her, wearing a black suit. Theroen put a hand under her chin and raised her face to look at his.

"I like what you've done with your hair," he said, and Two laughed, incredulous and still weeping.

"You're really alive," she said.

Theroen nodded.

"I'm not dreaming?"

He shook his head and smiled. "No."

Two leapt forward, flinging her arms around his neck, pressing her lips against his, wrapping her fingers into his hair. She kissed him with a raw passion that she had honestly forgotten she was capable of. Theroen kissed back, put his own hands in her hair. Two could feel the twin points of his elongated canine teeth as he pulled gently at her lower lip. She sighed and shivered, holding him to her, kissing and kissing. Theroen wrapped his arms around her lower back and lifted her off her feet.

At last, Two spoke around his lips. "Don't you ever, *ever* leave me again, you asshole! You don't get to die without me twice."

Theroen laughed, kissed her, set her down. "I will try to avoid it."

Two at last moved her lips away from his and stood with her arms around him, face against his chest. Theroen glanced over her head at the other party in the chamber.

"It is good to see you, Naomi. I feared you were dead."

Naomi smiled, nodded. "I am glad to see you as well. It has been far too long. How do you feel?"

Theroen contemplated this for a moment. "I could use a shower."

Two laughed against his chest. She was trying to make herself let go of him, embarrassed by her own behavior, but was having a hard time doing so. Finally, she forced herself to take a step back, letting go of Theroen's waist but taking his hands in her own.

"I think she was worried more about the whole screaming thing," Two said. "Are you all right? Does it still hurt?"

417

"No, the pain went from excruciating to ... gone, in a blink. I am hungry, and I feel somehow different. I must also confess to some confusion. I don't know how to say this, but *when* is it? Time must have passed. It *must* have, or Naomi would not be here now, and you would not be a human, and Abraham ... what happened to Abraham? How long has it been?"

"You've been dead for nearly two years," Naomi said in a gentle voice.

Theroen was silent for a time, contemplating this revelation. "Two years," he murmured. "Dead?"

"It's a long story," Two said.

"It feels like *yesterday*," Theroen said. "It feels like it was just last night that Abraham ... I remember nothing. There were no dreams, no thoughts."

"You were dead," Naomi repeated. "Your heart stopped. Your breathing stopped. Your brain function stopped. The only thing preventing you from rotting into the earth was the trace amount of blood that Abraham left in you."

"And now, somehow, you have brought me back," Theroen said. "But it has been two years and I ... I do not feel the same."

"You're not the same," Two said.

Theroen pressed the heel of his hand against his forehead. "There is much you need to tell me."

"That is a serious understatement," Two said.

Naomi's cell phone began to ring and she flipped it open, holding it to her ear. Two and Theroen paused, listening.

"Stephen. Yes, we're still here. Yes, it worked. No, not yet. What do you need? Oh! Stephen, are you serious? Yes, we'll be there as soon as we can. Yes, bring her in if they start before we get there. No, no, I don't advise that. No, not while they're waiting. Yes, that'd be best. We'll leave right now. Goodbye."

She closed the phone and looked at Two and Theroen. "I hate to do this, but—"

"But there is something urgent that you must attend to," Theroen finished for her. "Yes, that's fine. We're going to New York?"

"Yes," Naomi said.

"Then we will have plenty of time to talk along the way."

"I'm sorry to do this, Theroen. You should have had time to adjust, but I think you're about to be thrown forcibly into vampire society."

Theroen shrugged, smiled. "It's been four hundred years," he said. "I guess it's about time. Let's go, Naomi. I spent more time in this chamber than I cared to even before I was buried here."

"No time to shower, I guess," Two said, and then laughed, a bright sound that made both vampires turn their attention to her.

"What, Two?" Naomi asked.

"Doesn't matter!" Two said, and she giggled. "The whole place is burned down,"

"It is?" Theroen asked.

Naomi nodded. Two grinned up at him. Theroen rolled his eyes.

"There is much you need to tell me," he said again.

Two squeezed his hands, pulled him toward her, kissed him on the lips. "Yup."

"Let's go," Naomi said, and she turned toward the stairs. Theroen and Two followed.

* * *

Nearly an hour had passed since the trio had begun their drive back to the city, and Two had spent most of it filling Theroen in on everything that had happened since that cold November night when Abraham had drained his blood. She had tried not to skip any details, other than those pertaining to her relationship with Naomi. She wanted to discuss that with Theroen in private, both for her own comfort and because she didn't think it was fair or appropriate to do it with Naomi sitting there. If the vampire girl disagreed with Two's decision, she didn't speak up.

Two finished the story by telling of their meeting with Ashayt and her revelation about the possibility of bringing Theroen back to life, and of their journey together back to the United States. At the end, Theroen spent some time sitting in silence, staring out the window, lost in thought. Finally he said, "This is a great deal to consider."

"It's pretty nuts," Two said, and Naomi laughed from the front seat of the car.

"Yes," she said. "That's one way to describe it. The emergence of the sole surviving *Ovras* vampire, and the creation of a new one. Not exactly a typical week."

"Is that what I am now, then?" Theroen asked her. "*Theroen-Sa?* A source?"

"That's what Ashayt believes."

"And pretty soon you'll have a *Theroen-Chen* of your very own," Two said, grinning. Theroen glanced down at her with concern.

"Two, we do not even know what I *am* yet ..."

"Don't give a shit," Two said, still smiling.

"But—"

Two turned, leaned in, and kissed him. "Shut up. Listen, I brought you back from the dead, so you owe me. We'll get you all filled up with blood, and then we'll get me sorted out, and it will be *fine*. Nothing we did to you should make you unable to make me into a vampire, so relax."

Naomi was watching them in her rearview mirror, smiling for the first time that night. Theroen looked over at her, saw her grin and sighed.

"I am not going to get any support from you in this, am I?" he asked, and Naomi shook her head.

"Not a bit. She's going to be your first, *Theroen-Sa,* if we have to knock you out and take the blood by force. We've spent too much time trying to get this done."

"That appellation is going to take some getting used to," Theroen commented. "Abraham kept me in the dark about so much. I am only now coming to understand how significant my status as *Eresh-Chen* apparently is ... or was. Now I've become something that will be even more prone to drawing unwanted attention."

"Do you *feel* different?" Two asked.

"Yes."

"How?"

Theroen laughed. "I don't know if I can explain it. It's ... when I awoke, my mental abilities were gone entirely; I couldn't even feel your minds, much less read your thoughts. That was a bit disconcerting, but I believe I can feel those things coming back."

"Good," Two said. She was anxious to reconnect with Theroen on the same level as before, to feel his presence fully.

"It may be some time before we know everything that's changed," Naomi told them, and Theroen nodded.

Two looked out the window. Trees and the lights of other cars were rushing by as Naomi sped down the highway. "Where are we going, Naomi? What's the rush?"

"I was wondering that myself," Theroen said.

"The council is meeting tonight. Not only are they meeting, but Stephen said that from his observations, the gathering was neither organized nor is being run by Malik."

"Who, then?" Two asked.

"He said that it seems to have been organized by William, the man for whom I served as apprentice ... the one who should have inherited the council from Abraham but chose instead to step down."

"And now he's staging a coup?" Theroen asked.

"That's how it seems," Naomi agreed. "It doesn't sound like William to me, though. Something must be happening that we don't understand."

"I'm *sure* that throwing Ashayt and Theroen into the mix will just calm everything down," Two said, and Naomi laughed.

"We'll find out soon enough, but first ... Theroen, there's a mall a few miles away. You can feed there, and we'll get you dressed in something that didn't deservedly go out of fashion in the nineteenth century."

"It was Abraham's choice," Theroen said, his voice dry.

Two giggled. "It's cute. In a kind of ... you know ... it's ..."

"Not cute?" Naomi finished for her.

Two glanced up at Theroen, trying to look solemn. The left side of his mouth curled up in a little smirk, and Two laughed at him.

"Two and I aren't dressed for council, but I think they'll forgive us," Naomi said.

"Doubt they'll even notice," Two said. Naomi had pulled off the highway and was now navigating surface streets. Two could see the mall in the distance.

"We definitely need to stop soon," Theroen said. He was clenching and unclenching his fingers. Two took his hand in hers, forced him to stop.

"Hungry?" she asked.

"It's growing worse by the moment. It is like something is inside of me, gnawing away. It burns. You should stay away from me, Two. If it gets worse, I could ... I might ..."

Two was having none of it. She shook her head. "You're not going to hurt me."

"The blood is working on you," Naomi said. "It is reshaping you, making you whole, and it needs fuel."

They pulled into the mall's parking lot, still brightly lit and filled with Christmas shoppers. Naomi found a parking space and they stepped out into the crisp December air, heading for the mall's entrance. Two and Naomi left Theroen at the men's bathroom, sparing him from having to walk through the crowded mall in his antique suit. They returned in less than ten minutes with a basic pair of black slacks and a red button-down shirt, socks, and black leather shoes.

"Hope you're not still in your all-black phase," Two told him.

"I had been meaning to branch out," Theroen told her.

He took his first blood as an *Ovras* vampire while stray price tags still hung from the clothes he was wearing. A wandering security guard had heard women giggling in the men's room and decided to investigate. Theroen, well beyond caring whether his victim was male or female, leapt upon the man as Naomi shoved the door closed and leaned against it.

Two could see that Theroen was ravenous, but also that he was struggling to retain his focus and not kill the man. At last, she stepped up next to him and pulled him away, whispering in his ear, assuring him that there would be more. Theroen forced the thirst down, licking his lips, and let the guard drop to the ground. In less than an hour, his coworkers would find him there, wake him, and raise him on shaky legs. With no memory of what had happened, the episode would eventually be dismissed as a case of food poisoning.

They went next to the bathrooms by the movie theater. Theroen found no one in the men's room, but Two reported that there was someone finishing up in the ladies' room. Theroen wasted no time, but he was somewhat gentler with this one, leaving her standing in swoon in front of the mirror, a cell phone in her hand, its text-message half-complete. The entry of a gaggle of teenage girls a few minutes later would rouse her.

They stopped once again in the parking lot, where Theroen mesmerized and drank from both a man and a woman; a couple who had come to the mall to catch a late showing of a movie. He left them in the back seat of their car, entwined together, and they slept there for hours before waking in confusion.

"How are you doing?" Two asked him as they got back into Naomi's car, and Theroen smiled, breathed deeply, and nodded.

"Vastly better," he said. "Not so weak and hungry, and I can feel your minds again."

He touched his fingers to Two's forehead and closed his eyes, asking, "Can you feel it?"

Two closed her eyes and tried to sense him in her mind. She thought perhaps that yes, she could feel something, but it was faint, like the distant fluttering of wings.

"Not much," she said. "Not yet. I'm still human."

"That will change."

"Not now," Naomi said as she sat down in the driver's seat. "We have little time. The meeting must have started by now."

"Didn't take long the last time," Two commented. "I mean ... we could do it while you're driving."

"We have no idea what it will be like this time, Two," Naomi said. "The process is different for each strain. It takes hours for an Ashayt fledgling to rise from trance, and I really would rather not leave you lying in the car while we go to this meeting."

Two grimaced, but sat back in her seat and nodded. "OK. Shit."

Naomi angled them back toward the highway. "I know you're anxious. It won't be much longer. When we are done with the council, you and Theroen will be free to ... well, to do whatever you want, I suppose."

"Unless, of course, they choose to detain us," Theroen said.

"I would love to see them try that," Two muttered.

"I'm inclined to agree that that won't be a problem," Naomi said. "Attempting to hold us would be nearly impossible."

"Would it?" Theroen asked.

"You need to meet Ashayt," Two told him. "She's uh ... kinda strong."

"You've a gift for understatement, Two," Naomi said. "Theroen ... Two can't sense it yet, but you're throwing off power like a blaze. I think they would have a hard time containing you alone, and if you're a fire, Ashayt is the *sun*. You will understand when you meet her. No one will stand in our way so long as she remains on our side."

"They shouldn't have any reason to be mad at us, should they?" Two asked.

"I highly doubt it. We've done nothing wrong and anyway, William is my former mentor and a good friend. He is held in much greater respect than Malik, and the other vampires will defer to him. I am much more concerned about whatever it is that's forced him to call this meeting."

"That is a plus," Theroen said. "I would prefer not to introduce myself to the council by fighting with them."

They were quiet for a time. Two leaned against Theroen, who had his eyes closed as if he were listening to something. Naomi drove, weaving expertly between cars on the highway. They had almost reached FDR Drive, now, and from there it would only be a few minutes.

"There's something ... I feel something between the two of you that I don't understand," Theroen said, his eyes still closed. Neither Two nor Naomi acknowledged this statement immediately, and Theroen opened his eyes, glancing at them each.

"Not now," Naomi said finally. There was an ache in her voice that she could not disguise, and Two felt guilt flare up inside of her. She sat up, leaning away from Theroen and rubbing the back of her neck with one hand.

"I'll explain everything after the meeting," she told him.

Theroen looked at her for some time, considering this, and finally nodded. "Very well."

Silence descended again upon the trio, and they sped on toward the city and their meeting with the council.

CHAPTER XXVIII

Before the Storm

"Oh," William said. "Oh my dear God."

Stephen's smirk widened to a grin, and he stepped up to stand beside Ashayt. "Never thought ye'd live to see this, did yeh, William?"

A nervous murmur was making its way through the crowd of vampires as they realized the significance of what was happening. Stephen turned around, glancing at the assembled council, gauging their mood. He was enjoying springing this surprise upon them, but he didn't want to start a panic.

William's mouth worked, but his voice was nothing more than a dry noise, like wind rattling through reeds. He closed his mouth, passed a hand across his brow, swallowed, and tried again. This time, his voice was there.

"This is the greatest honor of my long life, Mother."

Ashayt smiled, bowing her head slightly in acknowledgement. She stepped forward, hand extended, and William took it, marveling at her.

"You are of my blood," she said, and William nodded.

"I am, Mother. Descended of Alexander, part of Eadwyn's line."

"I remember Alexander," Ashayt said, tilting her head. "You are too young to be his fledgling ... who was your sire?"

"Isabelle."

"I did not know her. A pity ... does she still live?"

William lowered his eyes for a moment, and when he brought his gaze again up to the elder vampire, his expression was one of old, deep sorrow.

"She took her own life. I ... I could not stop her."

Ashayt lowered her gaze momentarily, frowning. "The curse of my blood," she murmured.

She looked back up at William and shook her head. "You blame yourself for this, my child – I feel it – but it is not your fault. It is my blood. I am *Ovras,* and all troubles of this line stem from my own failings."

William found himself again at a loss for words. Stephen, sensing this and rarely afflicted with such troubles, stepped in.

"There's a time and a place for dwelling on the past, my dear, and I'm afraid 'tis not now. This meeting was called to order for a reason, one I'm curious to hear more about. What has happened to Jakob?"

William looked at Stephen, surprised. "You've not heard?"

"We've been in this country for but a span of hours, William, and I spent most of those sleeping. You'll forgive me if I've not had time to check my email. Do fill us in on current events, would you? That way I can give Naomi the short version when she arrives."

"Naomi is here?"

"I've told you this. Not *here*, here, but on her way. Good Lord, William, has something happened to your brain?"

Stephen's caustic tone seemed to cut through William's daze. He glanced at Stephen, smoldering, and then rolled his eyes. "You've a way with words, Stephen."

"It's a talent. Brevity. Simplicity. Honesty."

Ashayt covered her mouth, but Stephen saw that William had seen the motion and knew that Ashayt had moved to cover the beginnings of a smile on her lips.

William smiled, laughed a small laugh, nodded to Stephen. "Very well."

"We will sit, William, and you can tell us a story."

"Yes, but not one you want to hear. That is, if I remember your political associations correctly."

"I don't make political associations," Stephen replied. "I make friends. Should we introduce our guest to the rest of the group?"

"It would probably be better to get it out of the way," William admitted. "I think they've guessed that something important is happening, but most have not studied their history. They don't know who you are, Mother."

Ashayt seemed unfazed by this. "I have spent millennia in seclusion. That my name is remembered at all is something of a miracle."

The assembled vampires around them had been silent, sensing that something of grave import was happening. Few had taken the time to read the old scrolls, though, and Stephen knew that most could only guess at Ashayt's identity. Those who knew seemed to be waiting for whatever was to happen next. He stepped down and took a seat in the shadows. Ashayt moved to stand next to William, who turned again to address the council, but before he could speak, Malik stepped forward.

"With an elder present, I must formally raise protest," he began. "These proceedings are an egregious—"

"Shut up!" Stephen roared, leaping to his feet.

Malik and William, both startled by this breech of etiquette, could only turn and stare, mouths agape.

"I tire of this bullshit," Stephen snarled. "I tire of protocol and formality, of rules and restrictions. I tire of deferring to my elders when they've not the common sense necessary to pull their heads from their very arses and make a decision. The European council makes their choices in the time it takes you, Malik, to make your opening pronouncement. I have seen how they operate firsthand, and it is *better* than this. So I beg you, for the sake of us all: shut up. Sit down, shut up, and let us address whatever problem it is that's caused this meeting."

"Of all the—" Malik began, and Stephen overrode him again.

"I know. You believe I am an impertinent fool. Even William, who likes me far more than you ever will, thinks I am a fool, but I am *not* a fool and I will not sit here while you waste our time. Jakob is missing. Sasha is standing here with some *human child.*

Something has gone wrong. Naomi is not here to contain me, as she normally does, so I shall speak my mind. Shut up. Sit down. Let William tell us what has happened to Jakob, so that those of us who are capable of action may take it."

"I—"

"SIT!" Stephen roared, stabbing a finger at the nearest empty chair.

Malik looked to Ashayt for help, but the elder vampire simply looked back at him, a small expression of sorrow on her face. She shook her head once and said, "I have not come here to assume control of this council. It is not my place to take sides or pass judgment. I cannot help you."

Malik's face hardened. "This will destroy the council!" he snarled, and he whirled on his heel, striding toward the exit. His apprentice Theresa looked startled, caught off guard by this action, and scurried after him.

"Good," said Stephen, and then shouted it at the departing figures. "Good! Too long have we huddled in this church, ignoring the world around us!"

"Stephen ..." William sounded old and tired, his tone that of someone who had seen too much, felt too much.

"Oh ... get on with it," Stephen growled. He sat back in the shadows, arms crossed, and only Ashayt saw the small tick at the right corner of his mouth as he, too, suppressed a grin.

There will be changes, he had told Two, and it was true. Her entrance into their world had changed everything already, and it was only just beginning. Stephen, for one, could not wait.

* * *

"Some of you have studied our history and others know only bits and pieces, but I believe all who sit here before me know that a moment of some significance has come to pass," William said, staring out at the council members from his podium. "Before you stands the elder vampire Ashayt, known in the old scrolls as the Girl from the Desert, quite likely the eldest among us all, and the only living *Ovras* vampire."

Ashayt bowed her head momentarily before looking up and out at the council. "I extend my greetings to you all."

Her words were met with a kind of soft rushing noise, the sound of a crowd lost in awe and, perhaps, fear. Ashayt had become a vampire during the height of the Egyptian empire's power. Even the eldest of the vampires assembled before her were, by comparison, mere children. William held his hands up, hoping to calm the crowd before the murmur could become a roar.

"Please, Mother, if you could make it clear that you are a ... a benign figure, it would be very helpful. There are those here who will fear you and the powers you possess. You are a name out of legend, for us."

"I hold no ill will toward any here or elsewhere," Ashayt said to him, and turned to the crowd. "Children, you have less to fear from me than from any other vampire in the world. I have not taken a life, human or vampire, in more than four thousand years. I have sworn on my very soul that I will never do so again, even if it means my own death. I am an emissary of peace and wish only that *all* of my people, be they of my line or any other, might live together in harmony."

"How are we to believe that?" called a voice from the crowd, and Stephen recognized it as Leonore's. "You've been gone for thousands of years, and now you're back at the side of a rogue Ay'Araf bent on tearing apart the council. Are we to rejoice at your coming? How can we know that your vow is real, that your words are not lies?"

"If she wanted us dead, idiot, we would already be so," Stephen said from the shadows in a quiet, exasperated voice. William gave him a disapproving glance, but also nodded.

"My friends, I understand your concern," he said. "Here before us is a legend come to life, returned after millennia of absence. You are right to fear her power, but you must understand: if she had come to us with the intent of doing harm, then all who she wished to eliminate would be gone. She is *Ovras,* and before her not even Abraham would have stood."

"I am here only to observe," Ashayt said. "I am here only to advise. I will not make decisions for this council, nor take sides in any argument. Events are occurring now in our world which will ripple outwards. They will eventually touch the vampires in Europe, Asia ... everywhere. No other *Ovras* vampires remain to help, to act as guides in this time of danger. I have stayed too long in seclusion, it is true, but I hope that you will forgive me and accept my aid."

"What dangers do we face?" the British vampire, Peter Markham, asked. He at least seemed unafraid, and his words were couched in a tone of deep respect.

"The vampire Aros has built an army," William said. "He has abducted Jakob and two human beings who are friends of Two Majors, the fallen *Eresh-Chen*. You know this because Sasha brought it to your attention at the last meeting. He intends to use his army as a weapon against the Children of the Sun, the religious cult of humans bent on destroying our kind. We fear that he will provoke them into a full-scale war, and that whichever group proves victorious will come then for us and those we care about.

"Even should Aros and the Children not prove a direct threat, there is always the possibility that their fighting will alert the human world to our existence. I don't think I need to explain to any of you why that would be tremendously dangerous. We live in an age of GPS tracking and instant communication to all corners of the globe. There will be nowhere to hide if they decide to wipe us out.

"We must therefore strike first, in order to prevent full-scale war with one or both of these armies, or at least so we may wage it on more favorable terms. I have asked you to come here tonight so that I might propose—"

William's words were cut off by the loud crack of wood on wood as the church doors were thrown open. The council members stood as one, turning to see what had caused this distraction. From the shadows, a woman's voice giggled and said, "You don't know your own strength yet."

At these words, Molly, who had been sitting quietly and following along as best she could, leapt to her feet.

"Two?!" she cried, racing up the carpeted aisle. "Is that you?"

"Yeah. Who's asking? Molly?!" Two came into the light, caught the girl in her arms and hugged her, looking baffled. "What in the hell are *you* doing here?"

431

"The vampires took Mom and Dad and I had nowhere to go so I went with Sasha and she took me here and then let me stay at her place and they wouldn't go get them so we had to go ask William for help and he said he'd hold this meeting and then the elder vampire lady showed up and everyone was like 'holy crap!' and then we were just really getting started but now you're here!" Molly spoke in a rapid rush, without pause for breathing. Two's eyes grew wider and wider.

"Wait, slow down. Calm down, Molly. What are you talking about? Vampires took *who,* now?"

"Everything will be explained if you'll come forward," William said from the podium. "Your timing is most fortuitous. Is Naomi with you?"

"I am," Naomi said, stepping also into the light and bringing Theroen with her. She and the others made their way forward, stopping before the podium. Molly sat back down on a bench, watching with curiosity.

"I suppose it worked, then," Stephen said from his place in the shadows, and Naomi nodded at him.

"It is good to see you, Naomi," William said. "I do not recognize your friends."

Naomi smiled at William, looking at home and in her element. Two was glad that returning to this council chamber brought comfort to her friend.

"You've never met. This is Two Majors, the *Eresh-Chen,* but I think you've guessed that already. Two, this is my mentor, William."

"Pleasure," Two said, shaking William's hand.

Theroen held his hand out and introduced himself. "My name is Theroen Anders, first child of Abraham, and also an *Eresh-Chen,* which I'm told is of some significance."

William gaped openly at him. "But you're dead."

"I was," Theroen said, still holding his hand out. After a moment, William shook it.

"I am glad to meet you, Theroen. How is it you came to be ... less dead than previously reported?"

"The lady here gave me her blood and the blood of Ay'Araf himself," Theroen said, indicating toward Ashayt. "Two injected these gifts into my body, and they have combined with the blood that has shaped me these past four hundred years. They have made me into something which does not have a name yet, something new."

"*Theroen-Sa,*" Ashayt said, and Naomi nodded. Behind them, the assembled vampires murmured in confusion, their voices again tinged with the sound of fear.

"If I am a source, an *Ovras,* then it means no more for me than it must have meant for Ashayt, or Ay'Araf, or even Eresh herself once." Theroen was pitching his voice loud enough to be sure that the council members seated behind him could hear. "I am not a god, not an ancient, not possessed of heavenly powers. I am just Theroen Anders."

"Few of us know anything about Theroen Anders, though we all know of your sire," William said. "Naomi speaks well of you, which is enough for me, but if you could take a moment to reassure us that you are ... well ..."

"That I am not my father's son?" Theroen asked, smiling. "Yes, I can say that. No one on this earth is more pleased than I am that Abraham has been sent to his death. If I had thought it at all possible, I'd have attempted the act myself. Abraham murdered my first love, split me from my friend Naomi, and sequestered me away from vampire society for centuries. He attempted to kill my second love more than once, and had she not survived, he would probably reign still over this council.

"Abraham was evil, and it is a good thing that he has passed. I have no intention of following in his footsteps, and I happily submit myself to the council's laws."

"Let's not go too far," Stephen said, and Naomi shot him a glance. Two gave a small laugh.

"You probably should have a spot on the council," William mused. "Certainly your age warrants it, and if you are truly an *Ovras* ..."

"We can discuss that some other time," Theroen replied. "For the moment, I would prefer to observe. It is clear that we are in dangerous times, and that decisions must be made this night. I would not stand in the way."

William nodded, said, "If you would take your seats, then, I will explain, and we may come to a decision on what actions to take."

Naomi led Two and Theroen to the bench where Stephen sat, and Ashayt followed. After quickly introducing Theroen to Stephen, Naomi left to take her seat among the council members.

"Fun night?" Stephen asked Two as she sat down next to him.

"It's had its ups and downs," Two replied. "Do you know what the hell this is all about?"

"William will explain it, give him a moment. Prepare to be unhappy."

"Great."

William stepped up to the podium again and cleared his throat. The murmuring from the council members quieted.

"A quick summary for those who just arrived," William said. "The Burilgi vampire Aros Kreskas has formed an army and is preparing to make war on the Children of the Sun. We fear that this war will spill over into our ranks or alert the general human population to our existence. In addition, he has kidnapped our fellow council member Jakob and the two humans Rhes and Sarah Thompson, because he wants Two for some reason and believes she will come after them."

"He's right about that," Two said. "What the hell are we doing sitting around here?"

"That's what I've been wondering," said Sasha from her seat amongst the council members.

William tapped on the podium. "The purpose of this council – the entire reason for its existence – is to make sure that we avoid making rash decisions. If we leapt into action at every hint of danger, we would risk bringing too much attention to ourselves. If we act rashly, if we expose ourselves, we risk destruction. This has always been true."

"Yes, but William—" Naomi began, and the elder vampire held up his hand, stopping her.

"Clearly, this is a special case," he said. "Jakob has been abducted. That will not stand, and I am so confident in my belief in

434

this council that I hardly feel it necessary to call a vote. Still, a vote we shall have. Sasha has obtained information on Aros's whereabouts. I propose ... I make a motion that we task a small group of vampires with going to this place, liberating Jakob and the humans, and bringing Aros here to face trial for his crimes. Do I have a second?"

Sasha and Stephen gave their affirmation simultaneously.

"Very well. The vote, then: all those in favor of the motion?"

William was greeted by a strong, if not universal, "Aye."

"Motion passed. Sasha, please take the lead in assembling the group."

Sasha glanced around the room. "I assume Stephen's coming unless we chain him down. I'd also like Peter and Kanene's help, if they're willing."

"We are," Peter answered.

"I'm going," Two said. "He's got my friends."

"She's not going anywhere without Theroen and me," Naomi said. Sasha raised her eyebrows at this.

"I may not be much of a fighter," Naomi said, "but I've learned how to take care of myself from Stephen, and I will happily wager on Theroen's strength and Two's ... utterly perplexing indestructibility. Besides, I didn't fly halfway around the world and spend the past year reuniting these two just to let one or both of them get killed."

Sasha smiled, nodded, turned to William. "That should suffice. Too many would just be difficult to coordinate and would make stealth impossible."

Ashayt coughed and stood, stepping forward and glancing first at William, then at Sasha. "With your permission, I would like to accompany you as well. It pains me to see my people fighting, and if by my words or my reputation I might prevent it, I would like the opportunity to try."

"A wise stance, Mother," William said. "I am sure it will not be a problem. Sasha?"

"Of course not. I would be honored."

"Very well, then," William said. He glanced at his watch, frowned, looked to Sasha.

"Not enough time," Sasha said.

"Sadly, no. Tomorrow night?" William asked.

"Yes. We will wait through one more day, and tomorrow at sunset we will set out. Is that acceptable to everyone?"

There were murmurs of assent from all of the involved parties.

"Excellent. I have no further business for this evening," William said. "I would like to thank everyone for coming. We are living in a most unusual time, and drastic steps were needed. Once we have rescued Jakob and brought Aros to trial, it is my fervent hope that we can return the council to its normal state."

This pronouncement was greeted with muttering from the council members. It was clear that the political implications of this minor coup would not be fully sorted out for some time.

"Does anyone have any further business to discuss?" William asked. After a few moments of quiet, he nodded and wished the council goodnight. Most of the vampires stood and began to file out of the cathedral. A few stopped to speak briefly with Ashayt, and she greeted each with pleasure, but it was not long before they were gone and the emergency meeting was over.

The only people remaining in the church were Two's band of companions, William, Sasha, and Molly. William stepped down from the podium and joined the others, who were clustered together at the back of the cathedral near the table of wine and blood.

"Well," he said. "It seems that we are living in interesting times."

"That would be one way to describe them," Naomi said.

Sasha turned to Theroen and Ashayt, who were standing next to each other, each holding a glass filled with blood.

"Forgive me for not expressing the appropriate amount of awe upon meeting either of you, Mother Ashayt and *Theroen-Sa*. My mind has been over occupied this night."

Theroen smiled. "I cannot speak for Ashayt, but I find your current level of awe not only acceptable but completely appropriate. Your name is Sasha, yes?"

"Yes. I am Jakob's fledgling."

"Jakob is the vampire we're meant to rescue?"

Sasha nodded. "Yes, along with Molly's parents."

"Why have the Burilgi taken them?" Naomi asked.

Sasha shrugged. "We are not entirely sure. We know that Jakob was not the target. Aros wanted the two humans as bait for Two. Jakob was just in the wrong place at the wrong time."

Two, who was standing on Theroen's left, spoke up. "Why the hell would he want me?"

"That remains a mystery," William said. "I know Aros. I sat with him on this council for decades before he abandoned it. He was not exactly of sound mind then, and all indications are that he has only grown worse with time."

"Fantastic," Two said. "I wish we could go now. I hate waiting."

"As do I," Sasha said. "We are already risking very much by sending so small a group into a situation that we know is meant to be a trap. Doing so during the daylight, when it is so debilitating at least to the Ay'Araf among the group, would be insane."

"I know," Two said. "Theroen hasn't even gone through a sunrise yet. Who knows what it'll do to him? Of the bunch of us, I'm the only one who's really built for daylight work."

"I am, too," Molly piped up. Sasha glanced over at her.

"I believe we agreed that you would stay in my apartment," she said.

"Yeah, well ... I mean ... Two's going!"

"I fail to see how that changes anything," Sasha replied.

"So do I," Two said.

Molly made an exasperated noise, throwing her body into an aggravated, sulking posture. "You guys suck," she said.

"Life's a bitch," Two replied. Molly stuck her tongue out.

"Molly has given me her *sincere* assurances that she won't try to stow away or otherwise join us," Sasha said. "I'm holding her to her promise."

"Yeah, yeah," said Molly. "Fine. OK. Can we go now? I'm tired."

"Yes, we should probably finish up for the evening," Naomi said. "Speaking of which ... Two, Theroen, you're welcome to sleep on my couches, but I'm afraid I don't have any further space."

"We'll find accommodations," Theroen said, smiling slightly. "Do we need to find space for your friend, Two?"

"I'll stay with Sasha," said Molly. "If he's really been dead for two years, I bet you guys want to have some ... alone time."

Two felt her cheeks warm. "Thanks, kiddo. You'll be all right?"

"Long as you bring everyone back safe, I'll be fine."

"We'll do our best. Guys, we're going to go find a hotel or something. We'll see you here tomorrow night just after sunset, right?"

"Yes, please," said Sasha. "Theroen, it was nice meeting you."

The others echoed this sentiment, and there was another round of hand shaking before Two could usher Theroen out into the street. Once there, standing on the curb and peering around, looking for a taxi, she smiled up at him.

"Finally have you all to myself," she said.

"Yes," Theroen said "I must admit to looking forward to ... how did Molly put it? Some alone time?"

Two's smile widened to a grin, and she put her arms around Theroen's midsection. He put one arm on her back, holding the other up to hail an oncoming cab. As it slowed, he turned to her with an embarrassed expression on his face.

"I just realized that I have no money. Abraham didn't put my wallet into the pockets of the suit he dressed me in, and with the rest of the mansion burned to the ground I doubt we'd be able to find it now."

"I've got it covered," Two said, opening the door. "I sold a lot of stuff from the mansion before it was burned. I uh ... sold your Ferrari. Sorry."

Theroen looked pained as he sat down in the cab next to her. "Please tell me you got a fair price for it."

"I could tell you that, but I'd probably be lying," Two said. "Where the hell are we going, anyway?"

"The W Hotel, Union Square," Theroen said, loud enough for the cab driver to hear. The man nodded, hit a button on his meter, and began driving.

"How trendy," Two said in a dry voice, and giggled as Theroen turned and raised his eyebrows at her.

"I know the manager and have a deposit box in their safe," Theroen said. "Not only will we have a place to stay, but it will provide me with a driver's license, passport, Social Security card, credit and ATM cards ... all of the necessities."

"Nice," Two said. She nestled in against Theroen, leaning on his chest in silence for a time. Finally she said, "I can't believe you're back."

"I can't believe I've been gone for two years," Theroen said. He was staring out the window, watching the city go by. It was nearly one in the morning, but the streets were still crowded with Saturday-night revelers.

"You really don't remember any of it?" Two asked him.

"It seems like last night. I'm sorry, Two, I know it must have been hard for you. There is so much to catch up on, I hardly know where to begin."

"I can tell you anything you want to know."

Theroen was quiet for a moment, considering this. Finally, he said, "How long were you in a relationship with Naomi?"

Two took a deep breath and pulled away from Theroen, frowning slightly. "You're going right for the throat. OK, it was about ... ten months. When did you figure it out?"

"Near the end of the meeting. My mental abilities are coming back to me, and I could sense some kind of connection while we were in the car, but didn't understand what I was feeling until we were taking our leave. Two ... she *loves* you."

"Yes. Yes, she does."

Theroen glanced at Two, and she could read his concern on his face. "And how do you feel?"

Two shook her head. "I've only ever loved one person in my entire life. Naomi is ... I don't know what happened, Theroen. I was lonely, and she was interested, and holy shit, I can't believe how lame this sounds. Did I really just say 'I was lonely'?"

"I believe you did," Theroen told her.

"I hear it, too!" the cab driver told her in his heavy accent as he pulled over in front of their hotel.

"Really earning your tip ..." Two muttered, handing him a twenty dollar bill. "Keep the change."

The cab driver thanked her, and Two stepped out onto the curb next to Theroen. A few people were mingling around the front of the hotel bar, smoking, not paying any attention to the new arrivals. Theroen was watching her with interest, waiting for her to finish.

"I've loved you every minute of every day since the first night I met you," Two said. She shrugged. It was that simple. "Naomi is a wonderful, amazing person and I care about her very much. I know that I ended up hurting her, and I'm sorry for that ... but I don't love her. I love you."

"And she knows this?"

"She knows. She knew the whole time. As soon as we found out there was a chance of bringing you back, she and I agreed to end it. Theroen, I never said I loved her. I couldn't say it to her or to anyone else."

Theroen considered this, saying nothing. Two stared back at him, some strong and terrible emotion welling up inside of her. She could feel tears stinging at the corners of her eyes. Had she come all this way only to lose him now?

"Please tell me you can forgive me," Two said. "I thought you were dead. I thought you died for me, and I couldn't stand it. I couldn't stand being alone, so I went looking for something ... someone, and I found her."

Theroen stepped forward, standing directly in front of her, and pressed the pad of his thumb against her left cheek, wiping away a tear. He tilted his head, looked into her eyes, smiled his inscrutable smile.

"Let's go inside," he said.

* * *

Theroen's penis was warm and hard in her hand as Two took it, brought the head to her damp and slippery labia, arched her back, and wrapped her legs around his body. Theroen moved his hips forward, parting her, entering her and pressing his teeth against her neck. Two put one hand on the back of his neck, gasped, murmured his name.

Theroen began to move within her, creating a slow and delicious friction that Two wished would never end. He kept his teeth pressed against her neck until she brought her left hand up from between her legs, wrapped her fingers in his hair and pulled gently. Theroen lifted his head, looked into her eyes, continued to thrust slowly within her.

"Hi," Two said.

Theroen seemed to consider this for a moment before asking, "Do you come here often?"

"Keep doing what you're doing, and it'll be my first time," Two replied. Theroen stared at her for a moment, eyebrows raised, then buried his head in her neck again, this time stifling laughter. Finally, he looked back up at her.

"Very nice," he said.

Two put her hand on his cheek, caressing lightly. His skin was smooth, and she wondered if he had shaved after his shower, or if his beard simply hadn't grown at all during the two years he had been dead. Something about this thought struck her as both hilarious and awful, and she closed her eyes, taking her hands from her lover and covering her face.

Theroen paused in his motions, watching her, concerned. "Are you all right, Two?" he asked.

"Theroen," she said. "I ... it's ..."

Theroen began to pull up from within her, and Two grabbed his back.

"No, don't leave! Stay with me. It's OK, I'm just ... it's been so long. I know it feels like yesterday for you, but for me it's a little overwhelming."

"I shouldn't have rushed you," Theroen said. Two laughed, kissed him, began to move her hips again.

"I *wanted* you to rush me! I'm not mad. It just all caught up to me at once. But trust me, if you ... mmmm ... just go slow and keep doing what you're doing, everything is going to be just fine."

Theroen smiled, kissed her lips, continued to make love to her. Slowly his motions sped, the warm friction he was making inside of her becoming more like a blaze. Two remembered their first time together, lying in a patch of grass on a forested hill. As they had neared orgasm, Theroen had turned and pressed his teeth against her neck, like he was doing now.

"Yes, my love," she whispered into his ear. "Take me. Make me one with you again. Make me whole."

She had come so far and waited so long, but now here at last was what she had wanted all along. Not just the blood, but the warmth and love, the connection that had been taken from her. Abraham had murdered a part of her when he murdered Theroen, but now her lover was back, here in this bed with her, and soon his teeth would pierce her flesh and unleash her blood. Soon he would drink, and drink, until Two was an empty vessel waiting to be filled. Soon he would make her his, and this time it would be forever.

Two dug her fingers into the skin of Theroen's back as his thrusts began at last to take her over that final edge. Her whole body was tingling, nipples hard and dark, flesh hypersensitive, craving this contact yet barely able to stand it. She gasped and panted, breathing in the scent of his skin, his hair, extolling him in whispers and sighs. Theroen, too, was nearing his climax, and Two struggled to hold on, wanting to share it with him, wanting to know that he was feeling the same pleasure that she was.

"God," he growled into the space between her neck and shoulder, stiffening, and Two answered with "Yes," and she let herself go. Her body clenched, tightened, shaking, and Two closed her eyes, lost in pleasure and desire, lost in her love for this man. Theroen, coming inside of her, drove his teeth into her neck, but the pain seemed to originate from somewhere outside of her, and it was dim and distant.

Within moments, as Theroen drank the blood that gushed forth from her jugular vein, the pain had left entirely, and there was only the pleasure. The initial short, powerful spasms were being replaced now with longer, slower, deeper sensations that seemed timed with her heartbeat. Theroen drank, and Two lay with him, legs wrapped loosely around him, hands resting on his back, eyes closed, tears leaking from their corners, a small smile on her face.

"Oh, my love," she whispered as he drank. The darkness was closing in on her again, and she felt like she was falling into some deep, black chasm where there was no bottom. She would fall like this forever, tumbling through the inky blackness, unconcerned and unafraid. Theroen was with her, at last, and that would be enough.

CHAPTER XXIX

The Burilgi Horde

Rhes Thompson stared at his friend Two in frank disbelief, unable to speak, paralyzed by an indescribable combination of surprise, rage, confusion and the almost uncontrollable urge to laugh at the absurdity of it all. If his vocal cords hadn't been locked solid, he might have done so. Instead, he merely stared.

Sarah, however, was apparently having no such difficulties. She whirled in the direction that Two's voice had come from, hands balled into fists, and Rhes had little doubt that if Sarah could have seen the girl, she would have punched first and asked questions later. Instead, she simply unleashed a snarling stream of invective at Two.

"Where the *fuck* have you been, you stupid, crazy, selfish bitch?!" she roared. "Do you have any idea what you've put us through? Do you even know what you've done? How dare you show up here, now, sounding like nothing's happened and everything's great in the world? How dare you?! You're lucky I can't see you, or I'd fucking strangle you to death right here!"

Two weathered this verbal attack without comment, waiting for Sarah to finish, a small, sad smile on her face. Rhes had time to observe the changes in his friend. There wasn't much that was markedly different about Two, and yet it seemed that everything was just a bit off. Her eyes seemed greener. Her face seemed paler. She had chopped most of her hair off, but what was left seemed fuller, thicker somehow. She was standing with her arms crossed, listening to Sarah, looking more calm and at ease and *alive* than Rhes thought he had seen her since before she had ever become involved with heroin.

"Hon ..." Rhes began, but Two stopped him without a word, holding up a hand and shaking her head. Sarah continued to rage.

"My house is torn up. My dog is dead. My daughter is shacked up with some fucking vampire. I've missed multiple days of work already and will be lucky to keep my job ... where were you?! Where were you when Rhes was getting the shit kicked out of him and I was lying there, scared out of my mind? Where were you when these fucking vampire shitheads were breaking into my house and killing my dog? You were out bouncing around Europe with your vampire buddies, living it up, not a care in the world, right? Right?! Fuck you!"

Sarah finally seemed to be finished. She stood in front of Two, frowning, hips set defiantly, waiting for a response.

"I deserve all of that," Two said.

"Fucking right you do," Sarah replied.

"And I wasn't trying to make a joke out of all of this, when I said 'hi' ... I was just so happy to see that you guys were still alive. You're not hurt, are you?"

"We're all right," Rhes said.

"Yeah, fine ... great," Sarah spat. "Here we are, safe and sound. Everything's terrific, isn't that right?"

Two sighed, shaking her head and staring at the floor for a minute. "I'm sorry for everything," she said. "I'm sorry for dragging you guys into this, and then turning away from you. I was trying to keep you distant ... trying to keep you from getting hurt, but it didn't work. It just made things worse."

"No, it didn't work. Jesus Christ, Two ..." Sarah couldn't seem to find the right words to continue. She took her glasses off and rubbed her eyes, giving a disgusted sigh. "I don't even know how to explain how angry I am right now."

"I'll do anything I can to make it up to you," Two said.

"Good! Leave us alone! That's what I want from you. Just fucking leave us alone. Leave us out of your insane vampire drama and let us live our stupid, boring, human lives. OK? Is that cool? Can we do that?"

"If that's what you want, that's what I'll do."

Something in Two's voice seemed to get to Sarah, and she bit off whatever it was she had been about to shout next. She lowered her head for a minute before bringing it back up to address Two again.

"You missed our wedding," she said, her tone still angry but no longer out of control.

"I know," Two replied.

"You missed Molly's adoption party."

"I know."

"You missed *everything!*"

Rhes tried again to calm her, saying her name and placing a hand on her shoulder. Sarah turned to face him.

"Don't do that," she said. "Don't let her off the hook. You always do that! I know you think she's the baby sister you never had, but she's not. She's an adult woman and she needs to face up to what she's done."

"I am one hundred percent on your side on this one," Rhes said. "I'm pretty sure Two's at least ninety percent on your side."

"I'd go with ninety-five," Two muttered.

"So why are you trying to calm me down?" Sarah asked him.

"Because her friends are done, uh … well, murdering everyone, and I'm worried they'll be mad that you're yelling at her."

"No one's going to touch either of you," Two said. "We're here to rescue you, not hurt you."

"All the same—" Rhes began, and Sarah cut him off.

"Are you a vampire now?" she asked Two. "Did you get *that* done, at least?"

"Yes," Two replied. "Yes, I'm a vampire now. Finally. It's … a long story."

"Halle-fucking-lujah," Sarah said. "You can tell it to us sometime when we're not trying to escape from a lunatic and his army of super-soldiers, OK?"

The left side of Two's mouth perked up in a small smirk. "So that means I don't have to stay out of your lives completely, then?"

Sarah paused for a moment, caught by surprise. Finally, she gave a small laugh, shaking her head. "You know what? Fine. Fuck you. Despite everything, despite knowing that I'm going to regret saying this, for some reason I am *still* your friend and I *still* don't hate you. That isn't keeping me from wanting to punch each of your teeth out individually, though."

"Just leave her two of them," said a vampire with long, reddish-brown hair as he came up behind Two. He had an Irish accent and was not much taller than Sarah. "She needs them."

"You're the original King of Comedy," Two told him, glancing over her shoulder. "You enjoying yourself?"

Stephen was covered in blood spatters and grinning broadly. He nodded.

"It's been a while since I saw this sort of action. In a way, I feel like I should thank Aros for the opportunity."

"Let's hold off on thanking Aros for anything," Sarah said. "Two ... who is this?"

"Oh, right," Two said. "Stephen, this is Rhes and Sarah Thompson. Rhes and Sarah, this is Stephen Connelly. He's been helping me out for the past year or so."

"I was caught up in the whirlwind that seems to trail behind your friend," Stephen told them. "I would shake your hands, but ..."

"But yours are covered in blood, right," Rhes said. "It's uh ... nice to meet you."

"Two ... what the fuck?" Sarah asked. "Seriously."

"It's not usually like this," Two said. "I swear to God, it's mostly totally normal, except the drinking blood part."

Stephen gave a short laugh and turned, wandering over to the other remaining vampires. There seemed to be no Burilgi soldiers left alive. Jakob was talking to a young woman with long brown hair who was clearly thrilled to see him, but also clearly upset about the wound in his side. For his part, Jakob seemed unconcerned and was spending most of his time staring at a tattooed black woman with an expression that looked like awe. There were four more vampires, two male and two female, also standing with the group.

As if sensing the scrutiny, one of the men glanced up at Two and began to walk over. He was tall and thin, lanky but not awkward, with short, dark hair and what looked like light-brown eyes. He was wearing a pair of navy jeans and a white button-down shirt and, unlike Stephen, he seemed to have avoided getting even the merest spot of blood on his clothing.

"This must be Rhes and Sarah," he said as he came to stand beside.

"Yup!" Two said.

The vampire regarded them for a moment with a calm curiosity, smiling slightly. Rhes thought he seemed familiar but couldn't identify him immediately.

"Two has told me much about you. Mrs. Thompson – Sarah – I heard you yelling earlier, and I must apologize. This situation is as much my fault as it is hers."

"Don't be ridiculous," Two said.

"If I had been around—"

"You were dead. It's not your fault."

Sarah held up a hand. "Dead? Wait, who is ... are you ... you can't be who I think you are, right?"

"My name is Theroen Anders," the vampire said. "I don't know if that's who you think I am, but I'm very pleased to meet you both."

"You aren't dead?" asked Rhes, shaking Theroen's hand.

"Not anymore," Two said.

"You want to explain that?" Sarah asked. "I mean, I know you guys are different than us, but I had the impression that dead was dead, whether you're a human or a vampire."

"It is, for the most part," Theroen said. "Especially if the body is burned or chopped apart. If it's intact, and the remaining blood within is powerful enough, the body doesn't decay immediately. It's sort of like suspended animation."

"OK, and so Two brought you back?"

"Like I said, it's a long story," Two told her. "This is kind of a once-in-five-thousand-years thing. There was some blood from a couple of ancients, and then the injecting and such, and—"

"Jeeeeesus Christ," Sarah said, cutting her off. "That's great. That's all super great ... can we get out of here? I want to find Molly, go home, drink about three bottles of wine, and sleep in my own bed ... assuming we're safe from Aros and his nutcase friends."

"I believe Peter and Kanene are going to take you home," Theroen said. "At least, that was the plan we were formulating a few minutes ago. I'm sure you can stop at Sasha's apartment and pick up your daughter."

"Where are the rest of you going?" Sarah asked.

"We've a bone to pick with Aros," Jakob told her, as he and the rest of the vampires joined them. Two quickly introduced them all to her friends, and Rhes and Sarah found themselves shaking hand after hand. At last, Jakob continued. "We're going to go find Aros. You're going to go home."

"Are you going to kill him?" Rhes asked.

"We're hoping to avoid it," the vampire girl with the brown hair, Sasha, said."Don't try too hard," Sarah muttered. "Two, why can't you and Theroen take us home? No offense to your friends, it's just ... you know ..."

"You know me, I understand," Two said. "But I can't go yet. The whole reason all of this is happening is because of me. Aros wants me, for some reason, and he's not going to be satisfied until I at least explain to him that whatever he thought he was going to get from me, it's not happening."

"He wants your blood," Jakob said.

Two paused, considering this, eyebrows raised. Finally, she shrugged. "Yeah ... not happening."

"Why does he want her blood?" Theroen asked.

"He believes he can merge his blood with her formerly *Eresh-Chen* blood, within himself, in order to create some new race of vampire. Supposedly, Abraham gave him the secrets to do it in exchange for this Burilgi army he's been building."

"Abraham was almost certainly lying to him," Theroen said.

Jakob gave him a wry grin. "That's exactly what I told him, but he wasn't terribly receptive to the idea."

"He's out of his mind," Sarah said, "and you should stay far away from him, Two. He's not just looking for a little drink or something. He wants *all* of your blood. Also, I'm not sure how many you are – I think I counted eight – but he's got like a hundred guys or more up there on that base."

"There will be seven of us, when Peter and Kanene have left," Sasha said. "That should suffice, especially if … well, we believe we can get most of Aros's guards to stand down."

"That'd be an accomplishment," Sarah said.

"Excuse me," Rhes interjected. "Your name is Sasha, right? Are you the one that helped Molly?"

"Yes, I am. Your daughter helped *me,* as well. It was through her connections that we found this place."

"Thank you for taking care of her," Sarah said. "Is she all right? We were very worried after the attack the other night."

"She is just fine," Sasha said, smiling. "She wanted to come along on this little adventure, but we thought it best that she stay home."

"Yes, thank you, we don't want her anywhere near here," Rhes said.

"What connections were you talking about?" Two asked Sasha.

"She took me to see Jerry, a 'fixer' who lives—"

"Oh, Jesus, you had to go see *that* motherfucker?!" Two exclaimed. "I am so sorry. No one should have to deal with that disgusting pedophile asshole, especially not Molly."

"It was an unpleasant experience," Sasha agreed. "Molly did very well, and it proved useful. If not for her connection to Jerry, we wouldn't be here right now."

"And we'd be dead," Sarah said. "We're not, so I guess I can accept that Molly had to go through some tough times for that."

"All's well that ends well," Jakob said. "So let's end this well. Rhes and Sarah, I believe we can all agree that getting the two of you far, far away from here is an excellent idea. Peter and Kanene are people I would trust with my life, and they will be happy to take you home."

"There's no way we can convince you to stay away from Aros, is there?" Sarah asked Two, who shook her head.

"I'll be fine," she said. "Seriously, guys, get out of here. Go get Molly and go home, and I promise I'll visit soon and start figuring out how I can make all of this up to you."

"We'll have you under guard until we're sure that Aros is no further danger," Jakob said.

Sarah sighed, nodded, took Rhes's hand in her own. "OK," she said. "Yeah. I want my life back. I want to get home before Rhes's vacation time ends and he gets fired. I want to hug my daughter. Let's do this."

Peter and his apprentice Kanene took a few moments to say goodbye to the rest of the group, shaking hands and wishing them good luck. Rhes and Sarah said goodbye to Two and turned to Jakob.

"I am very glad you made it through this," he said.

"Us, too," Rhes said. He shook Jakob's hand, and Sarah hugged him.

"Don't get yourself shot up anymore," Sarah told him. The vampire grinned.

"Not planning on it. Rhes, Sarah, take care of yourselves."

Rhes and Sarah nodded, waved once more to the group, and took their leave with Peter and Kanene. Soon they were gone, and the seven remaining vampires began to make their way back through the tunnels toward Aros's complex.

* * *

"This is where it gets difficult," Jakob said. They were standing at the end of a hallway, just past the room where he had fought with The Rat and The Dunce, looking at the doorway that led to the staircase.

"Why's that?" Two asked him.

"By now Aros must be aware that something has gone wrong, since his Burilgi haven't returned with my corpse, nor those of your friends. I suspect he will have gathered the rest of his people to him and will be anticipating some sort of attack. Also, I can only guess as to where in the compound he might be found."

"I may be able to help with that," Ashayt said. She was standing behind the rest of the group, looking both sad and serene at the same time. "If a large group is together, I should be able to sense it from a distance."

"Thank you, my lady," Jakob said.

Two noted the breathless awe still in his voice and was amused by it. *I'm never going to get tired of introducing her to new people,* she thought. *It's like touring Jesus around the Bible Belt.*

With Jakob leading the way and Sasha close behind, they began to ascend the staircase. They had met no resistance since wiping out the Burilgi troops in the warehouse, and they emerged from the stairwell into a dark and empty office building. This seemed to confirm Jakob's suspicions that Aros had drawn the rest of his people close.

"I feel something to our left," Ashayt murmured as they descended toward the building's front door.

"There is a rather large building in that direction," Jakob said. "I think it was a garage once. Perhaps they've gathered there."

"We just gonna ... you know, bust in on them?" Two asked.

"I would strongly prefer a diplomatic approach," Naomi said. She had spoken little on the trip so far, and Two wondered if perhaps she was regretting coming on an expedition that had already involved so much violence.

"If his guards will let us walk in without a fight, I am happy to do so," Jakob said. "But, Naomi, I wouldn't get your hopes up. Aros has been preparing for this day for a long time, and he will have surrounded himself with his most loyal soldiers."

"If we have to fight, then I will fight with you," Naomi said. "Forgive me if I hope for the best."

"No one here is hoping to fight—" Jakob began, but Stephen interrupted him.

"I am."

"No one here who is sane," Jakob continued, rolling his eyes, "is hoping to fight. I don't begrudge you your optimism, Naomi."

"Is your side OK, Jakob?" Two asked him.

"There's a bullet stuck in one of my ribs ... so it's been better, but the bleeding stops whenever I'm not fighting, so I think it will be fine," Jakob replied.

They were making their way across the open courtyard, not trying to hide. There were no other vampires in sight, even in the places where Jakob would otherwise have expected guards. However, they could hear the rumbling of a crowd from the building ahead of them.

"Sounds like a lot of people," Two said.

"Hopefully fewer than the thousands he could raise if given the time, but we're about to find out," Jakob said. He pushed on the large set of double doors and strode into the building, the rest of the group following behind him. A crowd of Burilgi vampires immediately swarmed around them.

"Let them pass!" a voice roared over the general rumble of the crowd, and slowly the mob of surly, angry-looking vampires gave way, forming a sort of corridor that lead to the far end of the large room. Two was not sure exactly how many Burilgi they were facing but thought that three hundred might be a reasonable estimate. There was no possible way that they could fight all of these people and win.

It'd really suck if we just walked into a deathtrap, she thought with a scowl.

The rest of her companions, with the notable exception of Stephen, looked equally concerned. Even Ashayt, who rarely appeared to be in any state other than "serene," was frowning. She moved up to join Jakob at the head of the group, and they began to make their way through the crowd of staring, grumbling vampires that encircled them. At last, the group reached the end of the room, where a blonde-haired, delicate-looking vampire was sitting on a leather couch, doing his best to look nonchalant.

"So you're still alive, Jakob," the vampire commented as they arrived. He stood up, arms crossed, watching them as they made their way forward.

"Surprised, Aros?" Jakob asked him.

So this is the one who wants my blood, Two thought, observing him. He was not what she'd expected; the vampire looked like he'd be more at home wearing an expensive outfit, sipping on luxury vodka, entertaining women in a chic Manhattan nightclub. If Two hadn't been surrounded by members of the man's army, she wouldn't have believed him capable of raising one.

Aros shrugged. "I expected you to fight off the execution squad, but I must admit I'd thought that the group you met underground would have been enough to finish you off and bring the humans back to me. It seems your friends arrived in the nick of time. Is this really all that the council could muster?"

"It's all that they felt was necessary," Jakob said.

"They underestimated."

Ashayt spoke up. "We are not here to fight," she said. Two could feel her aura once again radiating off of her in waves, and could see in the faces of the Burilgi nearest to them that it was having an effect. Most seemed fascinated by her. Aros, however, seemed to be unaffected. He glanced at the elder vampire, raising his eyebrows, and turned back to Jakob.

"Who is this woman? You can tell her that her transparent efforts to mesmerize me are wasted."

"You know who this is," Jakob told him. "You've read the scrolls."

Aros looked again at Ashayt, and Two saw the jolt of recognition run through him, as it had through so many of the older vampires that Ashayt had met. For a moment, just one small instant before he recovered, Aros's expression betrayed him, and Two saw in it a look of hopeless, helpless fear. Then it was gone, and the casual, arrogant look returned.

"So you've dug up an *Ovras*. How marvelous for you. Hoping to cow me into submission? It won't work. I spent hundreds of years living by the laws of the scrolls, and it brought me nothing of value. I hold no respect for them or for the elders who wrote them."

"I am not here to command your respect," Ashayt said. "I seek only the chance to advise, to—"

"Save it, *my lady*," Aros snarled. "I've no interest in the senile ramblings of a long-lost ancient."

Naomi spoke up at this. "Aros, please, be reasonable."

Aros looked over at her, unimpressed. "Naomi Ames, isn't it? Yes ... I remember you. Weak and servile, enamored with the political games of the council, prone to whoring around with humans ... Why should I be reasonable, Naomi Ames? I have more than enough people here to tear you all to shreds, *Ovras* or no. Do you have something to offer me in return for being reasonable, or are you simply trying to appeal to the good nature that you've surely been informed I do not possess?"

"We're not here to bargain," Jakob told him.

"Then what are you here *for?!*" Aros cried. "Why are you here wasting my time, when you should have died or fled with the humans to huddle in the darkness, awaiting the inevitable?"

Two took a step forward and made her way to Jakob's side.

"I'm here to find out why you kidnapped my friends," she said. "Let's start with that. You wanted me, so here I am. What was the point?"

Aros's eyes narrowed. "Who are you?"

"I'm Two Majors."

"Don't waste my time with your lies," Aros said. "You cannot be the *Eresh-Chen.*"

"Why not?" Two asked.

"Because you're a *vampire*, idiot," Aros snarled. "The *Eresh-Chen* is a human. My informants in Europe know that she was turned away by the council there."

"I was," Two said. "They turned me away and sent me to Ashayt. She gave me what I needed."

"I don't know whether to be insulted or amused," Aros said. "That woman is thousands of years too old to make fledglings. You are not her daughter."

"Not hers," said Theroen, and he too made his way to stand next to Two, Jakob, and Ashayt. "Mine."

Aros stared at him for a moment before saying, "I know you ..."

Theroen nodded. "Yes. We've met once before, though I didn't know it until I saw you just now."

Aros looked taken aback. "This can't be! I ... you can't be alive."

"I can't be, but I am. Shall I prove it was me?" Theroen asked. "It was a night in early summer, perhaps ten years ago. You came to meet with Abraham, a *tête-à-tête* that didn't include me, but I let you and your companions in. I also cleaned up the mess after one of your men went wandering, against my recommendation, and Tori ripped him to pieces."

"Zachary. She killed my fledgling Zachary," Aros said, his voice barely audible, an expression of shock on his face. "No. How is this possible? You are supposed to be dead, like your father. That line was ended."

"I have returned by the grace of the lady Ashayt. Her blood and the blood of Ay'Araf have combined within me to make something new. I am no longer *Eresh-Chen*. I am *Theroen-Sa*, and I have made Two *Theroen-Chen*."

Aros had gone pale, even for a vampire. His hands were balled into tight fists at his sides, and his eyes had taken on a wide, glassy, manic look that Two did not like at all. He turned slowly, looking first at Jakob, then at Ashayt, then back at Jakob.

"Is it true?" he asked, in voice strained and barely above a whisper. Jakob nodded.

"This is Theroen Anders, son of Abraham, brought back from the dead by the grace of the lady Ashayt."

"She gave him the blood," Aros murmured, and then uttered his shrieky, disquieting laugh. He turned to glare at Ashayt. "You gave *him* the blood!"

"I did," Ashayt said.

Aros spoke again, his voice rising, becoming a shout. "I have spent seven hundred years waiting to escape the curse of my blood. Abraham promised it. He swore that he would give me that which I needed to be reborn. He promised it to *me*, and you have given it to this *worthless corpse!*"

"It was never his to give—" Ashayt began, and Aros again cut her off.

"Witch!" he screamed. "You foul ... you evil, black, rotten *thing!* You've taken what is rightfully mine and thrown it away!"

"It wouldn't have worked, Aros," Jakob said. "I tried to tell you that. Two's blood would have done nothing for you, nor would the blood that Ashayt gave to Theroen. Abraham lied to you, like he lied to everyone. You made him an army, and now in return you have exactly what he would have given: nothing."

Aros had put his hands over his face, and now his shoulders slumped. For a moment, Two thought that it had ended, that the Burilgi lord would simply give up and come quietly with them to face his trial. She felt almost bad for him. She knew what it was like to want something with every fiber of one's being, only to have it denied.

Then Aros straightened, removed his hands from his face, and looked out at them with eyes ablaze with hatred, and rage, and madness.

"I will have what is mine!" he roared. "Kill them! Kill them all, and bring me each of their hearts!"

"Children ... wait!" Ashayt cried as the crowd of Burilgi soldiers surged forward. She held her hands up, and Two felt her aura surge outward, washing over them in all of its power. The soldiers closest to her faltered, coming to a halt, staring at the elder vampire in surprise and fear. Those behind them came to a stop as well. Somewhere in the background, Aros was still howling, ranting at his men to ignore the witch and murder Two and her companions.

"It does not have to be this way," Ashayt said, and her voice now came to Two as it had before in Silifke, both as a sound her ears could perceive and as something more, something that seemed to originate within her mind. The force of it nearly brought Two to her knees as Ashayt continued to speak.

"I know that your lives have been hard," the elder vampire said to the crowd. "I know that for too long the American council has ignored your wants and needs, your trials, your rights. Know this: the American council is no longer the tool of Abraham, bent at every turn to his evil ways. The change has already begun, and at last you will have your time.

"Children, each and every one of you is free. Aros does not own you. He does not control you. You can choose to put down your weapons. You can choose to leave this place, to work *with* the vampire world instead of against it. You must accept responsibility for your own actions, consider the consequences, and make your choice. If you blindly follow Aros, you can bring only war, and war can lead only to destruction.

"I have lived without taking a life, human or vampire, for four thousand years. I will not now do violence against my own people, even if it means my death, but I beg you, please, my brothers and sisters … do not do this. Put down your weapons, turn away from this place, and renounce the violence that Aros would have you do at his command."

"She lies to you!" Aros roared at them. "They will never accept you. They will never give you all of that which you deserve. Kill them now or die eventually at their hands. This is how it has always been: they hold one hand out in peace, while the other holds the sword behind their back."

Ashayt glared at him. "I speak no lies. The dictatorship of Abraham is ended, and instead of celebrating that fact, you would simply replace him. You desire equality no more than he did. It is not enough for you to be a member of vampire society, is it, Aros Kreskas? You wish to *rule* these people and to eliminate any that would stand in the way."

"I will bring them absolution. I will bring them redemption!" Aros cried.

"You will make them slaves."

Aros seemed to have no reply to this, and so they stood for a moment in quiet, each side waiting to see what the other might do. Two felt Ashayt's aura slide away, vanishing as quickly as it had come. The Burilgi soldiers began to murmur among themselves.

"Aros would command you," Ashayt told them. "I will not. I give you choice. That is the difference between us. You can leave now, and the American council will accept you without judgment. Or you can do as you're told and murder your brothers and sisters at the command of a would-be dictator."

The muttering among the Burilgi increased. Some of the soldiers stood their ground, but many more began to withdraw. Two heard the clattering noise of weapons being dropped to the ground. Someone said, "Forget this."

"Fools!" Aros hissed. "Idiots! You're signing your own death warrants. Don't think I won't remember this. I know each of you. I will remember!"

The Burilgi ranks were thinning as many of them made for the exits, abandoning Aros and their fellow soldiers. It took only a few minutes before what had been a group of more than three hundred became one of less than fifty. Aros looked around at the men and women who still obeyed him and gave Ashayt a thin smile.

"Very well," he said. "You've cowed the lesser of my people into abandoning me, but there are those here who remain true, my best and strongest who have been with me for so long. Will you plead with them some more, *Mother Ashayt?*"

"I have offered my choice," Ashayt said. "There is no more that I can say. But you, child, can still make your own decision. You can choose to turn back from this path."

"Aros," Jakob said. "The lady is right. There is no need for further violence this night."

Aros turned and looked at Jakob with an expression of disgust and hatred. The two stared at each other for a moment, unspeaking, and then Aros grinned, and the strange, mad light returned to his eyes.

"I want each of their heads laid at my feet," he said. "Save the witch for last. I want to see if she'll really die without a fight."

With this, Aros turned his back on the group and walked to his couch. His soldiers, needing no further exhortation, roared as one, and charged.

A few of the Burilgi had guns, but none were firing, perhaps afraid that they might hit their companions on the opposing side of the circle. Some had blades, and others seemed prepared to attack simply with claws and teeth. They were moving quickly, leaving Two and her companions little time to plan. Two's group had not come unprepared to fight, however, and they braced now for the impact of this oncoming force. Each had a long, machete-like blade, even Ashayt, though hers remained hanging at her side.

"Oh, damn it," Naomi swore, holding her own blade aloft. She looked determined but also terrified, and Two didn't blame her.

There were only three experienced fighters among them. The rest of them would have to rely on luck and natural ability.

Stephen, who was holding not one but two blades, looked back over his shoulder. "Stay loose, remember what you've been taught," he shouted at Naomi and Two, and then there was no further time. The first of the Burilgi soldiers, a shrieking harpy of a woman with what looked like open sores all over her face and arms, was upon him. Stephen spun in a pretty movement that looked almost like dancing and severed her head with a single swing of one blade.

Naomi, Theroen, and Two were quickly separated from the rest of the group. Ashayt, faster than any vampire among them, was using her talents to avoid conflict, expertly dodging away from attackers, always moving, leading them around and around the large garage. Stephen, Sasha, and Jakob had disappeared into the crowd, tearing apart the less-experienced Burilgi soldiers and, like Ashayt, moving constantly to avoid being overwhelmed or targeted and shot.

"This is not how I wanted to spend the night," Two snarled, swinging her blade at a vampire, who easily avoided her blow by jumping backwards. This brought him close to Naomi, and she took the opportunity to stab him in the side. He screamed and lurched away into the crowd, blood jetting from his wound.

"I shouldn't have come," Naomi said with distaste. "I hate this."

Two wanted to speak some words of encouragement, but before she could, they were separated by another wave of Burilgi soldiers. She found herself next to Theroen. He was faring well, his strikes finding their mark again and again, the Burilgi falling at his feet, dead or howling in pain.

"Get away from me!" Two heard Naomi scream, and looked to see her friend surrounded by four soldiers, each holding a blade. Naomi spun in circles trying to parry their probing blows. Two reached behind her back and drew from her waistband an old friend, the GLOCK that she had taken from Darren two years ago. She pointed it at one of Naomi's attackers, who turned to face her.

"I don't want to shoot you," she told the Burilgi, a deformed, barely human-looking thing with long arms and legs like a spider's.

"So don't," the creature chortled, and it advanced on her, waving what looked like a hatchet. Two leveled the gun at him and pulled the trigger, firing the first shot of the battle. The bullet punched in the right half of the Burilgi's face and he pitched forward, falling to the ground in a heap.

Two spun and targeted another of the vampires that had surrounded Naomi. Without further warning, she fired again, hitting this one in the shoulder. He fled into the crowd, snarling and cursing. Theroen came up behind another of Naomi's attackers, a tall woman with flaming red hair, and split the back of her skull with his blade. Jets of her blood sprayed out on either side of the weapon, and her entire body went rigid before dropping to the ground. Theroen, with an expression of slight sadness on his face, stepped on her neck for leverage as he removed the machete from her skull.

Naomi had a large cut on her arm, where one of the Burilgi's blades had nicked her, but was otherwise unharmed. The last of the four who had surrounded Naomi charged her, shrieking and swinging his claws. Naomi ducked neatly below them and stabbed him in the belly, pulling away as the soldier fell to the ground. Two and Theroen moved to stand by her side.

"Thank you," Naomi said. "I can handle one or two at a time, but four was asking a bit much."

"Glad to help," said Theroen.

Two nodded. She glanced around, surveying the scene. The Burilgi numbers were thinning, but those who were left seemed almost as talented with their weapons as the three Ay'Araf vampires. Stephen was fighting two at once, one with each hand, and Jakob was still managing to hold his own despite the wound in his side.

Two heard a scream of pain and turned her head to see Sasha staggering away from a muscular black woman who was carrying something that looked like a medieval broadsword. Sasha had a large gash in her belly, and Two thought that she had probably been lucky to escape disembowelment. The Burilgi woman roared in triumph, leaping forward, and Sasha instinctively held her left arm up to ward off the blow. In another instant most of the arm was gone, and a ragged stump, severed above the elbow, was jetting blood onto the concrete floor. Sasha fell to her knees.

"Leave her alone!" Two shouted, running toward the Burilgi and firing her gun wildly. None of her shots hit home, but they were enough to make the woman back off, snarling and turning her face away. Two reached Sasha and grabbed the Ay'Araf girl's good arm, tugging her to her feet.

"We have to get that wrapped up or you're going to bleed to death," she said to Sasha, who made a groggy noise of acknowledgment.

Two heard Theroen shout her name and turned in time to see a blade descending toward her head. The soldier who had cut off Sasha's arm had caught up with Two, and if Theroen's call had been any later, she would have ended up dead on the concrete. Instead, she pulled herself backward, falling over and landing on top of Sasha, who cried out in pain.

The blow missed her by less than six inches. Two watched as Theroen, enraged, buried one hand in the woman's curly black hair and jerked, exposing her neck and running the length of his blade along it. The soldier's throat opened like a floodgate and crimson blood poured forth, splashing all over Two and Sasha. Theroen hurled the woman's corpse aside.

In a moment more Theroen was kneeling down, asking if she was all right, and it was Two's chance to scream out a warning, one that she knew even as she began would come too late. Behind Theroen's kneeling form, Aros had suddenly appeared, his right arm raised above his head, hand holding a large dagger, eyes filled with glee and malice and rage. He was going to stab Theroen to death right in front of her and there was nothing she could do about it.

Aros swung the blade downward, but at the last second, another hand caught his wrist and held him, stopping the blow that had been aimed at the back of Theroen's neck.

"No yeh *don't!*" Stephen screamed, twisting his hand, and Two heard the bones in Aros's wrist crack and break. Aros shrieked in pain and the dagger fell from his hand, bouncing off Theroen's shoulder and clattering to the floor. Stephen grabbed Aros's collar with his left hand and dragged the vampire up, pulling his face in close.

"Shoulda done this a long time ago," he growled, letting go of Aros's broken wrist and reaching for one of the blades that hung at his side.

"Keep waiting," Aros hissed, and brought his left hand up. In it was another dagger, and he drove it into Stephen's breastplate, just to the left of center. There was another cracking noise as the blade passed through bone, and Stephen's eyes went wide. He made a strangled noise and released Aros, falling backward to the floor.

Naomi shrieked and ran toward the pair. She fell to her knees as she reached Stephen, skidding and tearing the fabric of her jeans on the rough floor. Aros backpedaled, grinning wildly and cackling his insane laughter. Not looking over his shoulder, he ran directly into Jakob, who grabbed Aros's good arm and whipped the vampire around, slamming him against the sheet-metal wall.

"Aros Kreskas," Jakob said, "this council finds you guilty."

He brought the gun he had stolen from Aros's guard earlier that evening up underneath Aros's jaw, pressing into the soft skin there. He pulled the trigger twice in rapid succession, and Two watched from her position on the floor as the top of Aros's head blew out, jetting its contents upward in a chunky red spray. Aros's eyes went wide and glassy then rolled upward, and his body went slack. Jakob watched for a moment longer, as if to confirm that Aros was really dead, and then threw the body to the floor.

* * *

For the moment, it seemed that there was peace. Two could hear no noise but the sound of Naomi's sobs and some low murmur of comfort from Ashayt. She could feel Sasha struggling underneath her, and Two realized after a moment that the Ay'Araf woman was actually trying to remove her own belt, presumably to use as a tourniquet. Two rolled off of her and began to help. Theroen knelt down next to her as Jakob moved toward Stephen's prone form.

"The last of the Burilgi are fleeing," Theroen told her. "Are you all right?"

"Fucking peachy," Two said, pulling the belt around Sasha's left bicep. "Worry about the girl who's missing an arm."

"Wrap it through twice and ... yes ... cinch it tight," Sasha hissed through clenched teeth. "Ah, good Jesus that hurts."

"Are you going to be all right?" Two asked her. "I mean, are you ... you're not going to ..."

"No, I'm not going to die," Sasha said, her voice hoarse. She struggled to a sitting position. "So long as I don't bleed out, the wound will scab over eventually. Give me ... tear that dead Burilgi's shirt off and give me the fabric."

Two did as she was instructed, handing the torn shirt to Sasha, who pressed the fabric firmly into the stump of her left arm and held it there, hissing in pain as she did so.

"Jesus Christ," said Two, staring wide-eyed.

Naomi's voice came to them from a few meters away, tightened with fear and grief. "Stephen, don't! Stay with me!"

Sasha held out her right elbow, indicating that she wanted to stand up. Theroen helped her to her feet, and she leaned against him for support. Along with Two, they made their way over to the rest of the vampires. Jakob glanced up at them, saw the state that his fledgling was in, and moved to help Sasha stand, freeing Theroen to come up next to Two.

"Oh, God," Naomi was moaning. "Oh, God. Oh, no. Please ..."

Two looked down at the sight before her and felt tears immediately well up in her eyes. Stephen was lying in a pool of his own blood, looking pale and haggard, barely breathing. The hilt of the dagger Aros had stabbed him with was protruding from his chest, quivering there in a way that seemed almost obscene. With an obvious effort, Stephen reached up and put his hand against Naomi's lips, quieting her. He shook his head.

"Don't," he said in a wheezing voice. "Be strong."

"I can't. I'm not!" Naomi cried. She was kneeling next to him, weeping so hard that the force of it was like physical blows pounding at her body. Her pink tears dripped down onto his blood-spattered shirt.

Stephen laughed, coughed, and a trickle of blood made its way down the side of his face. "Yes, you are," he said.

"I can't lose you," Naomi whispered, pressing her lips to his knuckles.

Stephen stared at her for a moment, his breathing growing more shallow with each intake of air, and Two knew that her friend had only moments left in his life.

"August ... eighteenth. Nineteen-seventy," Stephen said, and Naomi opened her eyes, looked down at him.

"Yes," she said. "I remember. But you wouldn't—"

"There was only ever you. Only you."

Naomi sobbed. Pressed her lips to his hand again. "Oh ... Stephen. Please."

"Let me go," Stephen said, his voice now barely a whisper. His eyes were far away. "Be strong. Let me go."

Naomi made a wailing noise of despair, but she did as he had asked, placing his hand gently on his chest, away from the dagger. Stephen stared up at the ceiling and took a final breath, deeper than those that had come just before it.

"It was a good fight," he said to no one in particular, and he smiled. With those words, he exhaled, and the exhalation became long and rattling. Surrounded by his friends, lying victorious on the field of battle, Stephen Connelly died.

Naomi put her face in her hands and gave in to her grief completely, sobbing. Two wanted to reach out to her, wanted to offer some comfort, but knew that she could give none. Weeping herself, she closed her eyes and bowed her head. She felt Theroen move away from her side and looked up to see him bending down to put a hand on Naomi's shoulder.

"Naomi—" he began, his voice quiet and comforting, but the vampire girl whirled on him, throwing his hand from her shoulder.

"Get away from me!" she snarled, her face distorted in rage and hatred. She stood, turning fully to face him.

"I don't—" Theroen began, but Naomi cut him off again.

"What else do you want?" she cried. "What else can you *take*?! First Lisette, then Two, now Stephen ... I have nothing left for you! You've taken it all, so leave me alone. Leave me *alone!*"

This last was a shriek, and Naomi shoved Theroen in the chest, pushing him backward. She whirled away from him again and stormed off to the edge of the room, where she leaned against the wall, covering her face with her hands and sinking to a sitting position, knees drawn up against her chest.

There was a moment of surprised silence among the remaining companions. Two sighed, held up her hand to indicate that the others should wait, and made her way over to her former lover.

"That wasn't very fair," she said in a gentle voice, and Naomi glared up at her.

"Oh, here she is to talk about what's fair," Naomi said in a caustic tone. "You want me to say I'm sorry, is that it? You're here to demand that I apologize to your lover because I hurt his feelings? Go away, Two. Go hold poor Theroen and tell him that it's all right, that everything will be *just fine!*"

Two was quiet for a moment, watching as Naomi went back to staring at her lap. Finally she said, "Naomi, what do you want from me?"

Naomi looked up again, rage and grief naked on her face, her mouth twisted up into something that looked almost like a grin.

"I want you to *love* me! I want you to tell me that it meant something to you, the time we spent together, the times when we fell asleep holding each other, the times when I put my face in your cunt and made you come. I want you to tell me that you weren't just using me this whole time, treating me like a toy, something to be tossed to the curb as soon as your real lover returned.

"I want that, but I can't have it, can I? You never loved me. You never said *those* words. You made it perfectly clear that I was a stopgap, a holdover solution, an answer to a problem and nothing more. Once you had what you wanted from me you were going to leave anyway, weren't you? Wasn't that the plan all along? Pretend that you wanted to be with me until I gave you the blood? So, fine. You have what you want. Go away. Go back to *him* and leave me where you already left me. Leave me alone!"

Two stood for a moment longer, trying to think of some response, something she could say that would take away Naomi's pain and make her understand that Two hadn't wanted any of this. She could think of nothing and so, at last, she turned and made her way back to the rest of the group.

"There's nothing more to do here," she said to them as she walked up, "and there's nothing any of us can do for her. Let's just … be done with this. Let's go home."

CHAPTER XXX

Healing Up

"Blood or no blood, that arm isn't going to grow back," William said, glancing toward the table at the back of the cathedral. Sasha was there, collapsed in a chair, alternating sips from a large glass filled with blood and another filled with vodka. A vampire surgeon that Two didn't know was stitching the flap of skin that had once covered her elbow over her wound, and Jakob was watching from behind him, peering over his shoulder. If Sasha was feeling any pain, she wasn't showing it, but Two could see the dark circles under the Ay'Araf woman's eyes from all the way across the room.

"She's got a pretty good cut on her stomach, too," Two said. "I think she's lucky to be alive."

"How nice for her," Naomi commented under her breath. William glanced at her with an expression of pity but chose not to comment.

They were sitting in a rough semi-circle, the five of them: Two, Theroen, Naomi, Ashayt, and William. With the exception of Jakob, Sasha, and the surgeon, the cathedral was otherwise empty of living beings. Stephen's body lay nearby, carefully placed on one of the church pews, wrapped in a blanket.

William had received a phone call from Peter Markham, confirming that Rhes and Sarah had been reunited with their daughter and that the trio had been delivered safely home. They would remain under guard until Jakob decided otherwise, but with

Aros dead and the Burilgi army scattered, it seemed unlikely that they would fall under any further threat.

Two looked around at her friends. Ashayt was the only member of the strike force who had managed to avoid looking like something out of a horror show. Two was drenched in the blood of the vampire whose throat Theroen had cut, now dried to a tacky, sticky mess. Naomi's arm was soaked in her own blood, and most of the rest of her was covered in Stephen's. Even Theroen, who had managed to avoid getting his clothes dirty in the first battle of the evening, was covered in stains, a testament to the number of Burilgi he had killed.

"Jesus Christ, what a fucking night," Two said with a sigh. She felt exhausted, too tired even to properly grieve for the loss of her friend. She knew that the reality of Stephen's death would hit her at some point, swamp her, leave her huddled up and sobbing somewhere. She wasn't looking forward to it.

"Terrible things have happened," Ashayt said, her voice quiet and calm and sad. "It grieves me to see violence done between vampires, and more yet to lose so brave a warrior. Stephen will be missed."

Naomi made a noise that sounded like a sob but seemed to force her tears away. She was staring at the floor, hands in her lap, her mussed and bedraggled hair hiding her face from view. Two wanted to take her hand but didn't dare. Instead she glanced again at the rear of the cathedral. Sasha had left with the surgeon, presumably to go home and rest, and Jakob was making his way down the aisle toward where the others sat. Part of his shirt had been cut away, and there were bandages where the bullet had hit him.

"At least she's right-handed," he said as he sat down with them. His voice carried little humor.

"I should have sent a larger force," William said to no one in particular.

"Maybe," Two replied. "I doubt it would've changed things. You could've sent two hundred people, and none of them would have been able to stop what happened to Stephen. He was too close to Aros, and it happened too fast."

"But Sasha—" William began, and Naomi cut him off, speaking without looking up.

"Sasha knew the risks. A big rescue party would just have set off the alarms before we saved Jakob, and then he and the humans would be dead. If you hadn't convened the emergency meeting, Sasha would have gone off to find Jakob on her own and gotten herself killed. This was the best way to do it. She knew what she was getting into, and so did Stephen."

Naomi looked up at them now and smiled an ugly-looking smile. Her eyes were bloodshot, and her tears had cut clean tracks through the dirt and blood on her face.

"Our indestructible *Eresh-Chen* survived, though, and so did her friends," she said. "I hope it was all worth it."

Two, unable to meet Naomi's gaze, looked away, shaking her head. "I know that I'm responsible for this."

"Two—" Theroen began.

"No, Theroen … in the end, it all comes back to me. That's the truth. I killed Abraham. I came looking for more vampires. I dragged Rhes and Sarah into this. I was the one Aros wanted. I insisted on coming on the rescue mission even though I'm not trained to fight. I was the one who you were trying to save when Aros got the drop on you, which is why Stephen had to save *you*, which is why he's dead."

She looked back at the group now, and she could feel tears at her eyes again. "That's all of it, right? Did I miss anything? Naomi?"

Naomi didn't respond. She was staring at her lap again.

"I fucked up everyone's lives. Rhes, Sarah, Molly, Naomi, Stephen, Sasha, Jakob … thank God Tori's in Ohio."

This statement was met neither with agreement nor denial, but rather with an odd silence. Two glanced around in surprise, noting that Jakob and Naomi in particular seemed unwilling to meet her gaze. After a moment, Theroen spoke.

"Naomi … what have you done?"

"Oh, Theroen, no!" Naomi cried in a miserable voice, and covered her face with her hands. She began to sob again.

"Naomi? Nao—Jakob, what the hell is going on?" Two asked. "What haven't you told me?"

Jakob took a deep breath and looked up at Two. "Around the time that you found Naomi and became involved with the council, Tori's parents were found murdered in their kitchen."

"What?" Two asked, unable to believe what she was hearing. "Mona and Jim? That's crazy. Who would want to kill Mona and Jim?! They're, like, the two sweetest people I've ever met!"

"Someone cut their wrists, slashed their throats, and left their bodies. The daughter – Tori – she reported discovering them the next morning. She had an alibi, but it certainly seems like the work of a vampire."

"Oh, Jesus," Two moaned. "Do you ... are you saying she did it? Are you trying to tell me that she killed her own parents?"

"No. We don't believe she did it," William said.

"Who then? The Burilgi? Did Aros kill them, too?" Two could feel rage and hatred rising within her, feelings so strong they seemed almost to tint her vision red. She tried to force herself to stay calm.

"That's one possibility," Jakob said. "But I think that if Aros had known where Tori was, he would likely have had her abducted for her blood."

"Haven't you tried to find out?"

"We made inquiries, but nothing came of it. Whoever was responsible, they didn't leave a shred of physical evidence. We were keeping an eye on Tori, hoping that the guilty party would return for her, but we lost her."

"What do you mean you 'lost' her!?"

Jakob sighed. "She disappeared shortly after you met Naomi. Our scouts lost track of her. She left a motel room one morning and never came back."

Two found herself speechless, flabbergasted by this news. They had known about this since before she had ever met with the council, before she had agreed to go to Europe, and they had told her nothing.

Theroen, who had remained silent the entire time, seemed to sense Two's growing fury. He put his hand on her shoulder, but she knocked it away.

"How could you keep it from me?!" she cried. "Naomi ... how *could* you?!"

"You would've run!" Naomi shouted back, still crying, her face contorted with grief and pain. "You would have run to Ohio, and we would have had to follow. We didn't even know where she'd gone at that point!"

"And you know now?" Two asked.

"A person fitting her description has been leading the groups that are abducting Burilgi," Jakob told her. "That's the entire reason that Aros was mobilizing his army. We believe the Children of the Sun are responsible, and we believe that he was going to strike at them directly."

Two ran a shaky hand through her hair, trying to retain some level of composure. "You fucking bastards. She's my friend. She's ... do you have any idea what she went through with me? *For* me?!"

"We agreed as a council that it should be kept from you," Jakob said. "It was not solely Naomi's decision, nor mine. It was put to a vote, and it passed. Unanimously. We had no idea where she had gone. Two, if you want my apologies, you have them. If I knew then what I know now, we might have done things differently. We were trying to protect you."

Two covered her face with her hands, forced herself to breathe. Forced herself to think. *Be calm,* she told herself. *Be calm and do the right thing. For once in your stupid life, try not to make things worse than they already are.*

"What can I do to help her?" she asked at last.

"You can start by treating us as your friends," Jakob said. "The council wants nothing more than to find Tori and stop her from continuing down this path. It's going to be difficult. We've been studying the Children of the Sun for decades, and we don't even know where their center of power is. They're extremely secretive, and they've taken Tori to somewhere unknown."

"So it would be pointless to go to Ohio," Two said.

"Pointless *and* stupid," Naomi muttered. William glanced over at her again, shaking his head.

"This is a poor time to discuss this," he said.

"It's a poor time for anything," Jakob agreed. "If we weren't all drenched in blood, I'd have already insisted that we break up this delightful gathering and go home. We need sleep, so that tomorrow we can do Stephen the courtesy of organizing the funeral he deserves. My men will be here with new clothing very soon."

"Fine," Two said. "Yes. Stephen's funeral comes first. Then we're going to figure out how to find Tori."

"You'll have the help of the council," Jakob said. "In truth, you both should have seats. Theroen and his apprentice ..."

"I offered," William told him.

Theroen shook his head. "No. Not yet. Forgive me, but I've been held back from vampire politics for more than four hundred years. I've only been back from the grave for two *days*. I'm not ready to jump headfirst into this council."

"I'm not much better than Stephen is ... was ... at sitting around and debating," Two said.

"That's not all we do," Naomi said. The last of her tears were gone, and she seemed almost relieved, or at least less beaten-down than she had been. Two supposed a weight had been lifted from her, with the truth finally revealed.

"The invitation will remain open," William said. "You are a new strain of vampire, the two of you, and the council welcomes the participation of all strains."

"Have you returned to lead the council, then, William?" Jakob asked.

"Only until Malik returns," William said.

"What if that never happens?" Two asked.

William sighed. "If that is the case, then I will do as we all have done: that which I must. In the end, is there ever any other way?"

No one answered him, and for a time, silence descended on the group. Two picked up Theroen's hand in her own and stroked his fingers gently. She was sorry for knocking his hand away earlier and tried to make this obvious in her thoughts. If Theroen could read it he gave no indication, but she hoped that he understood.

At last, there was the sound of the cathedral's front door opening, and Jakob stood.

"My men are here with clothing," he said. "Let us all change and get on our way. I would like for this night to be over."

* * *

"She didn't mean the things that she said."

Theroen was standing at the entrance to the hotel room's bathroom, naked except for a towel tied around his waist, leaning against the door frame. Two, more thoroughly soaked in blood than he had been, had taken the first shower. Theroen was now done with his, and Two had been amused to hear him humming to himself as he brushed his teeth. She recognized the tune not as something from his long past, but rather a pop song that had been popular just two years ago.

"Who?" she asked now, glancing up at him from the bed where she had been reading. "Naomi?"

"Yes."

"Of course she did."

Theroen was silent, looking at her, waiting for her to elaborate. At last Two sighed, setting her magazine down on the bed.

"You know what Naomi learned from what happened to Lisette? She learned not to make waves. She learned to play politics, follow the rules, and not piss anyone off. It kept her alive even when she was just a fledgling with a dead master, stuck in the middle of Europe with no friends and no idea what to do next. She went to the European council, and they put her in touch with other vampires who could help her. That was how she learned to be a diplomat, and how she learned that if she didn't have something nice to say, she probably shouldn't say anything at all."

"I'm not sure how that coincides with her screaming at you," Theroen said.

"That's the point, though. Listen, Naomi couldn't admit to me that she blamed you for Lisette. Even when we were lying in bed together she said she didn't blame you, but that wasn't the truth. It took Stephen ... it took him getting killed for her walls to finally come down enough for her to tell us the truth about how she felt."

"I wish I could help ease her pain," Theroen said. "But I don't see how I can. She is right to blame me for Lisette's death."

Two shook her head. "Oh, baby, she doesn't blame you for *that*. I know you blame yourself, but it wasn't your fault. It was Lisette's fault, and Abraham's fault, and Naomi understands that. What hurt her ... what's *still* hurting her is that Lisette chose you. She made Naomi her fledgling, but she *loved* you."

"I never knew," Theroen said. His eyes were distant, and Two guessed he was going back through his memories of times long ago, searching for clues that he might have picked up as to Naomi's true feelings.

"She kept it inside," Two said. "She didn't want you to know. She was happy for the two of you! She ... it's complicated. Love is fucking complicated."

Theroen nodded.

"As for the rest of it, I mean ... is it any surprise she was upset that as soon as I heard we might be able to bring you back, it pretty much nuked our relationship? Blaming you for Stephen was unfair, but it's probably the only thing she said that she didn't mean."

"What about the things she said when you went to talk to her?" Theroen asked. Two had told him about that on their way from the Cathedral to the hotel. She had seen no sense in hiding it from him.

"What, that I'm a horrible, ungrateful, manipulative bitch who never loved her like she loved me, no matter what she did to make me happy? That's all true."

Theroen left the doorway now and sat down beside her on the bed. He took her hand, pressed his lips to it, and smiled.

"I don't think it's true," he said. "Or at least, I don't think your actions were anywhere near that intentional and malicious."

"Sometimes people can be pretty malicious without meaning to," Two said. "I ... I need to be a better person, Theroen. I need to be less selfish and impulsive. I need to make up for all the shit I've caused for so many people. I owe it to people like Melissa and Stephen. Naomi. Rhes and Sarah and Molly. I owe it to *you*. All of those people believed in me."

"We still do," Theroen said. He leaned over and kissed her. Two kissed back, broke away, closed her eyes and put her face against his neck. His skin was warm, his heart beating. He was here, real, and that fact seemed to fill her with a strength she hadn't felt in so long.

"Will you help me?" she asked him. "We're together in this now, right? You and me? Will you help me to be someone better than I am now?"

Theroen put one hand in her hair, traced the other up and down along her back, said, "I will help you to be whoever you wish to be."

"You're not going to leave me again?"

"I am not going anywhere."

Two wrapped her arms around him, clutching him to her, holding him tight. Theroen returned her embrace.

"My love," she whispered.

* * *

Members of the American council of vampires held services for Stephen on Christmas Eve. William led the event, as Malik had tendered his formal resignation from the council the previous evening. The funeral was attended by many Ay'Araf vampires, and not a few from the other races. For all his abrasive qualities, Stephen had been well-respected among the vampires of North America.

Naomi had declined the opportunity to present a eulogy, not wanting to break down in front of her fellow vampires. She was sitting in the first row, next to a man Two did not know but who looked equally devastated. Two thought the man might be Stephen's sire.

It was Jakob who delivered the principal speech of the evening, and he took the podium with an expression of deep sadness, looking out over his fellow vampires for a moment before addressing them.

"Stephen was my friend and I will miss him," he began. "I will miss his experience and his insight, his humor and his sarcasm. I will miss sparring with him, with words and with weapons. Most of all, I will miss his honesty – the knowledge that whatever his opinion of the subject at hand, I was sure to get it without filters ... of any sort."

The crowd chuckled at this. Even Naomi managed a laugh through her tears.

"It pains me so very much to have to stand here today," Jakob continued. "It pains me to acknowledge that I will never see him again, never laugh with him, never argue with him. It pains me, yet it is the least I can do for him. The very least.

"Stephen Connelly was a good man, a good fighter, and a good friend. He gave all that he could in the service of his fellow vampires. In the end, he gave the most precious thing he had to offer: his life. Today we honor him. We will not forget him, nor the sacrifice he has made so that others of us might live. Goodbye, Stephen. Goodbye, my friend."

Jakob's voice cracked on the last sentence, and he bowed his head briefly as he attempted to regain control. Eventually he made his way back to sit down next to Sasha, who looked tired and pale. Her left arm was still heavily bandaged and partially bound to her body to immobilize it. She leaned her head on Jakob's shoulder and he took her good right hand in his.

Two had started crying only a few moments after walking through the cathedral doors and had been unable to stop since. She was weeping now, holding a tissue to her eyes with one hand, the other clutching Theroen's. These were not the hard, harsh sobs of anguish that she had gotten out of the way earlier, first standing under the shower at their hotel and then kneeling, leaning against the tiled wall, her legs no longer able to support the weight of her grief. Instead, it seemed simply that her eyes would not stop leaking tears, no matter who was speaking, or what the subject was.

Two listened as William told of Stephen's many contributions to vampire society and the work he had done on behalf of the council on both sides of the ocean. She listened as some of his Ay'Araf friends told stories about him. She listened as the man who had been sitting next to Naomi, now proven to be Stephen's sire, told of the young and brash human he had once known. At last, the service came to an end. Stephen's casket was brought away by a group of Ay'Araf men and women, Jakob among them, and the funeral attendees stood, breaking off into small groups to talk among themselves. Two was surprised to see that Naomi, now somewhat more composed, was making her way over.

"Hi," she said as she reached Two.

"Are you OK?" Two asked.

Naomi smiled a little, sniffled, dabbed at her eyes with a tissue. "I've been better."

"Yeah. No kidding. Look, Naomi—"

Naomi held up her hand. "No, wait. Let me go first. I ... I've spent some time talking with Mother Ashayt, these past few days. She is helping me to deal with what happened. Not just Stephen, but all of it."

Naomi glanced down at the floor. Two and Theroen waited, silent, letting her gather her thoughts.

"It was wrong of me to say the things I said ... to both of you," Naomi said at last. "That's not ... it's not the politician talking. I'm not trying to win points or ... or smooth feathers. Do you understand? It's just me. Just the stupid, needy, pick-pocket servant girl who's been hiding behind the façade for all these years. What I said was wrong."

"Under the circumstances, we can hardly blame you," Theroen said.

"Stephen and I ..." Naomi shook her head, sighed, and looked like she was about to begin crying again but forced it away. "In nineteen-seventy, in August, he and I went to Ireland together. I'd known him for two years and we'd become quite close. We toured the countryside by night and ended up staying just outside of Galway, on the western coast, near the place where he was born. One night, just after the sun had set, we went down and walked on the same beach he had walked as a child, and I kissed him. I told him I loved him, and I kissed him.

"He stopped me, of course. We went through all the usual things that people say when they don't want to start a relationship. He told me I was wonderful, that it was because of his issues and not me that we couldn't be together. He told me he wished it could be different, but that he would never be right for me. He said I deserved someone who would want to see plays and read poetry with me. He said I should find someone who could love me in all of the ways that I could love them. I didn't know what he meant, not then, but I do now.

"He knew he couldn't make love to me, and I think he believed that would eventually drive us apart. He never said it outright, and he never even tried asking me how I felt about it. I guess he didn't believe that I could stop, even if I wanted to. He was probably right, and I don't think he could stand the idea of me being with someone else in that way, not if the two of us were together. Not if I was 'his.'

"We never talked about it again, after that night. I never stopped loving him, exactly, but I stopped wanting him and needing him in that way. Others came and went, like they have for so much of my life, and he never said anything. I always assumed that the truth of it was that he just didn't feel that way about me. That's what I thought right up until the night he died."

"August eighteenth," Two said, her voice barely more than a murmur. "That's what he said, right? That since then there was only you."

Naomi sobbed. Pressed her hands against her face. Nodded.

"He loved me all this time," she cried. "He loved me, but he kept me away, and now he's dead. I couldn't do anything to stop it. I couldn't do anything but stand there and watch him die!"

Two moved forward, standing up on tiptoes and putting her arms around her friend. Naomi stiffened at first, then hugged back, weeping. Eventually, with a great deal of effort, she regained control of herself.

"The two of you have something important," she said, looking at each of them in turn. Her makeup had run, forming dark circles under her red-rimmed eyes. "Don't lose it. Don't walk away from it or forget it or let it die. Don't let something stupid get in the way. Just ... just love each other."

"OK, Naomi." Two said. "Is there anything we can do for you?"

Naomi shook her head. "I'm going to take Stephen's ashes to Ireland. There will be another service there, and then I'm going to take him to that little strip of sand, and cast him into the wind. I think it's what he would have wanted. Then I ... I'll be back. William is taking over the council, and he'll need an apprentice. Making peace with the Burilgi is going to be a lot of work, and we still have to find your friend. There's so much to do ..."

"We'll be here to help," Two said. "Theroen and me and all of your other friends."

Naomi gave Two a small, sad smile, but she nodded. "Yes. You and Jakob and Sasha. We'll work together. Just forgive me if I ... sometimes it's ... I don't know."

"It's complicated," Two said.

"Yes, exactly. Complicated."

Someone called Naomi's name and she glanced over her shoulder, gave a small wave, and turned back to Two and Theroen.

"I suppose I should mingle," she said. Two nodded.

"Us, too. Have to introduce Theroen to, well, everyone."

Naomi smiled, dabbed again at her eyes with the tissue, then rolled them when she saw the amount of eyeliner that had come away.

"I must look ridiculous. Oh, well. Stephen would laugh at me and then tell me to get over it."

Two smiled, nodded. Naomi closed her eyes and breathed deeply. After a moment she opened them again, and Two could see a steadiness in her gaze that hadn't been there before. Naomi the politician was back, shutters closed tight over the windows to her soul.

"I'll see you both soon. Two, we need to introduce Theroen to L'Obscurité. I'm sure Thomas has missed us terribly."

With that, Naomi turned and made her way off into the crowd. Theroen turned and gave Two an appraising look.

"What?" Two asked.

"Are you all right?"

"Well, I'm awkwardly patching things up with my ex, in front of my boyfriend, at a friend's funeral," Two said. "This is life, right?"

Theroen nodded. "This is life."

"Yeah. Well, then I guess I'm all right."

"I am pleased to hear it," Theroen said.

"Good. OK, let's go meet people. Let me know if you see Jakob, too. Stephen was going to teach me to fight, and I'm pretty sure he'd be pissed off if I didn't see it through. I'm hoping Jakob will be up to the challenge."

Theroen smiled, took her hand, and together they made their way toward the crowd of people gathered at the back of the cathedral.

* * *

"They cut off her arm?!" Molly cried. "No way!"

"I saw it happen ... it was awful." Two told her. She was sitting in an arm chair in Rhes and Sarah's living room. Molly and her parents sat across from Two, on the couch. Two had spent most of the past hour and a half filling them in on what had happened since she had first encountered Naomi at *L'Obscurité*.

"That sucks," Molly said. "Is she going to be OK?"

"I think so. They stitched her up and gave her some blood and sent her home. At least she's still alive. Aros killed my friend Stephen."

It still hurt, saying this out loud, but Two knew she had to acknowledge it. She had to accept it, had to deal with the pain and the grief that Stephen's death brought her. She rubbed her arm across her eyes, which had gone suddenly wet with tears.

"I'm sorry you lost your friend, Two," Sarah said.

Two nodded, shrugged. "It happened. It's awful, and I wish I could change it somehow, but I can't. Aros got what was coming to him. Jakob shot him twice in the head, and the rest of his people took off."

"He didn't deserve any better," Rhes said.

"No, probably not," Two said. "I just wish ..."

"That it hadn't cost so much," Sarah said.

"Yeah."

"But now it's over?" Rhes asked. "I mean, no offense, Two, but we'd really love to get back to normal life. Sarah almost lost her job, Molly missed a week of school, and I got to lie to our other friends and tell them that I surprised the girls with an unplanned trip upstate, where Sarah and I somehow managed to both lose our cell phones."

Two put a hand to her forehead. "Christ ... yeah, I wouldn't blame you if you just wanted me out of your life entirely."

"The thought has crossed our minds," Sarah said.

"Not mine," Molly said. "I don't want you to disappear again, Two!"

"I wasn't serious," Sarah said. "At least, mostly. For better or for worse, Two, you're our friend. You're in our lives, and we like that. It was because we wanted you in our lives that we went out and got involved in this in the first place."

"OK," said Two. "And thanks. Honestly, though, it's going to be weird. I mean ... I'm a vampire. It still feels strange to say that, especially to all of you, but it's not like you don't know it. I can move faster and lift more than I'm supposed to. I'm not going to get sick or age. Sunlight makes me tired and kinda burns when it touches me. I drink *blood* for Christ's sake. I had some on the way here."

"You didn't, ah ... kill anyone, did you?" Rhes asked.

Two smiled a little, shaking her head. "No ... whatever it is that Theroen made me, it's not like before. I don't need that much and I can break away pretty easy. I just lured a guy into a Starbucks bathroom. I'm ... *pretty* sure he enjoyed it. He made kind of a mess."

"OK, that's gross," Sarah said. "Moving on ..."

"I think you're going to have to be, like ..." Rhes found himself searching for a way to explain. "You know that crazy uncle in The Nutcracker?"

"Drosselmeyer," Sarah said.

"Right, him. The guy who swings by once or twice a year with tales of exotic trips and brings weird gifts. Magical nutcrackers and talking coconut monkey heads and all the crazy shit that we're not supposed to believe in, but now we don't have any choice because our friend's a friggin' vampire."

"Too much exposure to me would be bad for your kids," Two said, smiling archly.

"It'd be bad for the illusion of normalcy is more the problem," Sarah said. "You're hardly the worst thing our kid has been exposed to."

"One time this guy on the J Train exposed himself to me," Molly said. There was a moment of silence following this declaration before Two burst into laughter, then clapped her hands over her mouth. Molly looked perplexed.

"What?" she asked. "He did!"

"We believe you, dear," Sarah said. "It's just not the best thing to mention in polite company."

"Since when am I polite company?" asked Two.

"Since we promised the state that we'd take care of Molly and try to raise her right," Rhes said, grinning. He leaned back on the couch, yawned, glanced around at the others. "So ... what now?"

"I think now I get out of here and leave you guys alone for a while," Two said. "You need to go back to real life. Theroen and I ... we don't know what's going to happen yet. I don't have an apartment anymore, so we're staying at a hotel, but we'll probably find someplace to live and get my stuff out of storage pretty soon."

"You going to bring him around some time?" Sarah asked. "We didn't have much chance to meet him."

"Definitely. He thought maybe you wouldn't want *two* vampires showing up so soon after the whole ... Aros thing."

"Sounds like a considerate guy," Rhes said.

"He is."

"So what the hell are you doing with him?"

Two laughed, shook her head, shrugged. "No idea!"

"What about Tori?" Sarah asked.

"We're going to work with the council to try and figure out where she is and what we can do to help her. I don't know what the hell these Children of the Sun people have put in her head, but there's gotta be a way to change her mind."

"If you can find her," Rhes said.

"Right. It sounds like that's going to be tough. Jakob says it might take years to track them down."

"Years? Wow. Well ..." said Sarah, "at least you have the time."

Two thought of Theroen waiting for her back at the hotel, sitting and reading or perhaps watching television, catching up on the time he had lost. She thought of the life they could now build together, free of Abraham, free of Aros. She thought of the things they might do, the places they might go, the sights they might see.

At last it was true. At last she had what Theroen had promised her more than two years ago. Love and safety and time; at last she had the time. Two smiled at her friends. Nodded.

"All the time in the world," she said.

EPILOGUE

The wailing, cowering things that kneel before her are not human.

This is not a trick, not some mental exercise used to prepare herself for the things she is about to do. This is not self-deception, so often essential to the psychological health of those who kill for a living. This is not her living, but her very *being,* and she needs no such cerebral trickery.

The things that are huddled in the corner of the room, knowing they are dead but not yet ready to accept it as fact, are not human. Their teeth are sharp and built for piercing. Their internal organs can process only blood. All of them are pale; all are also twisted, their affliction having caused horrible growths, extended ears and fingers, other deformities.

She waits, not out of sympathy or any desire to prevent what is to come, but only because the order has not yet been given. These creatures' cries mean nothing to her. In truth, she is unable at this point to equate them to anything human, or even anything alive. They are making the sounds of the dead. She has heard these sounds before, she thinks, though the past comes to her now only in flashes and fragments.

Memory is difficult. The day begins with meditation and the needle, ends with practice. For many months this practice was held against inanimate targets, machines, or even humans wearing protection. More recently, they have begun to bring her these things that scream, that spray when she stabs or slashes, that thrash and howl and beg when she shoots. Their bodies shake with seizures as they react to the poisons in her darts. In all cases, in the end, they die. This is her purpose, the thing for which she has been made, and she takes righteous and savage pleasure in performing her duties.

This journey began with death. She knows that, though she can no longer see the faces of those she seeks to avenge. She does not know if she would recognize them, even if shown a picture or video. It doesn't matter. The past has been driven from her, or buried deep and locked tight. Now there is only her master, and her mission, and the dead.

Her body trembles. Excitement and rage, joy, a need that is almost like lust. These things wrestle within her, yearning for release, as she waits for the word that will let her unleash the hate within her. She will work until she is empty, a hollow vessel that, by this time the next day, will be full once again.

The voice of her master comes. "Kill."

She leaps forward, and the wails become shrieks of terror. Her body sings with excitement and release. She works with the blades she holds in both hands, though she could just as easily use the guns at her side or the darts strapped to her chest. Each choice has its merits, each has its time.

Today she wants the blades. They are eighteen inches long and made of carbon steel, honed and cared for with reverence. They are not elegant weapons; there is little aesthetic value to their design. They are brutally effective devices, built to pierce and slash and kill, augmented only with the most rudimentary of hand-guards for catching or deflecting incoming attacks. She is capable of maneuvering the blades deftly, at startling speeds, with either hand.

The first vampire dies as she brings the right blade up in a long arc that begins just below his gut and ends with the very tip of the metal skidding along the bone of his sternum. The blade tastes air for a moment between the creature's chest and chin, then cleaves through the flesh and bone of his skull. The head falls apart like two halves of a ripe melon.

The second of the creatures has time to scream a name, presumably that of the dead thing lying on the floor, still twitching. She hears this and her left arm, which had been pressing the pommel end of the weapon against her chest, shoots out and to the side, catching the vampire in the throat and impaling him against the wall. His cries become harsh coughing noises and his fingers scrabble at the blade for an instant before she yanks it sideways, ruining the neck and sending blood spattering against the opposite wall.

The motion spins her to the right, which allows her to note that the third and final vampire has decided – laughably late – that his best option is to stand and fight. He is charging her, but he is so slow. She almost takes a moment to smile at this comical attempt, but there is work to be done, so instead she drops to her knees. The outstretched arms pass harmlessly above her head, and she catches him in mid-stride, driving the left blade up and into the vampire's crotch, burying all eighteen inches of it in a near-vertical thrust.

The force of this attack combines with the vampire's momentum and causes him to flip forward. She takes the opportunity to drive the other blade into his skull and end his miserable existence. The body thuds to the ground as she stands.

It has been only moments, but all three vampires are dead. She waits in the center of the room, soaked in blood, eyes closed. She is not even breathing hard, has not worked up a sweat. Her heart is barely beating any faster than it was before the killing started. The only thing that has changed is her hate; it has gone to where it goes to grow again, and she has been left hollow, shaking with relief and the pure joy of killing.

Eyes still closed, she allows herself a small smile.

"Good," her master says. "That's very good."

* * *

To Be Concluded in Book 3: The Children of the Sun

Keep Reading for a Sneak Preview!

AFTERWORD

I started writing this book with the same words on which it still opens, "Tori Perrault shifted position," and since then many things have changed, but those have stayed the same.

That was sometime in the summer of 2004, and Blood Hunt's predecessor, The Blood That Bonds, was just a manuscript that had been through a couple of drafts and a copy-edit, and had been read by perhaps a dozen people scattered across the country. I would end up working on the first draft of Blood Hunt – a much longer and more ambitious book – for two years, off and on, before leaving it aside, still waiting for an ending, in late 2006. Both books sat on my hard drive untouched for another two and a half years.

When I published The Blood That Bonds as a free eBook in October of 2009, I was hoping to do a thousand downloads. That, I told myself, would definitely be something to consider a success. When I hit that milestone, a couple of months in, my wife and I went out to dinner and celebrated with champagne. No bullshit.

It's been almost two years since then, and The Blood That Bonds has been downloaded more than 150,000 times that I can be sure of (there are many distributors who don't provide me with any numbers). That's astonishing! It's astonishing, and gratifying, and exciting, especially when you consider how well-reviewed the book is on its various websites. People seem to enjoy my writing, and they like this girl, Two, that I've introduced to them.

They wanted more of her story, and they were quite vocal about that fact. I realized it was time to get off my ass and finish Blood Hunt.

Well, then. Here we are. Three drafts and two copy-edits later, and I'm sitting in my office just a little more than a month from the book's scheduled release date, typing this note into the document that will eventually become the official eBook. By the time you read these words, you will have bought Blood Hunt and (hopefully) read it to the end. You'll know all about Naomi and Stephen, Ashayt, Theroen ...

But me? I have no idea how this book is going to do. The Blood That Bonds was free. Blood Hunt is not. The Blood That Bonds was short. Blood Hunt is not. The Blood That Bonds was basically a love story that ended unfortunately. Blood Hunt is ... something else. Will people like it? Will they demand the third volume as they demanded this one? I don't know. I hope so, but all I can do is put it out there and then wait.

Thank you for reading this book. If you paid for it, thank you even more. If you didn't, well, I hope at least if you've read this far, you liked it enough to consider buying a copy, or a copy of the final installment.

The Children of the Sun is already in progress. I haven't finished the first draft yet, but I know much of what's in store for Two and her friends. Not everything ... these books have a habit of writing themselves, and "little" things like Theroen dying were unplanned. It just happened. I don't know who will survive to the end of the final book, or what shape they'll be in.

All I know for sure is: The Children are coming, and when they arrive, things are going to get ugly. I'm excited to find out how it ends.

Hope you are too!

-Christopher Buecheler

MORE INFORMATION

There's lots of ways to stay in touch:

- Visit Christopher Buecheler's Writing Blog
  http://writing.cwbuecheler.com

- Follow @cwbwriting on Twitter
  http://www.twitter.com/cwbwriting

- Like Christopher Buecheler on Facebook
  http://on.fb.me/iOAdA1

- Subscribe to the CWB Writing Newsletter
  http://writing.cwbuecheler.com/newsletter

ABOUT THE AUTHOR

Christopher Buecheler is a professional web designer / developer, a published author, an award-winning amateur mixologist, a brewer of beer, a player of the guitar and drums, and an NBA enthusiast.

He lives a semi-nomadic existence with his wonderful French wife and their two cats, Carbomb and Baron Salvatore H. Lynx II. Currently they reside in Providence, Rhode Island.

You can visit him at http://www.cwbuecheler.com

THE CHILDREN OF THE SUN

Sneak Peak

The man's name was Matthias Vanden. He was an Eresh vampire, more than six hundred years old, and he had come to America for a few years at the request of his two fledglings, both of whom had visited the country often and thought he would enjoy it. Thus far they had been right. The three of them were staying in a luxurious apartment that took up the entire top floor of its building and offered views of Lake Michigan, the Sears Tower, and several other Chicago landmarks. They had been in the city for six months and had not yet tired of it. When and if they did, he thought, perhaps they would try Los Angeles or New York.

The two younger vampires, both Dutch, both in the middle of their second century, were in the living room now, entertaining two women and a man. The humans had become frequent guests, happy to provide their blood to the vampires in exchange for the ecstasies that came with being bitten. Matthias wasn't worried by this; at the end, the humans would remember little of their time with the vampires except that it had been extremely enjoyable.

He sighed, filled with the pleasurable melancholy that came with reminiscence. He no longer needed the blood in such volumes, no longer yearned for it with the passion of an insatiable lover. The centuries had left him able to subsist for weeks on but a few drops, and he rarely interacted with humans. Still, though, he could recall how it had been, the blood pouring forth in hot torrents as he drank and drank, fighting against the swoon that had threatened always to envelope him. He envied his young fledglings this experience, even while he appreciated his freedom from the need to drink every night.

He was reclining now on the gigantic bed in the apartment's master bedroom, watching the television with the volume turned off and the closed captioning on, aware of but not really listening to the music from the other room. He and his fledglings had spent the early evening walking along Navy Pier, enjoying the throngs of people around them. Then there had been the bar. A curious place in a mostly commercial downtown area, it had specialized in martinis and played lesbian pornography on its many screens. Matthias could remember a time, not so very long ago, when the bar would have been burnt to the ground for such heresies. He had found it deliciously scandalous, and his fledglings, more comfortable in this modern age, had in turn found his reaction highly amusing.

Matthias leaned back on the bed, grinning, remembering their laughter. He looked up through the skylights, where he could see a thin crescent of moon and a few bright stars. He could also see the lights of a nearby office building and a flashing red beacon that he thought was meant to warn airplanes and helicopters of a radio tower. He could see something else, too, something that he did not immediately recognize. It seemed to be getting closer, however, and in a moment more Matthias realized that he was looking at a human form, plummeting down from a great height and angled directly at the glass windows above him.

Matthias leapt from his bed as the body fell through the skylight, and even as he was thinking that this must be some sort of suicide attempt, he realized that the body was not crashing to the floor in a jumble but rather landing on its feet, absorbing the impact with its knees, and springing forward. He saw long blonde hair streaming out behind it and there was a bright flash of metal. Matthias heard a woman's snarling cry as the figure grabbed him by the neck and threw him up against the wall, pressing the tip of a blade to the soft spot below his chin.

"Move an inch and I will cut your head from your body," the woman told him, and Matthias looked at her in surprised awe. He knew few people who could have performed that landing and the follow-up leap forward, and all of those were vampires. This woman was not a vampire, though he did not know if she was exactly human, either. She was certainly a trained professional of some sort, dressed head to toe in black combat gear.

2

How very remarkable, he thought to himself, but he said nothing, afraid that if he moved then the blade she held to his throat would pierce into him and let his blood out all over the exquisite Oriental rug upon which he stood.

There were crashing noises now from the living room and a woman's screaming that was cut short by a loud thud. Someone – Matthias thought it was the human male – voiced a protest at this, but his cry was choked off midway through. In another few moments, there was a knock at the door.

"Enter," said the woman who was holding him against the wall, and Matthias watched with a kind of horrified curiosity as the door opened and a young, dark-skinned woman stepped in. She too was clothed in black. Rather than blades, she carried in her hand a silenced pistol and at her side, hanging like fruit, were two oblong, textured objects that Matthias thought were hand grenades.

"We've got the other two bats contained, and the humans have learned to shut up and mind their manners," the black girl said, and the blonde nodded.

"Good."

"You want us to bring them in here?"

"No. I'll take him out. Go make sure they don't get any stupid ideas."

The black girl turned on her heel without another word and strode back into the living room. The blonde turned to Matthias, and he saw that her eyes were a clear and brilliant blue.

"We're going to walk into the living room," she told him. "You first, me behind you. If you try to run, or attack, or do anything else that upsets me, I will put this blade right between your shoulders. It will come out just above your collarbone, it will leave you alive, and it will be excruciatingly painful, especially when I start twisting it. Are we clear on this?"

"Yes," Matthias said, still mindful of the metal point pressed into the flesh under his chin.

"You're an old Eresh, so you must be fairly fast. Do I need to tell you that I'm faster?"

"No." Matthias had seen her move after she came crashing through the skylight. He knew very well how fast she was.

3

"Good," the woman said. She took the blade away from his skin and held it unsheathed at her side. "Go."

"Are you going to kill me?" Matthias asked her.

"If you don't start walking, yes. If you do exactly what you're told and stop asking stupid questions, you might get through this."

"Please," he said. "I don't ... kill me if you must, but leave my children. They've hurt no one."

The woman gave him a disgusted, mocking laugh, and she pointed toward the bedroom door. "Get moving."

Matthias did as he was told, moving slowly and deliberately so that this woman holding him hostage would know that he did not intend to fight. Matthias had never been much for fighting; that sort of thing was best left to the Ay'Araf. He was Eresh and not a warrior, though he thought he might soon be put in a place where there would be no other alternative.

His fledglings were sitting on the living room's large sofa, flanked by two black-clothed human men. Adrianus, the younger of the two vampires, looked disgusted and angry. Mikel, older by twenty years and more even-tempered than his brother, seemed to be in control of his emotions. He was looking at one of the human women. She was lying on the floor, a trickle of blood running from her nose to the carpet. She wasn't wearing a shirt, and her bare breasts were not rising and falling in the way that they should have been – they were still, and Matthias knew she was dead.

The other two humans were each being held with their hands behind their backs by a member of whatever strike force this might be. Both were still fully clothed, though the man's shirt was unbuttoned. He had a black eye and livid red marks around his neck, just below the edges of his long, dark hair. The girl next to him, a tall woman with a large mass of tightly curled red hair pulled back in a ponytail, was weeping quietly but seemed unharmed.

The black girl who had come into the bedroom was standing at the far end of the apartment, looking out at the city. She glanced over her shoulder as they came into the room, watching Matthias's ⁻low progression forward, and then resumed looking out the ⁻low.

"What a lovely scene," The blonde girl commented from behind him, and Matthias could hear the sarcasm in her voice. He came to a stop in the middle of the room, and she didn't seem to object to this.

"Girl wouldn't shut up," said a tall, burly man with brown, crew-cut hair.

"So you thought you'd break her neck?" the blonde woman asked.

"I got a little overzealous, Captain," the man admitted.

"Right. Next time, wait for my orders."

"Yes ma'am."

"Are you the one in charge, here? What the fuck do you want?" Adrianus demanded in his thickly accented English, and the blonde woman turned to him.

"You'll speak when spoken to and you'll do so respectfully, or I'll have them kill another of your blood-whores."

Adrianus said nothing, merely glared at the woman. The human girl's sobbing had redoubled at the confirmation that her friend was dead, and for a moment it was the only sound in the room.

"Please," Matthias said. "We wish to avoid any further trouble. Tell us what it is you want from us."

"What I want is for every single blood-drinking piece of shit in this country to die," the blonde-haired woman said. "But that's not what I'm here for tonight. Tonight I'm here to send a message. You're going to deliver it for me."

"A message to whom?" Matthias asked her.

The woman moved in front of him now, holding her blade at her side.

"You're going to go to the American Council of Vampires in New York. You're going to tell them that the day of reckoning has come."

"I do not know anyone on the Council. I am not from this country," Matthias said.

"Then you'd better figure out how to find them," the woman replied.

From the couch, Adrianus made a sound of annoyance and muttered something under his breath. The blonde woman turned to him.

"What did you say?"

"I said 'this is ridiculous,'" Adrianus told her. "I will not be held captive and given orders by a group of humans with delusions of grandeur."

"Adrianus, please ..." Matthias began, but his fledgling overrode him.

"You invade our home, murder our friend, hold our patron at swordpoint and threaten him, and now you expect us to deliver your ridiculous message to this group of vampires we don't even know? Go away, human. Go away before something terrible happens."

The woman frowned at him. "It's a bad idea to speak to me in that tone, and an even worse idea to try and give me orders. I serve only one master: the Emperor of the Sun. I am an instrument of his light."

"I tire of this nonsense," Adrianus snarled. He stood up from the couch, and the humans on either side drew their guns, pointing them at him. The black girl turned from the window she had been staring out of, an odd smile on her face.

"Put your guns down," the blonde woman told her fellows.

"But, Captain ..." began one, and the woman glared at him.

"What part of the Captain's order didn't you understand, Janus?" the black girl asked from across the room. The man who had spoken glanced at her and, after a moment's hesitation, lowered his weapon. His fellow guard, the man with the crew cut, did the same.

"Adrianus, do not do this," Matthias said. "You are making a terrible mistake."

"I do not fear these humans," Adrianus told him.

"That is the mistake," Matthias replied, but Adrianus wasn't listening. He was striding forward toward the blonde woman, gaining speed with each step.

"You should have let them shoot me when you had the chance!" Adrianus roared, leaping forward. The blonde woman stood still, ready, and at the last possible moment she ducked.

Adrianus's arms passed harmlessly over her head and he tripped on her outstretched leg, stumbling forward.

Moving now with that same impossible speed she had shown before, the blonde girl stood and, even as Adrianus was falling, swung her sword in a downward arc. The blade cleaved his head from his body and it rolled away, throwing fans of blood against the wall and coming to a stop near the bedroom door. Matthias watched as the corpse – a thing which had moments ago been his son – thudded to the ground, arms fluttering, spurting blood from its neck.

Matthias could hear himself screaming, but the sound was warped and distant, as if it was echoing down to him through a long hallway. He stood rooted to the ground, unable to move, unable to do anything but voice his horror. Mikel, too, was screaming, but he had leapt to his feet. The humans were shrieking, struggling against their captors.

Matthias didn't know whether Mikel would have attacked or not, but the blonde girl did not give him the opportunity. Lightning-quick, still in a crouch, she reached to a clip at her breast and pulled from it two darts, which she flung across the room in a single motion. One hit Mikel in the chest, another in the arm, and his cries became immediately strangled. He took one step toward her and then pitched forward, twisting in the air as he did so, landing on his side.

Matthias watched in horror as his fledgling's limbs began to seize up and a great torrent of bloody foam gushed forth from his mouth. Even his eyes had begun to bleed, and he was making choked cawing noises of agony that seemed to pierce Matthias like knives.

"Please!" Matthias cried, begged. "Have mercy on him!"

The blonde girl, up on her feet now and striding toward Mikel's shuddering, jerking form, glanced over her shoulder.

"There is only one mercy for him now," she said, and she held the blade up over her head for a moment before driving it down and into his chest, piercing Mikel's heart and ending his pain. She stood, cleaning the blood from the blade with a dark cloth. Both humans were sobbing now, wrestling with the men that held them but making no real headway in their attempts to escape.

"It's always a pleasure watching you work," the black girl said, and the blonde woman favored her with a sardonic smile.

"Thank you, Vanessa."

"Oh, God help me," Matthias moaned. He was still rooted to his spot, standing now between the bodies of his two dead children, shaking and unable to move. The blonde woman turned to him.

"There is no God," she said. "Even if there was, He wouldn't want anything to do with you."

Matthias felt a surge of rage and hatred run through him, and in that moment he almost threw himself at this woman despite her superior speed, her obvious skills as a fighter. At least then it would be over; he would be dead like his children, gone to whatever afterworld awaited. He tensed and the woman tilted her head, studying him intently.

Then he thought of Hell, of the punishments that might be waiting for the things that he had done in his youth, newly made a vampire and intoxicated with power and the need for blood. The desire to fight passed, replaced by a sort of hopeless anguish, and Matthias felt his body slump. He was a coward; he knew it and he could see from the blonde woman's eyes, her smile, the set of her body, that she knew it too.

"Will you take my message to the Council?" she asked him. "Or will I leave *three* dead vampires behind me tonight?"

"I will deliver your message," Matthias told her, his voice hoarse. "I will find this Council you speak of, and I will tell them what happened here, and surely they will send better men than me to hunt you down."

The blonde woman favored him with a savage grin. "Surely they will."

"Captain, what about these two?" the black girl, Vanessa, asked. She indicated with her gun at the two human captives.

"They're tainted. Put them down," the blonde girl said, and at this the humans redoubled their struggles. The red-haired woman was weeping, saying 'no, no, no,' shaking her head as if by such an action she could negate the things that were happening.

Vanessa walked over to the two of them and said, "You are still human, so I will make it quick for you."

"Tanya, I love y—" the human man began, and Vanessa put the gun to his temple and pulled the trigger. There was a small popping noise, and most of the man's brains came jetting out from the opposite side of his head.

"Oh, Jesus *God!*" the red-haired woman screamed. Vanessa turned, placed the gun against her forehead, and blew the back of her head out, too. Matthias, who had not vomited in centuries, felt the urge to do so now and fought against it. The men who had been holding the two humans let their bodies drop.

"Let's go," the blonde woman said, putting her blade into the sheath strapped to her back.

They moved as a group toward the balcony, and Matthias watched as one by one they took hold of a rope that had been attached there and climbed over the edge, disappearing from sight. The blonde woman – the Captain – was the last to go. She looked at him for a long moment, not a trace of sympathy or regret in her eyes, and then she favored him with a long, angry smile. *What a terrible place her mind must be,* Matthias thought to himself.

With one swift movement she was gone, and he was alone with five bodies, two of which had been his children. Matthias felt his knees unhinge, felt himself fall to a sitting position. He covered his face with his hands, his stupid, cowardly hands, and began to weep.

* * *

The Children of the Sun are coming. Find out more:
http://www.iiamtrilogy.com/

9

2091731R00274

Printed in Great Britain
by Amazon.co.uk, Ltd.,
Marston Gate.